Going Down Swinging

BILLIE LIVINGSTON

RANDOM HOUSE CANADA

Portions of this novel first appeared in the following periodicals: *sub-Terrain*, *Grain*, *Imago* (Australia), *TickleAce*, *The Capilano Review* and *The Malahat Review*.

Canadian Cataloguing in Publication Data

Livingston, Billie, 1965-
    Going down swinging

ISBN 0-679-31000-2

I. Title

PS8573.I916G64 2000   c813'.54   C99-931434-3
PR9199.3.L58G64 2000

The Author and Publisher gratefully acknowledges the following for permission to reprint lyric excerpts.

Band on the Run
Words and Music by McCartney
© 1974 Paul and Linda McCartney
Administered by MPL Communications, Inc.
All Rights Reserved

Brand New Key
Words and Music by Melanie Safka
© 1971 EMI April Music Inc. and Neighborhood Music Publishing Corp.
All Rights Controlled and Administered by EMI April Music Inc.
All Rights Reserved   International Copyright Secured   Used by Permission

Circle Game
Joni Mitchell
Copyright © 1966 Crazy Crow Music (Renewed)
All rights administered by Sony/ATV Music Publishing, 8 Music Square West, Nashville, TN 37205
All Rights Reserved   Used by Permission

Cover design: Karen Satok
Interior design: Sharon Foster Design

Printed and bound in the United States of America

10 9 8 7 6 5 4 3 2 1

Going Down Swinging

Eilleen One

No ONE EVER believes they'll sink So Low. *So Low* is someone else's life, someone else's man, someone else's job. Everyone imagines little rubber bands hooked at the shoulder, springing back to safety just before the life-sucking bedrock.

Now Danny's gone, your man, the guy you called husband. And you're wandering in the haze between dazed and terrified. Flat broke. Flat out. Just flat; a reasonable hand-drawn facsimile of your former self. Somewhere along the line, you got weak and sickly, sucked dry. And he got necessary.

He's always had a kind of crafty power—everyone wanted him and no one could push him. Not until they took him away, at least. Why did you start up with him again? If he hadn't've been busted two years ago, you would've dumped him. So then, what'd you go and do in the meantime, you idiot—went out with one too many assholes until even Danny sounded good.

And Charlie's gone and fucked off too—mind you, for all intents and purposes, she's been gone two years now. Couldn't wait to get out of the house—all that hash and acid floating around

the streets, all those micro-minis and fishnet stockings. Fourteen
years old when Danny ended up in jail, and without him to make
her, she wouldn't do a goddamn thing you said. She got pissed off,
sometimes smug, always bitching, sitting around lazy or walking
off and coming home late. It wasn't supposed to be that way. She's
been cruel ever since. She won't look after you and you can't look
after her and she won't let you. She's sick of you and your wine
and pills, and screaming retaliation every time she mouths back.
Thank god for Grace. She loves you. She clambers all over you
and says so.

Now it's just the two of you again, you'll celebrate her seventh
this month, alone. And you'll have to work, find work for bills,
and landlords and food and rent and Grace and the hydro and the
phone. You've been sober all of one week now—too sick to get a
job again, to go back to teaching—that was someone else, that
woman. Sick when you do drink, sick when you don't. Nauseous
and sensitive—skin hurts, and your hair, you can feel each hair
move when the air shifts. And the mess, everything's dirty—you
can't get up the strength or the will to clean. You'll have to get
welfare again. At least for now.

You pace all morning, trying to get up the nerve, the strength to
go down to the Welfare office. Pick out the right clothes, now, or
they won't believe you. They'd have to be morons. He never kept
you like a queen—you refused all hot merchandise in the form of
furs and jewels—stupid-stupid-stupid.

By noon, a social worker is looking over your application. He's
sweet somehow, so careful with you. His little round bald head,
his soft voice. Seems foreign now, another language; gentle, artic-
ulate. He puts *g*s on the ends of his verbs. None of Danny's crowd
could ever string together five words of proper English. It's always
boozin', screwin', fuckin'—or more likely *f(ee-iz)uckin'*—they've
got to throw that *ee-iz* smack in the middle of anything illegal or

obscene, just in case the walls have ears. But you can't imagine this man ever uses those words.

He gives you the emergency assistance cheque. You'll soon receive a cheque every month: $269.67. For you and one dependant. You start to cry. The social worker doesn't understand. Or maybe he does. He just doesn't know what to do but yank tissue after tissue. Each one gives a sympathetic little gasp as it pulls free, until both you and the Kleenex box are hoarse from hyperventilation.

Guilt is coursing through your arms, up your neck and pounding at the back of your eyeballs until you want to scream, rip it out of your wrists like ropy veins. It's pointless, guilt is useless. It just wasn't meant to be, that's all. You and Danny shouldn't have bothered again and Charlie should've just kept doing whatever she was doing: screwing with her foster mother's head or robbing every kid in the group home blind. Christ, stop thinking such shit—it's not her fault, it's not your fault, it just is. You just couldn't get along— used to start up as soon as you came in the door, the screaming. Fights were getting worse and worse and you were scared it was going to get as bad as it got before she took off the first time. Scared of getting your hair pulled and your mouth slapped and scared of doing it all back.

The night before Charlie left for good, you didn't come home. But it was about time that kid took some responsibility. Maybe it was time *she* found out what it was like looking after a seven-year-old in this insane asylum with a man who wouldn't come home for three days running half the time. It was your turn to bugger off and take a break. It's not like you were drinking much. And you were trying to go to AA now and then.

Just before noon when you came in, and no one was home; it was a school day and Danny was probably out with his cronies somewhere pretending to be a real estate agent. You were standing in the kitchen. The room looked as if it'd spat up on itself: a chewed-on dried-up piece of bread lay in a puddle of crumbs on the table beside a chewed-on twisted straw, dirty pots on three out of four burners, white plates covered with dried orange slop, macaroni pieces on counters, a milk carton tipped on its side, spoons in every pot, forks on every plate, a butcher knife on the counter and cheesy orange fingerprints all over the fridge door. You started to seethe. *Christ, I live in a house full of assholes.* They couldn't even make a pretence of cleaning up, couldn't even stack dishes in the sink, not even near the sink—they're punishing you, you thought, this is what happens when you don't come home.

Remember yelling *Fuck*? Who were you hollering at? Yourself? For crawling out of a stranger's bed at ten in the morning and straggling back to house and home. Huh! No. Why should you feel guilty, everyone else stays out all night, big deal. It wasn't like Grace was alone. Danny said he'd stay home with her while you went to your meeting. Said it with a sneer, of course, said it like, *Sure I'll stay home and look after your kid, because you're too weak and ineffectual to stay sober on your own.* So. So there. So you met someone who was nice to you, so Steve/Dave (couldn't get his name straight) with the nice bum, who turned out not to be named Steve or Dave but Karl (of all things), turned out not to be queer either. And not bad in bed either. And furthermore, it was a nice change to be in bed with a man with a decent-size dick who knew what the hell to do with it. And for godsake, who was kidding who, the only reason you and Danny were living in the same house again was for Grace. He was hardly ever around. Wasn't as if his stony little pea-size heart would be broken over this.

The front door slammed. It was noon exactly.

Hello? Charlie. What was she doing here? Oh yes, a school day, she must have been out running the streets.

Hello.

You listened to her denim legs rub toward you. She walked into the kitchen looking like a badger with a bone to pick.

Where the hell have you been? you asked her.

She squints in the uniform teenage-face-of-disgust. *Where the hell have I been? You're the one wearing the same thing you left in last night.*

How would you know? When's the last time you deigned to show up in this house?

For your information, I was here last night looking after Grace. Dad had to go out. And you never came home. I looked after Grace, fed her, and put her to bed.

Oh. Well, that would explain why the place is such a pigsty then.

Are you for real? You fuckin' never came home last night! Where the hell were you—we thought you were dead, but I guess not, eh? Yeah right, an AA meeting, you look hungover if y' ask me. What'd you do, find yourself some poor slob in a bar?

Before you realized, you'd already slapped her face. *How dare you come into this house and talk to me like that, and you of all people—talk about the pot calling the kettle black, the only reason you ever ran away from home in the first place was because you were a horny little slut and you couldn't keep your pants on to save your —*

You stupid whore, don't ever touch me again. Who —

Shut your mouth, and you're a goddamn thief too—you think I don't know you've been stealing from me. Well, you've got another thing coming, you treat this place like a flophouse, stop by to eat, steal some money, take my pills —

What!—I never took nothing of yours! You're nuts!

Liar!

Nothing's ever gonna change with you, is it? I'm getting the hell out of here—I wish you were dead and I'd take Grace with me. I should take her with me anyway.

The front door opened and closed, but you were both too furious to shut your mouths.

You just try laying a hand on one hair of that kid's head and I'll slit your throat. And there was a knife in your hand, the butcher knife. Charlie's eyes were huge and incredulous, brimming hot water. But you meant it, no one was taking the baby anywhere. No. You could feel her in the room somewhere, that door-slam was hers, you could feel her but you couldn't peel your eyes off Charlie.

Charlie opened her mouth, there was a strand of saliva running between her jaws; she looked about to choke, but words came: *You're crazy.* That's all. And she turned to run and then Grace's *No-o-o Charlie-ee,* and crying and Charlie running for the front door and Grace chasing after, bawling her sister's name and you squeezed the knife once and let it fall and thunk linoleum and yelled, *Grace, you stay in this house.* But the door opened and the screen door banged in its frame and feet scrambled down wood steps. And there was nothing to do but push palms into eye sockets until the black screen turned psychedelic and you couldn't hear your own moans. It's all your fault, you thought again, again, everything's your fault; he'll blame you when he comes home. And Grace will hate you for making Charlie disappear again. Can't change anything, even when you change it. And then you were up and running to the living-room window, terrified she really would take Grace.

They were just a little ways down the sidewalk. Dead leaves scraping cement, scuttling past them onto neighbours' lawns. The sky was slate and about to pour any minute. You could faintly hear their voices, mostly crying. Charlie shook her head and Grace was hysterical, face blister red, wet with tears and snot and saliva. She threw her arms around Charlie's waist, pushed her face into Charlie's stomach, the back of her head covered by Charlie's hands, hands running over and over silky child-hair, and the both of them stood inside the same square of sidewalk and wailed and mourned for minutes or hours. Charlie's lips were moving, *She's crazy*s and *I love you*s dropping onto your little one's head.

Numb.

For the next few days you didn't move much, except the occasional rocking. You brought Grace to bed with you most nights and held on, breathing deeply through her child-smooth hair as though it were an oxygen mask, her little body a scuba.

She is the last thing, the last possession; she is the padding on the wall that keeps you from beating your head to bone and mash. So often you catch yourself whispering in her ear, making plans, the primary request being that she never grow up, that she remain small, pliable and loving.

Now the house feels colder, as if there's been a death. It's this decade, this fucking sixties hangover, this time. Every time you turn on the TV, another insufferable teenager with centre-parted limp hair hanging dreary down the sides of her sulky face, giving it the look of a mooning teardrop, spouting off about Vietnam, about the consent she never gave to her own birth. Their sit-ins, love-ins, beads and flower power. Fuck them. Fuck them for making you cry every time you see a teenage girl on the street, every time you nearly call out to a strange girl with dark welling eyes.

She's right maybe, maybe you're out of your ever-lovin' mind. Or maybe not so much. But how many people threaten their children with knives, order them out of the house? Then again, how many children threaten to steal their sister from home? None of it's right. Nothing will ever be right again. Every time you hear the words in your chest, hear that day, you want to go upstairs, just go upstairs and take something. Before it all cracks into a thousand million splinters. It's all too clear and ugly. A person's got to take something, prescribe a nice smoky film on things—when things are too clear, the world is a closed glass door; you don't see what's coming until you're already shatters and shreds.

Refer: (Mrs.) Lilly Darling
File: 56722

February 1, 1972

Child Protection Agency of Metropolitan Toronto,
(Mrs.) Dagmar Lindlay,
Executive Director
333 Wellesley St. E.,
Toronto 5
Ontario

Dear Madam:

> RE: <u>HOFFMAN</u>, (Carrington) Charlotte
> born 3/7/56
> c/o Mr. and Mrs. Daniel Hoffman
> 560 Woodfield Rd.
> Toronto, 8 Ontario
> <u>Telephone: 465-7879</u>

We are writing with regard to the above-mentioned
girl to you for follow-up service.

Charlotte was in our non-ward care from 1970 until
January, 1972, when she was discharged from our care and
returned to her mother in Toronto. Charlotte's legal name
is CARRINGTON, but she goes by the name of HOFFMAN, which
is the name of her mother's common-law husband.

This girl has severe emotional problems and is, we
feel, close to a breakdown. Just prior to leaving
Vancouver, Charlotte (aka Charlie) was admitted to the
Health Centre for Children at Vancouver General Hospital,
suffering from acute anxiety and depression. She was

then seen by Dr. Evelyn Kendle, a psychiatrist who works closely with the Vancouver CPA. Dr. Kendle felt that Charlotte was close to a breakdown and unworkable in an outpatient capacity. She was making arrangements for Charlotte to be admitted into the psychiatric wing of VGH when Charlotte decided to return to her parents in Toronto.

Mr. and Mrs. Hoffman have a very stormy relationship. Mrs. Hoffman is an alcoholic with many problems who has had several hospital admissions because of emotional and alcoholic problems. Still at home with the Hoffmans is a younger half-sister, Grace.

Charlotte is very resistant to receiving our help, but, we are quite concerned about her and felt you should be aware of her arrival in Toronto in case there are further problems.

For more information you can write to Dr. T. Benson, Child Protection Medical Clinic, 1550 Oak St., Vancouver, B.C., or Dr. Evelyn Kendle, M.B., B.S., C.R.C.P., Metropolitan Board of Health, Vancouver, B.C.

Thank you for your help in this matter.

Sincerely,

(Mr.) G.H. Pretty

(Mr.) G.H. Pretty
Director,
Broadway Branch

Lilly Darling
_____
(Mrs.) Lilly Darling
Social Worker

GHP/pl

Refer: (Mrs.) Lilly Darling
File: 56722

August 10, 1972

(Mrs.) Dagmar Lindlay,
Executive Director
Child Protection Agency of Metropolitan Toronto,
333 Wellesley St. E.,
Toronto 5, Ontario

Dear Madam,

RE: Carrington, Eilleen (neé Ellison)
known as Mrs. Hoffman
Child: Carrington, Charlotte Anne,
Born July 3, 1956
Status: Care of the Child
Protection Agency of Vancouver

    The above-named daughter of Mrs. Carrington was apprehended under the Protection of Children Act by our Agency, August 5th, 1972. The Hearing date has been set for September 9, 1972

    We apprehended Charlotte as she had returned to Vancouver on a transient basis. We did not have new non-ward consents for Charlotte as the previous agreement expired as of January/72 when she returned to her parents in Toronto.

    Enclosed are Court Notices of the Hearing: please serve Mrs. Carrington with the original Court Notice, complete the copy marked Exhibit "A" and the Affidavit of Personal Service in duplicate before a Commissioner and return to us by September 9, 1972. Also have Mrs.

Carrington sign the Enclosed Affidavit of Parent not
appearing in Court, before a Commissioner, and return to
us with the other documents.

Thank you very much for all your help in this matter.

Sincerely,

Lilly Darling
_____
(Mrs.) Lilly Darling,   (Mr.) G.H. Pretty
Social Worker   Director, Broadway Branch

GHP/jl

Grace One

APRIL 1973

S HE STOOD in front of the bathroom mirror, with a beer
on the counter, and painted black lines over her top lashes,
then thinner ones under her bottoms. She was going out man-
hunting and I sat on the toilet with my heels on the seat and got
a picture in my head of her going slinky like a tigress through the
alleyways. She painted blue on her lids and rubbed some lipstick
on her cheeks to look rosy. The last part was the most important;
even if she didn't have time for anything else, she got her face
right in the mirror and made a sharp shiny lipstick-mouth. I swallowed and swallowed, trying to think of something good to say.
She looked at me in the mirror and said, "What's the matter, you
look like you're about to cry."

"Can't you stay home, can't we watch TV or something? or play
a game?"

"Honey, just let me get out for a while and I'll be much easier to be around. Maybe I'll find us a nice man who'll take me for
dinner and take you horseback riding and be sweet to us." I didn't

say anything, so she asked me, "Are you going to stay up here so you'll feel closer to Frank and Janet?"

"No." I didn't feel like being down the hall from stupid Frank and Janet, all gooey-lovey and doing whatever they were doing in Charlie's room. Since they moved in, Mum was either hating them for every second they spent in the bathroom or loving them for being last-minute babysitters.

"Do you want to bring a pillow and blanket downstairs and watch TV and then I'll bring you back up when I get home?"

I didn't say anything, just nodded. "Grace, why are you making such a production out of this? It's not as if I've never gone out at night before." I nodded. "Oh, come on now, stop with the crocodile tears." I started hating that expression of hers since I found out it meant fake. I dropped my feet onto the yellow mat that hugged around the toilet. There was a space of tile where its fluffy arms were coming away. I crushed it back and stomped out.

From my bed I could see into her room, so I left my door open: I wanted to watch her go back and forth getting ready. Except she hucked her own door almost closed, so I had to listen instead. I listened to her pulling on pantyhose then swear and yank them back off and rummage for different ones. Skirts and hot pants shushed over her hips, the zippers zedding up and down every time she changed her mind. Then, what sounded like sweaters pulling over her head; my favourite one had a short zipper right at the neck. Then the sound that told you she'd almost made up her mind: the clunk and zipper of her boots coming on. First just one—she always did it that way: high heel on one foot, boot on the other, leg up, leg down, other leg up. And down.

Another zipper. It'd be boots tonight. She bought two pairs a couple months before, one red, one white, both made of shiny crinkle stuff that was clingy on her legs. The boots usually meant hot pants. (Skirts got high strappy shoes—rain or sun or snow.) It was still wintertime, so probably the red; she didn't think white was right for the winter, even though I tried to tell her it went good with the snow. I listened to her go around her room, she usually did that—prowled around, turning in the mirror to make sure.

Her boots came down the hall toward my room. There was a pause as her heel snagged the carpet. A snap when she yanked free. She poked her head in my room. I was pretending to read *Danny Meadowmouse,* one of the books Charlie sent me for Christmas from Vancouver.

I looked up. She had on my favourite outfit: black hot pants, a tight red turtleneck and a black tam. Plus the red boots. She sat down on the edge of the bed and patted her belly. "I'm getting fat."

I put the book down. "No, you're not." Her stomach did bulge a little under her sweater, but it looked pretty. Her boobs, her belly and her hips, all pointed at you like soft round fingers.

She sighed and patted my leg. "It's almost spring and it's still winter. Leave it to bloody Toronto." Mum picked a lint off her sweater and kept talking. "When you were a baby, in Vancouver, we used to take you and Charlie to the beach, and you used to run around in the nude, giggling your little head off. And your dad would chase you and threaten to unscrew your belly button and let your bum fall off. And you'd scream and hold your bum; you were such a funny little bird."

Mum always makes it sound like it used to be fluffy heaven when I was a baby. Like we used to have a real family. The pictures make it look like that, but mostly I remember yelling and the house being always dark. Mum looked at my hand. She said I was going to grow into one big dog with hands that size. I tried to think of more stuff to talk about.

"Will you sing me songs before you leave?"

"Oh god, sweety, I don't feel up to it. You're getting too old for bedtime songs anyway."

"Please …?"

She sighed. "One. I'll just sing one fast one, and then I have to go, OK?"

"The piggy song."

"Oh god, the piggy song. I haven't got it in me tonight, honey … just … OK:

There once was a piggy who lived in a sty
and six little piggies had she.
She waddled around saying oink oink oink
and the little ones said wee wee wee.

Now six little piggies grew skinny and lean,
and skinny and lean grew they
from trying so hard to say oink oink oink
when they only should say wee wee wee.

She leaned and kissed me. I grabbed round her neck and held on till she tried to straighten up and still had me hanging off her. She patted my back. "OK, sweety, that's enough, come on now, give me a kiss and let me go. Grace, enough now, you're being silly." She yanked my arms off her neck. "For goodness sake, what's with you tonight?"

"Don't want you to go. Can't you just stay?"

"Come on, angel, I'll be back in no time flat. And Janet and Frank are here, it's not as if you'll be all alone."

I listened to the quiet when she quit talking. She kissed my cheek and my mouth and told me she'd bring me back a happy. That's our name for treats, *happies*. When she got up off the edge of my bed, my mattress sucked back against the wall. The hallway floor creaked and hangers clanged each other in the closet when she got her coat. Her boots came back to my door. "OK, lamby, I'll see you later, don't go to sleep too late, OK? You're OK? Lock the door after I go, but don't put the chain on." I stared. She sighed, "OK, I will be back soonly."

She kissed the air and waved. Her boots stepped downstairs. I could hear her keys—probably checking to make sure she had everything. She called, "Bye, angel," and I jumped off the bed and ran down the steps. Tears were coming—I was being a baby.

"Mummy? Mum?" She had the door open, and she turned. "Can I have a kiss goodbye?" I couldn't think of anything else. She leaned and squeezed and kissed beside my eye, said "I love you," and then I started—tears and tears. I couldn't let go, couldn't stop begging and dragging at her neck and choking on the tears and guck going down my throat.

She looked mad at me. "Honey, stop now, stop, don't do this, please. Why are you crying? Honey, this is ridiculous—come on, Grace, I shouldn't have to feel guilty for going out one night— one night!" I sucked my breath in. She squished off the tears under my eye with her thumb, said, "What's gotten into you?" and kissed me again. "OK now, everything's fine. I'll be back in a few hours." She stepped backwards, kissed the air and waved, and closed the door behind her.

It felt like wet Kleenex going through my chest. I ran to the window, saw her coming onto the sidewalk from our path, saw her move her tam down on her forehead, look at me in the window and wave again. My hands went against the glass, and crying noises came out of me like hiccups. I couldn't stop calling her and begging through the window. She was leaving and she wasn't coming back.

She looked up again and frowned and stopped. I could see her mouth moving, making "Stop it" shapes. One boot stomped and her head fell back and she looked at the sky, like she was yelling at God or the angels or someone. She looked at me again and then away, shaking her head. She stomped with both her feet and then her purse hand dropped and her bag bounced against her knees.

She took two hard stomps away, then she bent forward at me in the window, mouthing, "Grace, stop it-stop it-stop it." She turned and stomped back up the sidewalk. I was too glad to be scared.

She slammed the door shut behind her. "All right, OK, I'm staying. There, OK? I'm not going anywhere! Happy?" I ran to the hall, shoved my face in her belly and held. She ran her hand over the back of my head and called me "Weird little creature."

After Mum called her friend to cancel their plan, we sat at the kitchen table, me with hot milk and honey and two pieces of cinnamon toast, Mum just taking bites off mine. She played with one of my feet in her lap, and after a while said, "Let's take a trip. Let's go see your nanna and grandad in New Brunswick."

"When?"

"I don't know. In a couple weeks."

"Fine by me," I said, and slurped and held some hot milk on my tongue until my throat had to have the sweet honey-pain against its back.

Eilleen Two

MAY 1973

I T'S GOING ON MORNING and you are on a Greyhound to
Saint John, New Brunswick—well, Montreal actually, and
then from there you'll connect with one back home, the womb.
Is that what you're doing, bussing it back to the womb? Grace is
passed out in the seat beside you—bare feet and you're hardly out
of April—filthy feet, dirty nails. No wonder she's got kids at
school calling her stinky, telling her she's got cooties. Why is it so
hard to keep one kid clean? Why will you never hear the phrase,
Mummy, where are some clean socks?

S'pose it doesn't matter, you touch her bangs, the angry bit
springing off to the side, watch violet colour her skin through
the window, street lights and trees, high beams and clouds, shadow
then strobe. She's the one thing that keeps you from saying *I
wish I'd never laid eyes on that prick in the first place*—son of a
bitch wouldn't even give you money to go visit your parents. Tried
to tell him, *This may be the last time I see them,* but he didn't be-

lieve you, or didn't give a damn. One day you're not going to wake up, they've told you that, doctors have. *Take another drink and you're dead.*

Just have to get out of godforsaken Toronto; just have to get the cash together, that's all. You can do that—got bus fare together for this trip, didn't you?

The bus is pulling into a depot. Six-thirty in the morning. It's supposed to be Montreal but it looks like nowhere. A gravel lot just off the highway. Christ. You wake Grace, her face is winced but she's still pliable; lead her off the bus and into the station.

Place is deserted. Now, sit her down with the suitcase on a bench, go to the ticket guy and ask about the next bus to Saint John.

Newfoundland? he asks. *Saint John not St. John's,* you bark. He says not till 10:07 a.m. 10:07? You say you were told 7:15. He looks at you, his French is better than his English and he's disgusted with both of yours. He says he *don' know who gived dat time at you, uh? but it not de true one—dix heures sept.* Screw dix heures sept—how 'bout sept heures quinze? You flop down beside your kid, tell her the story. *Now what,* she wants to know, *can we sleep here for a while?* Forget it. Liable to have some thief grab your bag or your kid—terrible things happen in bus stations. You stomp back to the ticket wicket, ask which way's east. He raises his lids, just enough to get you in his pupils, then points.

The two of you start out, up the gravel hill to the road, you dragging the suitcase, Grace hobbling barefoot over the rocks carrying an overnighter. *Where're your shoes?* She doesn't know. *What do you mean you don't know?* She thought you brought them. *You thought I brought them?* What kind of cockamamie excuse is that? You can't keep track of everything, can't even handle travel arrangements let alone someone else's footwear. *You thought,* you say, *you thought. Well, you know what Thought did ...* It's the family retort to all assumptions made, and the family reply when an answer is requested: He planted an egg and thought he'd grow a chicken. Grace asks, *What?*

He shit his pants, you tell her and she nearly busts a gut. Ah, dirty jokes, they make it all a little brighter. She's giggling and hopping and wincing over sharp rocks, and you kneel down and offer her a piggyback; her and her bag and your suitcase all dragging off your sickly pack-mule self as you lumber up the hill. Nearly twist your ankle again in those asinine boots. You'll have to change before you get to your parents'. No point walking in looking like the Jezebel who ate New Brunswick.

At the highway, you drop your bag, let her slide down your back and off your bum. She wants to know, *What're we doing?*

We're going to hitch ourselves a ride and blow this joint, that's what. She gets a sly smile on her face. She likes doing bad stuff sometimes, no telling when. You've got her missing school for this trip: today, Monday and Tuesday. And that was OK with her. Maybe because her teacher's got her in with a little batch of geniuses, reading ahead of the others into grade 3—maybe she's getting a swelled head, thinks a few days away from the dumbos won't set her back much. You tell her not to tell her dad when she sees him.

Now stand there like this, hip out—provocative but not too sexy, or maybe the other way around; and hold your wee child's hand. Who could say no? Thumb out … Whoosh, a single car careens on by, not even a glance—what was he, a child-hating queer?

Don't despair, look pleasant but with a touch of ennui … Not another car in sight, not going in this direction. Grace's smile is fading, she looks blue again. *Sing me a song, old thing*, you tell her. She says she doesn't know what to sing. May as well go for the cheap laugh again. *I know one. Wanna hear a dirty one? Us kids used to sing this when we were about your age.* You tap your toe and take up with a Southern twang:

Once knew a lady lived out west,
she had moun-tains on her chest,
she had a bird's nest 'tween her legs,
where a cowboy laid his eggs.

She giggles, then *What eggs?* she says. An-n-n-d presto! Shhh-oo, crunch, car slows onto the gravel a little ways down, a male silhouette glances over his shoulder. There now, this is travelling.

This first guy says, in bare English, that he's going to Lévis then over to Quebec City, and he sits with a hand on his gearshift, gripping with gusto while he fixes on your thighs. Well, that's the French for you, no harm in looking. Thank god for your baby, though, she puts her head up over the back seat every few minutes, every time a French version of a familiar song comes on, and now and then an English one, like now, that one she likes, "*I got a brand new pair of roller skates*"; she's half-crawled over the seat, trying to get closer to that wiggly girlish voice on the radio. The driver is frowning at her, guess she's making him nervous hanging over his shoulder like that. You mimic the shudder in Melanie's voice: "I ride my bike, I roller skate, don't drive no car, don't go too fast but I go pretty far. For somebody who don't drive I bin all around the world; some people say I done all right for a girl. Ba ba ba ba yeah. Oh yeah. Oh yeah-h-h-h." He smiles out of the corner of his eye.

By nine in the morning you're driving toward St. Léonard with an older man. He finds Grace's bare feet quite charming and striking to the funny bone. His English is good. He offers to stop in Edmundston and fix her up with some shoes. Now that's charming.

He waits in the car outside the shoe store; you were hoping he'd offer to pay. He does at breakfast, though, takes the two of you to some family dining place and picks up the check. Just outside St. Léonard, he invites you to stay with him for the day, before travelling on. Or come back with him to St-Jean-Port-Joli, where he lives—you'd like it there, he says, lots of artists, says he'll buy you a woodcarving and laughs softly. He's got heavy gentle hands and his hair is silver fluttering into black just at the nape. Part of you wonders if he takes you seriously. Or if he just wants to fuck you. Maybe either way would be OK, though, feel loved for a few years or a few hours. Feel like someone wants you bad, what does it matter why? But you stand with him outside his car and say goodbye. Seems wrong leaving a woman on the highway like this, he says. And you laugh and shrug and he does too and there's a long silence before he kisses either cheek and touches at the outer corner of your eye, the curve of bone before your temple. Looks in deep as if he's soul-hunting; feel like telling him it's at the shop. He smiles at the pavement, puts a card with his number and address in your palm, folds your fingers and kisses them shut. Gives your hand a final squeeze for punctuation.

The next guy is young. Good-looking and he knows it. Tries to be even louder and more jocular into the back seat at your cowlicked girl. Tries to show he's fun for the whole family. She's not buying it, though; her laugh's a little phony. She takes her hands off the front seat and relaxes into the back, closes her eyes. He's English, anglophone, he says, says he speaks French but not that great. *I hate trying to practise in Quebec, these guys can be such assholes.* He's in sporting goods, the rep for about half of Southern Ontario. Says something about being young and how it's a positive thing in this business, given the market. He's not working now, just sort of a vacation to see some buddies in Fredericton. You went to teachers' college in Fredericton, you tell him. He thinks that's interesting. Seems to think your boobs are pretty interesting too.

You've been in the car about forty-five minutes when he says, *You look tired. I was thinking I wouldn't mind stopping at a motel and resting for a couple hours.* You smile and look out the window.

Feels nice, all this good old-fashioned lust. He lets loose a grin and asks what you do for a living, anyway. You tell him this and that. He asks if you're strapped for cash right now. Huh, that was pretty bold. You could use the money, to get back or put toward getting out of Toronto for good—rather swallow your teeth than ask your father for money. *I mean, we could just sleep, I could just stretch out along the bottom of the bed.* How cute—your pause for thought nearly scared his preppy little pants back on.

Grace's head and shoulders come hurtling over the front seat. *OK, no funny business!* What does she mean? Well, you know what she meant, but how could she know what she meant?

The guy looks startled. You both giggle. You pat her cheek and smooth fingers over her forehead, say, *Out of the mouths of babes ...* and the subject is dropped.

Some family-man sort drove you the last jaunt from Fredericton to Saint John. Wanted to take you right to the door; you had him let you out down the road. No point leaving yourself open to a lot of questions. It's almost dark and you've got Grace by the hand, hopefully by the ear. *We took the bus here and then a taxi from the bus station, OK? Don't forget that. I'm serious, sweety, don't slip up.*

But aren't they gonna see us walking? There's not gonna be a taxi car, they're gonna know.

They won't even ask. It would never even occur to them.

Yes they will, they'll think it's weird, they're gonna know. They're older than you.

Oh, pipe down, Grace, you're making me nervous. You let go your daughter's sweaty little mitt and bring the back of your hand to your lips, dab at them for an overabundance of red, glance down your blouse, do up another button, avoid another stumble, this time over grass growing out of the sidewalk, say out loud, *Step on a crack, break your mother's back.*

What do you mean?

Nothing. Haven't you ever heard that expression?
No. It's kind of mean.
Not if you don't step on any cracks, it's not.

She begins making wide strides across all pavement connections before your parents' house. Your eyes coast from her feet to their door and see a face, see Grace's woolly eyebrows on an old face. Oh shit—shoot—heart's going love and terror; a smile splits your face. *Mumma!*

The screen door opens and she rushes down three steps to the sidewalk. The space she leaves makes room for Dad. Drop your suitcase and run to the ohs and my goodnesses and *How was your trip, did you take a taxi from the station? We could've come and picked you up. How did you get here?* Grace checks her shoes for crack evidence, then smiles politely at an old lady, an even older man. God they're old—how did they get so old, everything's white and lined like school paper.

Your father moves with prepared stiff strides toward you. Greets you with that firm pat of his, his gaze eased with a nod that you try to make pass for *Baby girl, let me look at you, is this my granddaughter—she's adorable!* or something like that, something human and loving as opposed to the stoic face of an old British schoolteacher. As opposed to a mouth that you can't recall ever saying you were so much as interesting. Oh Christ, run, just run before you get in that house and every cruddy, insensitive, stingy remark he ever made hits brick-deep in the back of your head. He takes your suitcase—What! What is wrong with the way you look? Didn't say anything but he looked you up and down, and you're not imagining it. Oh god, it's like falling down a hole. Down some muddy fucking rabbit hole. You can't go home again.

You're sitting up straight, trying to be well-mannered by memory: the prodigal daughter. Haven't seen them in seven years, not since after Grace was born, and you don't remember how to do this, be with them. It's suppertime and the four of you are at the kitchen table, just you, Grace and them. Tomorrow night'll be the big family dinner in the dining room.

Scooping a dollop of mashed potatoes onto your plate, you look over at Grace's. Mum's just put a kid-size portion from every serving dish on the table in front of your child—House Rule Number 1: *At mealtimes, you must try a little bit of everything.* Grace is gawking down at the mashed potatoes, fiddleheads and broccoli beside her roast beef. She's already announced she doesn't like the first three and her grandfather refers her to House Rule Number 1. Her jaws start working and she twirls a lock of hair round and round.

You feel like telling them your kid's got the taste buds of a cat and you've just never had the energy to force-feed her. Besides, you did it with her sister and look where that got you. But they're too busy wondering where they went wrong with you to handle that information, and your rambling thoughts are interrupted when Grace grabs the slab of beef off her plate and starts salting it in her hand. Dad raises his penguin eyebrows.

Quick, be motherly, show some authority. *Here, honey, let's try putting this down and eating like a good girl instead of a chimp-girl,* and she giggles and fidgets. You take up her fork and your knife and commence cutting her beef into bite-size pieces as if you do this all the time, before you hand her back the proper grandparent-friendly eating utensil.

How come? You're the one that's always saying fingers were invented before forks, she yaps at you, because god forbid she should just go along with you on this one.

Dad smiles at her and swallows a fiddlehead. *Better learn to eat with a fork and knife, young lady, or your boyfriends won't want to take you to any fancy restaurants when you grow up.*

Good, your kid says, through a mouthful, *we can eat pizza all the time then.*

Dad's eyebrows rise again and Mum chuckles and says, *She's got you on that one, Wilfred!*

Ha, they're laughing. See, it's not so bad.

It's quiet a minute, except for some cutlery against plates. Grace is staring across the table at your father and finally says, *You sure got long eyebrows.*

Mum giggles again, holding her lips until all her food is swallowed, pats Grace's arm and says, *Thank you sweetheart, I've been trying to tell him about trimming those things for goodness knows how long now. But he won't let me near them.* She leans over to Grace's shoulder and whispers, *You think his eyebrows are bad, wait'll you get a look at his ears.*

Grace shrieks, *You got long hairy ears too?* The table erupts. Everyone's laughing, even your father. It's almost strange seeing him laugh; it's never the way you picture him. Your child goes on, *You know what, this kid in my class, Parmjeet, has really really really long hair, like around down to her bum and*—oh god, your heart stalls: you kids were never allowed to say the word *bum.* Dad's just listening, though, looking old and tired as Grace rambles—*and oh and her dad has this cloth thing on his head that's like a hat only it's called a turbine and Parmjeet said* his *hair is even longer than …*

She prattles on and you sit, relieved not to have to run for cover re: *bum.* She talks so long and so fast, they can only listen and you get a temporary reprieve from having to speak, come up with the answers as to how or where Grace's father is.

Everything's wonderful until you realize that all the food's been eaten except for your child's dinner. House Rule Number 1B: *The little bit of everything must be entirely eaten off one's plate.* You look down at your own: clean, not a morsel. And you're sure you've only consumed like that out of some flashback habit.

Grace glances around whilst simultaneously edging her plate away, the fiddleheads, mashed potatoes and broccoli rearranged but not nibbled. *Mashed potatoes make her gag, she only likes 'em baked, and fiddleheads and broccoli—well, you can forget them altogether.* That's what you'd like to say, but this would only serve to remind them what a cruddy mother you are, that you screwed up with one kid and now you're working on a second.

Dad looks at Grace, says, *Better finish up now or you won't get any dessert.* Friendly but stern.

She mutters she doesn't like it and you smile and wink at her. Try to feed her a buggy, curling fiddlehead off your fork, but she purses her lips and tucks her chin looking like she's going to vomit. It's not long before your father tells you to come join them for tea and cookies in the living room, adding that Grace can join you as soon as she's finished her dinner. And something about all the children in the world who have nothing.

Your mother starts clearing plates and you jump up to help, glancing over your shoulder at your baby, her eyes welling. Remember? It was always like this—

Jo and Larry and George and you sitting around that dining-room table. Mumma's right arm, practically raised Josephine yourself, not to mention George and Larry. And Larry, poor bloody Larry—he was such a little bugger and Dad was always beating the hell out of him. Used to want to scream in Larry's face when he came home late or broke a neighbour's window—*Can't you see what he's going to do to you when he finds out?*—but he just couldn't help himself. As if he had to prove that he was smarter, cooler, tougher, better than Dad. And Dad had to prove Larry wrong. Prove Mum wrong for loving him so much. And that night—the night at dinner when Larry was late and Dad was simmering at the head of the table, your brother George cracked the air with, *Hey, did you hear about the fight in the bakery?* You kids sat holding your breaths—everyone knew that joke—he couldn't have said what he just said. Not in the house where you couldn't say *bum* or *damn*—nothing *smutty*. George sat up straight and, with this cocky toy cat grin, said, *The bun kicked the doughnut in the hole.*

Silence.

One two three seconds, then Mum laughed this listing heh-heh and stared at her plate. No one said a word until Dad ordered George to go to his room. The screen door opened just as George left and it was Larry, thirty-five minutes late. Sat through the rest of dinner listening to Dad beating on Larry, trying to get a scream out of him, Mum shielding her eyes with one hand as she ate, Jo moving food around her plate, tears streaming, and you, stone-faced.

Why did you come here, this is no escape. You didn't need this right now.

Mum has the tea ready and soon you are following your parents out to the living room. Like a scared sheep. What the hell are you so afraid of? Screw it. Just say something—*Actually, you know what, I'm just going to go check on Grace and see if I can't get her to finish her dinner any faster.*

You hear a sigh through Dad's nose and your shoulders stiffen. Who cares? Just go, what's he going to do about it, spank you?

You walk back in the kitchen and sit kitty-corner to Grace, in your mother's seat. She gnaws inside her lower lip and stares up at you like a dog in the SPCA. You reach over and swipe at her cowlick before taking the fork from her hand. Glance back at the kitchen door and raise a *ssh*ing finger to your lips before shovelling her swamp-cold vegetables in your mouth. Chew, chew, chew fast. She's giggling, you're holding your finger to your lips again, watching the door, nearly gagging now on the lumpy mash, listening for footsteps. *Finished! Good girl. (I'll smuggle you a peanut butter sandwich later.)*

He's barely looking at you. All this goddamn effort, clean and sober, you've been sober since January, almost four months, but no, that's not good enough. Nothing's ever good enough. He doesn't even seem that crazy about Grace. Your mother likes her, she taught her how to knit this morning, but Dad's too busy being whatever it is that he is—concerned but indifferent, or not letting you get your hopes up by building them—them or your self-esteem, because you're just who you are and you don't have a lot to offer. Don't think about him, think about how good it feels to see George and Larry again.

Tonight's the big Saturday-night, welcome-home dinner at the dining table and everyone's just sat down. No Jo, though; she's in Calgary these days and rarely comes home. Got married and high-tailed it out of here just as soon as she was legal. George lives just outside town with his wife, Lorna. Lorna couldn't come tonight; their youngest has whooping cough. And Larry's just here to see you. He's a cop in Charlottetown now, divorced.

You conned your mother into making things that Grace would like and so far it's coming off without a hitch. Larry's telling about one summer when the family was out in the country looking after Uncle Sam's haunted farm and how you kids all sat huddled in Jo's room pretending to comfort her but scared out of your minds from listening to spooks drag god-knows-what around the attic. Then George tells about the rat who used to come into the out-house every time he sat down.

Everyone's laughing at the visual in their head: Little George sitting there staring at a fat grey rat staring at him.

George is cackling, trying to pry some outhouse rat stories out of the rest of you. But the rest of the table denies any knowl-edge of said rat.

George swats the table. *Oh, come on! So you mean to tell me,* he says, *none of you saw that rat. He never came in while you were there?*

Larry snorts. *Must've been that sweet music you were serenading him with.*

You're laughing yourself stupid until George starts talking about Darnell Woods, one of his friends in high school who was heart-soaked with you. Heart-soaked, he says; never heard that one before. He says, *Imagine if you'd married Darnell, Eilleen— that guy's loaded now, he owns about six gas stations in Fredericton.*

Larry interrupts with his usual sardonic lilt. *Nope, Eilleen's always been a sucker for snakes.*

George chuckles and cuts himself off. It's a joke, get it, Eilleen? You used to catch snakes as a kid and you married one as a grown-up, an almost grown-up. *Jake the snake,* you say out loud with a bitter ha-ha, and suddenly you are vaulted into 1952, over twenty years ago. Christ.

Had just finished teachers' college in Fredericton when you met Jake Carrington. God he was beautiful. A beautiful bastard. Every girl in town had her eye on him. And it wasn't as if he was just some lowlife either, his father was Joseph Carrington, a Member of Parliament. Jake could have had anyone he wanted and he did, every time he wanted. Before him you'd never thought much of drinking, no one in your family drank at all. Jake was always soused, though, and after a while you started drinking for him and despite him.

The grand beginning, your first real drunk, was spent crouching alone behind the dance hall with a bottle of lemon gin. Jake had claimed he was sick that night, but he was in there all right, and you were going to sip and wince until you had a snootful, and then—well, then you'd just waltz right in and show him who's boss. You had the tightest outfit you owned on and in five minutes you'd wipe yourself on the first good-looking guy you saw, right under Jake's nose.

It didn't take much, really, till you felt it in your wrists, singing up your arms, the sweet pulsing, going up your thighs, making things sparkle and go numb, and you thought, *Jake-Jake, Jake the Snake—This is Magic, I can make Jake do whatever I say, I could tell my father to go take a flying fuck at a rolling doughnut*, and that sent you into giggle fits you couldn't remember having since you left teachers' college and came home to this godforsaken hole in the world. You swigged back a little more—just walk right in and catch him there sucking on a bottle. And some tramp.

Drank about half and stood up and things kept moving, but you lifted your chin and thought, *I'm Betty Grable, I'm Jane Russell and Lana Turner*, and boy, could you saunter.

In you went, found some girls you knew who said that Jake had already been and gone.

Huh, well, that was that, tough titty for him, you'd just stay anyway and have a grand old time. And looking around at all those guys, you had yourself convinced. And you danced, and someone bought you a Moosehead beer, and it was all fun and games. Until Jake came back at midnight with lipstick smeared all over his mouth and the two of you had it out in the middle of the dance floor. He insisted he had come looking for you, though— some drunk girl had kissed him outside, he said, and he felt guilty, so he came looking for you. And you believed him.

God, what a knack for self-deceit.

Like the day you were walking with your brother downtown and saw Jake across the street, drunk, with some woman slung around his neck. In broad daylight. Couldn't think of anything else to do but drag Larry over and introduce them. Ridiculous. What did you think you were doing? *Larry this is Jake; Jake, Larry.* Was that supposed to make the woman disappear? solidify something, show proof? Were you trying to say, *I'll see your loose broad and raise you one brother. You'll have to love me better now, I have*

family. Jake slurred out a nice-to-meet-you, shook hands and staggered away and there you stood: single, white and twenty-one,
looking down the street at what you'd hooked your wagon to: the
town reprobate. And your brother beside you looking straight
ahead, face hard. The same expression that passed through your
family when you announced the engagement.

Just bigots, you thought, just because Jake's Catholic. You'd
had it with being pushed around, told what to wear, what to say,
what jobs you could hold, how many squares of toilet paper you
could use. They'd stopped telling you what time to come home
since you'd started working, but it was still implied. Mostly your
father and that look of his, the one somewhere just the other side
of indifference loping toward disgust. Marriage would be the
ultimate putting-down of your foot, the stomp to end all rules.

So, Jake drank, so? So he hit, and lied, cheated, stole—nobody
had to know that, and in the meantime you'd fix him. Marriage
would settle him down.

You converted, and joined with him in a lovely Catholic cere-
mony. Even got a job substitute teaching for a Catholic school—
they paid less, but you thought you should try and *be* Catholic.
Meanwhile, Jake sold pots, pans, magazines, vacuum cleaners,
gadgets; he sold door to door and in department stores; he could
bark like a carny or gently soothe open their wallets. And he never
wore his wedding ring. Women were more likely to buy if they
thought a man was single, he said.

Then one Sunday, after a be-fruitful-and-multiply sermon at
church, you decided that maybe if you had a baby, things would
be different. How could a man look in a sweet baby's face and
think of anything else? The two of you needed to build a family
together, you figured. How could two people grow if they weren't
working together towards something? Then wham, you got pregnant with Charlie.

When there was enough money you both drank, but mostly he drank because mostly you were in the process of trying not to be evicted again as a result of Jake not paying the rent or because he'd broken another door when he was drunk or smashed a window or generally disrupted the neighbourhood. And every place you moved into was further north than the last, until you were living in off-season cottages because they were the only places you could afford. Sometimes, when the two of you were laughing and carrying on like kids, you'd think, *God, I love him*, and then the booze would run out and so would he. Just get up and leave. Usually he'd show up the next morning. And usually it was better if the booze did run out because the times it didn't he just got drunker and started hitting.

Of course, months later Charlie was born and nothing changed, you just gained a shield. Now, when he got out of control and staggered and insulted, you could run for the baby. No one would hit a woman holding a baby.

Took you three years, a barrel of sleeping pills and a whole lot of black eyes to get out of that.

After dinner, Larry volunteers the two of you to wash the dishes.

He's drying. *So, what's the story, morning glory? I hear rumours, but I should probably get it from the horse's mouth,* he says.

Rumours, eh? You been talking to those miserable bitches in my neighbourhood? and you scrub at the bottom of a pot.

Jesus, you've got a mouth worse than mine now. What the hell are you doing these days anyway? You're not teaching. Are you going to start teaching again or what?

*I've thought about it. I'm just—I'm not up to it now. Danny's buggered off, and—well, I kicked him out, truth be told. He hardly slept at home anyway. I figured we may as well go through the formality of having him actually move his belongings out. And—*Take a breath, don't know whether to just let it all hang out or what. This is Larry here, after all; he must've done a lot worse than you have. *And Charlie's gone. When Danny and I—*

I thought Charlie was in a foster home still, from the last time she ran away.

*She was. She took off when Danny left the first time. Then he came back. Well, he got out. He—*Do you want to let it hang this far out? *He did two years in Kingston for grand larceny. Everything went to hell while he was gone. And when he got out, we tried to make it work again. I didn't know what else to do.* You hand Larry another clean wet plate. It all sounds so pathetic when recounted this way. He's just drying, no *uh huhs*, no nothing. You go on. *So. Danny brought Grace and me out to Toronto from Vancouver and then, when it started sinking in what a mess Charlie'd become, he got it in his head that he wanted her there too—he raised her for the most part anyway, Jake was never around—so Charlie came out to Toronto and … Ah. It didn't work. I don't think anybody's heart was in it anyway. Charlie's been running around on the streets for two years now and she's not about to let me* or *him tell her what to do. I think she went to school about three days of the six months she was back home and then she just got sick of us again and took off back to Vancouver. Danny actually tried to head her off at the pass at first. He found out what train she was on, caught up with her and dragged her off at a station along the way. Didn't sound like she put up much of a fight. I think she liked it, I—*

Larry's not moving. He's got his dishtowel stuffed in a glass and he's standing there, staring.

You go on. *I think I just didn't want her back, maybe,* and your voice breaks. *I did, I did want her, but I didn't know what to do with her. When they threw Danny in the joint two years ago, I just—I lost control of her. Everything's just such a f(ee-iz)ucking mess.* Larry's shaking his head now, putting one glass in the cupboard, picking up another. *What?* you say, *why are you looking at me like that?*

Ah. He shrugs. *You. You listened to yourself lately? You sound like one of them. You're an elementary school teacher, or you were, and now you sound like a jailhouse rat. I'll tell you something, since we're standing here playing Truth or Dare and all: I looked up Danny's record. I made a couple calls and, uh—huh. Christ. He was wanted for everything from petty theft to—he was charged with kidnapping and extortion a few years ago, you know, but they couldn't make it stick. Whole thing fell apart. I kept wondering if you knew. I thought, she couldn't know. How could she knowingly hang around with this kind of garbage? He just did time for conning old people into giving him their life savings. Did you know that? Did you know he was stealing from eighty-, ninety-year-old ladies?*

You're shaking now and shoving your hands deep in the dirty soapy water, gasping back the tears and hysterics that threaten up your throat. *No,* that's all you can say. Not really. You knew some things. Cops came and searched your place once while Danny was out. One of the other wives called to let you know they'd just left her place. It was all—well, what could you—it was better than being alone—he was better than the one before him.

Remember how repulsed you were by the women in that crowd, Danny's crowd, the look of their skin, the way they spoke. Scenes from the gutter, you thought. And then you started to feel foolish around them, the way they mocked you, called you a squarejohn broad. Twenty-eight years old and there you were trying to act cool and tough. Trying to show you could be bad as all hell. Wonder if Larry knows about your record for stealing a steak and a half-pound of butter for Chrissake. God, they laughed at you for that, all the hookers and girlfriends of thieves and arm-breakers, card sharps and hustlers.

Thirteen years later and now look—you're a squarejohn broad with a jailhouse mouth. Nice combo, lady.

Larry puts the dishtowel down and takes your shoulder, dances you around so that his back's against the sink and you're against his chest like a child or a lover. He holds you and says, *You're better than this, sweetheart.* Rests his cheek against your head. *Whenever I come back to this place, I start seeing what turned us all into such assholes.*

You shake your head no in his chest. *Don't say that.*

OK. I'm just saying … look, you've got Grace still and she's a great kid. You're going to have to pull yourself up by your own bootstraps, honey. I'm talking from experience and I'll tell you, you've got a little Wilfred in you, Eilleen, we all do; start using it to make your life work instead of screwing it up. If you've gotta get out of Toronto, do it, do whatever it takes, just don't stay in this life of yours, the way it is … don't do it, sweetheart. He rubs your back while you sniffle, tilts your chin up and says, *Ah, you're no big sister, you're my little girl.* And you laugh and duck your head.

Grace Two

JUNE 1973

T WICE, AN AMBULANCE showed up and took her away, unconscious. Frank and Janet from upstairs called them both times, before I knew what was going on and, both times, they hung around at the front door, hard-faced, telling the ambulance guys how old Mum was and what she took. I told them twenty-eight and Janet came behind and told them forty-one. I told them aspirin and Janet said, "At least a bottle of wine and God knows how many of these," handing them pill bottles, some empty and some rattling. I wouldn't look at Janet afterwards. She was a traitor and she may's well know it, I figured.

Stupid Frank and Janet. When my dad moved out, he put a fridge and a hot plate in my sister Charlie's old room and rented it out to these newlyweds called Frank and Janet. They almost never came out of their room and mostly you wouldn't even know they were there, except for sometimes when it was quiet, you could hear a whimpery noise, sort of like a puppy or a parrot or something.

Anyways, after that, Frank and Janet left. Because of me, probably, me ignoring them. But they deserved it and they shouldn't
have been in Charlie's room anyhow. But then, just when it started
getting good, with them gone and Charlie's room empty in case
she decided to come back to Toronto, Mum got in a big fight with
my dad over the phone and she was madder than when she told
him to get out in the first place. She spat out one last thing and
smashed down the receiver, so I asked her what he said.

She stared at the rug. "Your father's got short arms and deep
pockets."

"What?"

"He's kicking us out is what it amounts to."

"What do you mean?"

"He's moving us into some dive of his down on Gerrard Street.
He'd rather his child live in a dump than forfeit the jacked-up rent
he'll get for this place." Our house on Woodfield was pretty nice,
like other families' houses, like with a matching rug and toilet-seat
cover in the bathroom and big long curtains in the living room
and wall-to-wall carpeting. Mum liked wall-to-wall carpeting cuz
of us seeming more rich and cuz it keeps your feet warm when you
get up in the morning.

"Is he still giving you your 'lowance?" Mum got five bucks a
week for a 'lowance when my dad lived with us and Charlie used
to get two and I got seventy-five cents. It was mostly mine I
wanted to know about, but Mum was in a crabby mood so I was
being not-selfish.

"Screw him and his *lounce* ... We don't need his crap." We did
so. I thought she should've acted nice to him at least for that. And
maybe even ask if we could get Charlie's still. We could've split it
maybe.

"Do you think Charlie'll come back again?" I wished I hadn't
asked that. I kept feeling like I was going to cry when we talked

about my sister. Every time I heard a plane growling overhead,
I imagined it was full Charlie. That she was coming back. I pic-
tured her up there fidgeting in the smoking section, complaining
about the food, her big deer eyes staring tough on anyone who
rubbed her the wrong way. I saw her in tight hip-hugger jeans with
a paisley blouse, and long hair hanging loose in her eyes, thinking about me and singing, "Sock it to me, baby, let it all hang
out." But every plane kept going and took her someplace else and
she'd press her hands against the window, crying, and I'd lie in my
bed and cry back, like we were talking to each other with ESP,
kind of.

"I don't know," Mum told me. And I started getting a stran-
gle in my stomach. Charlie was sixteen—old enough to do anything she wanted. I wondered if she'd come back or if, from now
on, there'd just be us two.

Mum took a breath the way she did when she was trying to
get her mind out of a bad memory.

The new house was on Gerrard, the closest big street. It was beside
an old empty gas station and around half the size of our old house.
There weren't any bedrooms, just a place between the kitchen and
front room that seemed more of a room to eat than sleep. We
crammed Mum's bed in there, though, and slept together. The
front room was dark and traffic-loud with a kind of greasy-look-
ing wood floor. The kitchen was the last room at the back. It
smelled like basement, like the rest of the place but stronger and
wetter. A curtain went around a toilet and shower in the corner of
the kitchen. The shower stall was tin and inside there was a fight
in the corners between the rust and the mould.

We had to share the house with Dad's other renters, Nelly and
her son Dale—they had the upstairs, we had the down. Nelly was
mean-looking with kind of see-through skin that always looked a

bit dirty. She had egg-coloured hair—white bits and yellow bits that she brushed and hairsprayed hard, down the back of her neck. I always wanted to lift just one piece to see how much would come with it.

Nelly's son Dale bugged me the same way Nelly bugged Mum —they were like the kids at school that win every fight because they don't care if they bash up their own selves or not. Dale had a couple years on me, he was nine I think, and had reddy-black hair and a cowlick in the same place as mine, except his stayed shoved off to the side and sproinged up only when he had one of his mad yelling attacks at squirrels or crows or telephone poles. His arms and legs were always jerking and looking for stuff to break.

It was summer again and I was boring; school was out and I felt like I had no friends any more. I decided to take the bus to the Riverdale Zoo and wander around. I spent practically all day staring down in the bear cages that were really just super-deep cement boxes in the ground. The bears were mangy and looked lonesome, walking round and round under the world—they only saw us when they looked up for sky. At lunchtime, zookeepers threw down bags of white bread to them, the kind I wasn't allowed to have because Mum said it had no nutritional value. I watched and wished for handfuls of bear through the black bars over their holes; I wanted to get down there and curl up in their dark fur and lie in the corner with our noses tucked together so tight we wouldn't notice the lousy kids over us throwing stuff even though the signs said not to. When the sun started going down and making everything yellowy, I figured I better get home.

Back to being bored cuz of there being nothing good to do at home any more. I never went to the park at the top of our old street once since we moved and the friends I had six blocks ago seemed a million years away—I couldn't remember what it was we used to do and if they'd still want to do it when I got there. TV was boring. I tried playing with Shadow but he was boring—he was more Charlie's cat than mine anyhow. And Mum was super-boring: she was lying on her bed again, like scribble on a crumpled sheet. Seemed like she was always sick and sad. When she wasn't flat on her back, she sang in the kitchen with Patsy Cline or Julie London or sometimes alone into a tape recorder. Lots of "Crazy" and "Cry Me a River," or else a song she made up about love and men and needing a man. And at the end of each one she'd cry. I almost hated her for not being fixed by my I-love-yous, but I still fitted myself in her lap sometimes and rocked back and forth with her while she sang.

I went back out of the house and stood on our side of the chain-link fence. Dale from upstairs was over on the old gas station side, on his knees, sharpening a stick with a paring knife. He looked up while he was hacking and made the knife hit the ground. He squinted and said, "Whatdya lookin' at?"

So I shrugged and told him, "Nothin'."

He held up the stick. "Yeah you are, you're lookin' at a murder weapon." I didn't say anything; he looked at the point of his stick and started jabbing the air. "Better watch your fuckin' cat, kid."

I looked over my shoulder, worried my mum heard and afraid Shadow was out. I hated the push in his voice. I tried to make my voice hard and told him, "Better not touch my cat or you're dead."

Dale made a phony howly laugh and went, "You and whose army?" Then he said, "Hey, what's your name again, kid? I forget your name."

"Grace."

"Oh yeah, like 'Hey Grace, come sit on my face'?"

"I'd rather stand on it."

He gave me his fake-shocked face. "You better watch it, little girl," and he shook his stick and stabbed the air then gave it a yank like he just stuck it through me and wanted it back. I watched and wondered what it would take to make Dale think I was crazy. My dad said that once—make 'em think you're crazy and they'll leave you alone. I wrapped my fingers in the fence and rested my cheeks and looked past him.

"Wanna do something?" he asked me. "Wanna climb the tree in the back." I shrugged. He looked like he was getting pissed off. "Why not, you're always out there sitting in it. You look like a skinny ugly squirrel up there." He threw his stick over the fence into our backyard. The knife was still beside his feet. He looked at it too. "I'm not gonna hurtcha," and he kicked it across the pavement. "Come on."

I came through the opening in the fence onto the gas station part. He picked up a rock and threw it at one of the old pumps. "I betcha ten bucks you can't hit the hose part on the pump with ..." he leaned and snatched it off the pavement, "this rock."

"I don't bet suckers, I eat 'em."

"Yeah, yeah, just cuz you can't."

I went close enough to get the rock from him and eyeballed the hose. It was around twenty feet away. He watched me aim and miss the pump by a mile, then he laughed his over-loud cackle again. "Ahha, ten bucks, y'feeb. You throw like a girl."

"So. I am one," and I wandered off to look inside what used to be the garage. He followed and stood beside me trying to spy through the dirty window. There was nothing in there but part of an old car's insides.

Dale leaned his forehead against the glass. "I could take a car apart and put it back together, you know."

I moved along the garage to a side room where the cashier's desk was. "Could not."

"I fuckin' could so, eh. I'm a really good driver. I'd have my licence if it wasn't for the stupid cops—my brother even told me. And he should know, man, he's a race-car driver."

"Really? Where is he?" There were posters on the wall of the Michelin Man and red cars that looked like sharks, and one of a red-haired lady in tight shorts holding a wrench to her lips. I had to move before Dale saw her.

"He's with my dad. In the States. In New York. They're both race-car drivers." Dale followed after me. "Where you goin'? We should break in and get some stuff."

"There is no stuff. What do you mean, break in?" He was crazier than I could even fake.

"Just bust in, man, it's all glass, just bust in." I walked away, not wanting to be there if he did it, scared he was going to follow me and scared he wasn't. He came along to the side of the building. "Come on, there's a cash register in there, maybe there'd still be money in it or else they hid money under it or something, or maybe there's stuff in the back like a secret compartment or a safe." We walked up to a sheet of glass leaning against the garage with a chunk the shape of a telephone broken out of the top. I could hear Dale starting to breathe all weird when we came to it, and he barked "This is mine" at me as if I was going to steal it.

"Why do you have a piece of broken glass?"

"I mean it's mine, like I'm saving it." I asked him why. "Cuz. Cuz there's days like today, man." He was getting more fidgety. "Back up," and he shoved me off to the side. Then he faced it, took a couple steps back and did a sideways jump, busting through the sheet to the wall. Glass flew everywhere and I screamed and turned my back. Pieces whacked against my T-shirt and fell. One hit low on my calf and slashed so that blood dripped down to my heel. It wasn't that deep, but seeing it made me scream even more.

Dale was on the ground from losing his balance. His voice was shaky a little. "Shit."

I had bare feet and there was glass all over the place around him, so I moved back trying to find a place where it wasn't. "Are you OK?" I asked him.

He got up off his arms and rested on his knees to see what he did to himself. His jeans saved his skin but the tank top didn't.

There was skinny pins of glass stuck in his skin up to the elbow and blood crawled out where they were shining. The piece that did the worst of it fell on the ground and left a big gash on the underpart of his elbow. I got butterflies watching the red streams come down his arm.

Dale had mouth-twitches while he concentrated on picking all the pieces out. I started to cry. He looked up at me with his eyes all watery and smiled.

"I'll get your mum," I told him.

"No." It came out of him like a bark again. He kind of looked like his mum for a second, the way her eyes scrunched when she left a cigarette hanging out of her mouth. "She's not home."

"Yes she is, you might have to go to the hospital." I was sure I heard her up there earlier.

"She's not home, just forget it. I'm fine." He held his arm to the sun trying to make sure he found all the glass.

"Well, I'll tell my mum then." I didn't know what mine would even do, the way she was.

"Don't tell your mum nothing—she's a whore." My mouth dropped and he said, "She is, my mum told me; your mum's a hooker."

"No! She *is not*." I squinted back at him. "No she's *not*."

Dale stood up. "Yeah she is, my mum told me, she knows your mum is and quit walkin' away from me, y' little baby; if you tell her I told you that, you're dead."

I glanced at Dale's arm; I didn't care any more. "I'm not, I just don't want to stay outside any more. What if someone comes and sees what you did? I don't wanna be there when you *get it*."

"I mean it, you tell your mum and I'll kill you—and don't think I won't know."

"I'm not, I'm just going in. Cuz anyway, she's sick today." I backed up some more, watching the ground.

"You mean she's hungover." He took a couple steps toward me with his wrist in the air and blood coming off his elbow like drool.

"No, she has the flu." I went back toward the house.

Dale hollered after me, "I mean it, kid: tell her and you're dead." Glass skidded on the ground behind me.

It was hot when I came in, but I locked the door and closed the window. I pulled the blind by our bed. Mum was the same: on her back with her mouth open and her head tilted back in her pillow as if she was trying to get as much air as she could without working that hard. I sat down beside her, watching the door and crouched in near to her ear.

"Mum? Mummy." She whimpered. "Mummy, Dale said you're a hooker." She mumbled. "Mum?"

"I can't hear you." Her tongue smacked the roof of her mouth trying to get wet again.

"Shh! Dale said you're a hooker."

"I can't hear what you're saying, honey, get me some water."

I hissed at her, "I can't talk loud, I'm not supposed to tell you because he said he'd kill me—he said you're a hooker." The phone rang. I pushed her arm. She asked for water again. I flicked hard, where I pushed her. And she went, "What! Get the phone."

It was Charlie. In Vancouver. Mostly we wrote letters, but I loved it the best when we got to be on the phone together. She said, "I miss you, Grace-face," and asked how I was. I felt all babyish like I was going to cry from her voice and I wanted to just be normal and tell her how much I loved her. All I said was I was OK. Charlie said I didn't sound so OK. I was OK, just that Mum was sick, I said. That way maybe she'd feel sorry for Mum just in case she was still mad at her. I looked down at the back of my ankle. The blood was pretty much dried. "And I cut myself."

"Oh no. Are you OK?"

"Yeah, it's OK."

"What's wrong with Mum? Sick with a fever or sick lying-on-her-back-throwing-up?"

"Lying on her back."

"Oh," and she got quiet a second. "I'm calling because I wanted to tell you that I saved up some money and I'm going to come back to Toronto for a little while. Day after tomorrow. Maybe we could go to the zoo or something, like you said in your letter. Or maybe we could go to the museum and look at the dinosaurs. And no, I'm not mad at Mum. Your letter sounded all worried."

I looked at Mum heaped in the sheets. The two of them together. If I could just have them separate. "Um, where will you stay when you come?" I felt guilty or more like mad, I guess, at my dad for making us move so we didn't have Charlie's room any more.

"Well, I don't know. Your place is pretty small now, eh? I think I might stay at a friend's place."

"OK. But you're going to phone right as soon as you come, though, right?"

"Of course, baby. I miss you so much." Her voice went funny and she took a breath for a second. "Well … um … can Mum come to the phone?"

"Mmm, she's sleeping."

"OK, well, you can tell her, I guess. So, uh, so then I'll see you. Wednesday, OK?"

"OK." Mum looked practically dead. I whispered "I love you" to Charlie.

"Oh." Her voice went warbly. "I love you too, baby. So much. OK? I have to go now."

On Wednesday afternoon, Charlie showed up full of piss and vinegar. She was excited since we talked on the phone because of her plan to come help Mum and help me clean up the house a bit.

Mum was still in bed, but she was talking more now and eating. They seemed OK so far, no fighting: hugs and kisses, and kind of mushy. Except for when Mum said that Charlie's jeans were so tight they were crawling up her arse. Charlie looked like she wanted to leave almost. She changed the subject to how messy the house was and said we'd have to scour it from head to toe. I nodded. Mum reminded Charlie that she was sick, so she couldn't help it being messy.

Charlie was all weird like a super-peppy maid or something, and she wasn't there an hour before she had the kitchen floor all swept and me filling buckets, hunting for a mop and cloths, going to the store for Dutch Cleanser and Mr. Muscle. When the floor was done she started on the dishes, then changed her mind and opened the fridge. "Maybe we should take a break and have a sandwich or something." She leaned in and her fingers went squeamy from everything they touched. "Grace, there's nothing in the fridge but mouldy old crap! God. What've—The milk is sour, it's two weeks out of date." She handed me the bottle and I dumped the lumps down the sink. "What have you been eating?"

"I don't know, hot dogs or fried egg sandwich sometimes, or there's cinnamon, I make cinnamon toast and I know how to make french toast now, you know, and— there was other milk, it's just that I finished it, and there was other stuff, there's Dad's oatmeal cookies, and maybe some Dr Pepper left from last night and apples. And bread, I think."

She took the bread off the top of the refrigerator. "Grace! It's mouldy, look at the crust, it's blue!"

"Well, some of it's still good. At the front slices and the back ones you can cut that stuff off—and there's wieners in the freezer. And relish and ketchup. And canned something—Mum was trying to get me to eat those Bing cherries in the can, but I don't like them. Anyway, sometimes we just order pizza."

Shadow skidded into the kitchen, playing with a cork, slapped it into Charlie's foot and crashed into the brown paper bag she'd set up for garbage beside the fridge. Charlie grabbed the cork off the floor, looked at the tip, all pink from wine, and threw it in the bag. She hucked the bread in after it and wiped her hand hard off her forehead. I picked Shadow up off the floor and held him a second; the room was sticky-hot. "It's OK, I can go to the store. I just forgot. Plus it's almost time to get cat food."

Charlie swooped past me into the middle room. She stood over Mum with her hands on her hips and said in a nicey-nice voice, "Are you ever going to get out of this bed and try looking after Grace or are you just going to lie there until she starves to death?"

Mum's eyes flicked open. "What are you talking about?"

Charlie grabbed an empty bag off the floor and crumpled it up. "Nothing."

"No—what did you just say?" Mum's voice was coiling up like a mad snake.

Charlie chucked the bag on the dresser. "You! You should be charged with neglect, that's what—goddamn house is a pigsty, place smells like cat piss, there's no food in the fridge—not even milk. What the fuck is she living on?—wieners and chocolate bars? Do you give a shit about anything in this world but men and booze!"

Mum struggled her head off the pillows. "Look who's talking! Grace is fine, no thanks to you. Coming and going whenever you damn well please—why don't you just stay the hell away so she doesn't end up crying for a month because you fucked off again. She's healthy and fine now and I don't need you barging in here trying to run the show. Person can't even be sick in their own home. Nobody asked you to come here, so why don't you just get the hell out of my house."

"Christ you're a bitch—kid's seven years old and she's looking after herself while you—"

"Get out! I want you out of my house before I damn well kill you. I swear to Jesus, I'll kill you!"

Charlie's face went white. "Grace! Grace, go get the knives."

I was in the doorway between them and the kitchen. "What? What do you mean?"

"Grace, do what I say." Charlie looked crazy-scared.

Mum hollered over her, telling her not to order me around and to get out of the house before she had to get carried out. Charlie screamed louder, "I hate your guts—you should be locked up! Grace! get the knives, get all the knives and scissors out of the drawers and hide them in the backyard."

I didn't move. Charlie backed away from the bed. I couldn't believe either of them. I mostly couldn't believe anyone believed Mum's killer threats. She could hardly make it to the bathroom, never mind stab someone. I tried to explain. "But Charlie—"

Mum dragged her back up off the bed, her chest crumpled forward on her thighs, until she got up the strength to dump her feet over onto the floor. Charlie screeched, "Grace, get the knives!" and she chased me back to the kitchen. Mum's voice came after us. "Get out of my house. I mean it and if you touch one hair on that kid, I'll kill you."

My sister yanked open the silverware drawer and started pulling dirty knives out of the sink, shaking and stuttering, "Where's the scissors?" I shrugged. "Well, where's a dishtowel?"

I grabbed one off the counter and she wrapped all the sharp stuff she could find in it, handed them over and said, "Here! Go. Take them out back and bury them."

I took them from her, trying to move faster so she wouldn't get mad.

Bury them? I walked out into the long grass in our backyard; the cherry tree took up most of it. I could hear their screams going over each other in the house and I dropped the stuff in the grass and sat down. There was a butter knife, a couple paring ones, ones

with edges for cutting meat and the scissors—the scissors that were
too dull to get through the cardboard in the back of Mum's pantyhose packages. I wondered if Mum even got off the bed yet. I
pushed myself up and kicked through the grass to the back door.

The place was quiet. Shadow was hiding behind the kitchen
door and Mum was sitting on the edge of the bed with her head
in her hands and her back shaking from crying inside. I could see
the open front door from where I was, so I creeped back out and
around the side of the house.

Charlie was out front, sitting on the broken old fence that separated our place from the sidewalk. Streetcars rattled past us. She
jumped when I touched her arm, and her face was red and clenched
up. "Can you please go back in the house and get my leather jacket
and my bag." I nodded and walked up the porch steps.

Mum's feet were still at the side of her bed; she said my sister's
name before looking in the front room at me. Then asked me if
Charlie left. I said yeah, that I was just getting her stuff. So she
croaked, "Yeah, well you tell her—Nothing, don't tell her anything. And don't you go anywhere with her either!"

"I'm not. Leave me alone."

"Hey ... watch yourself."

I went back out the front door to Charlie, handed her her stuff
and sat down on the fence. I didn't know what to do, so I held her
hand and squeezed it to keep from crying. "I'm sorry about not
changing the cat-pissy litter box. Do you have to go back to
Vancouver?"

She made a weird smile and pressed her fingers against her eyes
and held that way a few seconds. I looked at her lipstick. It was
practically the same as Mum's. Or maybe she was just tall like
Mum so stuff only seemed like Mum. Really they didn't even look
the same—Mum didn't have big deer-eyes or hair like a horse
mane. Maybe it was just that they said my name the same way, it
melted out of their mouths like warm chocolate—not like my dad

or other people who ever lived with us. And we were holding each other right now and I could crawl inside Charlie the way I could Mum. Charlie wasn't drunk or sick and she wasn't crying, like normal. She was something else. I looked at her jeans tucked into her big black boots that my dad got her when we were still all together. She looked like she could kick the crap out of someone with those boots. Like she could bleed and smile.

She said, "Yeah soon, I guess. I have a couple friends I know here that I'm going to visit.... We could still go to the zoo or something."

"I'm not allowed."

She shook her head and laughed sort of clunky. "Oh yeah. Perfect. What the hell. Wh—OK, well I guess I better go. I'm sorry, baby. I'm really ... sorry. That you're still here in this."

"It's OK, you know, she's just in a bad mood and she has the flu and plus Daddy moved us down here and she really hates it so she's not feeling good. And plus, me not changing the litter box and everything. You just caught us at a bad time."

Charlie laughed again and folded her leather coat over her arm to go. I felt bad for her, having to carry a coat in that heat.

CANADIEN OUEST/CANADIEN FEDERAL

TELECOMMUNICATIONS

CANADIAN WEST/CANADIAN FEDERAL

Child Protection Agency
Metropolitan Toronto

333 Wellesley St. E.
Toronto 205
Ontario   June 25/73 (1.22)p.m.

Request check Mrs. Daniel Hoffman 1416
Gerrard St. Toronto Phone 466-2727 re care
being given daughter Grace born 24/11/65.
Complaint received here by daughter Charlotte
who recently returned Vancouver. Mrs. Hoffman
history of alcoholism and emotional problems.

Signed: Darling C.P.A. Vancouver

| | plein tarif | lettre de nuit | mots | coût |
| | full rate | night letter | words | tolls |

Nom de l'expéditeur, adresse et numéro de téléphone • Sender's name, address and telephone number

HOFFMAN, Anne <u>Eilleen</u>

7.7.73 (L. Barrington) Received letter from CPA
Vancouver regarding Eilleen Hoffman and the welfare of
daughter Grace, born 11.24.65. The letter was sent by
Lilly Darling, case worker of Mrs. Hoffman's older
daughter, Charlotte (in care since 1970), who has had
a roller coaster relationship with her mother over the
last several years. After a recent trip to visit her
family, Charlotte returned deeply concerned over the
well-being of her younger sister.

7.9.73 (L. Barrington) After several failed attempts
to contact Eilleen Hoffman by phone, I went to the
residence for a home visit. There was no answer at the
door and a neighbour from the other side of the
property (dwelling is a side-by-side duplex) came out.
I informed her of my purpose there. Neighbour is
Arlene Kensit, 1418 Gerrard St. E. Her daughter
apparently plays with Grace Hoffman. Mrs. Kensit
informed me that she wx was not surprised, that it was
"only a matter of time before the Child Protection
got involved." She told me that Mrs. Hoffman wasn't
much for looking after Grace, that the child is often
unkempt-looking, face dirty, uncombed hair, T-shirt on
backwards. She told me that various men come and go
from Mrs. Hoffman's home at all hours of the night and
confirmed that Mrs. Hoffman is an alcoholic and often
bedridden by her frequent "benders." She recalled a
day when Mr. Hoffman, who owns the property, came by
to pick up Grace. Mrs. Hoffman had company, two men
with whom she was drinking on the porch. Mr. Hoffman
tried to come up the stairs and Mrs. Hoffman slurred
out that her rights as a tenant stated that the land-
lord would have to give her 24 hours notice before
appearing on the property. Mr. Hoffman said he wanted
his child. Mrs. Hoffman told him that Grace wasn't
home and as he tried to climb the stairs, one of Mrs.
Hoffman's companions pushed him back down. Mr.
Hoffman left saying he'd be bb back.
    Incidents such as these can only be damaging to a
child. Apparently, Grace was not there to witness this
as she was playing out back with the Kensits' daughter,
Pearl. But Mrs. Kensit says she has already seen
evidence that Grace is becoming "messed up." She told
me of seeing Grace tie her cat to a skipping rope and

swing him round and round out back. This went on for
a considerable length of time until Mrs. Kensit went
to knock on Mrs. Hoffman's door. There was no answer
and Mrs. Kensit again expressed concern over the lack
of supervision with Grace. Mrs. Kensit also mentioned
an incident where Grace pushed another child down on
the sidewalk. At this point in the interview, the
Kensits' daughter Pearl came outside and interjected
that Grace was retaliating over a name the other child
had called her. Nevertheless, I feel these incidents
speak of maladjusted aggressive behaviour, common in
children of severe alcoholics and/or children in
violent family situations. Will attempt another home
visit tomorrow.

7.10.93 (L. Barrington) Knocked at Hoffman's door
at 9 a.m. to no avail. Returned at 11 a.m., knocked
louder, calling Mrs. Hoffman's name. This time,
daughter, Grace, answered the door in her pyjamas.
She seemed to be very protective of her situation and
closed the door to get permission to allow me in.
Mrs. Hoffman was in a nightgown still and asked me
to wait outside until she was dressed. I had the
distinct impression that this is some sort of game
Mrs. Hoffman plays with those she perceives as
authority figures.
     When finally allowed into the home, I was shocked to
see the disarray -- the kitchen mess, the floor ~~flit~~
filthy, a litter box that must not have been changed in
weeks. The bathroom seemed to be a part of the
kitchen although curtained off -- can't imagine that
this is legal with respect to health regulations.
Living-room floor covered in crumbs ~~am~~ and dirt. Mrs.
Hoffman obviously is in no shape to care for a child
in her state. She seemed to be hungover, the previous
night's makeup still half on, breath sour.
     The child was very reluctant to leave her mother in
order that Mrs. Hoffman and I might talk alone. Both
mother and child seem very anxious and protective of
each other. I spoke at length with Mrs. Hoffman about
the complaint received by CPA and her current situation.
The idea of putting Grace into care while she received
help seemed to be disastrous to her. She sounded
somewhat dependent on Grace, who found several excuses
to come back in and eavesdrop in the half-hour I was
there.

Mrs. Hoffman has been in and out of AA and claims recent illness to have kept her from meetings lately. She agreed to begin attendance right away if we found her transport. I insisted on the importance of removing Grace from this situation until we could get the house back into shape and her mother into some sort of detox ~~x~~program. We settled on the idea of my contacting Mr. Hoffman regarding Grace's care and Mrs. Hoffman seemed to have no problem with his involvement whatsoever.

7.11.73 (L. Barrington) Met with Daniel Hoffman today, Grace's father. He was tidy and well-dressed, his manner quite congenial and ~~aple~~ apologetic regarding his wife's condition. He said he would have her in a detox program immediately but that he would not be able to keep Grace in his apartment as it is too small and he will be away on business as of this Sunday. He has suggested Gloria Carnaegie of 337 Greenwood Ave., who is his first wife, and apparently a good friend of Mrs. Hoffman's as well. Gloria Carnegie is single with one son and is quite fond of Grace. Mr. Hoffman will be making arrangements as soon as possible to have Grace stay there. Spoke with Eilleen Hoffman. She is comfortable with this arrangement.

7.12.73 (L. Barrington) Spoke with Mr. Hoffman again today. Grace is now staying with Gloria Carnegie and Mr. Hoffman has contacted a treatment facility where Eilleen Hoffman can be admitted this week. Assuming the situation improves before summer's end, Grace's schooling shouldn't be an issue.

7.14.73 (L. Barrington) Made arrangements yesterday with the chairman of the Gerrxard East Group, an AA group that meets every Tuesday and Thursday night. A member will be picking up Eilleen Hoffman tonight to take her to the meeting. Spoke with Mr. Hoffman today. Grace is well and happy at his former wife's home. There are apparently many children her age in the area. Will contact Gloria Carnegie tomorrow to check situation.

7.17.73 (L. Barrington) Met with Miss Carnegie today. House was very clean and bright on a nice tree-lined street with many children about. Miss Carnegie herself was very clean and bright though a bit hard-edged and with a distinct cynicism regarding Daniel Hoffman's involvement in Grace's care and well-being. She told me that Mr. Hoffman dropped Grace off the other day without so much as a word about when he'd be returning or even staying a while to make sure she was okay. He brought next to nothing in terms of clothing: one extra outfit in a paper bag and a teddy bear. Miss Carnegie went shopping for Grace the following day and called Mr. Hoffman after the fact to ask for reim reimbursement. He apparently showed up the next day with cash for her, and, as she put it, "He barely said a word to Grace, didn't sit down with her, didn't so much as take her for an ice cream." She added that this incident has caused her to lose an all respect for Mr. Hoffman. What Mrs. Hoffman lacks in cleanliness, she said, "she makes up for in love of that kid." Miss Carnegie is, indeed, quite fond of Grace.

Eilleen Three

NODDING AND NODDING to yourself, pacing around the house, thinking and making shaggy zigs and zags, trying it out in negative then positive, blueprints and tooth-crushing nothing—Here's the thing—the thing is, is, they're going to keep your kid if you don't do something. That's all there is to it. They've got her, but at least they've got her where you want her, where you can find her, just can't go near her that's all. Gloria's got Grace. Say that a few times to calm your guts. Gloria's got Grace. Sounds almost pretty almost.

Had to be Charlie, Charlie called them—who else would've? —mean-hearted bitch. Fuck-fuck-fuck. Charlie came, Charlie saw, Charlie phoned. Phoned the fucking Child Protection. How could she, how could anyone do that to you? Why didn't she just go rip the belly out of the sky and let it all drain white. Doesn't have to now, she's done it to *you*—you are the symbolic sacrifice to all her demons. They showed up at your door—Well, one did,

just one of them came to the house. Wretched old bat showed up
first thing; eleven Monday morning. And you and Grace were still
asleep. That really got her. She came bustling in, that barn-door
arse of hers bursting at the seams, said she was Mrs. Barrington
from Child Protection, that she just wanted to have a look around,
which she did and immediately set about tisking and fuming, saying things like *dreadful* and *hmm* and *This isn't good, Mrs. Hoffman,
this is just no good.*

Confusing, the whole thing, being woken up by a nightmare
like her. Kept trying to slide excuses in there, jam every babbling
orifice she had with excuses, but she was a flood not a trickle. She
looked at Grace, shook her head. Miserable cow—nobody shakes
their head at your kid. She told Grace maybe she might like to go
outside and play for a while while she, Mrs. Barrington, had a talk
with Mummy. *Go outside and play?* What was Grace supposed to
do, just go out and play with things at random? Stand out in the
parking lot and turn in circles till she passed out? Grace looked
bewildered/relieved/territorial—hard to single out just one face
on her. You told her it was OK.

The second you were alone, Mrs. Barrington slapped down
your file. Morning was still flapping around your brain, it was hard
to think clearly. *Why are you here, did someone call you?*

She said there'd been reports but that was confidential. She
opened the folder. *You should know, though, that as part of my in-
vestigation I have reviewed the file of your daughter currently in care
and I have spoken with your neighbours.* These broads always think
they're with the CIA or something. Apparently she interviewed
them to see if they'd noticed any odd behavioural tendencies in
Grace. Ah geez, here we go. Evidence from the parents of Pearl —

Not long after you moved into this sty, Grace started up a
friendship with Pearl, the little girl next door. She spent a lot of
time there. In fact you thought she must have been hard up for
friends seeing the two of them out there in Pearl's backyard singing

Pearl's favourite, *Country Road Take Me Home.* When you know for a fact your kid hates that song. Or, Grace told you, they played *Rifleman.* God knows what that entailed; now and then you'd hear Pearl call Grace *Pa.*—And now Barrington has enlisted Pearl's wingnut parents, who drink at least as much as you ever did, as informants—*And you know, it didn't take a wink for them to tell me yes that your child has displayed questionable behaviour. For instance, one afternoon they saw her tie her cat around the middle with a skipping rope and proceed to swing the poor animal round and round in circles. Mrs. Hoffman, your little girl stood there half an hour or more just swinging and swinging until they thought surely the cat would throw up or die.*

Barrington calculates your face, decides you are not duly shocked. *I can assure you, Mrs. Hoffman, cruelty to family pets is long past the first sign that all is not well.*

Piffle! What—does she think your kid was the first person to swing a cat? Where the hell does she think the expression came from? Children are curious and wicked, is that not common knowledge? Should've seen her at three—wait'll she turns thirteen.

Your new social worker went on to say that they, the Child Protection, were fully aware of your alcoholism and she inquired as to when you'd discontinued treatment. AA, that is. *Not long ago,* you told her. You were going—just that you'd been sick lately, hadn't been up to it, and then with Grace home for the summer, you wanted to spend as much time with her as possible.

Fish-eyes descended on you. Deadpan. *I see* and then *We can easily arrange someone through the AA Program to pick you up a few times a week and take you. Surely, Mrs. Hoffman, you're aware that things cannot go on like this, you need help and Grace needs a structured supportive environment.*

Grace would have to be taken into care until you and the house straightened up.

Shaking; could feel your bones chattering in the skin.

Then she asked about The Father. *Is the father present?* And it was the one time you thought better of publicly running him into the ground. You nodded, stuttered, *Yes, I mean, we're separated, but you can call him at work if you like.* And you thought, *Yeah, call him. If there's one thing Danny knows how to do, it's weasel people like you.* She cleared her throat and jotted some more, asking if it were possible for Grace to stay with him? Yes, yes, you told her, that would probably be fine—no idea where he was living these days. And you started rummaging for a phone number. If it wasn't possible, she said, Grace could be put in temporary care. Foster fucking care. No. Uh uh. That much you said, not your kid, *She has family.* You said again how you'd just been ill, sick, the flu. She took a last glance and scribbled, said she could arrange a cleaning woman to come and give you a hand, then riddled thumb against fingertips, flicked crumbs off the arm of the couch. Looked as if she were flicking fleas.

You called him fast, frantic, soon as you got Barrington out the door, and the next thing you knew, Danny had sweet-talked them, shown up at some office in one of his lovely and respectable suits and cast a lovely and respectable light on the whole mess. He explained your problem—poor him, saddled with such a beast as the mother of his child—said he would set you up at a treatment facility, said his place was actually too small to accommodate Grace but his first wife, Gloria, with whom he'd remained close and who had actually become a good friend of the family, would be more than happy to care for Grace. She has a teenage son of her own in quite a nice house in a good residential area where there'd be kids Grace's own age. Of course he wouldn't've said it just that way, it would have been wrapped in his bashful doddering cadence, grammatical errors endearing in light of everything else.

And so that's that. Gloria's got Grace, under the advisement of Mrs. Barrington. For three days now, she's had her. And you're supposed to be in treatment, not wandering back and forth from the front room to the kitchen, pondering what to do next. The next move is getting out of this godforsaken town, before they take her and don't give her back. This is temporary—Danny arranged it, this is definitely temporary. Just got to get your ass moving, get some cash together and am-scray.

Seemed like the last time Danny left, you weren't so totally alone, his friends still came by once in a while to drink and shoot the breeze. But that was Vancouver. They were all you had, his friends from The Life; the card players and dealers, loan sharks, hustlers, and their girlfriends. There was even a hooker whose company you didn't mind. Deirdra. She told stories that kept you amused for hours. Like the one about her masochist john, his wrists roped to a doorknob. *No matter how much I beg, don't stop.* It made you laugh when she mocked square women: *Well at least I don't give it away.* There was a group of them who hung around together, swapped stories and tied one on. You went to a birthday party for one, Penny or something—no, Patsy, her real name was Penny but she changed it to Patsy because she didn't want to sound cheap. That was a night all right. Got laughing so much you couldn't breathe. Turned out nobody remembered to pick up a cake for the birthday girl. And everyone was broke. The punchline came when the skinny blonde with all the boobs and hair (think her name was Molly) volunteered to turn a trick for cake money. She came back an hour later with a box full of angel food and all the girls gave ovations, stood up and hooted and cheered. Molly gave a floppy blonde bow.

Grace and Charlie didn't know who they were, didn't under-stand what they were talking about. You were only just beginning to understand their lingo yourself, that *ee-iz* language, mixed with bits of pig latin—they concealed so much in front of their own kids (and squares) it'd become second nature to them: *That f(ee-iz)uckin' astard-bay wanted an ee-fray bl(ee-iz)ow j(ee-iz)ob.* Used to make you cringe—hated that expression. Then again Deirdra never claimed to be Sandra Dee and more than once she came to your rescue with a bottle of wine when you were so sick you couldn't see straight.

And then when things got bad and you were broke and welfare wasn't going to feed your kids, you thought, *At least I don't give it away.*

You had. You'd given too much away. You'd fucked men whose names you couldn't remember without so much as a phone number to show for it. What possible difference would it have made if you turned it into a more pleasurable experience? It just so happened your immediate pleasure was money. You needed the cash equivalent of a night on the town, that's all. It wasn't so bad. What was the difference? It's your life and if you wanted to screw somebody and make a few bucks for your time and effort, who's to tell you you were wrong? Attractive, intelligent, you knew a few tricks —you should've been showered with cash and prizes long before.

So you called her, called Deirdra and invited her over for a drink. Couldn't do it alone. There was a right way to do this.

Deirdra brought wine and her expertise, along with her mouth. The first time you'd met, you thought you'd never heard such a foul mouth on a woman. She opened her purse when she sat and took out three Seconal. Thought you might need them.

That's why. Now you remember. That's what made Deirdra special. She gave a damn. And perhaps for the sake of comparison; you were afraid of who you'd become. But next to Deirdra, you were still clean, still an innocent, your confessions were commonplace.

Grace was outside playing. The house was quiet and your embarrassment echoed through the halls. Deirdra took it in stride. She was neither insulted nor enjoying your fall. Sympathetic but still matter-of-fact, she assuaged your fear. She knew some men, nice square johns she could fix you up with.

You told her how afraid you were, that you were glad she brought the pills, they'd help. You planned to get so drunk you'd be able to screw anyone. She cut you off, tough yet maternal. *For Chrissake don't get drunk. Stay smart. Keep the upper hand.* She took a swig of wine. Her Southern accent used to come out when she drank. Hard to tell if it was an affectation or real, but it gave the impression she could hogtie any sumbitch who came her way without hardly breakin' a sweat. *An' get the money up front fer Chrissake or you'll end up where you started; screwed 'n broke. I'll sendya some decent eggs but watch what yer doin', don't make a mark outa yerself. You squarejohn broads are so f(ee-iz)uckin' naive sometimes, I'm tempted t' take advantage myself. An' when you got yer money—here, look here, put it in yer purse and go to the bathroom. See this*—she pulled up her skirt to show you the inside hem, her voice lowered in anticipation of a trade secret about to be released—*take out a couple stitches and stick it right in there. No sumbitch's gonna find it there.* She smiled. You smiled. You started to feel brave.

You did it before, you can do it again.

You are standing on Jarvis in go-go boots—Yeah, go-go man, let's go. Almost funny standing here up to your eyeballs in whores when you *are* one. Jesus, the colours, lotsa hot pink and jumpsuits. Gotta get yourself one of them, it'd be a perfect uniform, a jump-me-suit and go-go boats—boots. kee-he-he—Quit your giggling, no one wants a giggling whore, 'specially one who snorts. Whore shmore, whores galore. God, it's spinning, your head is teetering shoulder-high, and dripping sky—Hey, you're a poet and you didn't know it; your feet show it, they're Longfellows.

Good Lord, it's wet out, summer-thick wet air, splattered all over the damn road, damn rain. How long have you been standing here?—hours and hours and what's it, twenty to ten o'clock and you got here at when, ten o'clock? no, ten to nine-thirty. What's that, an hour and …? No. Ten minutes? Jesus. Is it your imagination or are the fattest, sluttiest-looking girls getting the most action? Frankly, that's insulting. *Fool that I am, la-la-la la-la-la,* can never remember the words to that thing. A hand taps your shoulder, pulls back. You turn and find a nervous guy in officey-looking clothes, not that old, maybe thirty-some—quit singing, you're singing out loud, you're going to scare him.

Uh hi, wh—uh, are you working? He's nervous as hell. Looks like a number guy, a whatchacallit, a count-it guy.

Sure as shootin'! (Sure as shootin'? Where did that come from? Sure ass, shoot in, sure. Shoot!) And he says he has a car, so off you go to his shiny big auto, wonder if that's his name, Otto; he's got glassers, looks like an otter, or um—what?—and he opens the car door. You sit and wait for him to come around his side. (Smells mouldy in here.) Seems like he hustled you in here more to get you out of sight than out of chivalry—careful now, don't be seen in the open with prostitutes. Praw-sti-toot: cruddy word. Christ, it was his idea, he's the one who wants you; what are you, a leper? Nope, you're a leopard. Bet he'd wet himself if you growled right now.

He puts the car in drive. His glasses are lit up with store windows and street lights. He says, *So uh, actually, my apartment is not far from here, uh, so we could just go there and uh oh! how much are you, uh, that is to say, if I were to get a, for you to mm blow— me—a blow job, how much would that be?*

How much? Money. Shit. For cryin' out loud, you're disorganized—*I need thirty bucks for my mortgage.*

He stops at a red light and nods and nods like one of those floaty-headed dogs on rear-dashboards. Floaty-headed dog. That's him. Otto the Floaty-headed Dog.

Oop he's right, his place is nearby, he says this is it, you're right in front of his building. *We's here!* Where's here, gotta pay attention, get yourself in trouble if you don't start paying attention.

OK, everybody out. Door—where's the handle? And you fumble yourself stupid until he leans across and pulls the handle. Good job you didn't take another Seconal. This just takes the edge off; another one and you'd've been too out of it.

You get to the front door, he shuffles you inside, walks you through the lobby, down the hall, stuffs you in the door.

Not bad, sort of a cute little pad for such a square guy. *What do you do?*

I'm a pharmacist.

Really! Some of my best friends are pharmacists. Huh. Where do you work, which drugstore?

Downtown.

Oh. So how do—

Would you like a drink?

Sure, whatever you got, wine, beer ... so ... Don't suppose you've got anything in the house that you could part with—I have a bit of a nerve problem. Haven't had time to get to my family doctor this week.

Nerve problem?

Yes, I'm really nervy. Got anything to help me relax so I can sleep better?

You mean barbiturates?

Well yeah, I guess if you want to get down to brass tacks! haha.

He looks disgruntled, or was that disdainful—something gave him the face he's got on. He offers you a seat on the couch, hands you a glass of wine, sits down beside you, glass of something on-the-rocks in his bony mitt. Is he ignoring you? you have a regitimal leguest, legitimate—

So how long have you been doing this? he wants to know.

Why?—is he only looking at experienced streetwalkers? You look at your watch. *Not long. I mean I've done it a couple times when I ran into fina—um (pwahh, lip's got my tongue) uh, just money problems you know, and I have a little girl so I had to make sure she was fed properly. And it's that way now too, I need it for her. It's tough these days.*

He nods and jinks the cubes against the side of his glass, pats his other hand against his thigh. *That's too bad. How old are you if you don't mind me asking?*

How old would you guess?—oh never mind, that's a dumb game. Thirty-two.

Oh. Really. You're a year younger than me. I thought you were, huh, well thirty-two's a good age. And he sets his drink down, puts his hand in your hair, pulls your face over, starts to kiss. Hard, like he—christ, he's kissing like wood, lips like nose, all cartilage, stiff and bony, and then his teeth knocking—Watch the caps, buddy! What's he yanking? something out of his belly—his belt. His other hand grabs for yours, but it's full of wineglass so he plucks it, clumsy, splashes on your leg, bangs it down on the coffee table, and then back to your hand. He pulls by your wrist, sticks your fingers to his fly. Well re-fucking-lax, buddy, lemme get the button undone first. It's as if his parents'll be home later. Like he's seventeen, everything stiff and jerking, fastens your hand on his dick, faster faster, do it, now. He jams his hand between your thighs, fixes on your crotch and rubs like he's trying to get a stain out.

Cross your legs, get him the hell out of there.

Then he starts doing that thing, that school guy thing, pushing you down by the back of your head, steering you by the hair, thank christ you don't have a ponytail. Just do it—the sooner, the calmer.

Now you're down staring it in the eye. Ain't much; least you won't choke on it. And he's clean at least, looks the type that showers twice a day. You're so dry, muster some spit before you try and slide him back toward your throat. Lips tucked around your teeth so you don't bite him. You'd give anything to touch your tongue to the roof of your mouth right now.

And suck—

What must this look like, no lips, no teeth, like someone's gummy old grandma getting them off. Sucking and running him in and out—... *Fool that I am, la-la-la-la-la*—shit were you humming or did you just think it. *Hmm hmm hmm hmm*, almost monotonous enough to be therapeutic; think of it like the housework you never did; like vacuuming, trying to suck up those last bits of lint that just won't come. Except this rug moans and chirps. Come on, y' skinny bugger.

His thighs tense, start to shake, vibrate from the hips, and he thrusts and shoves your head down hard. You gag—good job he's not built or he would've shoved it through the back of your head ... aach, that taste, like bleach.

You sit back up. Ah the joy of tangible results. Should've been a bricklayer or something. He lets his head loll back for nine maybe ten seconds, then zips up and sits up, adjusts the collar of his shirt, and backs off a hair, just a bit, just so you know you're done. *So uh, should I call you a cab or are you just going to walk— oh here*—and he goes into his pocket for his wallet. Starts moseying through tens.

Oh. Well, I thought you'd be taking me back. I'm not really sure where I am.

You're right near where I picked you up, you're not even six blocks, you're just east. I—I can't, I have some work I have to catch up on and, I'm, expecting—here, here, take thirty-five and I'll call you a cab. Thanks. Thanks a lot for a—

For what, a job well done? Pathetic little grunt—soon as they get what they want, they want it to go away.

So you say, *OK, thanks, that's fine. So, well, before I go, uh, have you got anything in the house you might want to let me have—just a couple tranquilizers?*

Actually, if you wouldn't mind, maybe you could just flag a cab outside, I'd really prefer you did that.

Sure, OK, just, I'm just wondering if you could give me anything that might relax me a bit.

Look, you just—uch, and he storms off to the bathroom, comes back with a bottle of yellow. *Here, how many do you need?* and he goes to take the cap off. *Never mind, here, they're yours, there you go, thanks a lot, maybe we'll see you again sometime.*

And out you go with three tens, a five and a bottle of something or other. Can't see the printing, looks all furry, mm, fuzzy. Maybe you should pop one. Keep coming in and out, wanting something else because your brain's gone clear. How the hell are you supposed to get back to Jarvis?

Sunday afternoon and you're on your way to the bootlegger, walking down the Danforth. Pretty much sober; had the better part of a beer this morning to work through a Nembutal hangover. Maybe take it easier today. Take it any way you can get it. You stop for a red light. Young guy waits alongside you on the curb. Looks Greek or Italian or something. Sort of cute. Looks sideways at you—black dinner plates for eyes, crazy-long lashes like a Shetland pony. Light turns green. You eye each other, lift feet off the curb. You hesitate and pull yours back, he steps off, looks over his shoulder and curls a corner of his mouth up at you. You smile back, look down as your shoes saunter all silky across the road before you look at him again. He cocks his head at you. Nobody's said boo yet, but you follow in the direction he cocks. He slows his gait, lets you catch up, puts his hand in the small of your back. *Hallo,* he says, *it's jus up 'ere.* Guess he means his place. Wonder if you should tell him now how much. He hasn't asked. Maybe wait till you get up there.

You follow him up the front steps of a rundown house, through the outside door, down a short hall to the inside door. Once in, he just stands there, looks at you, tells you to take off your jacket. You drop it and your purse to the floor, lean back against the wall, wait. He says nothing, burrows those plate-eyes into your chest, undoes his belt, zips down. You start to say something, he says *shhhh*, takes a dark cock out, holds it in his hands a moment, tenderly, as if he's warming it in the light, never takes his eyes off you, and starts to massage, slow, then faster, works it to a steady pump. You shift your balance and he gets frenzied, yanking, jerks himself ferocious. He takes a sharp breath like he hurts, you expect it to tear, fall and stick to the floor. But he drags back a last slow gasp, pulls smooth till white syrup spits and hits floor. A single drop touches down above your knee.

The air comes out of him, punctured, limp.

Puts himself back in, does himself up, hands on his hips, nods at you and opens the door to the hall. Dismissed.

You open your mouth: no sound. Don't even know what noise you'd make if you could. Can't say about money, can't speak, can't think what garbage, what garbage you are. Nothing, just nothing.

It's six days your baby's been gone. And now nights and you're starting your seventh in a Mercedes. Getting so you wonder what a guy in a Mercedes wants with you anyway. Is he slumming it? He's still trying to make conversation, he's telling you about his youngest son at University of Toronto, the eldest is married with a son of his own. He asks if you have kids, how many? You tell him one, she's seven. Bad enough he's got a cheap hooker, may as well spare him thinking he's got an old one. He must be at least sixty, though. Clive. He tells you his name up front. Tells you his wife died of cancer three years ago. Clive finds it very hard to date now because he doesn't know how to talk to women any more who aren't his wife. You nod. *I know what you mean.* What do you mean you know what he means? Your wife didn't die.

You're easy to talk to, though, he says, *the most beautiful eyes you have, gentle and torrid at once. And your bones, cheeks like high rolling hills. Have you ever been to Ireland? Looking at you—you're a little like a place called Connemara—it's wild with deep still waters and one can't help but find a sweet kind of serenity in that.* May as well not burst his bubble, tell him you're pilled to the gills, you sweet surrendering thing.

Inside his house, his tone doesn't change. Around the living room are all the nice things his wife probably picked out, the vases and paintings and knick-knacks. Everything looks old and expensive. He offers you a cognac and the two of you sit on his chesterfield, cushions pushed into the small of your back, you in your new red jumpsuit, him in grey slacks, a white shirt, gracious and chatty. He doesn't notice the run in your pantyhose. Just talking and talking about marriage and books and women's lib—Old Clive's not for it, he won't give up opening their doors, buying their dinner, putting them on pedestals. *Isn't that why women were created? As beings to whom we men can cater?* True. Should be true. He gazes off every now and then and gives this easy Burl Ives kind of chuckle, then he asks if there's any way you could consider spending the night, what with your child and all. *I'd be willing to take care of you for your time.* You look up at the carved ceiling, tell him your little girl is staying with a friend tonight.

When you wake up, he's holding your hand, still in his pyjamas, and you're in the shirt he loaned you. God, you slept, feels like you've been dreaming and dreaming, all kinds of soft toffee stories, and now you've gone and woken up your old ugly self. He won't find you so serene and calm if he gets a gander at you now. *Like rolling hills*—he'll be talking about your gut. Guess you could bugger off, you got your money—that was the best part of the night, seeing him open his wallet and frown, then go to his underwear drawer. *Rita never approved of this,* he said, *silly old man keeping money in his drawers with his drawers, she used to say. Ha ha, my Rita.* And then he handed you two fifties, out-of-his-element hesitant. *Is this OK? just something to help with your rent and things. Terribly expensive, I'll bet.*

You looked at his hundred, kept up the stooge act—the shy leading the dopey—*Ah, yes, sure, that would be fine, thank you.* Felt like you didn't want to break anything, sully the atmosphere.

Here, maybe you could give this to your little girl. And he lisped another five out of his wallet.

He really is the darndest old thing. Rita must have been something to keep him still so in love. Two of them probably held hands in this bed every night, close, hardly moving, sweet breaths sifting in and out.

Wonder what kind of cancer it was. Wonder if it hurt, dying, hurt so much her husband's still got ghost pains. Poor Rita and her sweet old house and her silly old man.

You are on your way down to the courthouse. Swallowed half a mickey of lemon gin before Danny picked you up, trying to get up the nerve. Man, this is it, if they get you, it'll be on your record; if they throw you in the bucket, what's the likelihood of you ever getting Grace back? Jesus Jesus Jesus. Danny's driving. Humiliating, having to call him and ask, tell him you had to appear for soliciting. Didn't even act surprised, just pushed a breath out his nose as if to say, *Figures.* Yeah, well, it's none of his business anyway—if he were any kind of man he'd be helping out, he'd be paying child support and you wouldn't have been on the street to begin with. He's not saying anything, just driving and dropping. He offers you a Clorets.

In the elevator with two lawyers on your way up to the courtroom: two lawyers and an old man with a stack of papers. Seems both lawyers are going with you—are you getting two? You open your purse looking for another gum, can't find anything in this mess, seems like everything you own and nothing you need is in there. Take out the mickey, so you can at least see what you're doing. Got it under your arm when one of them starts snickering. The lawyers are giggling and shaking their heads; one leans over. *You might wanna get rid of that, or put it away.* The old guy glues his eyes to the numbers above the doors. It takes a second to figure what they're talking about, then you feel the gin in your armpit and chuckle too, stuff the bottle back in your purse. The lawyers laugh all the way to the courtroom. Turns out one's prosecuting and one's defending.

Ah, what're they going to do to you; probably nothing probably. Pimps get girls out every day. Never heard about anyone actually doing time that you recall. Used to hear those streetwalker gals saying *Ah they got me in on a vag c.* Vagrancy. Nothing ever happened. Dragged 'em in and let 'em go.

Just that what if someone finds out?

Most of the time in the courtroom you're not listening, it's too hard to concentrate, just lawyer crap, something about no prior convictions, or did you just remember that from cop shows? And a child and social assistance, think that was in there somewhere. And now the cop, that f(ee-iz)ucking cop is on the stand. The bastard who got in on the passenger side while you were in negotiating with the driver, the one who sandwiched you in and said you were under arrest for soliciting. Sitting on Jarvis betwixt two cops. Cops cops everywhere and not a john to fuck. Actually, this pig on the stand is the first guy, the driver, because he's saying you got in and told him you'd give him anything he wanted for thirty bucks. What a crock of shit, he asked you and you told him what it'd cost. It was only right! Your smartass lawyer isn't saying a word, so you holler, *You're a liar!* from your seat.

Doesn't go over well, judge threatens you, tells you to keep quiet, says you display a poor attitude, an attitude common among prostitutes. Fried yourself, idiot. So you stop listening. Let them hash it out amongst themselves, got nothing to do with you anyway, it's like a play about you where you never appear. Don't hear again until the gavel cracks and someone says *Guilty with Absolute Discharge*. A big finger shaking in your face. *Don't make me have to talk to you again, young lady.*

July 20/73
1416 Gerrard St. E.
Toronto, Ont.

Mrs. Lilly Darling, RSW
Social Worker

Dear Mrs. Darling,
While searching for a practical answer to my present
situation, I came across the letter you wrote to me on Dec. 1/72,
letting me know that Charlie was coming to Toronto. It
occurred to me that you might be able to help.

I'm alone now with my daughter, Grace. The situation
with her father was an impossible one. It seems to me that
to remain here another year would be a simple waste
of time. Charlie's not doing well, I know, and I'd like
to be there in Vancouver so that we can all be together.

Now, could you tell me, if I can find a way, financially,
to make the trip, would I be able to receive social
assistance on arrival? Whether or not I will try and
undertake some sort of retraining I have not yet decided.

I really see no point, outside of the fact that Grace
sees a little of her father, in us being alone in this cold
and friendless city without so much as a relative.

Charlie and I are in contact and I know you've been
wonderful with her. I hope you'll be able to advise
me as soon as you can find the time.

Sincerely,
Eileen Hoffman

HOFFMAN, Anne <u>Eilleen</u>

7.20.73 (L. Barrington) Paid visit to Mrs. Hoffman
today. Thanks to a visit from a homemaker and Mrs.
Hoffman's own efforts, the home's appearance is vastly
improved. Mrs. Hoffman herself appears to be on the
road to recovery, her attire and grooming much more
tidy. She has been to two AA meetings and feels that
she can do this without admitting herself into a
treatment facility. Will continue to monitor.

7.22.73   (L. Barrington) Saw Mrs. Hoffman again.
She continues to improve. There is a world of
difference from the situation I walked into two weeks
ago. We discussed Grace's supervision and how things
might change when Grace returned home. I recommended
that on Grace's return, some sort of routine be
implemented in her life, possibly some sort of
community centre with scheduled activities, a day
care or a summer school.

7.25.73 (L. Barrington) Grace has returned home.
The situation is immeasurably ~~impra~~ improved. I have
found a day camp available through a local church
where Grace can begin attendance immediately. We have
agreed to allow a brief interim for mother and child
to have time to themselves. Grace ~~if~~ is scheduled to
begin day camp 7.28.73.
    Although this family seems to have found its
bearings once again, I feel this home should be
monitored on a regular basis I will be going on
leave beginning 8.8.73 returning 8.22.73.

8.3.73 (L. Barrington) Spoke with both Mr. and Mrs.
Hoffman today. Home situation continues well, Grace
attending Saint Paul's Day Camp and enjoying herself,
Mrs. Hoffman attending regular AA meetings. Mr.
Hoffman sounds very pleased with the family's progress.
    I will go on leave 8.8.73. This family should
continue to be monitored

Grace Three

MUM WAS ALL perked up from getting well at the hospital and us being together again snapped her like sheets on a clothesline. The day she came and got me back from Gloria's, we went to Chinatown and wandered through stores, sniffing the baskets and incense, then into Woolworth's and picked around counters full of underwear and knick-knacks and plastic flowers and she bought me all the happies she could afford: a package of new plastic animals—Safari ones, pink nail polish, new jacks, Silly Putty. And she kept singing "I'm Back in Baby's Arms" while we pretended we were stinking rich and filled practically a whole Woolworth's basket.

We were both kind of goofy about being just-us again, but I couldn't help watching her; something about her felt like a big nervous laugh. She finally told me on my fourth day home, like it was just *by the way*, that the Welfare was nosing around still, asking how I spent my summer. They told her I had too much unsupervised time on my hands. Stupid buggers, she said. My heart started to go. I didn't want anything to spoil her mood, spoil the feeling that I was the only happy she needed—her forever shiny doodad.

We were riding the streetcar home from the Riverdale Zoo when she told me and, actually, I wasn't paying that much attention at first cuz I was still nervous that maybe she knew my secret. All afternoon, I wouldn't let her get near any of the popcorn and balloon sellers in case someone might recognize me and tell her about the stuff I used to buy there before I had to go stay at Gloria's. I was starting to feel like maybe I should just tell.

Whenever there was nothing to do, I'd been taking the street-car to the zoo. I liked how being by myself let me make up dreams about who I was and I'd sleepwalk all day long doing it. Sometimes I was escaping from kidnappers and had to lose myself in the crowd, or else I'd murdered the man who broke my heart and just needed time to get a plan together. But more and more, I was a rich kid with a mum or dad in one hand and a floaty high balloon-in-a-balloon in the other. I needed the balloon-in-a-balloon, though, for it to feel real, so I started taking change I found on Mum's dresser, or the kitchen table. Sometimes her coat pockets.

But then, when all the lying-around-the-house change was gone, I went into her purse. The money lying around seemed not that big a deal, but the purse was way worse. And now, here we were, clanging home on the streetcar and Mum was explaining the day camp thing and I kept looking away so she couldn't read my mind and hate me forever. Then she said, "I'm sorry, I know you hate this kind of stuff, being herded around by strangers—and I hate the thought of you being gone every day, but let's just do this and get them off our backs, OK? And it might be really fun; you'll probably have a grand old time with all those kids around. And you won't have to be stuck home with nothing to do but look at your boring old mother."

I skipped confessing, cuz this seemed worse all the sudden. "Did you tell them about Pearl?"

Pearl lived next door and we did stuff together. And her mum supervised us lots of times. Whenever I wasn't at the zoo we did stuff together. Some nights we sat on the front porch and watched the streetcars go by, counted red cars and hoped for lightning storms close enough to shake our chests. We wished on thunder the same way we did on railroad tracks when we drove over: crossing fingers, lifting feet, holding breath and closing eyes. On rainy days we organized my green plastic farm fences on Pearl's dining-room floor, and arranged the animals by how big they were. Or their teeth were. We added the safari animals when I got back home, and after that, when we set up the day's farm, we worked hard to keep tigers and stuff separate from the farm animals. Except for once there was a fence break that made a pig and some piglets get murdered and covered in ketchup.

When it was sunny we climbed the tree in my yard or went to Pearl's and made up plays about *The Brady Bunch* or else *The Rifleman* cuz it was Pearl's favourite. Or else sometimes we made up this show about two sisters called Julie and Donna. Pearl hardly ever said my name—the whole point was for her to go, "Julie!" and then I could turn and fling imaginary long hair out of my face like Julie in *The Mod Squad*. But she kept calling me "Sis." I guess cuz she didn't have a real one.

And now Mum was telling how the next day I had to start being at a day camp for my whole rest of the summer. Every single day, except Saturday and Sunday, I was going to have to take the streetcar to a church with a bunch of other kids whose mums were probably getting threatened by Welfare.

We were separated into six groups; we got group names and group stuff to do. My group was the second youngest (seven- and eight-year-olds), the Schroeder Shrimps. The younger group was the Sweet Peas, the older one was the Yellow Tigers. I would've gave all my cows to be a Pea or a Tiger.

We had activities every day and it always started out in the
basement of the church, then sometimes we took a school bus to
some place cheap or free. The Schroeder Shrimps had a kid that
was called "troubled." James. He hated the counsellors' guts and
waited until we got away from the church to get revenge. Our second swim day got cancelled right in the middle of getting-off-the-
bus instructions because James pushed his back against the kid
beside him and kicked with all his might into my favourite counsellor. The kid that was beside him got squashed and James kept
kicking Wendy's chest and stomach as hard as he could. Wendy
tried to be calm and grab hold of his ankle. Then Gavin, the guy-
counsellor, grabbed on James's other ankle and got a kick in the
mouth. They couldn't stop him, and Wendy and Gavin turned to
the rest of us and got us all saying, "Stop it James—Stop it James
—Stop it James" all together like the prayer at school. I mouthed
the words but no sound would come out. I wished I could rip his
legs out for what he was doing to Wendy, but James was red in
the face and wasn't listening to anything. It went on until they got
him pinned and asked the driver to turn us around. The bus was
quiet. The Shrimp beside me started to cry. There was still twenty
days left till school started.

When we got back to the church, Wendy and the kids went
off the bus and Gavin hung back with James. I lallygagged as long
as I could so I could hear what was going to happen. But I only
got Gavin's low talking-sense voice and James saying, "Shut up—
you're not my dad," before Wendy yelled to me to get a wiggle on.

Down in the church basement, Wendy went over and huddled
with the Sweet Peas' counsellors a few minutes before announcing
a softball game: Schroeder Shrimps and Sweet Peas all mixed in to
make two teams.

Our group, Group Two, was first up. I was supposed to be second at bat; the first kid was Kenny, one of the Peas, and he stood
beside the crossed sticks we laid down for home plate and bounced

at his knees, his head kept bobbing on his scrawny neck, looking around and up and down, swinging the bat and losing his balance. Gavin brought James back and put him on the other team with Group One. Which I was glad about. Especially seeing him warm up in the puny front-lawn outfield. I watched him throw the ball to first base, where one of the Peas caught it, dropped it and tried to huck it back, but it dropped a couple feet in front of her. James said, "Hey Pisspot, try throwing it here." Wendy clapped her hands. "OK, buddy-boy, enough of that or you'll be so far in the outfield there'll be no more field." Just to know James wouldn't be in line behind me made my chest looser. Instead he stepped up between the two rocks we were using for the pitching mound and winged his arm around, hung his tongue down his chin and yelled "Sucker" at home plate.

Kenny's face drooped a little, but his body never stopped bobbing. Someone called Batter-up and Kenny jiggled up to the crossed sticks, elbows wiggling under the bat.

James barked, "Ready, Pisshead? haa-a, sucker," and hucked the ball at him. Kenny ducked and swung at the same time, and his legs jumped right out from under him. He landed in a pile and the whole yard killed themselves laughing. James laughed so hard he couldn't think of anything to say.

Kenny jumped up off the grass, still holding his bat, stepped up and started his jiggling again like nothing happened. I imagined Pearl at home sitting in the first big V of my cherry tree, singing "Country Roads," and watched Kenny squeeze the bat. I didn't want to be up there next. I knew I wouldn't be able to take practice swings in front of James like Kenny did, I'd feel too dumb. James pitched the ball. Kenny swung again and just tipped the ball before he started running off to first base. I squinted up in the sun until something smashed my mouth. The ball hit the grass again and I heard "foul." The bottom half of my face burned. I touched my fingertips inside my lip and looked at the watery blood. James smiled as he wound up his next pitch.

I backed off, glancing around the yard, but all their eyes were on Kenny. I looked for Wendy, but she was laughing and clapping in time to *Ken-ny, Ken-ny*. I felt my lip to see if it was hard or puffy. It wasn't. Kind of raw inside, but there wasn't even that much blood. Kenny whacked the ball this time and sent it rolling out onto the road. Every Shrimp and Pea but me went crazy, screaming and clapping cuz Wendy'd said that any ball on the street would be an automatic home run and she'd go get it herself. I kept touching my lips, licking my teeth to see if they were chipped, hoping someone would notice. But they were all too busy cheering Kenny's home run.

I was almost to the sidewalk when Wendy called, "Next batter," and some other kid went up. I was supposed to be second. I licked at my lip again and started up the sidewalk. They were going to yell at me to come back; I could feel it on my back. Wendy called, "Strike," and I looked back. Nobody was even paying attention, just looking at the Shrimp swinging over home plate. I stormed up the sidewalk toward Gerrard Street and caught a streetcar home.

When I got home, the front door was open so the breeze would come through our screen door. Mum had a thing for breezes. Before I opened the screen, I could hear her talking, saying something about a hard decision. I ducked beside the door because I thought maybe she was on the phone with the day camp people and I wanted to hear if they got hell or if it was me who was going to get it for taking off and making her worry. It was quiet a second. Then I heard a man-voice, not my dad's though, more crunchy and with an Englishy kind of accent, say "Poor Gentle Eilleen," almost in a mushy way. I crouched down and put my ear against the screen door so I could hear better. Mum said, "Well, I s'pose her father's here … but he's a good-for-nothing."

A good-for-nothing? I didn't know who she was talking to like that, because usually she never talked about my dad without swearing. She was talking all nicey. Then she said, "I've been in touch with Social Assistance there so we'd be looked after—I can't help thinking it would be a brand new start." My heart started going cuz it sounded like she was telling secrets that she never even told me yet, and then the man-voice said, "You know I hate to lose you, but you don't deserve this sort of squalor …" He hated to lose her? My neck went hot—she must've had this guy over lots for him to think he could just hang around acting like she was his girlfriend or something and say she had squalor. And all while I was busy getting hit in the face with baseballs so the Welfare wouldn't have a hairy about me getting supervised any more. And then he mumbled some other probably mushy thing and Mum went, "Clyde, you're such a dear," all goopy, the way she did to me if I did something nice for her, like buy her an ornament with my 'lowance.

I stood up and stomped my feet as if I was just getting there now, and opened the screen door. Mum called, "There she is," from the kitchen, in the voice she used to call me angel. Not worried or mad or anything; this wasn't that voice. This was her voice that sounded like butterflies. I came in the kitchen and found her drinking tea at the table with an old man.

"Sweety, this is Clive, Clive this is my baby, this is Grace." I couldn't hear right what his dumb old name was, so I said, "Clyde?" and he said no, that was his brother's name, and Mum laughed like he was hilarious or something. "Clivuhh, Clive," she told me, and he smiled and said how lovely it was to make my acquaintance. I wanted to show her my lip but I didn't want him around.

She threw her arms open, grabbed my face and gave me a big kiss. I hissed and ouched and pulled back, the way I wished I did at day camp. She said, "Ouch? What?"

"My lip! A kid hit me in the face with a baseball and I got a bleeding lip. That's why I'm home early." She grabbed my face again and tilted it back to get a look. "Ow, you're hurting me."

"I thought you said it was your lip, not your neck."

"Yeah but—be careful."

"Oh yeah, I can see a little cut. Ah, poor sweety, let mamma kiss it." And she brushed her mouth across my lip. I rolled my eyes. I was home early on account of a wound. It was a *big* cut.

Mum threw up her hands and said, "Now what? I kissed it, didn't I? What do you want for a nickel, a bag of dimes?"

The old guy chuckled. I was ignoring him the best I could, but now he'd gone and laughed himself back in the picture.

Mum patted the table. "Come sit with us, poor injured birdie." I sat down opposite from Clive. Mum was in the middle, but closer to him, saying, "We were just—" when I interrupted her.

"I hate it there. I'm home early, you know—they didn't even check to see and they don't care that I'm gone—they're supposed to be *supervising* me—I could be anywhere! I don't even wanna go back any more."

Mum took a sip from her mug. "OK. So don't go. I miss your shining countenance around here anyway."

And that was all. I wanted a scene. I wanted someone to get mad about the way I got treated. Or to get hugged without old men in the room. Mum looked at me and grinned. I let my mouth be open a bit in case it might start to bleed again. She asked me, "Are you hungry? Clive brought over a whole truckload of fruit and vegetables and some pork chops and milk, and there's bread if you want a sandwich." She smiled over at him. I said I didn't feel like it, it was too hot, and I leaned back in my chair feeling like I was way at the far end of the table. Clive kept a smile on his face and kept moving his eyes on my mother's face like fingers. She backed her chair out a little and moved a bit closer to me so she was more equal between us and said, "So, sweety, we were just talking about how beautiful the autumn is there, and how warm it stays. There's hardly a winter."

"Where?"

"Vancouver. Didn't I say that?" The balls of her cheeks were pink and her eyes were glittery like fishes. She already decided, I could tell. That's what they were talking about and that's what I heard in her voice when I came in. I could see it in her hands, the way they flitted; if she was mixed up or scared, they hung in front of her like broken birds. I tasted the cut on my lip again and felt the running butterflies start in my belly. Then I remembered Clive and wondered if he knew that, when we ran away, it could only be us two.

"Well, I'm too hot already," I said.

Mum gave me a poke in the arm with her fingernail. "What are you so grinchy about, antface? You'll be crying for the sun in a few months when your hands are falling off because you've lost your mittens again."

Clive and I looked at each other. Clive smiled. He didn't fit in this kitchen. Everything on him was ironed and neat, like someone's TV grandpa, like on *Eddie's Father*. *The Courtship of Eddie's Grandfather*. I thought Pearl would love him. He looked at me and said to my mum, "Rita's sister had a little girl with eyes just like hers; Rita used to call them guppy eyes. She thought they were shaped just like guppies," and he chuckled some more.

"Who's Rita?" I kind of snapped it at him.

His eyes were watery. "She's an old friend of mine. They're lovely, your eyes, I meant no disrespect."

Mum reached over and pushed my bangs aside. "I always thought Grace had wolf eyes." I liked when she said that. It made me feel prowly and strong, like a snap of my jaws could rip out a man's throat. Her hands fluttered at the chain on her neck.

HOFFMAN, Anne Eilleen

8.24.73 (L. Barrington)   After returning to work on
August 22nd, I was disappointed to see that no follow-
up calls had been made to Hoffman residence. Checked
on residence myself today only to find that Mrs.
Hoffman had packed up and cleared out. She has been
gone nearly a week according to Arlene and John
Kensit. They claimed not to know her whereabouts.
This sudden lack of knowledge is suspicious given
daughter Pearl's closeness to Grace. Can't help but
think Eilleen Hoffman manipulated this situation in
order to make a smoother escape. The Kensits do did
say that Mrs. Hoffman was in much better condition
though. I cannot stress enough that CPA must continue
to monitor this family's situation.

8.27.73 (L. Barrington)   After several attempts, was
finally able to contact Mr. Hoffman. Mrs. Hoffman, he
said, has gone to Vancouver. He is understandably
disappointed as Mrs. Hoffman could not be persuaded to
stay and he has no means of contacting his daughter.
    I hope the breakdown in internal communications has
not jeopardized this family. Mr. Hoffman has given me
the address and phone numbers of family friends in
Vancouver that she will likely contact. I will write
and inform CPA Vancouver.

Child Protection Agency of Metropolitan Toronto

....

333 Wellesley St. E., Toronto 5, Ontario Telephone: 983-4545

....

September 20, 1973

Mr. G.H. Pretty
Executive Director
C.P.A. of Vancouver
2075 W. 7th Ave.,
VANCOUVER 9, B.C.

> RE: Mrs. Eilleen Carrington,
> known as Hoffman
> and child Grace Hoffman
> born 24 November 1965
> c/o Ray Collingwood
> 4788 Quebec St,
> VANCOUVER, B.C.

Possible Schools: General Brock School
_____ 4860 Main St., VANCOUVER, B.C.

Dear Mr. Pretty:

I am writing to alert you of a family well known to your agency as Mrs. Hoffman's daughter, Charlotte Carrington, has been a ward, and Mrs. L. Darling, Broadway Branch, was the worker.

Mrs. Hoffman was living in Toronto with her younger daughter, Grace but without informing us, she moved to Vancouver last month.

Mrs. Hoffman is an alcoholic and during July, she was drinking so heavily that we felt it necessary to ask Mr. Hoffman to remove Grace from her care. The situation improved a good deal and Grace returned to her mother in August.

We felt it necessary to refer this family again to your
Agency because of Eilleen Hoffman's instability and alcoholism.
The Collingwood family (see above address) are friends of Mrs.
Hoffman and should be able to help, but should you be unable
to locate her through them, Charlotte Carrington will be sure
to know where she is living.

As Mr. Hoffman is very concerned about Grace's welfare,
we would appreciate hearing from your Agency concerning her
present situation.

Thank you for your assistance in this matter.

Yours Sincerely,

L. Barrington   _I. Hereford_
(Mrs.) L. Barrington   (Mr.) I. Hereford, Supervisor

Eilleen Four

WALKING IN Chinatown with Grace, pumpkin shopping. It's coming on November. She's got one hand in her pocket, one hand in yours—it's just getting fall-nippy. You look down onto her hair and smooth a hand over, she looks up so you run it down her face, squash her nose and lips along the way. She giggles and hip-bumps your thigh. So you say, *Wonder what the poor people are doing right now.*

Why?

Cuz us rich peoples is havin' fun.

What do you mean?

I mean, it's a nice day—I wonder what those poor slobs stuck in Toronto are doing.

Grace stops to have a gander at a twisted orange head with what looks like a goiter on its face. She cups the lump in her palm, says, *This could be his chin, huh? If he was really fat.*

You laugh. Laugh laugh. Everything makes you laugh now. Feels so good just being. Here. Sometimes when she's at school you sit at home in the living room and touch the arm of the couch, the heavy furniture weave, squeeze till it hurts your finger bones a little, just enough to hang a *For Sure* sign on everything you own: your furniture, your dishes, your self. Your here. Vancouver, baby. Just so relieved to be back, so thankful to be here not there, thankful for the friends who came through—even the ones who are really more Danny's than yours, but they've stuck by you just the same—like Alice and Ray; the same way they put you up two years ago while you were waiting for Danny when he got out of jail, they put this together when you ran from Toronto. You owe them close to three hundred bucks between the first month's rent they fronted and the second-hand stuff Ray put together from his furniture store. But you're home again: Grace has her school right across the road, Ray and Alice just four blocks away. OK, it's only one bedroom and you are right on Main Street, but it's a start. It's free air through your chest—don't have to be afraid any more.

The two of you keep walking. Your child wants just the right pumpkin, as if she's picking a puppy. Can't even remember if you had a pumpkin last year. She stops to look at a bin of apples, says, *These are considerably cheaper than the supermarket, aren't they?* An old woman looks sideways at Grace and you chuckle, say, *Yeah, you're right. We'll get a load of stuff before we go. And I'm kind of thinking I'd like to pop over to Kripps Drugstore, we're almost out of lecithin and C.* That's your new language, Vitamins. Right after you got into town, back on the wagon, you picked up two Adelle Davis books: *Let's Have Healthy Children* and *Let's Eat Right to Keep Fit.* Saw her on tv, on *The Merv Griffin Show,* and you thought, that's it, we're going to start this life with a bang—Adelle Davis was going to get the two of you so healthy, you'd be jumping and leaping, shooting off brilliance wherever you went. Mega-vitamins, scoops of powdered vim and vigour were going to make you and yours radiant and robust. No more skinny kid—no more Alice and Ray holding both of Grace's wrists in one hand, comparing them to their own rugrats', telling you yours looked like one of those starving African kids. Every morning you swallow B-complex, kelp and halibut liver oil pills. The powdered vitamins, like the C and the brewer's yeast—you stir 'em up with grape juice and Grace downs it. Takes some coaxing, but she does it.

Mind you, maybe I'll just go tomorrow—if we get all these fruits and vegetables, we're not going to wanna drag them over to Kripps Drugs and then all the way home. And don't forget, Pumpkin Queen, not too big or we're not going to be able to carry it. And not too expensive—oh shi—shoot—I can't go to Kripps tomorrow, I have to work. Grace rolls a head off the shelf into her arms and cradles it a moment, pulls her chin up trying to free the apartment keys on the string around her neck. You ease them out from between the pumpkin and her chest and drop them down her sweater. She squeals on the cold metal. *Oh sweety, sorry, I thought you had a T-shirt on under there.* She glares at you ever so slightly, says this is the one, the pumpkin that stole her heart. You ask her how much it is. She frowns, *ummm,* as if she doesn't know and rotates the thing around till the black scrawled numbers show themselves. You squeal on the price. Tit for tat.

It's Monday afternoon and you are standing behind a jewellery counter at Eaton's department store. Christmas help. Bored out of your mind, nobody needs help with Christmas yet, no one's even thinking about it. You've got a VIP job here, through the Welfare—the Vancouver Incentive Program: they get you a part-time job and you're allowed to make an extra hundred dollars a month. Any more and it gets taken off your cheque. Seems like you should be getting more for two days a week, like you're being had. But at least you're out here, meeting people. Who knows who you'll meet during the Christmas rush.

Someday when there's a Christmas rush.

You've already started buying little doodads for Grace, stocking stuffers. You're going to really get into it this Christmas, there'll be tinsel all over the bloody place. Soon as Halloween's over, you're getting a wreath for the door. Already got Grace drinking eggnog —that's actually nothing to do with Christmas, you just told her that. Really it's to get two eggs' worth of protein down her gullet as quick and painlessly as possible. Adelle Davis says she needs thirty grams a day and by God she's going to get it. No more white bread, white sugar, white rice. Actually you never did let her eat white bread, but now you're serious.

Oh God … can't you just go take an extended lunch break; there's no one here, no one is shopping at eleven o'clock Monday morning. You're in the middle of a square counter, three sides of jewellery, one all drawers and a cash register. Jesus. Wonder if anyone would mind you bursting into a little jazz—skiddley wa-wa-a-a … You are staring through your fingerprints into the display case.

There are twenty-eight pairs of earrings under this glass.

Twenty-eight. Twenny hate. Twenty ate. Twaw twaw—that was one of your favourite ages, that's how many teeth you have, that's how many pickled peppers Peter Piper picked.

Time check: Eleven O Two. And a half Christ. This cannot be. You call over to the girl at the watch counter, ask her if she has the time. She says it's about five to eleven.

That's it, the universe is turning backwards, it's folding in on itself. Your eyes and teeth are going to leap out to escape the boredom of sitting in your head.

Now and then, Margo, the supervisor, minces over to see how you're doing. *Any sales? You might want to stand up rather than lean on the counter, it's more professional.* Old Margo's got to know you're a welfare case, the way she treats you, all phony smiles and impatient sighs. Yesterday you asked her where the keys to the next counter over were, the watch counter; someone wanted help and the salesgirl was gone. Margo flipped her hand over her shoulder. *They're in the drawer.* And you looked to a wall of thirty little draw-ers—started to ask her which one and then she exhaled, *Who is it that needs the help, Eilleen?* as if she'd better just do it herself. *The one with wrists,* you wanted to spit.

Ah screw the old bitch, don't think about it. Maybe they'll really like you by the end of this and you'll get put on full-time and you can move to another department. Not that working in a department store is your ultimate goal, but you'll start teaching again when you're strong enough. This is an interim. Gives you time to catch your breath, meet people. And gets you an extra hundred bucks to do with what you'd like. You'd like to have a nice Christmas. Maybe you'll buy a little two-person-size turkey. Or maybe a chicken and you could stuff it and make wild rice and baked potatoes and carrots or whatever Grace feels like.

She's really been pretty good about the whole thing this last couple months, all the new stuff, leaving the old stuff: she left her father, her friend Pearl. Had to leave her cat with Clive's youngest son. That last bit took the most convincing, she was determined, said something about taking a cat cage on the plane—Pearl told her she could—then started on a rant about how Shadow was like her child. She snapped at you, *Why don't you just go ahead without me.* Your mouth opened and she said, *There—see! How do you feel!* She was all mouth the days before you left, but you let it go, ex-plained sweetly that the two of you would have to live in an apart-ment, at least for a while, and here was Clive's son in Toronto with a house and a big backyard. It would be cruel to put that poor cat through a plane trip. Her eyes were bugging. *But I'll be with her, she won't be nervous if I'm there.* That clinched the deal; you ex-plained that the animals had to stay in the belly of the plane with the luggage and dogs and idiot baggage handlers tossing them around. She narrowed her eyes as if wondering what the hell you were trying to pull.

The morning of your flight, she and Pearl just stared at one another. Grace gave Pearl all those crazy little plastic sheep and pigs you'd bought her. The two of them used to sit on the floor hours on end playing with them. You were amazed Grace gave anything. Usually she's so territorial. Then they sat on the front step and exchanged addresses. Then they stared some more, didn't touch one another, just stared like two old men.

It's not that you disliked Pearl, but she was an incessant gossip. Had to keep her at arm's length. Although, as long as you weren't starring in her stories, her big mouth could be the best thing about her. The kid had the goods on everybody—wasn't two weeks before Grace got a carefully printed juicy letter telling all about Mrs. Barrington, the social worker, showing up. Apparently, the morning after you left Toronto, she banged on the front door long and hard, screaming *Mrs. Hoffman! Mrs. Hoffman! Open the door. Mrs. Hoffman I know you're in there so you open this door right now.* She even ran around peeking through windows on her way to the back door. Pearl said that Mrs. Barrington was so crazy mad, Pearl thought she was going to hurt herself. That letter kept you entertained for weeks. Grace would come up to the bathroom door nattering in whispered shrieks, *Mrs. Hoffman, I know you're in there. I mean it! This instant!* And you'd laugh yourselves dizzy.

And then Grace's father. She didn't have all that much to say about leaving him really. Danny came and took her for a drive before taking the two of you to the airport. Wonder if it was hard, that last hour or so alone with him. It gave you a little twinge, wondering if he would ever try anything; turn into a born-again father and not bring her back. But Gloria told you he never even bothered to visit when she had Grace with her. Gloria told you that put the kibosh on Danny as a human being as far as she was concerned. So you let him take Grace for a last drive. May as well leave your kid with a half-decent impression of him.

Tried to pump her for information afterward but she didn't say much, just that he took her for Kentucky Fried Chicken and a car wash. She said they didn't talk a lot but that he'd asked her if she was going to write to him. She said she would and asked him if he'd send her the money from the bank account he'd started for her. God almighty, two peas in a pod. Didn't think a cash obsession could be passed down the genes.

The thing is, it's not as if you didn't try and discuss it with Danny before you made the decision to leave. You phoned. *I think I'm going to go to Vancouver before things get any worse here*, you said. And it was silent at the end of the line, until he finally came out with a *Yeah*. You tried to give him a chance to not let go. *So, well, what do you think, I mean if you want me to stay, I'll stay. Just, what do you think?*

Deadpan voice, dull, nothing, he said, *It don't matter. You're just gonna do what you wanna do anaways.*

And so you told Clive. He didn't try to talk you out of it either. He said he knew it was something you had to do right now, that he hoped it wouldn't be the last he saw of you. Guess he knew the two of you didn't have much chance as lovers. Christ, he was nearly seventy—older than your father. It wasn't really sex that you had anyway, more like holding on to each other for dear life. Clive took you seriously though, seemed like he was falling in love a little. If it weren't for him, you might not of made it here, he gave you the other fifty you needed for plane fare and a hundred to take with you. Even bought you a suit for the teaching job you were going to apply for.

Margo taps you on the shoulder and tells you it's time for your break, you have twenty minutes, don't be long now. Straighten up (you've been leaning again) and brush off your skirt; it's the skirt to the suit Clive got you. Feels like you're casting his pearls before swine.

When you get home, Grace is already parked in front of the TV. Hard to peel her off the thing sometimes. Sometimes her concentration is so concentrated, it's cement; nothing gets through when she's got her eyes on a *Get Smart* rerun or *Scooby-Doo* on Saturday mornings. She hears you tonight though. You tell her *hi* before you go and hide the record you got her for her birthday. She's eight next month and has developed a mad crush on Donny Osmond. Her last allowance went on *Tiger Beat* magazine.

Album in closet, you join her on the couch in the living room. She's watching a *Brady Bunch* rerun. The one where the family goes to Hawaii.

Hey, I was thinking today, what would you think of having a birthday party next month?

She unsticks her gaze from Greg Brady and looks at you, with concern or nerves or something. So you say, *What's the matter? It'd be fun. We could make a list and you could invite a bunch of kids from your class and we could have a cake and play games.*

I don't really have much friends at school.

Why does she always think that? She never brings anyone home. *Oh you do so. You always say that. Even in Toronto, and your teacher there said you had lots of friends.*

Yeah, then how come they called me names and stuff.

Because kids are monsters, but deep down they're OK. So come on, let's do it, it'll be fun. We have to throw a party here so it'll feel more like our place. And we'll play corny games like Pin the Tail on the Donkey and I Spy. OK, pruneface?

She shoves your shoulder with the side of her head. And smiles. *OK.* When the phone rings, you kiss her temple, tell her in the

voice of one of her cartoon chickens, *It's going to be so much fun.*
She jumps up and runs to get the phone in the kitchen, yells back
that it's for you.

It's Stewart. You wait until Grace resumes watching television.

Stewart's craggy voice catches you at the other end of the line,
asks you what you're doing, if you're free tonight. You say sure, for
a little while, after dinner, you want to have dinner with Grace
tonight. And you want to see if you can find a babysitter. *How's
eight o'clock,* he says. *Eight's fine, I think, but just lemme call this girl
to see if she can come sit with Grace a couple hours.* He says, *Right-eeo,
dear,* call him back and hangs up. You sit for a moment thinking.

Sweety? … Sweety pie?

What?

*I think I'm going to go out with Stewart for coffee tonight. So I'll
phone Darlene—you like her, don't you? How's that?*

She doesn't look up. *I thought you had AA tonight.*

Shit, she's right. You tisk. *Yeah. Well. Well, I went night before
last. I'll go to an afternoon one tomorrow.* She says, *Yeah,* and keeps
watching the tarantula on screen, so you flip your phone book to
D for Darlene, the sitter you found through the office at Grace's
school.

Stewart's the only one you're still—well, with whom you have
this sort of relationship. Met him in Vancouver years ago, back
when Danny was in jail and you were short on cash. Called him
from Toronto when you were trying to figure out a plan, asked
him if he'd be able to front you money for rent. He said he would
but he never came through and you called Ray and Alice instead.
The only time he was reliable, as you recall, was when you were
there in front of him with your palm open. But he's not a—sometimes you just have lunch: he's more like a sugar daddy really. And
you wouldn't, but if you're going to buy all these vitamins and
meat and fresh fruit and vegetables and whole milk and keep the
two of you clothed, well, welfare plus a hundred ain't gonna cut it.

It's no big deal. Stewart's OK, he's bald and divorced and a little sad. Easy enough. And it's whatever you feel like at the time: fast or more social. He gives you whatever he's got on him, sometimes extra because he knows you've got Grace, sometimes fifty, sometimes more. And Grace thinks he's just a family friend. She never asks—sometimes you mention how much money he gives you and she believes he does it as a humanitarian gesture or something.

Hi may I speak with Darlene please—oh hi Darlene, I didn't recognize your voice, it's Eilleen Hoffman.

You wonder sometimes if Grace knows on some level. If she just doesn't say anything. She's met Stewart once, he was dropping you off just as she got home from school. She seemed indifferent to him for the most part. She thought he was a little on the dopey side, truth be told. She does dopey cartoon imitations of him after he calls. She kind of likes his big yellow car, she calls it the Yellow Submarine, and she likes it when he gives you an extra couple bucks *for the kid.* Anyway, a lot of women have boyfriends who take care of the bills; at least this one isn't getting in your hair twenty-four hours a day.

Just that sometimes you half expect someone to come tiptoeing up to your baby and whisper in her ear, tell her her mother is the unspeakable. Tell her something to make her never want to look at you again. You even told her a story once about being mistaken for a hooker, and you laughed uproariously, just in case. Just in case; you've laid the groundwork to roll your eyes with believable head-shaking frivolity.

Had a dream last week. Grace was tiny again, two or three. One of those slow thick dreams where your legs and arms are leaded and your voice is molasses congealed behind your tongue.

Holding her propped on one hip as you answered the door, you could feel her soft damp arms against your neck, fingers and wrists entwined at your nape. The strangers at the door were in dark suits, arms extended mechanically. The man on the left wore a charcoal fedora like your father used to. He reached out and pulled Grace from your hip. You could feel her fingers losing their grip but your mind was a tar baby and every thought you punched or yanked lay stuck in its viscous belly. Couldn't think or move, but you could hear the bawl of *mummy* and the man holding her turned and walked away, hysterical sobs erupting over his shoulder. The one still at your door jotted words in a pad with a china blue cover. He seemed to be writing notes on the condition of your home, your housekeeping skills. Your hand moved to your hair, which only called attention to your personal appearance. The fastest movement was his scribbling pencil. As he turned to leave, you made out Stewart's name and old Clive's, highlighted in yellow ink in his blue notebook.

You shake off the dream, pull yourself back in your living room in time to hear the Bradys' closing music, say, *Lamby? Why don't you come sit with me in the kitchen and make a guest list for your birthday party while I start dinner. Oh shit, just let me call Stewart back quick.*

CHILD PROTECTION AGENCY OF VANCOUVER

 **CPA** 2075 West 7th Avenue, Vancouver 9, B.C.

TELEPHONE 732-8282

Refer to (Mrs.) Lilly Darling
File: 56722

October 18, 1973

Child Protection Agency of Metropolitan Toronto,
Mrs. L. Barrington,
Social Worker
333 Wellesley St. East,
Toronto, Ontario

Dear Mrs. Barrington,

RE: <u>CARRINGTON</u>, Eilleen
(aka <u>Hoffman</u>, Ellison)
<u>Address:</u> 4789 Main Street,
Vancouver, B.C.
<u>Child:</u> HOFFMAN, Grace Anne
- b. 24.11.65

In reply to correspondence from Mrs. Barrington
dated September 20, 1973 regarding the above-named woman,
we are glad to be able to tell you that she appears to
be managing very well.

She has an apartment at 4789 Main Street and has
found a job at Eatons Department Store in the jewelry
department, which she is enjoying. She has also joined
Alcoholics Anonymous and attends meetings regularly, at
least twice a week.

Grace is attending General Brock School which is
very close to the home. She is doing well at home and
at school. She is receiving very good care and we feel
that Mr. Hoffman can be re-assured at this point.

Charlotte's progress is not good. She is our
Temporary ward but disappears periodically for days at a
time. We feel she needs a good deal of help. At this
point she is unwilling to accept it.

We hope that Mrs. Carrington will continue her
present good level of functioning and we will be in
constant touch with her; certainly at this time, Grace
is receiving excellent care.

If we can be of further help, please let us know.

Sincerely,

Mr. G.H. Pretty
Director,
Broadway Branch

cc: Mrs. Dagmar Lindlay,
    Executive Director

Grace Four

I T WAS SATURDAY and I was up in Sadie's room with her, playing Donny Osmond records while Mum was downstairs in the kitchen with Sadie's parents, Alice and Ray, and I was wondering how come we had nothing better to do. We'd been in Vancouver around five months and Mum was never sick any more—it seemed like we should've spent the day at Stanley Park or something. Instead I could hear Sadie's dad, Ray, laughing at my mum, making fun of her all afternoon—"Jesus-Mary-and-Joseph, Eilleen! You're a wingnut, you'd get lost in a phone booth"—while Sadie told me Donny Osmond would never even kiss me never mind marry me because I was skinny and bucktoothed and way too young. Sadie was nine. Nine and three quarters.

Then she sat down at her electric keyboard, in the spare room, and plunked out "Heart and Soul," the only one she knew off by heart. And right in the middle of it, she said how she was going to take ballet lessons at the community centre. I sat beside her and felt the music vibrate in my ears, expecting her dad to tear up the stairs any second just to plink out the sidekick part at the other end of the keyboard. Sadie's fingers plopping their way through "Heart and Soul" was practically a surefire way to get Ray to come play with her no matter what he was doing. He thought his kids were musical geniuses and loved to get both of them to sit and sing "Night and Day" into the microphone of this huge reel-to-reel tape recorder he had. But especially Sadie; he said lots of times how he was going to get her a voice coach—that voice of hers could take her places. I thought it might too, the way it cracked and snagged the music. In fact, I wished on the sore throats I'd been getting since the winter, that they'd give me the kind of Sadie-voice I was going to need if I wanted go places.

I sat beside her on the piano bench and watched her play, wanting like crazy to get my own lessons. Then I said how maybe I should take ballet too. Sadie laughed and brought one hand to the other side of the keys to play her own sidekick part. I followed her fingers and knew I was a feeb compared to her; Sadie was taller than I was with long thick almost-black hair and big black eyes, deep in her always-tan face. She wasn't clumsy like me; she didn't trip on rugs or knock stuff down. She was dead sure about everything and it made her seem tough and right all the time. Hardly anyone ever looked at Sadie and didn't say how beautiful she was.

She kept her eyes on her fingers and laughed. "But you're accident prone, even my mum says—yesterday she goes, 'Gees, Eileen picked a dandy of a name for that kid. Shoulda called her Thumper.' And it's true, man, you always got scabs on your knees from where you fell and you got no coordination and plus you're too skinny; my dad says you ain't got enough on your bones to even hold you up half the time."

It was hearing it from Sadie that got me saying "ain't" for a while. Until my mum made me stop by telling me that it was the ugliest thing about her: Sadie couldn't speak proper English—that and the fact that she was going to have a hawk-nose just like her dad. It kind of bugged me when my mum said that, because anyone would want to be like Sadie and that's why you'd do stuff to be like her so that everyone would want to be like you too—tough and pretty and getting away with stuff other kids would be in trouble for. On the other hand, though, it sounded like I could be smarter and prettier and sort of Sadie-*Plus* if I added Mum's big words and took out the ain'ts. But in the meantime, while I waited for her to be nothing but a pile of nose and bad English, I wanted to catch up. In a few classes I'd be leaping through the air in a crispy pink skirt; ballet was going to make me into a pretty, dainty girl-girl. It would make my teeth straight and flatten my cowlick and give me leopard eyes like Sadie's. She kept going with her sandpapery laugh, though, telling me more and more reasons why I couldn't take ballet. I missed Pearl all the sudden. Pearl would've wanted to do ballet to the song "Country roads, take me home" and she would've thought I'd be good at it.

But Sadie and me were still best friends and the fact was, she rather'd have me there than not. It was better to get up Sunday morning and trudge through the snow with me than to have to go alone.

The first morning of class, I waited at Sadie's back door with my boots leaking, trying not to melt on Alice's warm kitchen floor. Sadie was upstairs screaming, "Give it! Give it back now or you're dead! Eddayyyyy!" It was quarter to ten; class was starting in fifteen minutes. The house shook a little and Eddy thumped down the stairs with Sadie running behind, yelling, "Give it back, you friggin' nature! I'm tellin'—give it!" When he got to the bottom, he went sliding across the kitchen floor in his socks, jumping and swan-leaping and yodelling this noise, like Ethel Merman if she was falling off a roof, while he waved Sadie's new leotard over his head.

Alice, their mum, yelled, "What the hell is going on in there!"

right when Sadie got hold of her leotard and yanked. Eddy's socks slipped out from under him and he cracked his back down on the floor. So Sadie stood over him with her leotard and yelled, "Serves you right, y'lez!" in his face and stomped back up to her room. Eddy crunched shut his eyes and moaned his guts out.

Alice ran in the kitchen and went down on her knees so she could rock Eddy in her arms and holler, "Sadie! Get your smartass back down these stairs right now and apologize to him or you're not goin' anywhere, young lady," over his head. The clock said almost five to ten.

I got rocks in my stomach. There was no way I was going to walk in that classroom alone.

A few seconds later Sadie skipped down the steps, all bundled up and ready to go. Ray, her dad, came in the kitchen and looked bored at Eddy. "What's wrong with him?"

"You know damn well who's always the instigator in these things!" Alice was looking at Sadie and still holding Eddy.

Ray grinned at Sadie, like he knew for sure that she was going to be a star if people would just get the hell out of her way. Then Ray noticed me. "Hiya Grace, here's a nice good morning for you, huh? Geez, the two of you better get your rears in gear if you're going to make it to this ballet class." Sadie whipped past her mum and Eddy and pulled me with her.

We scuffed along the sidewalk, some of it shovelled, some with thick snow that got walked into being ice. We chewed gum in time to our steps and Sadie talked between chomps. "You know if you swallow your gum, it stays in your stomach for seven years." I didn't answer. She was probably right. She blew a bubble and said, "Is your mum still working at Eaton's?"

"Nope. It was just till January, till after Christmas." I looked sideways at Sadie's coat: fake fur with ear-sized black spots on top of silver-grey. Mine looked dull next to it now. Sadie's coat. It just bugged me—I couldn't believe she'd picked it when we were shopping in the Girls' Department at Eaton's with our mums. I tried on something black and belted; I thought it looked fancy and ladyish with the skinny waist. Then Sadie threw on this fat mountain of fur and spots. She looked like a dalmatian blob; it was the dumbest-looking thing I ever saw and there she'd gone and picked it on her own free will. I was so glad.

But then something happened between the department store and the first day back at school, after Christmas vacation. Something changed that clown-thing into a movie star coat. The other kids stared at Sadie, all jealous, and touched her sleeves. Grown-up ladies ran their fingers over her collar and wondered if they could find one in their own size. Sadie must've been praying for snow till summer.

I peeled my eyes off her coat and looked back at my feet going along the sidewalk, then asked her, even though my mum'd told me not to, "What'd you get for Christmas again, you never said."

"Umm, I'm not supposed to tell you—my mum said not to talk about what we got for Christmas because you guys are on welfare and you don't have a dad and your mum couldn't afford to get you as much as us."

My mum had told me the same thing, only she said that being an only child I was bound to get more stuff than Sadie and Eddy, and that Alice wouldn't be able to afford as much for both her kids. So I said, "Oh. Well, I got a brooch shaped like a dog with little green glass eyes. And I got a ring. Too." I pulled my mitten off to show her the blue stone. "It's sapphire," I told her, and drooped my hand to look glamorous.

Sadie glanced. "I got Spirograph."

I pulled my mitt back on. "And I got a black Barbie with an evening gown and high heels. And Monopoly—"

"Holy crow, you just got Monopoly now? We've had it since we were little!"

I was trying to think of another Christmas present worth bragging about when we got to the edge of Riley Park. There was snow and sticks on the bottom of the kiddy pool and three teenagers in red lumberman jackets on the other side of it. They had their backs turned and their shoulders scrunched into each other. "Glue Sniffers," we said together. It seemed like we had to say what they were when we saw them, to keep them away. Riley Park was full of Glue Sniffers: big kids from school and The Projects. Guys as old as my sister filled up baggies with glue, shoved in their noses and breathed until they got dizzy. Glue Sniffers were like boogeymen almost. We kept going toward the community centre.

When we got to the classroom, the clock on the wall was just hitting ten past ten. The rest of the girls sat cross-legged on the floor, all in leotards with white or pink tights. They sat super straight with their hands folded, listening to this skinny lady with a long neck that looked like a foot cuz of being all chicken-bone-stringy right down to her boobs practically. She had on a bodysuit and baggy drawstring pants. And ballet shoes. She looked up then at her watch. "Sorry we're late," we told her, talking all over each other.

"That's good, I hope you're sorry enough not to let it happen again. I'm Miss Stickney. Have you got your leotards on underneath?" We did. We yanked off our slacks and sweaters and sat down to change into our slippers. Meanwhile Miss Stickney got the other girls up and made them do stretches. Sadie watched out of the corner of her eye and got the giggles. My other slipper wouldn't go on and I got them too. I tried not to hear the squeaks in Sadie's throat, but then she started a mouse-voice of Eddy's Ethel Merman opera and we both shook from holding the laughs in. Sadie coughed to cover hers up and I bit my tongue to get the most pain without blood.

Our teacher looked at us, breathing, slow in/slow out, with her arms bent all funny like my black Barbie. "Come along, ladies, giggling on the floor is not going to get you warm enough to keep you from pulling a hamstring." We stood up, embarrassed, but then I got a picture of Sadie dragging a ham on a string and it was killing me. Sadie started stretching.

"What's your name, Miss?" Sadie told her. "And yours?" I looked to the other girls and copied their stretches so that my name would come out of someone who was trying her best and told her. "Well," she said, and dropped forward so her palms were down flat against the floor, "the sooner you two find out this class won't tolerate silliness, the better off you'll be." Miss Stickney told us we would be more flexible than she was in no time at all, that we were young and like rubber next to her. I thought she should know that I wasn't anything like rubber. The back of my legs were burning like crazy and my fingers didn't even dangle to my ankles and she yelled, "Knees straight!"

Then she arranged us in a circle, put music on, and we hop-kicked our way around and round the circle in time to violins. It seemed like we were doing some kind of furry-hat Russian dance thing, not ballet. We weren't doing anything that was going to make me more graceful, we weren't leaping through the air, and we didn't get tutus. We just kept kicking around the circle over and over until she clapped at us to stop and everybody fell back on their bums, panting. The class finished with more stretching.

I pulled on my clothes afterward, tired and crabby. My throat hurt and I didn't want to go back in the cold. The bones on the bottom of my feet hurt and I was mad at myself for getting a stupid short-sleeved leotard that made me look like a baby instead of the long-sleeved kind that made Sadie all long and tall and practically grown-up.

The next two Sundays were pretty much the same: squat kicks around the room and long breathy stretches. Except after the second class, Sadie brought along this other girl on our walk home. Then the third next class, she went over to the girl's house afterwards and I didn't get invited. I was kind of upset, like I was going to cry on the way home. Sometimes it seemed dumb even being friends with people. They'd just go off and be friends with someone else. Even if you tried to be like them. Or else they'd move. Or else you'd move. Or else they had a whole family who did stuff together, like, had dinner at a certain time or did church stuff and you could never be in the family, even though sometimes you could be one of the place settings at dinner.

When I got home, Mum was on a cleaning binge. I hardly ever saw her like that, moving so fast, so I stood outside the kitchen in my boots and coat and watched. Country music was blaring out of the radio on the counter and Mum rubbed a J Cloth on the floor on her hands and knees. She looked up. "Hey there, ballerina. How was it today?"

"Mmm. Same."

"No good? Hey! Goofball, you wanna take your feet off, you're slushing up my floor. I ain't just a-killin' time down here, ol' thang."

"Sorry." I backed up and took off my boots. "I hate these lessons. It's not even ballet. Just this kicking stuff like—" and I squatted and tried to show her.

She looked up, still wiping around herself. "Huh. Maybe she's trying to strengthen your legs."

"No. She's stupid."

"Well, you don't have to keep going, just do whatcha feel, shlemiel."

"Yeah, I know."

She kept wiping and said, "Your dad called today."

"He did? Why didn't you tell me?"

"I'm telling you now."

"Well, what'd he say? Did he say anything about me? Did you tell him about me doing ballet?"

"Yes, of course he asked about you and how you were doing and I told him you were at ballet—he seemed to get a chuckle out of that."

"What do you mean, a chuckle?"

"Well, I mean a kick, you know, he said, 'Yeah? boy that's real good, that's real good for her,' and I told him what they were going to cost and he didn't offer to pay for them. You know. The usual."

"Oh. Is he coming here?"

"Well, he said he might come in the spring. And pigs might fly, but they're very unlikely birds. He said Charlie's out there again. She's there with a guy, staying at some joint your father's got on Bloor Street. Apparently he's a pretty tough customer, the guy —his name's Ian."

"Ian?"

"Yeah. He's an albino."

"Like a rat?"

"Apparently."

Mum was right about Vancouver. By the end of March it was T-shirt time; kids were already getting tans on their faces. And I had a friend called Gabrielle. My sore throats ended up being the flu and I had to stay home from school for a whole week—it was Gabrielle who showed up at our door with a big envelope of get-well cards that the grade 3 class made. I knew our teacher made them do it and Gabrielle was just delivering them, but still, it was practically like she made them herself. Plus, it turned out to be that Darlene, my babysitter, was Gabrielle's big sister.

Gabrielle was like Pearl, kind of, but prettier. She lived a block and a half away, in The Projects, and she was one of hardly any kids from around there that my mum didn't say was riff-raff. Sadie and Eddy were riff-raff.

The first couple times I brought Gabrielle home after school, we had the place to ourself. We drank milk with Strawberry Quik and played cards at the kitchen table until she had to go home for dinner. The third time she came over, Gabrielle taught me snap. Gabrielle won every practice round and I made sure she knew they didn't count. I cracked my knuckles while she dealt our first real game. I planned on being one of those pool shark guys who stomped everybody when they played for real. I slowly turned cards off my hand until she waggled her finger at me, like Gladys Kravitz on *Bewitched*, cuz she said I was holding back, trying to see her card before she saw mine. Then she yelled, "Snap!" and grabbed both our twos and the piles underneath them. And "Snap!" again and the next time and the next. I was down to around eight cards and the sound of her voice was starting to bug me, that word—if she said it one more time. "Snap!" I snapped, but it was a four and an ace. Gabrielle giggled and snapped at the next pair. I was getting bored when my mother came home.

Mum was in a good mood; she was coming home from General Brock, our school, where she got a job doing volunteer work with the first- and second-graders. She tried to do teaching in Vancouver when we first moved here and found out she wasn't allowed to in B.C. unless she went back to school and did more classes. She said forget-it to that and then got this idea to do volunteer work, cuz maybe it'd be an *in*.

Gabrielle gave my mother one of her shiny blonde smiles, said hello and held out her hand. I never saw a kid shake hands with a grown-up before that. My mother looked all impressed and said, "Gabrielle," and rolled her *r* like she was French or something, "tu parles français?"

"No. Not really. My dad does. My sister and I were born in Montreal, but we've been here since I was really little."

Mum sat in the chair on the other side of her. "Oh, Montreal, I used to love Montreal; the way the women dressed—just fantastic! The French women really do have a way—I used to want to stay there forever just so it would rub off on me a little." Gabrielle was still smiling at my mother, glinting her with her glasses. Her glasses were too big and Mum's reflection practically took up Gabrielle's whole face, one of her on each side. "You have such pretty hair, Gabrielle, the colour of butter," and then she touched it. She put her hand on Gabrielle's hair and ran it all the way down to the middle of her back. She touched it the way she touched blouses she couldn't afford in department stores. "Goodness, it's like velvet!"

Gabrielle got even shinier the more my mum paid attention to her; all teeth and glasses. She said that her mother bought her a special conditioner that smelled like apples. Mum hmmed and went to the fridge to pour herself a Fresca. I asked what conditioner was. Gabrielle giggled and said you put it in your hair after rinsing out the shampoo. I fanned out the four cards I had left in my hands—kids were putting stuff in their hair that made it soft and I never even heard of it. Mum didn't say anything, just put the Fresca bottle back in the fridge. We didn't even use shampoo.

"What kind of conditioner do you use?" Gabrielle asked me.

"I don't know, let's just play."

Mum leaned against the counter and sipped her green bubbles. "Grace and I use good ol' soap and water. I never really believed in that racket, shampoo and conditioner and all that."

Gabrielle laid a card down. I laid mine slowly across from hers. "Snap!" She picked up both cards and cackled. "Grace isn't getting the hang of this that good."

"I am so."

"Well, you're not that fast, I mean. You keep losing."

"So you lost crazy eights, y'lez." The word fell on the table like dog poo.

Mum coughed on her Fresca. "What? What kind of talk is that? That sounded like a *Sadie* if you ask me."

Gabrielle blinked under her glass plates. "What's a lez?"

"People who put conditioner in their hair."

"Grace! for goodness sake. Sorry, Gabrielle, I think your friend
took too many crabby pills today." Mum gave me the look. I
wished she'd quit saying Gabrielle's name or quit saying it that
way, the way people say cream or caramel. She changed the subject. "So I had a nice interview with your principal, he's really
lovely. We had a terrific little chat—actually, he's kind of handsome, well, maybe more cute than handsome. And I start coming
in a couple hours a day next Monday! Isn't that great!"

I said uh huh. The phone rang and she went off to the bedroom. I watched Gabrielle's cards and wondered how I'd look
with glasses. "Snap!"—my first victory. I grabbed the cards over
to my side: four of her cards. Four captured cards. I wondered out
loud about the glasses thing. She smiled and pushed hers up.

"I don't know, you kinda have a nose like Fred Flintstone;
they might look funny." I rubbed a finger along my nose bone.
She explained, "Well, your nose kinda goes down and then boing,
kinda there, boings out in a round part on the end and glasses
might maybe make you look more like you're from Bedrock."

I looked at the clock. Gabrielle cranked her head around too.
She had to go, her aunt was coming over for dinner and Gabrielle
had to help, had to do things like set the table and stir stuff in pots
just in time for it all to be laid out at once. Probably things like
stew and mashed things, cabbage rolls; reasons I was too afraid to
go to other kids' for dinner. Mum came back in the kitchen as
Gabrielle was getting ready to go and told her goodbye, said how
nice it was to have met her, then touched the little blue flowers on
her cuffs and said, "What an adorable sweater," and asked if someone in the family'd made it. She told Gabrielle how my nanna
knitted too, that I had nighties and slippers she made. I wished
they'd shut up.

When the door closed, Mum folded her arms and smirked,
"Boy oh boy, somebody's a green-eyed monster today," and she
started into a song she sang all the time that went, "Jealousy, it's

crawling all over me," and didn't knock it off until I left the room. She called after me, "Come here, you monstrosity, I have to tell you something. Come 'ere—come 'ere … we have to talk about something." I stayed in the kitchen and looked in the fridge like I was hungry. She came in behind me and said, "Charlie called last night."

"What—why didn't you let me talk to her?"

"Because you weren't here, you were at the bookmobile." Every Tuesday night, a bus with a library on it came around and stopped for two hours on Main Street, two blocks from our building.

"Well, why didn't you tell me?"

"Just hold your horses. She's pregnant. And her son-of-a-bitch boyfriend's been knocking her around. And—just wait, don't get yourself all in a knot—she's OK, but she was talking about coming to Vancouver. She wanted to know if she could stay with us for a little while and I told her she could but to give it some thought and call me today. I didn't want to tell you until I knew for sure—you know how she is; changes her mind every mi—"

"So is she coming or not?"

"Keep your shirt on; that was just her on the phone now, she's coming. I don't know how she got the money, but she's catching a plane tomorrow. And I don't know what kind of shape she's in, but it's probably pretty bad if it's enough to make her leave this goon and come out here. So don't be shocked if you see her and she doesn't look too hot."

Grace Five

S HE DIDN'T LOOK too hot. My sister's face was still puffy with bruises. Her left eye was half shut, rock blue and purple down to her cheekbone. There were cuts across her nose and lip and stitches through her eyebrow.

Charlie sat at the kitchen table while Mum tilted her chin up and looked and sighed. I stood beside Mum and asked why he hit her and Charlie said, "Because he's an asshole. He's a fuckin' lunatic," and told us how Ian put her head through a wall, that he just kept hitting her and hitting her, and how screams had started coming out of her that she didn't even think were hers and she could see blood all over the place and it looked like poster paint. When the cops showed up, they separated her from Ian; one stood in front of him and the other kneeled beside her and asked what happened. She could still see Ian's eyes and they had the same look as the night when he held a gun to her head and asked her if she loved him. So Charlie told the cop that she fell down the fire escape. The one beside her was young with smooth chocolate-coloured skin, she said, and he kept talking softly, telling her she could press charges and have the guy put away. She could feel the blood crusting on her chin and hear the leather squeak on his holster and she thought how the good guy was the one in black and the bad guy was in white. And it didn't matter what she did, the bad guy had her by the throat. The cops finally gave up and took her to the hospital to get stitches in her eyebrow.

I wished I could wipe off the cuts and bruises, like they were dirt—give her one of Mum's spitbaths. My mother took a deep breath and growled it out, saying, "So where is he now?"

"I don't know. I didn't tell him I was leaving, I just pretended everything was fine and when he went out this morning, I packed a bag and grabbed the money under the mattress. I took the bus to the airport and flew standby." My sister's fingers came up to pick a pimple on her chin. "There was a hundred and sixty-five bucks under the mattress." Mum patted her hand away and Charlie hid her fist between her thighs. "I left him five."

Mum chuckled. Charlie tittered from her chest. Mum looked at her and giggled louder. Charlie laughed up her throat and through her nose, trying to hold her lip still so it wouldn't hurt. Mum burst out a giant laugh. Charlie put her hand over her mouth and squeaked through her lips and palm. I laughed too but I wasn't sure I got it, so I said, "It'd be enough to eat at McDonald's for lunch. And dinner." My sister howled now with all her fingers on her lip and doubled over, gurgling and making little acks and ha-has while Mum held the kitchen counter and wiped tears from her eyes. Our eyes flicked on each other and we got quiet and tried to hold back the noise still in our bellies, as if we were all hiding in a closet trying not to give ourselves away.

So then I said, "But why didn't you tell the police? They were there, they would've took him away." Mum corrected my English and Charlie sighed and looked down at her basketball tummy. She rested her hands there and let her hair fall over her face. I looked back at Mum, she opened a kitchen cupboard and grabbed Adelle Davis's *Let's Stay Healthy* off the counter.

"Charlie, we should put something on your face so it doesn't scar. And here, you should take some ascorbic acid, it helps you heal, so I'll give you some vitamin C … and B-complex and …" She sat down beside my sister with her arms full of brown plastic bottles. "First we'll put some vitamin E right on your poor little facey." Charlie looked at Mum's mouth and watched her nip the end of a vitamin E capsule. She let her breath go like she'd been holding it all this time and closed her eyes while Mum drizzled oil over the hard black threads in her eyebrow, the split in her lip and across her nose.

No maternity wear, no shopping for baby clothes, in fact she hardly talked about being pregnant at all. If Charlie looked like anything, it was tougher. She was still wearing the same tight jeans, except with the zipper down, big hippy blouses hanging over top, and her platform boots. And the boots seemed like they had their own scariness, like they were looking for a neck to stand on. She zipped all her money in those boots right along with her killer feet (she told me she knew how to high-kick someone right in the head now). She told me more than I ever remembered her telling, things I wanted to tell my friends with all the details right. My eyelids practically peeled back so I could see more of her when she told me about street fights she got in, gang fights, and how she learned to take care of herself from her boyfriend before last, the Hell's Angel guy. Her eyes were more flicky when she told those stories, like she thought the door might fly open and something bigger and wilder than her was going to knock us all down. He was Cree Indian, the only Indian in the Hell's Angels, she said, and he took her everywhere with him on the back of his motorcycle. She told me about dreams she had when they were together — crossing desert plains with feathers in her hair and a papoose on her back, straggling way behind the rest of the tribe. She didn't have moccasins and her feet were burning, but she just kept walking, playing with two speckled eggs in her hands and singing Indian songs.

It was her third night home and we were lying in bed, the bed where all three of us slept. Except Mum was out tonight. "His name was Shane," she told me. Her eyes were closed now and I couldn't tell if she was still in her dreams or back on the street with motorcycles. The swelling was down and the bruises were getting yellow, but the black slices on her nose and lip were still shiny with vitamin E oil and the stitches would be in for ten more days. "He had this thing for chicks with tattoos and I always thought they were kinda cool too, so-o ..." she rolled her back to me and yanked down the neck of her T-shirt. An orangey yellow ball as big as one of Mum's vitamin lids sat just on the back part of her shoulder. It had a red ribbon tied around it like a Christmas present. "It's a peach," she said. "Shane used to call me Peaches." She let her T-shirt go and lay back on the mattress. "Actually, he said my boobs were like peaches." I looked at her chest and thought about when we were all together in Toronto.

A little while after my dad came and brought me and my mum with him to Toronto, Charlie came out to be with us too. This one time in the summer, we were sitting on Charlie's bed, trying to think of something to do. Her sheets were rumply and warm and she was lying on her stomach complaining that she hated single beds cuz that's what she had. So I said, "Why?—is someone staying over?"

She giggled in her pillow, said, "That'd be the day," and pulled herself up and sat beside me against the wall watching while I peeled a big bubble of skin off my heel. I flicked it beside my knee. "Eww!" She elbowed my ribs. "I have to sleep here, y'know." I said sorry and put my legs straight so I wouldn't get tempted. My feet came to just past her knees. I looked over at her shins that got shaved so much, her bones shined. Like Mum's. Then I looked at my hairy sticks. Charlie took my arm closest to her and ran her finger along the skin. "Did you shave your arms?"

"No. My arms!" I looked at hers and wondered if her and Mum did that too.

"I just thought I remembered your arms being a lot hairier, like your legs—look at your legs—you look like an orangutan!"

I giggled cuz of how I like being called monkeys and apes. She grabbed me and tickled under my arms, singing, "Monkey-girl, monkey-girl, Grace-face is a monkey-girl." I doubled over, laughing and coughing and scrunching, trying to save my pits, scared she wasn't going to stop and I'd suffocate and die. I started to yell and she whacked her hand over my mouth, in case Mum might hear and know we were just goofing off instead of getting out of the house.

I fell away from her, still laughy, until I got my breath back enough to ask her, "So what do you want to do?"

"I don't know." She sighed like Mum. "It's kind of boring here."

I twiddled my toes on each other, trying not to be boring, trying to make Toronto be fun. I said, "We could go to the park. I saw kids up there catching bees yesterday, in a jar. They had a big pickle jar and they put flowers in it and holes in the lid with a nail and they'd open the lid and catch bees off those purple round flower things and they'd shake 'em down like this ..." I pretended a pickle jar and shook the bees to the bottom.

Charlie watched me and then opened her mouth and said, "Why?" through a huge yawn.

"Because you'd have a whole jar full of bees and bees and bees—probably a thousand—and you could put your ear over the lid and listen to them or you could make honey with them ... Or um, oh!—or my friend Shelly who lives up at the top of the road, near where the corner store is? her cat has kittens. Maybe we could go see them?"

"Really? Hey, do they have any black ones?"

"I can't remember. I only saw them once, in a box in their basement, and it was kind of dark."

My sister's big eyes bugged a little and her eyebrows bounced. "Let's get a kitten! That'd be so far out!" and she wiggled my knee-cap. "'K, let's go see 'em. Get dressed."

Charlie pulled off her nightgown and went over to her dresser and for a second I saw her from sideways. That was the first time I saw her totally bare naked since she came to Toronto. She bent forward to put on her underpants and all the sudden there was new jiggly stuff there. I got hypnotized.

Charlie saw me gawking at her new boobies and went, "What're *you* staring at?"

I wanted to keep looking, but I said in a bratty voice, "I see your boobies."

She turned her back and grabbed her bra from the pile of clothes on her dresser. I crawled to the head of the bed where I could see them again. Charlie crossed her arms and told me to shut up over her shoulder. But I couldn't now. "I see Charlie's BOO-OOBIES," and I cackled like Dracula. Her face got all mad and she called me a pervert and then yelled me out of the room. I was laughing so much, I couldn't hardly say the booby thing. She pulled a T-shirt on and stomped over to where I was and yanked me out of her room and slammed the door after me. And then she locked it.

I kneeled and peeked through the keyhole, and sang all low, "I see Charlie's boobies." Charlie grabbed a sock off the floor and stuffed it in the keyhole. I plunked down on the floor and stared up at her door. She was never going to let me see them again and it was my own fault.

But I couldn't help it—she just grew them like that. Whole new parts of herself. Like she was a starfish or something. They weren't big like my mum's, but they stuck out like snow cones and wiggled like Jell-O. I thought of her old boyfriend Dwayne, from Vancouver, before she ran away from home, and wondered if she had those then and if he knew about them. I must've saw Mum's a thousand times and never thought about them; maybe because they were always there, like her legs or her eyes.

Ever since then, I suppose, I thought they were my secret, her boobies. It felt weird now knowing some biker guy'd seen them, but I just said, "How come you didn't keep him, how come you started having *Ian* for your boyfriend?"

"I don't know. He was nicer than Ian. Ah, he was a dink too, though, they were both dinks. Every guy I go out with is a dink." And she spread her fingers on her belly and rubbed softly. "Feel it," she said, and I put my hands between hers. "Weird, eh," and she watched me try to squish the middle of her. It was so hard and tight, like a balloon, and part of me wanted to bite, or pop it— slap it flat so it'd be just us two again. Then, like she knew what I was thinking or something, she said, "Aunt Jo thinks I should give it away."

"When were you talking to Aunt Jo?" Jo was Mum's sister. She lived in Calgary with her husband and we hardly ever saw her— we never saw her.

"I talk to her sometimes. I wrote to her when I was in Toronto and told her I was pregnant. I don't know why."

"Aunt Jo? How come you told Aunt Jo? You didn't even tell *me*."

"I don't know. I guess I thought she wasn't so close to the situation or something, so she could give me advice. I don't know."

"Well, who would you give it to?"

"I don't know. Up for adoption. I probably wouldn't even get to meet them. She says I'm being selfish and there's lots of people

in the world that can't have children and here I am having one
when I can't even support it. I told her to fuck off. And then I
started bawling. I'm so stupid. I'm such a gimp. I don't know what
the hell I'm doing. But even Mum said it was none of her business
to tell me that. Shit. Do you think I'm selfish?"

I looked at her body and couldn't stop thinking it was just
stuffing under her T-shirt. I pulled it up to look at her ball. The
skin was yanked tight and tiny blue and purple veins showed
through and her belly button was pushed up even with her stomach. I patted and tapped and listened to the plunks it made. I put
my forehead against it, then my ear, and faced Charlie's chin. She
drummed my forehead with her fingertips. "Hey goofball, tell me
I'm not selfish."

"I don't think you're selfish. I love you. And I hate Ian's guts
for hitting you."

She smiled and scratched my head. "My baby," she said, "my
little Gracey-baby." I sprawled over her stomach and Charlie
poked at it. "Do you think it'll be a boy or a girl?" she asked me.
I sat up and thumped my palms on her again, a little harder. "I
don't know."

"What should I call it if it's a girl?"

"I don't know. Call it Sneezy," and I moved up beside her so
our faces were close.

Charlie pushed her head back in her pillow and giggled.
"Sneezy Hoffman." She turned her face to me. "Oh, who cares
anyway." She looked up at the ceiling. We rolled our heads toward
each other and stared. She said, "I thought about calling it Grace
cuz I thought that might make her special. But then I realized
there'll never be another you anyway. Right?" I didn't say anything,
just looked in Charlie's big deer eyes. "It's not going to be anything
like you," she said, "it won't have orangutan arms and it won't
smell like honey ..." She brought her fingers to my forehead and
flattened the cowlick.

"I don't want you to have a baby," I told her.

"Ohhh, Grace-face … are you sad? Come here and hug me—it doesn't matter if I have it, it won't really be my baby, not my real baby. You'll always be my only baby. I promise. I promise, cross my heart and hope to die, I won't love it. I only love you." Tears went down our cheeks and we fell asleep that way, holding hands between our chests, heads together, waking up just for a second when Mum came home and crawled in on the other side of Charlie.

My sister was with us around three weeks when I asked her to go with me to the bookmobile. She didn't feel like it. It was nearly May and the days were getting summery, so her and Mum were sprawled around the living room, legs all over the couch and chair arms, eating bread-and-butter pickles with crackers and cheese. Charlie bought treats and the three of us had picking-food for dinner: Cheez Whiz with celery, celery with peanut butter, Granny Smith apple slices, carrot sticks, cheddar cheese, Ritz crackers, Melba toast—and three Pep Chews, ice cream and Popcorn Twists for dessert. They were lazing and telling stories and Charlie didn't want to move. "Geez, Grace, I've had to go pee for an hour now and I haven't had the energy."

I left them laughing and went to get the phone in the bedroom so I could try and talk someone else into coming with me. I didn't bother with Sadie and Eddy, they would've called ages ago if they were planning on it. I had to go, though; the week before, the librarian 'd talked me into getting *James and the Giant Peach*. She promised I'd like it, so I took it, even though it was about a boy, just to prove her wrong. But I loved it and now I had to go tell her and show how I read the whole thing in six days. I called Gabrielle instead. Her mother answered the phone and said she wasn't finished dinner yet but she'd call as soon as she was done.

Twenty to seven. Nobody ever didn't get interrupted during dinner at our place.

The bookmobile would only be there until eight. I went down the hall to the living room. A news guy was on and Charlie and Mum were talking about his head. "Last time I saw a rug that bad, it was on my bathroom floor," and then this thing about Alaska came on and Mum said, "Hey, what do you call an Eskimo with a hard-on?" Charlie snorted before she even heard the answer. "A frigid midget with a rigid digit." They both screamed and Charlie started begging, "Ah stop, I'm gonna pee my pants."

By ten past seven Gabrielle and I were walking down Main Street. We could see kids coming in and out of the long green bus from a block away. Even tough kids came to the bookmobile. All of us did. I had *James and the Giant Peach* under my arm. Gabrielle had *Black Beauty*. I already read that one too and I told her so. Then she asked about my sister, where her husband was. I told her she didn't have one. I said it in a way that she'd see how cool my sister was, how no-big-deal this baby was. Her eyes looked worried. "What about the baby, it won't have a dad. Does she know where he is?"

I thought about whether to say this next part. It'd made my mum sigh and say oh-boy. It felt big though, and I wanted to try it out. "She's doesn't know who the father is." Gabrielle's face went limp like she was going to cry. "I mean she's not sure. She started going around with Ian, the one who hit her, right after Shane, the motorcycle guy, and she got pregnant right around then—she'll know when it gets born though; the old boyfriend was Indian, like the teepee kind, and the new guy was albino. Like a rat. And everyone in the albino guy's family has red hair anyway. So if it's dark, she'll know."

Gabrielle got white. All she said was "oh" and kept her eyes down the rest of the way.

There was about six kids on the bus, less than I figured. I let Gabrielle go ahead so I could look for the librarian with the long springs of black hair. I didn't want to return the book without thanking her and telling her she was right. People's favourite thing is when you say you-were-right to them. The only librarian was a lady with droopy eyes and a skinny mouth that went up at the corners every time a kid handed in a book.

I wandered down to where Gabrielle was standing staring at a shelf. "Find anything?" I asked her. She turned and smiled like she was embarrassed. I wondered if she was still weird about what I told her—God, you'd think it was her that got pregnant. She said, "I'm trying to find *Go Ask Alice*. My sister read it and her friends read it and they won't let me—I just want to see it."

I was one of the kids ahead of her on the wait-list. Everybody was. Charlie said she read some of it and didn't know how come us kids cared; it was all about drugs, she said. But it had sex and swearing *and* drugs. And anyway, Sadie'd read it and I couldn't stand her having anything over me.

"I'll go ask the lady," I told her, and a girl walked behind and tripped into me. I looked after her; she kept going. I whispered, "Excuse *me*," and went to ask the librarian.

The lady's eyebrows flicked up, but her mouth hardly moved. "Boy, you kids are sure crazy about that book. It's got quite a few reserves ahead of you, so you might want to check back in a few weeks."

I trudged back to Gabrielle. "Same as school with all the holds, but um, how 'bout—" and the same girl passed behind and shoved her elbow into my back. I whipped around.

"Oops. Scuse me," she said, and stopped to look at a shelf near the front of the bus.

Gabrielle watched after her and whispered, "That girl's mean, I saw her fighting with a grade 3er before. A boy. She's in grade 5, you know."

"Well, I'm telling if she does it again," I told her, and Gabrielle chewed the inside of her cheeks. "I forgot what I was gonna say." The grade 5 girl passed and elbowed me again, and pushed me into the shelf this time. I said, "Hey, quit it," at her back and she stopped beside her friend, who was littler with freckles and red hair. The friend giggled. The bigger one made fun of my "quit it."

"That's it. I'm telling." I ran and told the librarian that two kids were pushing me. Her mouth went up like I just returned a book. I waited.

"Well, just try to ignore them and they'll go away," and she nodded at me.

I went back to Gabrielle. I was kind of scared of kids I didn't know, kind of like how some people are about dogs. I didn't know what they'd do. I thought they'd do anything. The grade 5 girl was coming back, I could feel her moving down the bus. This time she kicked her foot into the back of my knee so my leg folded and I fell on the floor. Gabrielle made a choky noise. There were giggles behind me. Gabrielle mumbled, "We should go," through her hand as if her teeth might fall out.

I yelled at the grade 5 girl, "Leave me alone or I'm telling." I wished I could sound more tough.

"*Leeme alone or I'm telling,*" she imitated me all squeaky.

I looked down the bus, my face was burning and I wished I had powers like the girl in this movie, where she blasts the place on fire with her mind. When I got my voice back, it was the same one they used to imitate me. "That's it, I'm telling my mum and you're in trouble." I left Gabrielle there and tripped down the steps, grabbing the door to catch myself.

By the time I got to our door I was shaking and out of breath. It was locked and I ripped the key string out of my shirt and shook so much I couldn't get the key in. Charlie was still laughing inside. "I think my poor retarded sister is having trouble with the door," she called, and slapped her bare feet toward me. She flung open the door. "Hey bookworm, find anything dirty?" I cried at the sight of her. "Hey, hey! What happened? What's going on?" She hugged my head and led me to the living room. I looked at Mum and her eyes and her mouth went hard. "What happened?" they said together.

I told them I hated it here, hated The Projects and the kids and the whole place, then about what happened on the bus. My sister pulled me into her side. I looked down at her hands around my ribs, the carved leather bands on her wrists. She had changed into shorts and the feel of her bare legs against my hands made me cry harder. Mum stood up and paced around the floor, said, "That's it! ...goddamn neighbourhood," and went into the kitchen. She came back with the top half of the broom handle that'd broken off the day before. "Come on, let's go."

My sister and I looked up. "What?"

"Let's go! We'll just see about this."

Charlie squeezed and let go. "Yeah, come on, Grace-face, we should go have a talk with these brats."

Mum put her shoes on and stood waiting with the broom handle. I looked at my sister's leg. The shorts showed off another tattoo: a green lizard, the same size as the peach, on her thigh. I couldn't take my eyes off it. I followed after them and felt slippy green tails between my ribs. The three of us walked in a row across the sidewalk, me running now and then to keep up. Mum looked like a killer.

When we got to the bookmobile, we all stood at the bottom of the steps. Mum's voice got a tough cocky sound like the girl on the bus but meaner, and she slapped the broom handle against her palm. "OK, Grace, just point her out when you see her."

The sun was going down and orange light hit low on the stucco buildings around us.

"Maybe they already went. They prob'ly already left." I'd wanted this so bad and now I couldn't stand it—not knowing what they'd do, Mum with her stick and Charlie with her lizard. They could do anything.

"I doubt it," Charlie said. She stood on one leg, sticking her hip out. How could I not see a green lizard in three weeks of sleeping in the same bed together?

The last kids were coming off the bus. Mum checked my face every time. "Maybe we should go." I said it quiet so they wouldn't know if they heard it or thought it.

Mum heard me, though, and said, "Uh-uh. I've had enough of this crap. Nobody touches my kid. Right, Charlie?" My sister grinned at her with rosy cheeks.

After a few minutes, I figured the reason we were there was already gone. I was getting unscared and it was starting to be a letdown. I looked at my feet and down came our reason. I almost lost my voice again when I said, "That's her."

The friend-girl's face went frozen. The shover-girl's foot hardly touched the ground when my mum caught her by the arm. Mum shook her. "Yeah, you better look scared, you mangy little brat—were you bothering her? Huh? Were you bothering my daughter?" Shover-girl swallowed and stared at Mum's throat. Charlie stepped in closer and folded her arms. She bounced her eyebrows at the girl as if she didn't really want to kill her but what else could she do? I looked at the green lizard; its tail rolled when my sister moved her weight to that leg. Shover-girl's eyes flicked on the lizard. Mum jerked the girl's shoulder up closer to her ear. "Hey, smartass, look at me." She raised her broomstick. "If I ever … *ever* … hear that you laid another hand on my kid—*ever*—" she shook her hard on the last *ever*—"again, they'll find you black and blue in a ditch somewhere." The air went out of me. A tremble went down the girl's cheek and neck. She smirked. My sister tilted her head and tucked her chin, smiling snake-eyed at her. "Understand me?" Mum said. Shover-girl's mouth pressed together and she nodded. Mum shook her again. "What?!" The girl said a small yes and my mother spat air off her teeth then let her go with a little shove. The friend-girl tugged Shover-girl's sleeve and they walked away fast.

Mum bit her top lip, like she was holding a laugh, and nodded. Charlie said, "Christ, I thought she was gonna pee herself," and the three of us snickered our heads off. We stayed beside the bookmobile a few more seconds and I looked around to see who saw. The green doors closed and the engine grumbled awake.

Eilleen Five

YOU'RE PUTTING your face on, getting ready to go out with a guy you met at an AA coffee house downtown. Lining your lids; make it perfect ... shit—damn hands always shaking. Should take a Librium to calm your nerves. There. That's pretty good. Not bad for an old broad, for a *grandmother. Granny.* Hate even saying it—grandma, nanna. Christ. Old. Old-old-old. And you rub lipstick into the apples of your cheeks—barely forty-two. Just feels like more people to hide—been telling people, well, men, that you only have one daughter, one eight-year-old or, well, you don't exactly say she's all you have, but she's all you mention—at any rate, now you've got a grandkid born in the same decade. How are you supposed to pull off being thirty-five after you've divulged that. Seems like your entire existence is secret sometimes. Grace was irked before the baby was born, but she's handling it better than you are, now that she's an aunt—some perceived power out of the whole mess. Except she's mad at Charlie, mostly for leaving her again.

Charlie's boyfriend tracked her down through friends. He conned her, asking if he could come talk and she didn't have the guts to tell you until ten minutes before he was due. Suddenly there was his voice crackling up the intercom. Charlie buzzed him in. Grace got twitchy. And you stood up, folded your arms, fisted your hands, put them on your hips, folded your arms again, threw your chin out—you could take care of some pool hall punk. Could hear his feet scuffing up the carpeted stairs and you secured the phone's location in your brain. Charlie waddled to the door, pregnant out to here, and Grace followed. She hardly had the door open when the son of a bitch slammed it wide and kicked her in the stomach. *There, you fuckin' whore, fuck you!* Grace screamed and Charlie fell on the floor. Ian backed down the hallway. You raced to the door. *I'm calling the police, I mean it, I'm calling them now.* And off he went downstairs, piggy blue eyes squinting, barking over his shoulder with those colourless lips like liver that'd washed up on the beach, *bitch* this and *cunt* that. Neighbours were opening their doors up and down the hallway while you locked yours. Charlie curled on the floor crying while Grace stuffed her head in between her sister's chest and belly, rubbing and saying her name over and over. Jesus-jesus-jesus. The more things change the more they stay the same.

You went to the living room and looked down on Main Street to make sure he was gone and there he was on the front lawn staring up at the window screaming for Charlie. He wasn't leaving until he talked to her. You brought the phone over to the window to show him—See this and I'm not afraid to use it. He just kept yelling and you kept yelling back, *I'm calling the police, I'm calling them right now.* And Charlie and Grace made their way to the couch behind you and you glared down at Ian and picked up the receiver. Charlie told you to put the phone down, she was going to talk to him. And you popped your eyes. *Are you out of your cotton-pickin' mind?* and she said just to wait, just let her talk to him.

Grace pleaded with her, but she left and the next thing you knew the two of them were out there arguing on the lawn. He took a swing at her and missed and you called the cops anyway. After a few minutes Ian swiped the air as if Charlie's words were gadflies and stormed off before the police showed up. Charlie was back inside crying when they asked if she wanted to press charges, one of them looking at her all moony like some kind of fish-eyed lover, telling her his name twice in case anything should happen and she needed to be in touch. The other was a sullen by-the-book-er; he knew full well she wouldn't press charges and not only that, she'd likely go back to the son of a bitch.

Four days later, Charlie disappeared for two. Another fight. You and her. Another screaming, name-calling, neighbours-opening-their-doors to the tune of *you slut, you tramp, you whore.* Funny how your insults for each other are so similar. Identical. Could be arguing about anything: the way you dress, the way you raised them; the outcome is the same.

Charlie showed up two days later with a ring on her finger. She was glassy-eyed and sugar-tongued and told you that Ian was sorry and he really did mean well—he wanted to marry her and take care of the baby whether it was his or not. Grace wouldn't speak to her. Charlie moved out with Ian a couple days later and now they're living in some basement apartment. Turned out it wasn't his—baby was brown. Suntan brown and stone black eyes. You give it six months. Not even. Wouldn't surprise you if she called in a couple weeks to say that she and the baby were buggering off before he killed them both. Can't think about it—she's going to do what she's going to do.

Face on. Now hair. It's up in rollers now. Never mind hair. Figure out what you're going to wear. Your long dresses are too dressy, don't really have a casual long dress. A long casual dress would've worked, like Mary Tyler Moore wears now—dinner and a movie.

Should wear a skirt, though, show a little something—who was it that said you had well-turned ankles? funny expression. Or maybe slacks and a turtleneck, nice earrings, casual but sharp. Christ, he probably won't even notice. He runs an AA club on Pender Street; all he sees are drunks and ex-drunks, not known for their elegant sense of style. Then again men don't have to be; so long as they're not wearing a toe tag they're fair game.

George.

His name's George. Originally from Prince Edward Island. He's a fisherman and he looks the part; kind of portly. Sideburns, not too long. Heavy wool tartan coat, a black cap. They all love him downtown. He chairs the *meetin's* there and keeps the men swimming in coffee and the women in compliments. You've been going there a couple months now but he still calls you the new kid. Rumour's going around that George has a crush on the new kid. He thought it was pretty interesting that you were a teacher, said he used to teach, himself, years ago. You found that a little hard to believe, his grammar was so atrocious, but he says it was a one-room schoolhouse in the interior and he mainly taught math. S'pose one doesn't have to know when to use *whom* to teach times tables and long division. You told him how much you wanted to go back to teaching, how you'd started volunteering with the young ones at the elementary school across the road and everything fell apart when the teachers' strike started; people hollering insults at you when you crossed the picket line, waving their placards, calling you scab—and you were a volunteer, weren't even getting paid. What a hideous thing to call someone, *scab*. Scabious. Scabies. Couldn't take it, felt too personal, made you feel ugly and crusty and contagious. Guess it was supposed to. And it wasn't going to be an *in* with the Vancouver School Board anyway, so you threw in the towel. Volunteer work—*At least I don't give it away.*

Time check: seven-fifteen. You got fifteen minutes, kiddo. New kid-do. Till Prince George arrives. Slacks or skirt, skirt or slacks? Wish Grace were here, she's full of opinions, but she's downstairs with Josh. Maybe you could go grab her for a second. No, that's stupid, his mother'll think you're a nitwit. At least she's got another new friend, been hanging around with the boy downstairs. He's a year older than she is and he's sweet and well-spoken. She spends too much time with Sadie and Eddy and they're monsters, they wreak havoc on her self-esteem, calling her accident-prone and a lost cause and anything else that comes into their mean little lunkheads. Gabrielle was a nice change, but she's always got some family thing going on. That boy downstairs has hamsters named Rhoda and Carly—he's got crushes on Valerie Harper and Carly Simon, of all people. He sits with Grace, paper mâché-ing and making crazy gremlins out of clay instead of throwing rocks at people's windows and playing nicky-nicky nine doors. Unlike that wretched whining Eddy, who's grounded now (that'll last about two hot seconds) and owes Ray and Alice fifty bucks (allowance for the next ten years that they'll still give him anyway) for the window he smashed across the road. Josh, on the other hand—well, he doesn't say *ain't*. And he sings "You've Got a Friend." And he doesn't call every kid he sees a freak-in-nature—don't think goofy Sadie and Eddy even know what they're saying, running around screaming *Outa my way, you friggin' nature, y' homo.* Now Grace has all their little gutter remarks as part of her own repertoire. And you know she has no clue what the hell she's talking about when she calls Charlie's boyfriend a stupid lez.

Oh, maybe these, these crazy-big wide-leg pants you got last week. They're kind of dressy, though—God, why do you always do this, buy something with no idea as to how you're going to wear it. They looked nice in the store, but what are you supposed to put with them? They're silky black and the legs must be two or three feet wide when you hold them out. Maybe a turtleneck. Might look interesting, contrast the loose and silky with the tight and busty. Throw on a couple strings of beads.—Time! : Seven-twenty-five. Hurry up. Ah, he'll be late. They're always late. Go with the silky black things and the turtleneck. Oh Christ, it's summer, who are you, the grim reaper?—put a blouse with them, a white blouse and a belt, where the hell's that gold belt?—

11:40 p.m. Feeling good, it was a nice date and he walked you to the door. He took you for dinner and to a movie and bought you popcorn—love seeing movies, why don't you see more movies? When you get back, the lights are all on in the apartment; Grace is already back upstairs, on the couch reading.

Hey Petunia, how's tricks?

OK. Did you have fun with George of the Jungle?

Toss your coat on the armchair, go to the couch, pick your child's feet up by the toes, sit where they were. *Yup.* Let them fall in your lap. *And I told him you call him that, by the way.*

You did? Did it bug 'im or did he laugh?

He got a good chortle out of it.

Did you go see a movie?

Yup. Saw The Sting. *It was just terrific. Paul Newman is positively the most beautiful hunk of man on this earth. And we had the loveliest dinner, I had a big steak and a baked potato and asparagus and this deliriously good chocolate cake for dessert.*

Do you like him?

Kind of. I don't know. He's like a big bear. I don't know if I think of him like that. I'll see how I feel. He's nice, though. You'd like him, I think.

Did you kiss 'im?

Little kiss. No big deal. Next time I'll introduce you and you can tell me what you think. So, how come you're up here?

Mm, got bored. We watched Rockford Files *and then* Night Stalker *and then Josh started drawing stuff and I just wanted to read my book.*

Uh huhh, let me see. Said the blind man to his deaf daughter.

As he picked up his hammer and saw—I don't get that.

What's Go Ask Alice?*—this isn't that thing with all the drugs and crap, is it? I told you I didn't want you reading that.*

Why! Everybody's reading it. They already read it. Mummy! Give it back.

Give it back nothing—I'll have a look at it and I'll see if I want you reading it.

That's stupid! Sadie already read it and—

Oh Sadie, now there's a good judge of literature. That's just who I want overseeing what my kid gets subjected to.

It's not subjecting me. God.

And quit saying God, it sounds terrible.

Well, Jesus Christ—I just—

Grace! Not Jesus Christ either. For a well-bred little girl, you're sounding more like a little rounder these days!

Well, you interrupted me, what I was reading, and it's not fair, you never let me do nothing.

Anything. *And piffle on that—for goodness sake, I let you get away with murder, no other kid you know gets to do what you get to you saw* Earthquake *last week, didn't you? Can smartass Sadie go downtown all by herself and see a movie like you can? No, I think not. It's going on midnight, how many other eight-year-olds do you know up at this time of night?* and you stop talking as you open up *Go Ask Alice* to: "Never had anything ever been so beautiful. I was a part of every single instrument, literally a part. Each note had a character, shape and colour all its very own and seemed to be entirely separate from the rest of the score so that I could consider its relationship to the whole composition, before the next note sounded. My mind possessed the wisdom of the ages ..." And she wants to read this. "... I felt great, free, abandoned, a different, improved, perfected specimen of a different, improved, perfected species. It was wild! It was beautiful! It really was."

Christ, what the hell was she on? Bloody kids think they invented euphoria.

Great, this is all you need, like you haven't had enough trouble with Charlie popping her Black Beauties and smoking pot and god knows what else.

You pull your brain like warm gum out of the book; Grace is still babbling about something or other, something about tin cans, and you interrupt, *You are not reading this, you're too young.*

What! I'm not too young. I am not! All the other kids read it already.

Well, you can bet your boots their mothers didn't know. It glorifies drugs and you're too young to discern the difference between fantasy and reality. That makes two of you, but you say, *Come on, time for bed.*

The next morning you're in the kitchen making up a recipe for rice flour pancakes. Grace is lying on her stomach on the living-room floor watching Saturday morning cartoons. You've been reading about wheat allergies lately, how lots of people have them. Symptoms from hyperactivity to inability to concentrate and irritability—you've noticed Grace being irritable lately and she's been doing this weird thing where she clenches her fists and eyes and teeth at once. She looks as if she's going to have a fit. Then relaxes. You've walked in on her a couple times and caught her clenching everything so tight, her whole everything shook. Sometimes she forgets herself and does it when she's watching TV with you. Asked her what she was doing and why. *Making everything shut as tight as it can go as hard as I can till it hits the top—like that game thing you hit with a hammer and then the metal thing goes up and if you hit it really hard, it rings the bell.* And why? Because she likes it.

The way she looks, though, when it's happening—like she's out of her ever-lovin' mind. You told her you were going to take her to see a doctor, that maybe she had some stuff she needed to talk about with somebody. You asked Doctor Peters about a referral. He told you not to work yourself into a tizzy; seen it before, just a stage, it's normal.

But maybe if you changed her diet. Maybe she has allergies. Maybe wheat. The phone rings.

Grace jumps and runs for it. It's Pavlovian; only thing that tears her brain away from a television. Last weekend you bellowed to make yourself heard and she had the gall to turn around and *shh* you. Shhed by an eight-year-old. She never used to behave like that, it's that Sadie's influence, her and her whole crazy family. Probably her on the phone now. Although it sounds like Grace is answering a survey. *Yes, no, yeah, yeah. 'K, just a sec* and yells, *It's George.*

You take the phone, *Hello* into it and hear *Hello there, you lovely thing, what ya up to this mornin'?* He does have a bit of a Maritime accent, didn't notice it as much when he was standing in front of you.

Oh, not much, just puttering around. I'm attempting a new pancake recipe.

Oh well, why don't you save it for tomorrow and lemme take the two of you out for pancakes. Or bacon and eggs or whatever you like.

Oh! Uh, well. That's quite an offer. I guess I haven't actually started mixing anything. Hang on—Hey Petunia, how'd you like to go out for breakfast and meet George?

The Road Runner's on and she was just about to get up and change the channel anyway, so she willingly turns her head, gives you a suspicious sort of look. *When?*

I don't know. Now. Just—when? you ask the receiver, almost giddy. Can't remember the last time someone called on the weekend and said let's go for breakfast.

He says, *How's about forty-five minutes or an hour? Does that give you enough time?*

That's sounds just fine—Grace: an hour! She nods. You palm the mouthpiece away from your head. *So why don't you go jump in the tub and get ready.* She says *yeah*, doesn't move. Bring the receiver back. *OK then, we'll see you soon.* You hang up and attempt a cheerful whip-cracking.

The three of you are in Denny's, smiling into plates the waitress just set in front of you. Well, two of you are; Grace is busy separating food so that nothing touches. Fifteen minutes ago she gave the waitress very explicit instructions about her eggs so they would arrive the same as when you make them: Not scrambled, she doesn't like them fluffy, or runny, not over-easy, definitely not poached—stirred, she wants. *Do it like you're going to do the regular fried kind with the yoke in the middle but then break it up with a fork and stir it around. And don't add milk or anything. And cook it both sides, flip it over so that nothing's raw or moving around still. Do you get it?* You were slightly embarrassed: *Oh for goodness sake, Grace, just order pancakes why don't you.* But George cut in, *No, she's doin' good, let her go. And what would Her Royal Highness like to drink?* and the waitress laughed and maybe you should just calm down. After she got it all down on her little pad, she went off to shuffle the chef's brain to your child's way of thinking.

Meanwhile, Grace has warmed up to George considerably. Not that she's speaking to him yet, but you can tell by the curl at the corners of her mouth as she moves the edges of her stirred eggs as far as possible from the hash browns without touching bacon. And in her eyes. They rest on him now; before, they looked beside him, above him, into her hands when he spoke.

So, Madam, your mum tells me you like horses. Do you ever get a chance to go riding or go out to the racetrack?

He's hit the nail on the head so hard she nearly falls off her chair. *Yes. I mean no, but I want to. I watch them on TV sometimes and um, yeah. I watched the Kentucky Derby on TV when it was on.*

The Kentucky! You're more up on things than I thought. Gees, a friend of mine put a bet on the horse who won that, what was his name? George squints, thinking. He's got his forearms on either side of his plate, hunched a little across the table toward Grace.

Foolish Pleasure, and she draws it out as if she's doing an ad for something so decadent, it should be illegal.

George chuckles. *Gees, I think she's right, that's the name.* And he shakes his head and picks up his coffee.

I remember because I picked him, he was pretty and he had a big bum—I heard they go faster when they have big bums. And plus I liked his name. George is laughing and then you remember something about it yourself, telling Grace to stop being foolish and take out the garbage and her reply: *It would be my foolish pleasure.* Now you know where that came from; one down, ten thousand and four strange replies to go.

FAMILY REVIEW
CARRINGTON, Charlotte

Mother: CARRINGTON, Eilleen (known as Hoffman)

Father: CARRINGTON, Jake (Whereabouts unknown)

Social Worker: Lilly Darling

Date: April 12th, 1974

DATE NEXT REVIEW: MAY, 1974

A.   DATES & CONTACTS WITH CLIENTS & COLLATERALS

02.11.73 Family Court: Charlotte's temporary ward
status renewed for six months. Review Date 02.05.74.
Home visit with Mrs. Carrington 12.12.73; 23.01.74.
Charlotte AWOL from January to March/74. Office visit
with Charlotte 07.04.74

B.   PROGRESS REPORT OR PLAN

My contact has been quite minimal with Mrs. Carrington,
and almost non-existant with Charlotte. Mrs. Carrington
appears to be managing well. She is attending AA and
volunteering as a teacher's aid with Brock School.
Grace attending Brock School. Charlotte has been AWOL
for some time, however, though, I did locate her at
the end of March. She is staying briefly with her
mother. She is pregnant by some boy with whom she went
to Toronto in January. She left him there and returned
to Vancouver in March. She is determined to keep the
baby and Mrs. Carrington is supporting her in this
feeling, suggesting it may help her to mature. I
question this.

C. INFORMATION FOR COURT PURPOSES

Review Date for Charlotte set for 02.05.74. We will not recommend that ward status be extended.

D. RE-EVALUATION OF FAMILY FUNCTIONING

I am concerned about Charlotte's involvement with this latest boy. After her return from Toronto, she appeared to have residual bruising and cuts on her face. She refused to discuss the matter. She says her relationship with this boy is over. My concern is that she will continue to mirror the abusive relationships her mother has been in -- from what I can gather, Charlotte's father drank heavily and was physically abusive with her mother. Her father has been out of the family picture since Charlotte was a small child and I fear she will continue to seek out abusive males in an attempt to re-create her early family life.

Mrs. Carrington continues to function quite well and Grace attends school regularly. I do not feel that Mrs. Carrington is being very realistic regarding Charlotte's pregnancy. I feel that Charlotte has so many emotional problems that she could not be an adequate mother. With so many of her own needs unmet I do not see how she could capably parent a baby. However, perhaps with her mother's support, things will be alright.

E. WORKER-FAMILY AGREEMENT RE FURTHER WORK

This Case will be kept open until May when Charlotte is discharged. If Mrs. Carrington continues to function well, the family file can be closed at that time.

Grace Six

AROUND WHEN she met George, Mum bought a twin-size bed and put it in the living room. I still fell asleep in her bed but usually I woke up in the living room. And then George moved in and from then on I slept always in the living room. At first it bugged me. Cuz mostly it seemed like they were friends, I mean not all kissy-kissy or anything, so I wondered what they were doing in there that they had to be alone and have the door be closed. But I suppose it was cuz of Mum's thing about how adults need adult company like kids need kid company. And plus I didn't want to not like George.

George was different from most of the guys my mum knew —the ones I saw, anyway. He had a slow for-sure way of moving and talking. Kind of like a big old horse—like in *Black Beauty*, there was a big old horse who gave advice and didn't shy away from bushes or dogs or stuff. And George was like that, like he wouldn't just crumple up—you could climb on him and ask him anything you could think of and he always had a good answer.

Even if it was a guess, he'd say that, and it'd be a good guess too, and you'd think, yeah, I bet that's it. One time he said that Mum was a bird on a branch and he got that right too. She was, kind of, and every once in a while it seemed like she took a good peck at him just to get a rise. But George would just breathe his deep strong horse breaths and give her a deep old horse look until she gave up and flapped down the hall to the bedroom. I wondered sometimes if she didn't think much of him, the way she'd get all tisky and snappy, as if he was a dopey kid or something. Or maybe it bugged her that he was right a lot and smart, about the things she wasn't: people and money and the world and the kinds of stuff that twisted them all together. She could string together enough sparkly words to cover a Christmas tree, but George was in the war.

He worked on fishing boats—he'd go out to sea for a couple months, make a wad of dough then come home and do nothing for a while. After a couple or three months of living with us, he was making Mum nuts—always in her hair, she said, sitting around the living room with those creepy black-rimmed glasses, reading or watching TV. And for the first time, when it came to someone who wasn't us, I wanted her to get lost; I liked it when he put on his glasses to read, they made him look like a professor or something. And besides, half the time the glasses were on, it was for me. I'd lie flopped on the couch with my head on his lap and he'd read me *Paul Bunyan* or *The Black Stallion.* Or he'd be at the kitchen table flipping through one of my math books. The school year was almost finished and I was having trouble with "New Math." Mum got all pissed off just looking at it. "What the hell was wrong with the old math?" she kept saying, but George sat with me, squeaking the table every time he erased something, and explaining how come it didn't work the way I was doing it.

One night after dinner he was trying to get long division in my head. Looking out the bottom half of his bifocals, he wrote down number after number, under and on top of each other, splitting them, carrying them, bringing them down, and then suddenly he said, "Here, try it this way," and started with short division. It was making me feel stupid and scared that George wasn't going to think I was that great. And anyway, it was his fault for expecting me to know stuff we weren't even learning yet. So I said, "I haven't even figured out the first thing—we're not supposed to do it that way."

"Well, that's OK, give this a shot, just try it and see if it makes any more sense."

"It doesn't and I can't do it that way. You're doing it wrong, just show me what they want me to do."

"Don't get yourself all worked up, now, just take a look at wh—"

"No! I can't. I can't do it. I don't even understand how come in the minussing part with the subtraction before, you crossed that out and it's a nine; it was a zero before and now it's a nine."

He turned back pages and grabbed the scrap we were just working on. "Because you've borrowed from the number ..." and blah blah blah, then "You see?"

"No! I don't see nothing—"

"Grace!" Mum came stomping into the kitchen from the living room. "Look, if you can't just listen to what he's trying to show you, instead of contradicting every word, then maybe you should just go in the bedroom and do it by yourself!"

"Oh, go drink your Fresca," George told her, and squeaked the table again, erasing stuff. Mum's lips went tight and then opened and smacked shut again. She turned around and stomped back in the living room. George and I looked at each other; she wasn't speechless that often. I stared at the stuff he was scribbling and tried not to make any smirky noises; I could feel Mum crackling around the corner on the couch.

"Do you wanna take a tea break?" he said. "We can have a cuppa tea and take a look at tonight's racing form; a few of 'em'll probably be racing on Saturday too. Did you ask Josh? Do you wanna bring him along?"

I didn't. Well I did, but it was just that this would be my second time at the track with George—I never went to one before George came along and he was teaching me things: how to bet, how to read a racing form, what it meant when the odds were five to two or four to three. And I was getting it—I was becoming a horse-racing expert, and if Josh came we'd have to start right from the beginning again. And plus, what if they liked each other better? Maybe Josh would be smarter and make better bets and George would like having him around. Mum told me after we came to Vancouver that my dad wanted a boy before I was born and he said if I was a boy he'd teach me to be a thief or get me into acting. She told me that after she already let the cat out of the bag: I caught her on the phone saying, "When Danny was in jail those years ..." Jail! And all that time she made me go around thinking he was at camp. Whenever Mum said camp, I used to picture the army, like the army camps on TV, and figured that must've been where he was. She said he was working there. He never wrote, though, or called us from camp and he never talked about it afterwards. I asked him once, in Toronto, when he was digging a hole in the backyard (to build me the swing that never got built), how camp was. He said, "Camp? Oh. Oh, it was fun. We went swimmin' and fishin' and all kindsa stuff," and he grinned and kept digging his hole. No wonder he didn't want to hang around me if I was that dumb.

Then I find out it was Jail. I made Mum tell me everything afterward and made her say she was sorry—cuz the whole thing about her and me was how we didn't lie to each other and then she went and broke the code of honour. I didn't even care about

him being in jail; it sounded better than *camp*. Jail could be kind
of cool; cowboys and cat burglars got jailed. I imagined my dad
in a super-tall skyscraper, all in black, prowling down hallways in
soft unsqueaky shoes, in and out of windows, diamonds glisten-
ing in the palm of his leather glove. She told me he'd said he got
framed or they got the wrong guy or something and he knew
who the real guy was but as part of honours around thieves he did
the time. Either way, he was like the movies all the sudden. Except
for what I found out later about being a boy; if I was a boy he
would've taught me stuff. If I was a boy, he would've called more
probably or visited me. He might not have let me go to Vancouver in the first place.

"Umm, nah, I don't know if Josh likes horse racing. He likes
music and drawing and stuff. It's probably not his thing, I bet.
Let's just us go, 'K?"

The whistle on the kettle squealed. "OK. It'll probably be
more fun anyway. Do you wanna bring ..." He poured water into
our cups and nodded his head toward my mum on the other side
of the wall. I didn't. Lately, I liked hanging around with George
better, sort of. I mean, you could count on him to be there for
sure and also not to have to go pee every five minutes and complain about his back, sitting up in the stands. That's how it would
be with Mum. And every time someone lost two bucks she'd start
talking about money down the drain. I shrugged at first so I
wouldn't seem too mean, then made my shrug into a head shake
and mouthed *nahh*.

The next day after school, I went down to Josh's place. When
I started grade 4, I switched schools to the same one as Josh,
General Wolfe, cuz Josh said there wasn't so many tough kids at
General Wolfe—and I was super-sick of tough kids. But we still
never walked home from school together or stuff because Josh was
in grade 5 and I hated those grade 5er boys he hung around with.
They always made fun of me and Josh like we were boyfriend/

girlfriend and all that junk, so I said forget-it to them. Sometimes I got home first, so I'd go hang around with Josh's mum and wait for him. They were on welfare too, so she was home most of the time. She was there when I knocked on the door; Josh wasn't. His mum was Sheryl. Their last name was Sugarman. I said her whole name whenever I could just for the fun of all that *shhing*. She brought me in and offered me a cup of tea.

And then she said, "You just caught me, I was about to go to the supermarket."

"Oh. Should I go? I can come back later."

"Nah, sit, you've got tea coming. I'll wait with you till Josh gets home." She turned on the burner under the kettle and went to the fridge for milk. She made it the way Mum wanted me to drink it: half milk to give me more protein. "So, Miss Gracey, where's your mum today?"

"School maybe, or else she might've gone downtown to the AA club with George. I don't know. Was Josh painting this morning?" There were tubes and brushes all over the place on the living-room floor. A big square of Josh's art paper was taped on a foam board beside them, the top part all swirly with reds and oranges.

"Yeah. I refuse to put his junk away for him, so I left it. He's doing some autumn painting for his art teacher. He wants a girl in the middle of the woods with a horse—actually, I think he wants you to model for him. I guess because you like horses so much." I was all flattered. Josh could draw and paint better than any grown-up I knew. I asked her who was going to be the horse. She laughed. "Actually, he was thinking that maybe when you and George go to the racetrack again, he could come and do some sketches of the horses and you together."

"Oh. Yeah. Can you look at these math things? George was trying to help me last night, I mostly needed help with the sub-traction stuff, and then he got into this other dividing thing and I got all confused and then my mum started getting mad and then

—oh, it was just dumb. Here—these ones here, I just want some-one to explain this stuff about carrying the number. See how come you can just take a one from this one and suddenly it's a ten or whatever?"

Sheryl Sugarman went into a thing about digits and numeri-cal values and decimals and then I started hearing them again. The voices. She didn't know about them; I never told anyone. But they were yapping in my brain, in the background, kind of, so I couldn't pay that good of attention to stuff. My teeth clenched. It helped, kind of, if I clenched. Josh came in around then and they were quiet. They kept quiet around Josh. He said, "Hey, what're you doing here?"

"I live here."

He tisked at Sheryl and rolled his eyes. "Not you."

"I came to see you and to ask your mum about these math things. I think I get it now." I didn't get anything. I just didn't want to talk about it any more.

"Well, I'm gonna go for a bike ride, some of my friends are meeting up at Riley Park to ride around. You wanna go? I'll double you."

"Yeah, 'K." I slapped my book shut and left it on the table. I could feel Sheryl Sugarman watching me. She told Josh she might not be there when he got back, so make sure he had his key.

My head started getting more clear when we got onto Main Street. Josh was on his bike with his feet on the ground, stepping himself along with me walking beside him. "I'll double you as soon as we get down on the side streets, there's too many curbs and lights and stuff here."

"'K." I only knew Josh a little longer than George. I trusted him the same way, though; even when we argued and I couldn't stand him, I still wanted Josh around.

We crossed 33rd Avenue and someone whispered behind me. I looked back. No one was near. And then again—my name this time. I snapped my head around thinking maybe it was one of Josh's friends. Nothing. No one was anywhere near us, just cars and buses. It'd never happened around Josh before, he was my safe place.

"What's the matter?"

"Nothing!"

"Fine! Don't have a hairy. Is it the math? Don't you get the math still?"

"No! I get it!" Josh was a year ahead of me and he never had problems with math. Or anything. Kids liked him, he never got into fights, his mum didn't have to threaten them if they didn't leave him alone. And his art; anyone who saw his art-stuff slobbered all over it. He even won twenty bucks in a contest around when I met him. I never won any contests, but I had twenty-one dollars I was saving since Toronto in my drawer. I never bragged about that, though—only some came from my allowance, and five dollars from last time at the racetrack and the rest I stole from my mum's wallet a little bit at a time. My plan was to buy her something beautiful one day, something she'd never get for herself. Or else, if we got broke again, like in Toronto, with no food in the house and nothing in her purse, I would spring it on her and say something like, "Look, it's OK, I've got money for whatever you want." I imagined how her eyes would be so happy she'd start to cry and she'd squeeze me and say, "What would I ever do without you?" I was thinking about starting that with her nerve pills too, so she wouldn't get so upset when she ran out. But in the meantime I didn't want anyone to know about it. I figured she'd thank me in the long run.

Josh and I turned onto Quebec Street, past Sadie and Eddy's house. I sneezed and wondered how many sneezes it took to drop dead. Sadie'd told me on the weekend that every time you sneeze your heart stops. I didn't want to run into her.

"Do you wanna get on, I can double you now."

"No. I want to keep walking still."

"You're bitchy today." I didn't answer him. I hated when he used that word on me. "Well, if nothing's wrong then how come you got two big frown lines between your eyebrows—you're gonna look like an old lady if you don't knock it off. Don't worry, though, my mum's got tons of Oil of Olay so I can keep you young and beautiful—even when you're twenty-five, everyone'll think you're eight still."

"Shut up."

"Jesus! What's up your ass?"

And then the whispers echoed *ass and bitchy. ass and bitchy.* I yelled, "Shut up!" over top of them, and then told him, "Don't say that! I hate when you say that. Ass and bitchy. Don't say ass and bitchy."

Josh laughed down at his handlebars and said, "Ay ay, captain."

My head was quiet again. He coasted and I walked another block; we were getting close to the park. I was scared of having it start up again around those other boys. "Do you have to go right to Riley Park, can't we keep walking a bit?"

"Uh huh," and he leaned down, sort of folding his arms across his handlebars, staring into the front wheel while it turned and skipping his toes along the road, "if you quit biting my head off for a while."

"I am not. Can you just—um. OK, I'm sorry! I have to, can you just—'K, don't say anything, just, um. Do you ever hear stuff?"

He turned his head and looked at me. I looked back, then down at my feet stepping. He said, "Can I answer?" I rolled my eyes, so he said, "OK. I don't get it, what stuff?"

"Stuff. Stuff, like voices. Like sometimes someone whispers your name and you turn around and they're not there, nobody's there or else there's maybe someone there but you know they never said anything because it was a lady's voice and it's a man behind you."

"Um. Sometimes I dream it, like once I woke up and saw my zaidy sitting in a rocking chair smiling at me and he was wearing a red baseball cap. He never even owned a baseball cap. And then we got a call from the hospital that he died during the night. Weird eh? My mum says I dreamed it, but it was pretty real. I think he came to see me before he left.—Like that, like a ghost?"

"I don't know. No. I don't think so. Or sometimes just voices and no one calling to you or anything, sort of like people arguing in your head so you can hardly hear the people in the room with you."

Josh pushed himself up, put his hands back on his handlebar grips. Then he chewed on his bottom lip a second. "Uh-uh. Do you?"

"Kind of. Yeah. Promise you won't tell, not even your mum ...Um. Um. Mostly it happens in school when I'm trying to think, like during a test, times-tables tests and stuff." My fingers twisted on each other. I was scared he'd think I was mental or something. He asked me what they said, what it sounded like. "It sounds like tinkling and clanging, like there's lots of stuff, you know, like those fancy dinners *Columbo* goes to sometimes when he's solving a murder mystery. And they're all talking, they start talking over each other and they have rich people accents—English accents— and they start arguing. Especially this one lady, who's older and she keeps saying, 'Shu*tt* U*pp*' when people talk back to her and then they get louder and louder over each other until I can't hear anything. And they all have English accents, did I say that already?"

"Wow. Did you tell your mum?"

"No. I don't wanna tell her. I'm afraid she'll make me go to a psycho guy or something. She was going to before because of when I clenched, when I'd clench my teeth and eyes shut. Sometimes I just like clenching, though. It feels like I can't get still until I scrunch everything as tight as it'll go and then I can be normal again. Sometimes it helps make it be quiet, though. Or sometimes I can't get it quiet and I can't do anything."

"Man. Is that why you can't get the math stuff sometimes?"

"I don't know. Maybe. It happened with your mum when she was showing me stuff and I started to get all mixed up—please don't tell her, though, promise you won't tell her or she'll tell my mum and I don't wanna to tell my mum yet."

"'K. Maybe you should tell George?"

"No. I don't wanna tell George. It'll go away, I think I can make 'em stop."

Josh squished a palm in his eye for a second, then he bit a nail off and looked at me. "Do you want me to double you?"

"'K. Do you wanna come with me and George to the racetrack on Saturday?"

"'K. Do you wanna skip Riley Park and just go back to my place and listen to records? My mum got me a Joni Mitchell record for my birthday. It's all live from a concert she did."

When we got back, Sheryl'd already left. Josh got pillows from his bedroom and threw them on the living-room floor. I laid on top of the whole pile while he took Joni Mitchell out. He held it like a wet painting, putting it on the turntable. The record was from a concert and there was lots of clapping and cheering before she sang. Josh flopped down beside me and we propped up on our elbows and bounced our heads in time.

"I like this song," he told me, "it always cheers me up." And he started singing this song called "You Turn Me On Like a Radio." Next came "Big Yellow Taxi." I didn't like it; it didn't sound like the one I was used to. "Yeah, it's different, huh, here lemme play you this one, it's my favourite." Josh jumped up and snaggled the needle off.

I flipped on my back waiting for him to flip the record. "Do you have that song, "I gotta brand new pair of rollerskates, you gotta brand new key"? She sings that song, right?"

"Nope, that's someone else. That's kind of dumb, that song."

"No it's not, it's my favourite." I turned back over, lumps in my throat: one because he didn't have the song, and one cuz he didn't like it.

Josh looked in my eyes before he set the needle back down. "Oh, you mean that one that goes, um—" and he nahhed and hummed the tune for me. "Yeah, I like that one too." It was like he just gave me something cat-fur soft and pink and it made my throat ache even more. Then Joni Mitchell's sore-throat voice talked at us. She said everybody should sing along with her because this next song was made for out-of-tune voices, the more out of tune the better, and Josh nudged me. "See, it's perfect for you." I smacked him and Joni sang,

> Yesterday a child came out to wonder,
> caught a dragonfly inside a jar
> fearful when the sky was full of thunder
> and tearful at the falling of a star ...

and then I recognized the song.

> and the seasons they go round and round
> and the painted ponies go up and down
> we're captive on the carousel of time
> we can't return we can only look behind from where we came
> and go round and round and round in the circle game ...

"I don't wanna play this—" My words got stuffed-up at the back of my mouth and tears dripped my cheeks.

Josh told me, "It's OK," and hooked his baby finger under the cuff of my sleeve.

Eilleen Six

SEPTEMBER 1974

I T's SO HARD to strike that delicate balance between a dumpy slum and Better Homes and Gardens: Better Slums and Dumps. But presentation is nine-tenths of the law.

A social worker's on her way to look the joint over and you have just wiped off the kitchen counter for the third time. She's a new one. Coming to see how you and Grace are maintaining since Charlie's file was closed, to check your receipts, make note of any rent increase and, of course, sniff around for man-things. Then, if all is kosher, she'll sign you up for another year. Go check the living room again. How come everything looks like hell? Maybe because every time you pick something up, a goddamn man drops something in its place. Not *a* man, your man. Everything's covered in a layer of dust—can't he think to dust the mantle or the end tables? Damp cloth, need a damp cloth, she'll be here in fif—ten minutes! Shit. Oh, just give it a lick and a promise, she's not going to be inspecting your lamp for lint anyway—and go check your face, see that your lipstick's not smeared on your teeth.

Your teeth are fine, it's the mirror that needs work: toothpaste goop everywhere—can't those idiots keep it in their faces and do they have to load so much paste on to begin with? Goofy Grace wanders around the house trying to talk through a mouthful of foam, makes her look like a rabid dog, and George stands there in front of the mirror, teeth bared like the rabid dog's screwed-up cousin; rhythmic scrubbing up and down and up and down, in circles in circles in circles. Christ—look at this stuff, it's minty fresh cement—J Cloth, where's a friggin' J Cloth? Five minutes till five minutes before she's due to arrive. They are always early. There. Good enough. Oh shit, take off the earrings, they look too nice. Mind you, this blouse looks crummy enough, they ain't gonna mistake you for royalty exactly.

Just take a last look for man-stuff. You cleared most all of it out into the trunk of George's car this morning along with instructions for him to pick Grace up after school and take her for a drive through Stanley Park or something. Had to keep this thing stream-lined. Last thing you'd need is Grace forgetting the point of the whole exercise and trying to impress the social worker with a hi-larious George-anecdote or, in lieu of that, an apartment tour that leads straight to a George-shoe hanging out of the closet, or a George-shirt. Whole thing is starting to feel like one big goof on your part anyway, having him move in here. Drives you out of your mind, him sitting around, underfoot, in your hair. Got no time to yourself any more. There used to be so much space in the day, all those hours to hog every room in the place, suck up all the air for yourself, watch whatever you wanted on the boob tube, read, talk on the phone. Now you have not one but two other space-suckers to contend with. Hardly had Charlie out the door when you moved George in—what are you thinking sometimes? You should get your head read is what. Least he pays half the rent, though, and that's why his self can't be here when the Welfare comes a-nosin'.

Buzzer. That's her. You say *hello*, buzz her up, run to the mirror, put the earrings back on, need something to brighten up your
face, look like a nice mother in a neat home with no men in it.
Surely to god she'll know a three-dollar pair of earrings when she
sees them.

Thunking at the door.

Palm your hair back on the sides—oh shit, what did you do,
you look stupid now, your palm was wet, now it looks—knock
and clunk at the door—crap, where's a—just calm down, here,
have a Librium. Swallow. Jesus. Go-go-go, to the door.

Open it wi-ide ... *Hello* ... smi-i-le wide: a poor man's Doris
Day.

Hi, she says. *Eilleen Hoffman? Nice to meet you, Patricia Hearst.*

Her palm goes out to yours. You start to laugh. *Sorry; really? Is
that really your name? I mean I, you must have told me over the phone
but I just didn't—*

Oh, I probably just said Pat. She steps into your hall and smiles,
curly red-headed, sheepishly looking nothing like the gun-toting
heiress currently obsessing the planet. *I feel as if I've been going to
great lengths to conceal my full name, I've even started using Trish instead of Patty—the woman has been the bane of my existence the last
few months.*

You walk her to the living room. *I'll bet! Poor you. Can't turn on
the TV without her face smeared all over the place. It's really something,
isn't it? Now they've got her on hidden camera with a machine gun.
Would you like some tea or coffee or something? Juice, milk? Fresca?*

Tea would be lovely.

You mosey nonchalantly to the kitchen, leaving Patricia Hearst
in the living room, saying, *I think they've got her brainwashed. God
knows what they've done with her,* as you contemplate just how to
nab your own Patty Hearst, make her carry a gun for you, renounce
her bourgeois ways of living among the bureaucratic elite and join
your one-woman show, The Symbionese Keep-my-welfare-cheque-

and-boyfriend Army. *My little girl is fascinated with the whole thing. I think she finds it all a little romantic, a rich pretty girl being kidnapped and all that.*

Yeah, I s'pose half the country finds it a little romantic or they wouldn't be leading every news hour with it. Is your daughter around this afternoon?

No, she called home asking if she could go over to one of her friends' after school. Probably won't see her again till dinnertime.

Oh yeah, kids! So how have the two of you been making out since coming to Vancouver?

Oh, really well. You walk to the entrance between the kitchen and living room, lean casually in the doorway. *It's really more home to me than Toronto ever was; it's such a relief to escape those horrific winters. And now the summer, I can't imagine being back in that unsleepable heat wave—have you ever spent any time there?*

Uh, Montreal, which is pretty close, probably worse, so I know the feeling.

You nod. *Oh yes, I lived in Montreal years ago, it's kind of an old stomping ground for me.*

She unzips a worn brown briefcase. *You just have one other daughter besides, mm, Grace, have I got that right?*

Yes, Charlie.

And, let's see, she lived with you briefly while she was pregnant, and now she's on assistance and living on her own.

Yes. She has her baby now, Sam. They're, she's with, uh, him in a basement apartment not too far from here. You keep your mouth shut about Ian, don't know if they know about him or not. *She was by last week for a little while, I think maybe we're all getting along a little better these days.*

And are you currently in an AA program?

Yes, yeah, I'm part of a group down near Broadway and Cambie and I'm spending quite a bit of time at the Twelfth Step Club.

Oh, that sounds good, so you've got a bit of a social life together now. That always makes it easier.

The kettle whistles and you excuse yourself back behind the kitchen wall to dump hot water into a pot of two tea bags. Milk, shit, did you remember milk? Good girl—although not affording milk may score big points, but you ask her anyway. *Milk and sugar?* She says yes. Here, throw some cookies on a plate. Ah the lovely hostess, you're charming as hell. Wish there was a tray, no actually, make two trips, it will illustrate just exactly the daily struggle that is your life. And still you smile in the face of it all: Glow little glow-worm, glimmer, glimmer.

So are you still single, Eilleen?

Are you still single? Now, although *noneofyourfuckingbusiness* seems to be the correct response, pause here, *Yup*, you tell her, *a good man is hard to find.* Laugh here.

Your ex-husband hasn't been in touch with you at all? Ah, Jake Carrington? I guess he would be the girls' father?

Jake Carrington. Always sounds so elite and swish when other people say it. Sounds like he should've been lover to Katharine Hepburn, like he uses a platinum shoehorn. *Yes. I mean yes he's Charlie's father but no I haven't heard from him. Not in years. He could be in prison again for all I know.* In prison? she says, that's not in her records. *Yeah, he was in Kingston Penitentiary a few years ago for armed robbery. It's not as exciting as it sounds, he was a drunk and a reprobate—thought he could rob a bank with a penknife when he was sloshed out of his skull. His father was a lawyer and then a politician in New Brunswick but he passed away shortly after Jake and I divorced, though, so Jake had to pretty much lie in his own bed after that.* She looks vaguely intrigued, shakes her head ever so slightly. She asks about Grace's father. You continue, *Danny's no help, he doesn't even send her an allowance.* Don't look bitter, keep your smile and tinge it with a concerned frown, you trooper you.

You know, the government is cracking down on these deadbeat dads who don't pay child support. If you can supply us with the information, we could attempt to force him to look after Grace.

Ahh. Well. I—you and your big mouth. That's right, sick the Welfare on him. He'd fix you all right, have your legs broken and grab Grace so fast your head would spin and what bloody good would it do you in the long run; they'd take whatever he gave you off your cheque and you'd be no better off than you were to begin with. *I couldn't even give you a phone number. Now and then he phones from god knows where, says hello to Grace and disappears again. I can pick 'em, eh!* And you shrug and shake your head mostly because it's true. Even though you could track him down any time you wanted, but who'd want to. He can rot for all you care.

Then old Patty orders her papers, proceeds with the formality of asking a steady stream of questions she already knows the answers to, ticks them off on her sheet, mumbling your replies to herself: Are you living common-law with anyone currently? Is the father of your child sending support? How many children do you have? How much rent do you pay? Do you have receipts? For hydro? For phone? Are you still seeing that sugar daddy who was giving you fifty bucks for a quickie now and then? She never asked that last one, you'd have busted a gut if she did, though. But it's not one of the standards. You could truthfully say no anyway, not with George around. Poor old Stewart had to back off and find someone else to lunch with, look after his needs.

Let's see, is there anything we haven't covered? I see we have you down for extra allowance for a special diet. You're hypoglycemic, is that right?

Yes, I went for a five-hour glucose test earlier this year, so yes, being on a proper diet is a big help.

That's good. Umm, and everything's OK with Grace, she has no disabilities or anything, does she?

No. Well, she's got a bit of a sweet tooth, which makes me wonder if she's a little hypoglycemic herself, but I try to keep her diet similar to my own—Oh, I wanted to ask you about lessons. She's on a real lesson kick lately. She was taking ballet and now she wants to start with swimming—could we get any allowance for that? I mean, is there any recreational thing allowed?

Not really. Um. Well, we'll see, I'll see what I can do, let me just write this down, swimming ...

And baton.

And baton ... Well, that's good that she's getting into community things. It's often difficult for children when they move around. Uh, Eilleen, I'm just supposed to take a quick glance around the apartment to make sure everything's the, uh, like we have in your file, one bedroom and all that ... I'll just uh ... Patty Hearst gets up off the couch, averts her eyes and smiles. She walks through the apartment, down the hall, pokes her head in the bedroom, fine, one bedroom, moves on to the bathroom, glances quick. You look over her shoulder, the medicine cabinet is open: a brush, a comb, Noxzema, bottle of Librium, cough syrup, can of men's shaving cream, Pepto-Bismol. Both your eyes glue to the can. Shit. How could you miss shaving cream? Her eyes flick to the bathtub but her mouth opens and *shaving cream* foams out. Someone had to say it, just to name names, just to give the thing a good whack. Like a cockroach. *Yeah, it was on sale and I thought I'd try it out on my legs instead of plain soap. I do seem to get a closer shave with it.*

Oh really! She sounds overjoyed, relieved. *I'll have to try that sometime.* She turns back down the hallway. *I guess all I need is your John Hancock now and I'll skedaddle out of your way.*

The phone rings, you excuse yourself to hear, *Mummy?* It's Grace. She's talking fast, hard to catch what about, but she's going to hit you with something. She's like a used-car salesman sometimes: a lot of questions where yes is the most logical answer and you're yessing and yessing and then suddenly you find you've yessed yourself into car payments you can't afford and a clunker that hardly makes it around the block—*And you said before that maybe I could get one and George said he'd drive me and we could get all the stuff, like the litter and stuff and we already called the SPCA and they have some.*

A kitten? You smile at Miss Hearst, trying to keep up your fascinating hostess appeal whilst simultaneously being a good and caring mother—She did this on purpose, calling you in the midst of this. A kitten. How could she pull this now? *Sweety, can we talk about this later. The lady from the Welfare office is over right now. We'll talk about it when you get home.*

She says, *No, Mummy, please, you said I could and this way you don't have to do anything and if we wait until, if we wait, they'll get destroyed. They put them to sleep if they're there too long, Mum, please. I promise I'll look after it.* You stutter and smile into the phone. How the hell—who told her what happens to kittens who loiter at the SPCA? Goddamn George. This was none of his business. His job was to distract her today, not talk about death row for kitties. *Mum. Can't I please? They kill them. We could rescue one.*

Oh Grace! you whisper and say, *OK. OK, but don't forget, it'll be your job. I mean it now.*

You hang up the phone, want to holler *Fuck!* as loud as you can. Just because: shaving cream, areyousingle, earrings, Patty Hearst, canyousignhereplease, kitten-killers—the SPCA's going to gas you all.

You sign the bottom of the page, smile.

Patricia Hearst smiles—hers is glass too and you get the feeling that any loud noise could shatter every lip and tooth in the room. She straightens her papers, stands them up, cracks them against the coffee table, back in the folder, back in her case. *Well, it was a pleasure to have met you. I'm sorry, I know these things can feel like an ordeal.*

Oh no, I mean, you're a nice person, I mean you don't seem like a, what am I trying to say? You made it easier. She ducks her head to avoid flying compliments and smiles, picks up her briefcase, is walked to the door.

Closing it behind her, you walk down the hall and go sit in the bedroom. If it weren't for George, this would not have been near so nerve-racking. Yes, he means well, but you can't have a man living in the house. Run the risk of losing everything. Run the risk of being bored to death. Feels like you're sleeping with your brother half the time. Yes, he's good for Grace, but they could still visit. He could take her to the track or something once in a while. He doesn't have to live here. The ramifications, the consequences —just, it's just—you need your closet back. He's going off on the fishing boats soon anyway, end of the month. You should tell him he'll have to store his belongings elsewhere—you can't have shaving cream around and that's all there is to it.

You flop back on the bed. Oh to sit and flirt again, at a dance, a bar—wouldn't have to drink, just dance, have a good time. Be a *woman* again instead of somebody's *grandmother.*

Grace Seven

G EORGE WENT OFF again on the fishing boats. He took his clothes and shoes and all the proof that he ever lived with us cuz Mum didn't want to have to explain it if the Welfare showed up. I felt cold for a whole week after he left. Like the air was getting under my skin. I didn't cry, though. I just got mad and bare-naked-cold-feeling. Mum had to go fighting with him even when he didn't want to fight. And she kicked him out and said it was on account of the Welfare coming by to inspect the premises before they'd sign us up for another year. So there'd be no man-evidence, she said. Before he was leaving, George said, all calm to me, that he had to go out on the boats again for a while, as if he was coming back. But he wasn't. I knew it. Plus Mum kept saying, "Thank God," all over the place and how relieved she was to have him out of her hair. Even though he was the best guy ever. And even though when he first came to live with us, she was saying all about adults needing adult company. I guess I cried once.

She bought us a bunch of junk food and let me stay up late that night and said George was good for me but not so great for her and that when he came back from fishing I was still allowed to hang around with him. We could still go horseback riding or to the races or whatever. She kept telling me not to make her into a villain through all this, but I couldn't help it. Cuz as soon as you let people go, even for a little, they just don't come back.

It was Friday night and Mum was at the Legion Hall, dancing or whatever. I was downstairs with Sheryl Sugarman. Josh was doing his art stuff until *Rockford Files* came on, so Sheryl and I were talking and drinking tea. I was still mad at Mum a bit and Sheryl was trying to be cheery. She said, "So how did your mum like the Parents-without-Partners Dance last week?"

"She said it was boring and that there was too many young women there." Sheryl laughed. "She said it was worse than three AA dances put together. She said last week that she wasn't going to AA any more because it was full of boring goofs that were riff-raff and dullards. And that it's silly to say you're not going to ever drink again." Sheryl took a breath and said yeah, that I already told her that. "She's going to get sick again," I said. Sheryl didn't look at me, just in her teacup, and sucked on her bottom lip for a second. So I said, "She was already a bit sick after being at the Parents-without-Partners thing."

"Yeah? Well, sweety, maybe that'll make her change her mind then."

"But my birthday's coming soon, in a month and three weeks. What if she gets really sick and she can't even get me birthday presents or anything?"

"Oh, don't worry—that won't happen. When's your birthday —you'll be nine, right?"

"Yeah. November twenty-fourth. I hate the number nine—I don't even wanna be nine."

Sheryl laughed at me. "What do you mean, nine's a great age—we'll have a party and Josh and I'll be there and ... how 'bout Gabrielle, you haven't mentioned her in a while."

"Nah. I hardly see Gabrielle any more. I guess cuz of me switching schools and stuff and plus because of Mum firing her sister Darlene from being my babysitter. Darlene had boys over, 'member? and they were smoking and I told on her, so Darlene got fired and so then Gabrielle stopped calling me back when I left her a message. And anyway, she started acting all weird when she heard that Charlie didn't know who her baby's dad was. She stopped coming over, it seemed like. Who cares anyhow—I hate her and her stupid glasses and her dumb name. *Gabrielle.* Gobrielle. I should gob on her stupid head," and then I banged my teacup and spilled it a bit and said I was sorry all over the place.

Sheryl oopsed and said not to worry and went and grabbed a dishcloth. "Well, you're probably right, who needs her anyway if it's that easy for her to walk away! Don't be gloomy, my sweet, we'll have a great party—and what about your sister! She'll be in town for your birthday this year!"

"Yeah, except for Ian'll have to come. I hate Ian." I was still thinking about Gabrielle and her dumb sister getting kicked out from being my babysitter. "At least I got a kitten, though, at least I got Henry, so I don't really need Darlene being my babysitter. Plus I'm going to get bribed now."

Sheryl hucked the dishcloth across the kitchen into the sink. "Bribes! Someone's getting a bribe? I never get bribes—who's bribing you?"

"My mum. Didn't I tell you? Last week, she asked how I felt about bribes and I said I was for them so now I get a dollar an hour to babysit myself."

Sheryl frowned and squinted her eyes like she didn't get it. "What do you mean, babysit yourself?"

"A dollar an hour to babysit myself and Henry. I mean if I'm alone, like last week. She let Mrs. Void or whatever—the lady next door—know in case of emergency cuz you guys were out. And tonight, she came down to tell *you* she was going out. Or well, actually, I don't know if I'm supposed to still get money if I'm with you. Maybe I just won't say I was here unless she asks."

"I thought you had a babysitter last Friday." I shook my head and smiled at her. She probably figured I was smart as anything, not being scared alone *and* getting money from it. Then I started feeling hungry all the sudden and I asked if maybe we could have cinnamon toast. And then Sheryl all the sudden went, "So, Grace, do you eat your lunch at school every day?"

I looked over at Josh, but he wasn't listening. He must've told her or something. I said, "Yeah," to Sheryl but I was getting all nervous because of how Mum said she didn't want me eating so much junk food. Sometimes lately, I wasn't eating my sandwich at lunchtime and I'd get a chocolate bar instead. And then I'd just leave my lunch bag sitting in the cafeteria cuz Mum's sandwiches weren't that great but I felt too guilty to chuck them out. Or, if Mum was sick and I was supposed to make my own lunch, I just bought something at the store instead, like those rectangle-shaped chocolate-covered doughnut things.

So then Sheryl started saying, "Grace, I promise not to tell, I just was wondering because of something I read recently. I mean, lots of kids'll trade their sandwich for another kid's doughnut or for a cupcake. Do you ever do that?"

That didn't sound as bad so I said yeah to that. Sheryl told me that she'd been reading this article called "Could Your Child Be Hypoglycemic?" So I said, "Oh yeah, my mum's that. She thinks I'm that too, so she always wants me to have more protein and vitamins and stuff."

Sheryl said, "Uh huh. I remember her saying that, which is why this article caught my attention. They've been doing a lot of research on kids and nutrition. So it started out discussing the diets of kids who steal and get in trouble." I got a bit antsy in my chair on that one, but she couldn't know about the emergency money I was saving; I never showed it or told anybody. Not Josh even. It was top secret. Sheryl kept talking about how lots of juvenile delinquents have low blood sugar and how they didn't get that good nutrition growing up and stuff. "I've noticed how much sugar you like in your tea—you get a lot of sugar cravings—and this article was saying how a lot of kids, if they have poor diets, suffer from bouts of depression, dizziness, confusion, nervous twitches and the shakes. Sometimes they can't concentrate on their school work because they get what are called brain clouds, where your mind just hangs there and you can't get a clear thought. And some of them talked about getting songs in their heads or hearing voices—"

That did it! She was making this up on account of Josh's big mouth. Josh was suddenly paying attention now. We yelled at each other at the same time. He said, "I never told!" and I said, "You promised you wouldn't tell!" Then I started to cry. Josh got scared-faced and sat chewing on his pencil.

Sheryl took my hand across the table. She said, "Sweetheart, Josh did tell me but—"

"Mum! God!"

Sheryl looked at him and said, "Josh, it's OK. Grace knows you care about her and you were only trying to help." Josh kept saying, "Oh God," and he went and sat on the couch in the living room where I couldn't see him. Sheryl kept holding my hand. "Grace, Josh loves you and I love you and we were concerned. Then I remembered this article and I thought maybe I had an idea what might be causing that stuff with you." I was getting all weird and nervous and I couldn't hardly look at her, so Sheryl said, "I don't think you have to go to the loony bin, you know— I just thought maybe we could fix things if we talked about it." I nodded. She said, "It seems like you crave a lot of sugar. And according to this article, extreme stress can have the same effect as having too much sugar—and in turn, the stress can make you crave even more sugar as comfort food. And sweety, you've been going through a lot lately—just in the last few months—your sister came to live with you and she had some pretty awful stuff going on with her boyfriend, you had to watch her and your mum fight a lot and then Charlie moved out with her boyfriend and had a baby. And now you don't get as much time alone with her because of the baby. Then George came to stay and you really liked him and things didn't work out, so now he's gone too … This stuff is really hard on adults, never mind almost-nine-year-olds." I didn't say anything. Just shrugged my shoulders. But it made me kind of depressed, how she was talking about my life. It'd probably make anybody depressed, even if they weren't a hypoglycemiac.

She asked me how long I'd been having the voices for. I told her not that long. "I'm not sure, like maybe around a couple months or something."

"Well, what does it sound like when you hear it?"

"Actually, it's kind of like what you said before about the songs in the head. It's like when you get a song stuck in your head and it just keeps playing and playing until you want to scream. Or else a commercial. Sometimes I get the words from a commercial stuck in my head, like, 'Tastes so good, you'll think it was made from scratch!'" I told her about the rich-English-people dinner I got in my head sometimes and then I said, "And I know that they're fake. It's not like I think they're really in the room or nothing, or like they're telling me to go murdelize someone, like in *Search for Tomorrow* when that lady killed her boyfriend because a voice told her to. They just argue in my head." Sheryl said that made sense cuz of how my mum and Charlie and Mum and George would argue lots. It sounded practically normal when she put it that way. So then I said, "And sometimes, usually after school, when I'm coming home, I think I hear someone whisper my name."

"I bet you that happens when you've had a chocolate-bar lunch. I betcha it does. Because you know, Miss Grace, you're a pretty smart cookie, and it's only been lately that you've had a hard time concentrating and understanding—like when we've talked about your math homework, for instance." So Sheryl started explaining about how hypoglycemia worked and how if you have sugary stuff, your guts started pumping insulin in your blood to bring the blood sugars down and then there's so much insulins that it makes your blood sugar go really low and that's when stuff starts happening. And how, when I start shaking after not eating for a while, that means my blood sugar's on the floor it's so low. And it's the same with white flour and coffee and alcohol.

I said I quit drinking, so it couldn't be that. And then Sheryl started laughing her guts out. I asked her if she was going to tell my mum. She said no, she wouldn't tell on me about the sandwich stuff but only if I promised to start eating them again—the sandwiches not the chocolate—and she said maybe we should quit drinking all this tea because caffeine is really hard on your system too. I said, "But it's half milk, Mum said I could have it if it's half milk."

"All right, I won't deprive you of your tea, but just one cup and only if it's half milk. And only one teaspoon of sugar, not three. And promise promise promise you'll try going two weeks eating your lunch every day. And no chocolate bars. OK? Let's just try this little experiment. And if you feel shaky or you get voices in your head that you can't get out, try eating an orange or an apple. Bring some extra fruit with you to school and keep them with you so if you start getting confused in class you can eat some fruit and balance out your system again."

So I said, "This sounds a little drastic," and Sheryl started laughing again and she told me I killed her. So that was good. I don't know, I guess I didn't really believe it that much, though. But I promised I'd eat my lunch. So. I'd do that part. At least she didn't think I was mental or anything.

After *Rockford Files* and *Night Stalker* were over, I went back upstairs. I was really wanting some of that chocolate cake that I made a couple days ago, but I already finished it. I didn't eat it all, I brought a piece to school for Josh. And plus I brought a piece for Mrs. Annis, my new homeroom teacher, but she was still a big pig-head so she wasn't getting any more cakes from me, that was for sure.

I made myself a brown sugar sandwich instead, like Mum used to make me for a treat when I was little, with the light-brown kind of brown sugar and lots of butter. I thought about what Sheryl said, but it was just a sandwich, not a chocolate bar, and plus I made it with whole wheat bread.

I took it to bed with a glass of milk for extra protein. Since George went away, I was sleeping in Mum's bed again. I laid awake after my sandwich for a long time cuz I kept wondering about my birthday and Mum getting too sick before it, but I fell asleep counting how much money I was going to have by Christmas and thinking how, for now, it was a pretty good deal cuz Mum got to go out and be with adults and I was getting super-rich. Until I woke up from hearing different feet in the house and then a guy's voice that wasn't George's and my heart started going like crazy.

It was like she wrecked the bargain.

He sounded drunk the way he laughed all slow. Like Stewart maybe. After George left, my mum's friend Stewart started calling again, wanting to take her for lunch or a coffee or whatever. And I had to listen to his crunchy dumb voice when I picked up the phone. He always sounded like he was retarded or something, he tried so hard to make kid conversation.

I kept still, listening. And then it sounded like two guys. My arms went hot and I got butterflies in my ribs. I tried to make out some words, but they were all warbly and foggy. Almost like cow noises. Then Mum did that laugh like she used to do when she drank, the more-deeper, throaty kind.

Adults need adult company the same way kids need kid company. I kept hearing Mum say that in my head.

I squeezed my eyes shut and they flapped back open—I couldn't tell what time it was—stupid clock was supposed to be glow-in-the-dark but it always stopped glowing hardly any time after the lights went out. My toes and my teeth clenched and then I started sliding them back and forth over each other—toes with toes and teeth with teeth, I mean. Then I pretended that the clock was really crickets and I was in the country. Then there was more cow noises. Not Stewart. And they weren't George, they didn't give a care about her, they were going to make her drink and get her to do stuff. Same as how it used to be, until she got too sick to move. Same way as Toronto. I got a picture in my head of them out there trying to dump booze right down her throat. And then "Shutt Upp!"—and knives clanging plates, a skinny high laugh, mean English ladies, fork sounds on teeth, and spoons, and "Shutt Upp!" until I couldn't hear anything down the hall. Not even Mum's voice any more; I couldn't tell how many people were really there. I tried to hear through the rich-people dinner in my brain, treat it like a spaghetti strainer that would let through words I wanted, but it worked the opposite and all the voices got stuck in a tangled-up mess.

I squeezed my arms in hard against my sides until my pits hurt, clenching so my body wouldn't fly off the bed and bang down the hall and scream "Shutt Upp!" in all their faces. I forced myself heavy, until my arms went deep in the mattress and I fell

asleep, going in and out, sitting at the long table, seeing the hands
of the Shutt Upp Lady, her throat, and all the silverware clinking,
and bottles clinking and Mum's voice and laughing and my bed,
and a man's voice and then Josh's voice and Kolchak from *Night
Stalker* on TV. I was sitting with Kolchak and Josh in Riley Park.
And glue sniffers were there, but I wouldn't look at them; Kolchak
and Josh's shoulders and chest were big and thick and then they
were horses and they curved their whole selves around me like
walls.

The clock said just past seven when I woke up. There was still
voices in the living room, low jumbles like rolling clumps of dirt.
Mum never came to bed. I sat up and dumped my feet on the floor
and balled up the extra cloth of my flannel nightie in my fists. My
nanna'd sent it to me last Christmas and I was still a bit short for
it. I tipped my feet up and grabbed the hem-part in my toes and
then it sounded like my mother said, "The cat's shoulders squirm
in God's head." I went down the hall to the living room.

Mum and a guy were sprawled on the couch, another guy
was passed out in the armchair. She raised her head up and her
face turned slowly when I came in the room; her lids were sinking halfway down her eyes and she said, "Hiya. What're you
doing up to, darlin'? mm?" Her blouse was slipped to one side
and you could see her black bra-strap showing on her shoulder.
She had one foot curled underneath her and one sticking out
straight with a high heel hanging half off. Her other shoe was on
the coffee table. The way her legs were bent yanked up her skirt
and made it so you could see her garter belt and stockings and
everything. I suddenly got super-pissed-off with her for looking
that way, right in front of people, and I wanted to kick her: for
the lipstick on her chin and mascara and blue stuff all smeary
around her eyes.

Her mouth was dry and she twitched it sideways, made a
pout-face and looked around. She sat up straighter on the edge of

the couch, trying to push hair back out of her eyes. "Christ," crawled out her throat like a bug, "I gotta lie down." She stuffed both her fists in the couch cushions, but nothing happened; her body didn't notice. She wobbled her head side to side and gave our ceiling "the look" as if it was keeping her down. Then a breath and a sigh, and she looked at the guy beside her and shoved herself up. He watched her limp past me to the hallway, then shut his eyes and she scraped along the wall, limping till she kicked her one shoe off along the way. I followed after her.

She fell on the bed and dragged herself up to a pillow. I said, "Mummy," at her like maybe it might make her shake her head and say, "Holy cow, what am I doing?" She didn't answer.

"Mum!"

"Shhhh ... what. Lemme sleep, OK, sweety."

I went up near her face and whispered in case it'd get her attention more. "But those guys are still there, you know. Those guys are in the living room ... Mummy. Mum!"

"What."

"Those guys."

"Mmhmm. They'll go," and she fell asleep. I sat beside her a minute, chewing the inside of my cheek, then crawled in beside her. At least she wasn't moaning and groaning because of her head hurting.

The room stank like cigarettes and sour wine. I stared at the ceiling, let it go dark and then bright, gave it stripes, then leaves, then clouds, and hoped for footsteps and a door slam. Mum snored.

I wished it wasn't Sunday, I wished it was tomorrow so I could be getting ready for school. I started grade 4 almost a month before that. The kids were nicer at General Wolfe, but my homeroom teacher was a mean bag: Mrs. Annis. The whole class was scared of her. The harder she whacked yardsticks on desks, hucked chalk at loud kids and told us how unsufferable we were, the more crazy the room went when she left it: fighting, screaming, swearing, chalk-chucking, desk-dancing—and always, we put a kid to be lookout at the door who'd yell "Anus" when he could see her or hear her shoes coming around the corner. She was also the music teacher, and music was the only thing she made as big a deal about as us keeping our yaps shut; she did both at the same time sometimes. Like on Friday, when she gathered us all around her piano, handed out papers with the song notes and words and told us not to sing just listen. Only listen. She put her fingers on the piano keys and warned us over her shoulder one more time, "No singing now, just follow along on your sheet music." So we did. Then she played the piano and then, sticking her chest up the way she made us do, yelled out the lyrics to "Here Comes the Sun." She sounded like when Eddy pretended to be Ethel Merman and she kept watching our lips and eyes the whole time. I watched my pages but, cuz of how I have buck teeth and an overbite, my mouth comes open a bit and the next thing I knew, Anus smashed her fists down on the piano and screamed, "I said no singing!" All the kids' eyes flicked around like they were scared for whoever went and did it. "Grace! Look at me when I'm speaking to you. Did you hear me, were you listening? Do not sing! Now, put your music away and go sit down." I was going to explain but I just said forget-it in my head, and sat down.

I listened to Mum breathe, glad at least there wasn't Anus on Sunday. The only friend I had at school now was Josh, anyway, and he was downstairs. And I hated Gabrielle for not being my friend any more and Mum too for phoning their mum to tell her that Gabrielle's sister was fired because of smoking in our place. I was getting more lonely-feeling and I couldn't sleep, so I gave up and left Mum to snore her head off. I went as quietly as I could through the kitchen so I could see if those guys were still there. They were dead asleep now, right where I left them: one on the couch and one in the armchair. Both of them had long stringy arms and matching hair. The one in the chair lolled his head back and his mouth fell open with a snort. He had whiter teeth than I expected to be in that whiskery face and the parts around his mouth and eyes were bluish. The other guy laid on the couch with his face squished in the cushions, one arm behind his back, one dangling on the floor. He had an unsmoked cigarette lying in his floor hand. I backed into the kitchen and made a bowl of Shreddies and sat on the counter not swinging my legs and not banging the spoon against the side of the bowl, just listening to a wheezy sound from one of the noses in the living room. A few minutes later, I put the bowl in the sink, changed and went to find Sheryl Sugarman and Josh.

They were awake and I could hear them arguing before I knocked: "Josh, turn off the TV and clean that bloody cage ... Josh! Jesus, why do you insist on listening to that crap?"

"Cuz it's funny. Are there real places like this, like nearby we could go to?"

"Josh! Your hamsters are living in filth. And you're *Jewish*!"

"Wait, Mum, look, this guy's blind, watchthis watchthis— ahh-ha!" Josh's voice was coming from the living room. Sheryl made a growly noise and slammed a door at the other end of the hall. And then only Josh giggling and a preacher-voice on TV. I knocked quietly. He giggled again. I knocked again. Then he stomped his feet fast to the door. It flew open and he pulled me in by my sleeve. "Hey! Com'ere-com'ere, you gotta see this."

On TV was a guy with thick grey hair and gold glasses, pounding one of those high church-desk things on a stage. There were tall white flowers in gold vases behind him and a blue fluffy carpet you could see when the camera got far enough away to show the backs of the audience heads. All of them were nodding while the preacher-guy hollered at them. He was more scary than Anus.

I was glad for their sake he didn't have a yardstick. I sat on the couch beside Josh and listened: "That if thou shalt confess with thy mouth the Lord Jesus, and shalt believe in thine heart that God hath raised Him from the dead, thou shalt be saved!"

Josh whacked me on the forehead with his palm and yelled, "Black and tortured spirit leave thy body" and his hand yanked off, sucking my black spirit with it. I giggled. "You just missed the healings," he told me. "Next Sunday we have to go find a place where they do this, it'd be a gas—OK, look, see that chick there, she's—she was all gimpy and now she can walk. Cool, eh? This is way better than wrestling."

"Where's your Mum?" I said, for proof I was never listening outside their door.

"She's in her bedroom, I think. She's mad at me cuz I'm Jewish."

"What?"

"I don't know. She's weird. She's mad cuz I'm Jewish and I'm watching preacher guys."

"I saw this movie with my mum where this lady tries to take this man, who's Jewish, to a party and he couldn't go cuz it was restricted."

Josh peeled his eyes off the TV. "You mean like there were naked people everywhere?"

"Yeah, I thought there was going to be too and nobody was. They all had suits and dresses and then my mum was trying to explain, but it was stupid cuz how would they even know he was Jewish and why would they even care?"

"Well, if Jews had stuff like this, I'd go, though, to synagogue I mean, cuz this is cool. But any Jew stuff my mum ever tells me's boring; they don't even get Christmas trees. And plus, ever since my dad left, my mum says we're going to be more Jewish and we're not getting a tree any more neither. It's stupid. Who wants to be Jewish—they don't eat hot dogs or cheeseburgers, they don't do nothing. It's boring." I listened to him and watched Rhoda crawl

up over his shoulder and down his pyjama top. He reached in and
picked her out, hamster-noising into her face. "Where's Carly?" he
asked her nose. "You've lost Carly. And now she's pissed off cuz I
haven't cleaned the stupid hamster cage. And cuz she hates this
church stuff; she always has a hairy when I put it on."

I looked at Rhoda and something rustled under my hair. I
knew it was Carly but the shiver on my neck made me jump anyway. I turned and cupped her fat fluffy self up before she could
crawl between the couch cushions.

Josh watched us. "Carly, you frog!" and his eyes snapped back
to the TV. "OK, look, watch this—this is cool, people in the audience start rolling their eyes and stuff and moaning like they're
totally off their rockers."

The preacher-guy's face took up the whole screen all the sudden. My nose twitched; it did smell kind of zooish in the room.
The preacher-guy tilted his chin up and looked into the lights
overhead so that his glasses gave him flashlights for eyes. He pulled
off the glasses, tears dripped down onto his cheeks and he said, "I
am the alpha and the omega, the beginning and the end, the first
and the last."

Josh cackled. "It's like *Star Trek*, eh? There's a better guy on
later, like around lunchtime, but my mum'll go mental if I watch
this till then ... What do you wanna do?"

"I don't know. What do you wanna do?"

"I don't know."

So I helped him clean the hamster cage and then he doubled
me down to Riley Park and we rode around long enough to get
into a scrap about mink fur and Josh's paintbrushes and mink
farms and animal traps and what was the difference between a
mink and Carly and Rhoda and I said forget-it to him doubling
me any more and he yelled that I was such a goof he wouldn't let
my stupid ass touch his bike anyway and I stomped home by myself, all pissed off that he said ass again but kind of wishing he'd

chase after me and make me not mad so I wouldn't have to go
home yet.

I closed the apartment door behind me and looked down the hall
to the living room. Nobody was there. Then chuckles in the bedroom. I went to the door and poked my head in. Mum was sitting up in bed, sipping a beer, and the two guys were on the floor,
one cross-legged, one lying sideways, passing a joint around. She
looked up and smiled. "There she is," and she introduced her
friends. They both grunted hello through holding their breath,
and one of them passed the joint to my mother. I couldn't stand
watching her with that stuff. I'd seen her do it with Sadie's mum
and dad and listened to them giggle and talk and try to hold
smoke in their stomachs at the same time. I waited a minute anyway, watching the droopy moustache of the guy who was sleeping on the couch earlier. They were talking about swimming and
dying and being buried at sea and then something about *Jonathan
Livingston Seagull.* I read that one last month, while I was waiting
for *Go Ask Alice,* and part of me wanted to tell them that, that I
knew all about it, but more of me didn't want to say I read anything they read. The droopy-moustache guy my mother called
Gary asked if I ever heard of *Jonathan Livingston Seagull.* Mum
watched me with a smirk that I figured was a proud-thing, wanting me to show them what kinda kid she had.

"Yup, I read it ages ago," I told him. He asked if I knew what
it was about. "Reincarnation," I said. I saw a guy on *The Mike
Douglas Show* once talking about reincarnation, so I knew the
whole scoop on that. "Getting smarter and braver and flying
higher until you get higher and higher in heaven."

"Whoa," he said, nodding. He looked at Mum and then back
at me and back at my mum. "She's kind of a trippy kid, eh?"

Mum kept smiling. "Yup, she's a funny bird." They all burst
out laughing. I left and heard Mum mumble, "Uh oh—Honey,

we weren't laughing at you, you know. We're just being silly. Hon? you mad?"

"No, I'm just—doing something." I went to the living room and sat on the couch. The air was kind of like that smell that gets in your nose before you barf. There were glasses and empty beer bottles and wine on the coffee table and floor. Cigarette butts were floating in a glass of beer beside a pickle jar of ashes and butts. Dead matches and grey flakes were all over the place. Henry climbed up on the couch and yowled until I remembered to give him cat food.

I decided to go over to Sadie and Eddy's.

When I got there, Eddy was on the porch, leaning over a piece of paper, concentrating like crazy. Sadie stood against the railing eating a piece of watermelon. She spat seeds and watched me get near the house. Eddy didn't look up until I got to their bottom step. Then they "hi"ed at me together. Sadie sneered at whatever Eddy was looking at. Nobody said anything. It was kind of a long time since I even saw them and I thought they'd be more happy or something. But they were just their crabby old selves. So I said, "What're you guys doing?"

"Nothin'." Sadie took a bite off her melon and scratched some paint off the porch with her shoe heel.

Eddy poked at his paper and said, "I saw you swallow a seed, y'know, you're gonna grow a watermelon tree in your stomach, y'know." And she spat a black gooey one at his head.

"Achgg, frig off!" he screamed. Eddy balled up some spit as if he was going to gob it at her.

Sadie stared at him. "Try it, y' little turd, and you're dead." Eddy swallowed and went back to his paper.

When I got to the top step, I looked at the pieces of grass and twiggy things Eddy had glued on yellow construction paper. Sadie chucked the melon skin into a bush. "I hope one of 'em bites ya!" she said and went into the house, banging the screen door behind

her. I was Sunday-sad again and I even had it worse because Sadie
and Eddy were my only friends now if Josh wasn't around and they
didn't even act like they liked me. Eddy stuck his tongue out the
corner of his mouth while he added more glue. They were legs he
was gluing, not grass: spiders, flies, earwigs and one moth. Around
half of them were still alive; most of them were stuck by their
backs and wiggling their other stuff.

"Go get me a spider." He always tried to boss me when Sadie
wasn't around to do it.

"Get it yourself."

He glared and threw the page at me. I "eww"ed and wiggled
out of the way. It landed on the welcome mat.

"What's your beef, jerky?" That was my new comeback I
picked up off Josh's mum. Eddy didn't think it was so great. "Why
do I cast my pearls before swine?" I asked the air. I got that one off
my mum.

"You and Sadie, you think you're so big and Sadie super-even-
more now she's friends with dork-head Sarah."

Sarah was the girl from ballet. I almost never saw Sadie lately,
not since starting at the new school. I brought Josh over a couple
times in the summer but the three of them seemed different together. The last time, Josh said we should all play doctor up in
Sadie's room. He explained how it worked and I never brought
him again. No one was taking out or touching or looking at any
of my underclothes stuff.

Sadie came back out and walked down the steps. She was carrying a purse.

"What's in your purse, lady? Kotex?" and Eddy laughed the
way he usually did just before he broke something.

Sadie sucked in an *ahhh* and said, "That's it! Say you're sorry
or I'm tellin'," and she ran back up the steps and caught him before he could get away, slammed him down with her knee in his
back and twisted his arm till his elbow went to his backbone and

he yelled, "Mawwwwwwwm!" She twisted harder till he squeaked, "Sorry," and their mum hollered from inside the house. Sadie let him go and yapped, "Yeah, you better run," when he dived for the screen door.

I asked her if she wanted to go play or something.

"Play?" she said, as if it was the most babyish thing she ever heard. "Nope. Can't. I'm going to Sarah's. Her mum's out and she's got tons of makeup. So. I'll see y'around." She started down the steps.

"Um, hey, are you still gonna take swimming lessons at Riley Park?" I said. I didn't want her to just go and me be alone with only Eddy. I kept having the sour beer smell in my nose and it made my mouth taste like sick.

"Yup, Sarah and me are starting *Intermediate* together."

"Oh."

Eddy came up to the screen door, still bawling his head off. "You're in trouble, y'know. You're getting grounded for sure."

"Get lost!" and she practically waltzed down the block. I heard Alice call her and Sadie kept going like nothing happened. By the time her mum was on the porch, Sadie was a block away and Alice mumbled and slammed back inside. Why didn't Sarah want *me* to be her friend and put on her mum's makeup? and swim with her. Sadie wasn't going to get grounded for practically breaking Eddy's arm. She'd just go around being cool and everyone would do what she said. Including me.

Eddy didn't even look mad any more. He kneeled over his paper; there was hardly a bug leg wiggling any more. "Wanna help me get more bugs?" he asked. So I did until it started to rain and it seemed even worse to be stuck with Eddy in his house than to go back to mine. He went inside and I started down their steps and tripped when my name got whispered in my ear. I got up off the ground getting ready to be laughed at for being accident-prone. I tried to laugh before anyone else did, but there was no one there. Then a Grace-whisper came over my other shoulder, but I didn't turn this time. My knee was banging from the pain and I scrunched my mouth and tongue tight to keep from crying. I figured maybe I should go home and have an orange.

The apartment smelled even worse after being outside. It was quiet, though. There was no one in the living room. And in the bedroom, my mum was curled up under her blanket with a bucket beside her bed. I went down the hall to the living room and my chest jumped when the droopy-moustache guy came around the corner from the kitchen. His shirt was all unbuttoned and he had these shiny-from-dirt ripped jeans on. A cigarette hung out under his moustache and he scratched his sideburn, took his cigarette and held it lazy in his fingers. He was the skinniest man I ever saw. "Hi," he said, kind of shaky, and flicked ashes on the floor. "How y'doin'? Grace? Is that right?"

"Yup."

"Right." He said it like *ry-eeet.* "Your mum's still sleepin'," and he nodded and chuckled. "Rough night I guess, eh?"

"Yup." I sat down on the couch. The TV was on with no sound. I stared at another preacher-guy waving like crazy on the screen. He looked like he should be glued to a piece of construction paper.

Moustache-guy wandered over and sat on the couch beside me. "So," he said. "Mine's Gary. My name, eh?" and he chuckled again. I looked at the TV. He took a drag and I watched him blow smoke without turning my head. "So. You're not a real talker, eh? Shy?" I shrugged and kept watching the preacher. "What's this? mm, September? School's in, right? What grade 're you in?"

"Four."

"Right. Huh. So uh … so you got a boyfriend?" I shook my head and got up off the couch. Went to the window where Henry was on an end table, resting his front paws on the sill, staring out at Main Street traffic. I ran my hand down his fur, watching what he was watching. Gary stood up, so I looked back and saw him stick his cigarette back under his moustache so he could give his arm a good scratch on his way over to Henry and me. Henry and me looked out the window. Gary did too. "Nice pussy," he said, then giggled at himself. "Oops, I mean pussy *cat*, kitty cat. What's her name?"

"It's a he." I wished I had the guts to gob a seed on him, like Sadie. I opened the window instead.

"Oh yeah? ... *his* name then ... ha."

"Henry."

"Humm. Good name. So. Grace. So what're you gonna be when you grow up?" I shrugged some more and kept looking out the corner of my eye to see what he was doing. I wondered if he knew that drinking alcohol and eating chocolate bars was probably making him into a juvenile delinquent. He smoked and looked me over. "You gonna pose for *Playboy*? You got a cute little ass," and he patted my bum and did that dumb laugh again, flicking his cigarette butt out the window.

My arms went tight and I thought about being in every car that passed on Main Street. I forced my shoulders back; they hurt like hair being brushed the wrong way. I squinted at him and said, "Pff, no!" to Eddy in the Sadie-est voice I could and saw him for the stupid-friggin'-nature he was, then turned and walked to the kitchen. My bum felt clumsy and naked stuck out there behind me.

In the cold air falling out of the fridge, I stared at the milk and some shrivelled potatoes. I wanted to crawl in the fruit bin and pull the door closed. But I was Sadie. Sadie turned me around to look at him follow me into the kitchen. His eyes flicked and he picked up a deck of cards lying on the table, lazy-shuffling while he looked out the window into the building next door. I poured myself some milk, imagined the moustache it would make on

Sadie's dark skin and then, bored as she could look, I took it down the hall to Mum.

"Mummy? Mum? Do you want some milk?" Nothing. "Mummy!"

"Grace?" she croaked like she couldn't move. "Please, let me sleep. I'm sick."

I couldn't decide about what he said yet. Maybe it was just "ass" that bugged me. I should've told him the same way I would Josh. Sadie would've. I put her milk-moustache on as thick as it'd go and went back, acting normal, to the living room. I looked at him and his scrunchy-rumpled shirt and his reddy-brown whiskers and watched him walk around, shuffling cards. Sadie folded my arms.

"Know how to play cards?" he asked me.

"Duh. Everybody knows how to play cards. What about you? Can you do anything with them? Like magic tricks?"

"Na, not really …" He kept sliding them in on each other.

My Sadie-self was disappointed. I wasn't sure if it was to make him change his mind or if she was just miffed that he wasn't answering like she wanted. "You can't do *any* tricks?!" she said.

He looked up at us. "Well, yeah, maybe a couple, if you're good."

"Oh yeah? Why don't you do a disappearing act." His bottom lip dropped open and his eyes squinted. Sadie got super-smug; I got butterflies and tried not to smirk.

"You're a little cheeky, if you ask me. Your mother know you talk like that?"

"Where do you think I got it from?" Sadie was getting him good. I started to giggle and joined her. "So? Come on, Gar … disappear."

"I leave when I'm good and damn ready. You better watch your lip or I'll tell your mum."

"She's not gonna care. Maybe I should go tell her myself." Then I raised my eyebrows the way my dad's ex-wife, Gloria, used to do, and paused to get a good effect, then turned and walked down the hall to the bedroom. I closed the door behind me and sat as quiet as I could at the foot of the bed. Five minutes or so went by till I heard shoes come toward me, shuffle, and the apartment door open and slam. He stomped down the stairs of the building, down each one of my ribs until he exploded in a thousand tickles in my stomach.

Eilleen Seven

TAKE OFF YOUR COAT and get a drink down your gullet; steady your nerves. You get down on your hands and knees and gawk into the pot-and-pan cupboard for wine—ridiculous having to hide your own wine. Just seems like Grace is happier when she doesn't actually have to see it, though. Everybody's happier when you pretend you're not drinking—everybody's a hypocrite, all with their own crutches and they have the nerve to knock you. Stupid buggers. You stand up with the bottle and brush crumbs off your knees, grab a glass off the shelf, pour yourself a half a one and slop burgundy back at your blouse. Shit— dab it with cold water. *You've got great tits, Eilleen.* Chuck the cloth back in the sink. Screw it. You look back down, run a hand over the left one: tits'll get you a lot in this town. Tits'll get you a lot in any town. You take a big gulp. Reach into your purse on the counter, pull out the white prescription bag. *25 x 25mg Noludar Dr. L.B. Henighan.*

Twenty-five.

Should've given you a hundred, the fat fuck.

You down what's left and pour another one. It's not that big a deal. Pretty clever really—how many other women could've done it? You're no victim. You are a cunning seductress: *This is the third time this month, Eilleen, I don't know that I can do anything for you.* Asshole Henighan. If Peterson wasn't pulling his high and mighty medical practitioner routine lately, you wouldn't have had to see Henighan in the first place—him and his third-rate Hastings Street dope-fiend's paradise. Not to mention Goldberg and Chan —every goddamn quack you know is pulling this ethics shit, this holier than thou, I'm-sorry-but-I-can't crap. Going to have to put together a new stable, that's all. Screw 'em.

You fight with the bottle cap. Childproof lids, only way you can get the damn things open is to get your kid to do it. Push and lift, no push and twist and—fuck! Push and twist and lift. Huh.

Sit down at the table and pull out the cotton batting, tilt the bottle around in your hand, sip some wine and look at their little two-tone selves rolling around in there, twenty five of 'em. Little coloured cylinders, like teeny tiny cocks. Not much smaller than teeny tiny Henighan. Only teeny thing on him. You stare into space and watch black flecks float past your eyes like water bugs, until the kitchen blurs and you're standing in Henighan's examination room again, sitting up on his table with your legs crossed. *Maybe we should give you a physical today, Eilleen, rather than just rattle off another prescription.* A physical, he says, and starts jotting down god knows what on his clipboard, burying his first chin in all the others. Three pig-foot fingers slide the pen back in his breast pocket. *Why don't you take off your clothes, Eilleen.*

Wouldja quit saying my goddamn name! is what you want to say, but you just start unbuttoning blouse. He puts down your chart and watches. There is no nurse in the room. He watches each button slip through its hole; you raise your eyes and watch his jowls shift as he tilts his head. You slide off the table and unzip your skirt, let it fall to the floor, step out of it. He doesn't say anything yet, just looks at your crotch. You look down, flesh is buckling at the top of your pantyhose, tummy's sticking out a little. *S'pose I could lose a few pounds*, you say. *Not necessarily*, he says, *you've got great tits, Eilleen*. You hold your head up. *Well thank you Doctor, how kind of you to notice*, smile like you know what's what and wonder what the hell this bastard's up to. About three hundred pounds you figure, and chortle before you can stop yourself. He doesn't reciprocate, just takes two steps and puts his stethoscope to your breast plate. *Pardon the cold*, he says, looks at the floor; it's dead silent until his breath catches on something in his nose. He cups the metal in his palm, slides it into the left cup of your bra; his fingers wrap around as much boob as they can get. He shuts his eyes just longer than a blink, tucks his lips together, opens his mouth and you can see his tongue flicking lonesome hungry in that fat head of his. Then you see the cost of Noludar has just gone up. *Your heart sounds OK*, he says. *OK, Eilleen, what I'm going to get you to do is run up and down the steps and then I'm going to check your heart rate again.* Steps? Look around the room and step out of your shoes. You never had to run up and down anything before. This is ridiculous, if it's a f(ee-iz)ucking blow job he wants, why doesn't he just say so so you can get the hell out of here.

He walks to a block against the wall with two steps built into one side. He drags it out. *All right now, I just need you to run up and down for about sixty seconds and then I'm going to take your pulse. You might want to take off your pantyhose. And if you wouldn't mind removing your bra.* Son of a bitch—does he have to make you look like a goof in the process? You sigh, look at him. He looks back. His face is stone with a faint twitch at one corner of his mouth. You know a put-out-or-walk smirk when you see one.

Starting at the waist, you roll your pantyhose down, trying not to look like a moose when you pull them off your toes and throw them with your skirt. You reach back and unhook your bra, let it slide forward off your arms, feel your breasts falling. A sound comes out of Henighan, a kind of whimper, and your shoulders crunch forward like protective dogs; there is nothing you can do to call them back. You turn to the steps, put your hands to your breasts, try to hold them up, keep things from drooping and jiggling.

This is, this is silly, I can't do this, you say, turn and look at him.

Just for a minute, Eilleen, one minute, he says. *Keep your arms straight out to your sides.*

Foolish. You step onto the first step, boobs sway, the next step and back yourself down.

—and you step up and your boobs stay down—feel like they're trying to wrench themselves free and leave on their own if you're not going to take them.

—and back down you go and they slap to the side, flop up and down. stupid-stupid-stupid exercise in idiocy and it's starting to hurt—

—and up—

—and down. They fall hard again and your hands leap to cradle them and you stop and say over your shoulder, *OK, this is— I've had enough* and Henighan steps fast to the block before you can get to the floor. *Good girl*, he says, *good girl* and he pulls you backward into his barrel belly, one arm round your ribs, bringing your feet down on cold tile, other hand fumbling with something, the stethoscope, over your shoulder he brings the cool metal to your chest, his breathing is getting harder in your neck. He leaves the scope dangling and jerks his hand back around and under so that both his arms are under yours, one holding you steady while the other mashes the stethoscope into your boob. He's lurching and shoving you forward with his stomach, pushing you to the examination table. *Good girl*, he says, *good girl, listen to your heart, I'm not gonna hurt you, bend forward, put your tits on the table, oh your heart, lemme feel your tits on the table, lemme pull your panties down,* but you're not wearing any and he brings his empty hand between your back and his belly, thrashing around back there, trying to get his belt undone, he can hardly get his breath now. Christ, what a production, all that grunting to get his pants open, trying to get it out, *listen to your heart, Eilleen, let me in, let me in,* and then this wee bony thing poking from behind, *good girl, good pussy,* and he starts to cough and you think it must be a finger inside until that bulbous gut thumps twice against your tailbone and there's a thin kitten mew against your back. He collapses on your shoulders, squashing your face to the paper on the table, his arms splay past your ears and he lies back there, breathing, breathing. *You got off, now get off,* you think, but you want your goddamn prescription. You try to get some air when you realize there doesn't seem to be any in or out of him. It's dead quiet again and you feel his slow drizzle down the inside of your thigh. *Hey, how you doin'?* you say, terrified he's had a heart attack or passed out and you're not going to get anything out of this—or worse, you'll be left to suffocate—no one'll find you until they get enough people together to cart him away. This isn't the bang you wanted to go out with.

The water bugs come in focus and you are back in your kitchen with a pill bottle in your hand. He came to all right, did up his pants, straightened his tie and wrote *25 x 25mg Noludar.* Should report him to the Better Business Bureau. No other man on this planet would think you were worth less than fifty.

You glance past the bottle, jabber pills around inside and bring them down to twenty-four Noludar with a swig off your glass before snapping the cap back on. The buzzer on the intercom goes. Shit, who the hell's that? Maybe Grace forgot her key—nah, it's just three o'clock now, unless she had another row with that teacher of hers and stormed out.—*Hello?*

Hi, Mum, it's me.

Charlie?

Yeah. And you *oh* and stutter and buzz her up. Shit-shit-shit. Cork up the bottle and put it back with the pans, rinse your mouth. Where's your Clorets? Why is she showing up like this, unannounced? You check your blouse, look around the room, look for anything you could get in trouble for.

The light sound of knuckle on wood, you go to the door. *Hi!* she says. She's carrying the baby, leans and gives you a kiss, her nose twitches. Little bitch, she's not kissing, she's smelling. You *hi* back and touch the baby's cheek, close the door behind her.

I was visiting friends around here and I thought you might like to have tea with your grandson. She sets down a baby seat on the table, puts him in and sits her diaper bag or whatever that is beside him.

You mean you thought you'd try and catch me in the act while at the same time shaming me into being a grandmother, you think, but you just say *oh.*

She says, *Is Grace around?* and takes the diaper bag off the table, puts it beside her on the floor.

No, she's not home from school yet, she'll probably just be a few minutes. She's going to a different school now, so the walk's a little further.

Hmm, she says, and you can't help noticing, as she plops down into a chair, how big her ass has gotten since the baby. All right, you're a shitty mother, but there's a certain satisfaction in knowing she won't be parading her pert little tits and ass around in front of every boyfriend you get any more. She pulls her tight T-shirt smooth, reading your mind, and says, *How do you like my new milk jugs! Practically as big as yours now, eh!* and she laughs.

You laugh back. *Yeah, I guess you'll be watching your weight again now. God, when Grace was born I never stopped moving, always rocking her or walking her, and I had my figure back in no time.*

Charlie reaches and squeezes the baby's foot, says she wasn't really thinking about it. Adds, *But I'm young, I'll bounce back.*

There's a pause in the room and she says, *So. What've you been up to, you look dressed up today, you're not working again, are you?*

Not working again, are you—no dear, I'm still a worthless welfare drudge, just like you—*Ah, no, I looked into teaching again, but the rules are different in B.C. and my teaching certificate isn't any good here, I probably told you that.*

Yeah. That's a drag, and she looks you over, looks at your chest as if the sheer size of them proves you're a slut. Not like her new maternal breasts. The first time she had her creepy boyfriend, Ian, over, she was still staying here, and she had you change your shirt before he arrived. Had you change into something a little less showy. You laughed. *What would that young pipsqueak be looking at me for!* But you changed; after all, it wasn't a competition. Course he couldn't keep his eyes off them anyway. The experience was both gratifying and revolting.

Pull your brain back, change the subject. *Yeah. So. No, I just went to the doctor and, I don't know, I'm not that dressed up, am I? Guess I thought I'd throw on a skirt and heels and brighten myself up a little, I guess. Ha. Uh—oh, so did you want some tea or juice or something?—here, let me throw the kettle on. So how's Ian?*

She scratches at something stuck to the table. *Um. Fine. He might be getting a construction job next week. Maybe. I don't know. He—he wins a few bucks here and there playing pool.* She makes a smacking sound in her mouth as if she's just finished a toffee and picks your pill bottle off the table. *He's always out, though, or hungover ...* and rattles them, rattles you. Can't tell if she's pissed off at you for taking them or for not offering her some.

You loiter around the stove, Noludar kicking in, forehead getting cool, back of your neck gone wooden, fairy dust at your wrists and going all the way up. Can never decide whether you want to smack her or soothe her—hold her against your breast and smooth your hand down the back of her head, *Let me make it better, angel,* or grab her by the scruff, *How can you be so fool-ish?* So you do nothing, just stand staring at the kettle, mute.

Then she makes some sound like a big puff through her nose, sets the bottle back down. And yes, the Noludar's kicking in for sure; you're getting stupider with each passing moment. Why does she have to just show up like this out of the blue? She got herself into this mess—what are you supposed to do? She says, *So how's Grace doing, how come she switched schools?*

Well, a lot of those kids across the street were pretty rough, as you may recall ... And her friend downstairs was going to Wolfe, this other one, so ... She doesn't seem much happier now, though, at the new one. This woman she's got teaching her, Mrs. Annis—Grace calls her Anus—kills me whenever she says it. Charlie laughs and her face becomes almost beatific. Melting. Feel like reminding her Grace is her sister, her baby's on the bloody table. The fight the two of you had before Charlie ran off and engaged herself to Ian started out about Grace. Charlie had the ovaries to tell you she was as much Grace's mother as you were, that she'd looked after her when you were too loaded to know your own name. *Anyway,* you go on, *I went in to see her, the, uh, Mrs. Annis, at the parent–teacher day last week.*

You did?

Yes. Why is that so surprising?

Well, and she raises her eyebrows at the baby just as if he's holding up a picture of you and the very image of this face at a parent–teacher meeting is nothing short of laughable, *I don't know. Nothing. So what happened?*

You clear your throat. *Anyway, so I was saying to her, "Do you realize all these kids are terrified of you, I mean really terrified." I thought maybe she had no idea and she might—well anyway, she looked positively thrilled and said, "Good. I like to keep them under my thumb." Ha—can you imagine! I was speechless. So, and then she*

said Grace had been a little difficult at first but she's doing the uh ...
better now.

Charlie's head twists around as you're pouring hot water into
cups. *She is not difficult. She's just smart, that's all, she's ahead of her*
time. Stupid bitch.

Stupidbitch scalds you and you start and splash hot water on
your thumb. *Ow, shit,* whip on the cold water faucet and hold it
there a minute.

She sighs. *Mum, you're so accident-prone—I guess that's where*
Grace gets it from.

Well, you don't have to tell me off for it, I didn't scald myself on
purpose—I did it making your tea.

I'm not telling you off, I'm just saying. You're not that careful and
Grace is just as bad, always hurting herself. It practically is *like you*
do it on purpose, it happens so—

Charlie! For godsake, can't we not have a nice visit visout—with-
out, sigh, now you can't tell if you're stoned or just thrown off. This
was going to be a pleasant afternoon before she showed up. There's
a key in the lock. The baby's home, thank god. You turn the faucet
off, shake your thumb. Doesn't hurt that much, and that ladies
and gentlemen is the beauty of wine and pills.

Grace closes the door and comes in the kitchen. *There's my*
baby! Charlie says.

Grace squeals, *You made your hair red!* and kisses her.

Shit, she did, too. How could you not have noticed that, it's
redder than yours. Maybe because you're so used to looking at
your own. Or maybe it's the light. Maybe because you're a crummy
mother and you never do anything right. You try. *Oh, of course!*
Your hair! I couldn't think what was different! It's cute! but she
doesn't look at you. And more than a small part of you thinks,
Perfect. You've nearly got my tits, now you've got my hair colour, one
baby down, one more to go, as she pulls Grace onto her lap and

blows a loud raspberry into her neck. Grace laughs raucously and Charlie's baby starts to fuss.

Grace jumps down and goes to him. *Can I pick him up?* His mother says sure she can. Somewhere along the line, Grace has gone from seething jealousy to asking to diaper and feed him. Something like Charlie did when Grace was born.

She sits down holding the baby in her arms, rocking him like they do in cartoons. Charlie giggles at her. Well, aren't they all just too cute for words. Charlie says, *So, Grace-face, how y'doin'? I heard your teacher's kind of a creep.*

Yeah, giant super-huge creep. I hate her guts. You should've seen her today, she was in fine form—she's a big hag and I bet she has warts on her boobies, and she blushes and ducks her head into the baby as she giggles. Charlie giggles back. Why shouldn't she. She's *practically her mother.*

You bring two cups of tea with milk and sugar to the table, tell Grace one's for her, knowing she'll want it because she's such a big tea-hound. She says maybe she should put the baby in his chair so she doesn't burn his bum or something. Charlie laughs and helps her put the baby in his seat, adjusts his soother, and he's asleep before they can get back in their chairs. *Hey, I almost forgot,* and Charlie goes into her diaper bag, *I passed by a bookstore this morning and I saw something in the window you might like; I think you're old enough now.*

You're just settling into your chair as Charlie pulls out a thin green and white children's book that says, *Where Did I Come From, Anyway?* on the cover. *It's about how babies are made,* she tells her. Grace snaps it up before you get near it, flips it open and fans through pages of line drawings and thick print until she gets to one of a man lying naked between a woman's spread legs and stops dead, scanning the text till her cheeks flush again and she turns the page fast to a giant egg with dozens of sperm zipping toward it. Charlie giggles.

You pluck the book. *Anyone mind if I take a look at this first?*

Grace yaps a *Mummy!* at you and swings a paw to get it back, catches a page and you know she's not going to let go and this is not a fight you want to have in front of Charlie, who has just said, *Well, Mum, she's almost nine, it's probably time she started learning the facts of life now. Better than finding it out the hard way in five years!*

Exactly! her little sister says.

You let the book go, afraid it'll rip and all hell will break loose. *Yes, well. Honestly,* and you try to keep the tone playful. *I don't see Grace running the streets at that age.* Charlie's face drops, edges toward a glare. You say, *Well for godsake, I mean I've never kept any secrets from you kids, I answer every question she has as they come up and I just think, well, I just think I should be the judge of what she reads about this subject, that's all. I'm not being a prude, I'm just— I am her mother, after all.*

Well, I've read it and I think … I think it's comprehensive and progressive, really. And I think it's cool.

You glance at the back of the book in your child's paws and see *A comprehensive and progressive look at basic sexuality as told by Doctor …*

Well, be that as it may … you say, and the two of you lock eyes. Unbelievable—who the hell—Grace is back to staring at the naked couple, sees she's been caught again and flips to the front of the book.

Well, I wanna read it, it's my present, Charlie gave it to me, not you. Anyway, why shouldn't I read it, everybody's doing it—you, you had sex before! and she cackles and brings the book over the lower half of her face.

Charlie looks at you. *Look, see, she's curious, and now you've made her all embarrassed.*

Oh, for god's sake, Charlie, I didn't make her embarrassed, she's embarrassed because all her friends are embarrassed. Quit making everything about me.

She gives an exasperated sigh. *I just meant you won't let her see it. And anyway, I'm not making this about you, you're making it about you. I didn't make you feel guilty, you did. Because you don't want her to read a normal book about the birds and the bees. I bought it so she could just read it and you wouldn't have to feel all weird talking to her about sperm or whatever.*

Isn't this charming: your judgment usurped by a recently knocked-up, all-of-eighteen-year-old tramp, posing as a—as a what—an all-knowing earth mother. And you're supposed to keep your mouth shut. That's the beauty of it. You have to be civil and maintain decorum while she casts her eyes like aspersions and dares you to just try it, pick another fight in front of Grace—tell your children how you know best, as evidenced by your fabulous track record.

Grace gives you her cartoon smug-face. So you say, *Go ahead, read it, see if I care, I'm sure there's nothing there you don't already know.* And you do for Charlie your best imitation of Grace smuggery. And the tone of your voice is echoing in your head, are you talking too loudly? But Charlie's laughing some kind of laugh, the nervous hollow one the family uses for certain situations; can't remember which ones just now.

Grace Eight

I WAS IN GRADE 4 probably around two months when Charlie told us her and Ian, the albino guy, were going to move to the States. Ian's dad was American and worked with a sportswear company in Portland, Oregon—he said he could get Ian a real job, not just hustling in pool halls—Ian said he was going to take care of Charlie and her baby, Sam, even if Sam wasn't his. Charlie made it sound kind of fun in a way, like everything would be different once Ian got with his family. And he had a big family, a real one with a mum and dad and aunts and uncles and cousins.

The night after I heard, I laid awake trying to picture Portland. It sounded like Vancouver but better; people would live in sunny houses and have tans and boats and yellow jackets and good jobs with sportswear companies. I wished she could take us with her.

The day before she left, she brought me early birthday presents: *Winnie the Pooh* and *Charlotte's Web* and *Stewart Little*, all hardcovers, she said, patting them like kittens, and held me in her lap on the edge of Mum's bed. Mum was propped up on pillows.

Sam was in his baby seat on the floor watching us. Charlie's chest shook against my back and her arms wrapped around my ribs while she looked over my shoulder, keeping her cheek on the side of my head. Tears wheezed through her nose and she stuffed her face in my neck. My own throat was strangley and burning and I told her not to get snot on me. She giggled and wiped her cheeks and started to make scared-voice promises: she was going to start a new life in the States. She didn't have a phone number or an address or stuff yet, but as soon as she was settled I could visit her. She hugged my back to her front and whispered that everything would be different.

After Charlie left, I went back and sat on the bed, my feelings all mangled so I had no words, and weaved my toes in and out of each other. Hairs on my arms stuck up like cat whiskers testing for close stuff, but it was getting so hollow where we were. If we could just take off, go to some other city, Mum'd get better again, get a job again. And maybe George would come back and come with us.

Mum groaned and reached for her bottle of 222s. This was her best in three days of lying there; she was sitting up some and talking a little. "Well, that's that," she said, and she dropped her hands on the bed and stared at the ceiling. "She hates my guts, doesn't she?"

I said no, but I kind of wasn't sure. Charlie seemed like she wanted Mum to say something before she left, beg her out of it or tell her to come live with us again. But Mum couldn't take living with Charlie any more. Mum couldn't take anybody but us two.

"I love her, I do. I just can't stand her," and her chin and lips wobbled. We sat quiet like that a couple minutes, her wiping her eyes and me just staring at the air. Like a brain cloud, like Sheryl said.

Mum tried to sit up. "Oh shit." She ducked her head down and held on to her forehead with one hand. "Jesus-Mary-and-

Joseph," then "Will you go in my top drawer and find my yellow pills—um, in the left corner," and she fell back into her squashed pillow.

I put her last yellow one in her mouth and she jerked her head to help it down. She stared at the ceiling a second, then said, "What about dinner, have something good for you, have a carrot and some meat and—uh. Christ, my stomach feels like the bottom of an old birdcage."

"There's nothing hardly left, just, well, there's Jell-O, but it's kinda crusty at the top now. And there's cake, I made chocolate cake. And I was going to go to the store but there's no money in your purse and um—" I'd put ten of the secret emergency money in a bank account Mum started for me a few months before and the rest I spent on a new Danskin like Sadie's and a baton. I was going to start baton lessons next Saturday morning.

I picked at the Explorers badge on my blouse. I'd started another group the week before, kind of like Girl Guides, where we wore uniforms (a white blouse and navy blue skirt) and sat in a circle singing campfire songs with good manners and stuff. Today was my second once-a-week meeting. I got Mum to sew the badge on my blouse before she got sick, and it turned out we put it on the wrong pocket. I started to ask the leaders why it mattered, but they gave me the Anus look, the one about how unmanageable I was. Felt like all the girls looked at me that way—a whole circle of Anus faces. I figured I'd probably quit. Maybe after the Halloween party.

Mum moaned again. "Oh. I feel like a big pizza."

I was still depressed about Charlie. "We don't have any money."

"Where's—did we give Charlie her Family Allowance cheque?" My sister's cheques were still getting mailed to our place and I forgot all about the last one, which made me feel even more bad. "Sweety, come on, don't be sad, Charlie's not gone forever, you know she always comes back and she'd want to cheer you up if she

could. So why don't we cheer ourselves up. It's the least she could
do, walking out of your life yet again." I decided Mum was right,
Charlie was the one who left and besides, we couldn't get the
cheque to her before she went away anyhow.

Mum ripped open the envelope while I looked up *Pizza* in the
Yellow Pages. I wrote down all the stuff we wanted and Mum
signed the back of the cheque and "extra cheese," she said, "I feel
gooey tonight." I dialled Gigi's Pizza—the trick was to not ask if
they took welfare cheques until they showed up with a large with
everything on it.

We polished off everything except one piece and sat on the bed,
brushing off our hands over the box and laughing at what good
scammers we were. Mum told stories about when she was young
and I screened phone calls. She also let me take her old nail polish
off and paint on new stuff. Her hands were mostly stopped shaking, but I liked to be the one to paint her. I had to get rid of two
phone callers before I got a coat of *Peach Caravan* on every nail.

Being Mum's secretary was practically my favourite thing to
do. You had to have a good ear-memory and be able to tell who
the voices were plus remember if Mum liked them right now or
not. She was sick of most men and some women and my job was
to say she was out and have no idea where she was and then pretend to take a number and hang up. I could tape-record almost the
whole conversation in my brain, so after I hung up I could tell her
the words exactly and how they said them. Once in a while I got
to tell a guy to get lost, she didn't want to hear from him again;
that hardly ever happened, but it was the best.

Her nails were still wet from the second coat when her friend
Doreen called. I held the phone to her ear while she drooped her
hands out like rained-on flowers and told Doreen that her mani-
curist was on a tight schedule so be quick about it. I could hear
Doreen's loud gravelly voice from the earpiece.

I don't know why they suddenly got to be friends, but it seemed like they liked each other best when they were drinking. Doreen was a friend of Alice and Ray's, Sadie and Eddy's parents, and I saw her around their house or sometimes at Ray's used-furniture store. She was usually drunk and swearing and laughing at all the wrong times and wearing too-small clothes in super-bright colours that kept almost showing something every time she moved. She was around Mum's age with long black hair, high on top like a country singer, bright blue eyelids and frosty pink lips. Doreen was the only one lately who could get my mum out of bed by just talking on the phone a little. Mum talked a lot of pig Latin with her and the *ee-iz* language.

After three or four minutes she said goodbye and I hung up the phone. Mum stretched. "Well, I'm feeling not-too-baggy now."

"Wanna piece of chocolate cake? Actually, never mind, this one's no good, it's all salty, I think I must've put salt instead of sugar or something or maybe I put a tablespoon instead of a pinch or something."

"Yick. Why do you keep making chocolate cakes anyway? Seems like you've made about ten in the last month."

"I don't know. It's fun. I like measuring the stuff and I like icing it afterwards, making all those swirly-doos with the knife. And plus, it's nice to offer cake to guests when they arrive." I did like doing all the cookbook steps, but it was also because I kept hearing them say, "Tastes as if it was made from scratch," on cake-mix commercials and when I found out what it meant, I never wanted to buy another cake mix. I wanted to make my own just so I could say, "Here, would you like some Scratch Cake?" whenever I could. It sounded cool.

Mum snorted. "Guests! Well, la-dee-dah. Like who? Who comes over here?"

"Like. Well, guests! Like Josh maybe, or like Sadie and Eddy. Or Doreen even."

"You're one wacky dame, kiddo."

I cackled at her. I liked it when she called me a dame or a broad and I was just about to say we should pack up her pillows and blankets and go watch TV in the living room when she told me she was meeting Doreen in a while.

"Why! You're sick."

"Well, I'm not doing too bad now and I need some fresh air and the thing is, we haven't got a dime in the house." She sat up and pulled off her nightie and held it in front of her boobs. "Can you pass me my bra hanging on the doorknob there?—and a friend of mine owes me some money, so we're going to go over and say hi and maybe I can get us a little moolah."

I passed her her bra. She looked tired, her eyes were deep in her head and the skin was drooping off her arm-bones. It took ages for her to get her bra on and I didn't help, just told her, "Be careful of your nails." She asked me to grab her a pair of under-pants from her drawer. She wanted a good pair and I couldn't see much difference. I said that and "Who's going to see them any-way?" "Well, I might get in a car accident." Then she got up and went to her closet, turned back around and went through the stuff tangled in sheets at the foot of her bed. She found her baby blue sweater and held it up in front of her, looking for dirt. She sat at the foot of the bed to scratch off some crusty yellow gook on the sleeve, then pulled it over her head and did a fast makeup job before the garter belt, stockings, skirt and shoes came on. Then more scrounging in her dresser while she tried to bribe me— she said, "How 'bout tomorrow night we get some junk food and play switcheroo—it's a good TV night, isn't it, isn't tomorrow night when *Happy Days* and *Good Times* are on?" She dropped a string of beads over her head. Switcheroo was what we called it when we couldn't decide what to watch and one of us jumped up and switched fast to the other show during the commercials or when we got bored. It was fun and there was action, but I was crabbed at her right now. I shrugged and looked at a hunk of pizza crust on the floor. I knew I should clean up a little, at least my own stuff, at least change the litter box, but I didn't feel like it. I figured most of it was hers anyway—the bottles, and they were mostly her clothes chucked around the room. A lot were probably mine too, but I made chocolate cake yesterday, I cooked; my work was done. The sink was full of cake dishes and Strawberry Quik milk glasses and they were starting to stink, but I was more in the mood to bust them all and make her get new ones. I thought about going downstairs and remembered Josh had some hockey-thing tonight. He decided lately that he wanted to try and be a jock-guy. Which reminded me about my baton lessons starting and I figured maybe I should just stay in and practise. Last time I'd tossed my baton I busted a vase, so I definitely wanted to practise tonight.

It was getting light out when Mum came in the next morning. She stunk when she kissed me and I couldn't get back to sleep. There was another hour before I had to get up and my eyes were stinging from staying awake to watch a horror movie.

I got up and tripped over a beer box she'd left in the doorway. In the kitchen I hucked the pizza box off the counter onto the floor so I could sit where it'd been and eat the last piece; cold pizza for breakfast was the best. I thought about getting Mum to order it more on school nights so I could have it for breakfast. Fast and good-for-you. She was snoring. She snored more when she was sick like this. We should go to Portland, I thought, maybe she'd go back to eating vitamins and brewer's yeast and reading Adelle Davis and maybe she'd take up sailing and Ian's dad would introduce her to a tall guy with glasses like George.

When I got home from school, nothing was changed. Except she had a bucket beside her bed again and she was whimpering. I still never did the dishes and everything smelled like sour milk and cat pee. Henry was sitting on the kitchen counter meowing. His

litter box was in the corner of the kitchen and he went on the
newspaper under it instead of in it today. I figured it was a hint
that he'd go in my bed next if I didn't do something. The phone
rang and my mum whimpered again.

It was Eddy. "Hi, what're you do—" and then banging and
Sadie's voice, "He said for *me* to call, stupid—Grace! Guess what!
Your dad's here." I thought she was about to tell me some dumb
joke until her dad grabbed the phone. "Hey, Grace? Hiya, uh,
guess who's here, I got Sadie to call in case your mum answered—
your dad's here! At the store! He's sittin' right in front of me, right
this minute!"

I took the phone down the hall and whispered, "My dad?"

"Yeah! Can you get down here? He'll be here for a little while.
Don't tell your mother, now,—can you get down here?"

"Um. Yeah. At the store?"

I hung up and tried to get his face in my mind. I could sort of
see him. Or maybe just hear him. Actually, I didn't know if I'd
even recognize him. Mum coughed and asked who was on the
phone. I told her it was Sadie and I was going out to play. Then
the buzzer went. It was Doreen. Mum was too sick for her right
now, but I buzzed her up anyway.

I opened the door to Doreen wearing a silver coat with a bottle of wine under one arm and a white bag that smelled like food
under the other. Tons of makeup on, like she thought she was Miss
America, as usual. She barged past me, saying, "Hi hon," and
tromped her high heels to the bedroom. "Jesus, Eilleen, you look
like shit. But looky here, doll, I brought you a little hair of the dog
and a scrumptious barbecue chicken." Mum made a noise like she
was going to barf. Doreen untied her coat. "Christ, open the window; joint smells like something died."

When I got to the store, my chest was killing and my spit
tasted like blood from running so hard. I shoved open the door
and the bell jingled. Everyone was at the back of the store, so I

moved through the faded junk and old armchairs and lamps, throw rugs and wood cabinets, being careful not to bust anything. Someone whispered "Grace" behind me. I turned fast and knocked my head against a lampstand, then grabbed it before it wobbled right over. But there was no one there. There was no time for them now—no whispers, no voices. I turned around fast to make sure no one saw. I kept going to where Ray was chuckling and Sadie and Eddy were hollering at each other about whether white chocolate was really chocolate. Then the English Lady laughed in my head and said, "You are little more than a dog." Something got knocked over and what sounded like a million beans bounced on the floor. "Shut up!" I was grateful for her sometimes, like now when everything was loud like Sadie and Eddy and the beads bouncing and whispers. Except that I said "Shut up" this time, not her, I think. Because it got so quiet I tripped and fell on one knee.

A man on a stool swivelled around and watched me get up. It was my dad all right. "Yeah, you kids shut up back there," he said in a babyish voice over his shoulder at Sadie and Eddy. He grinned at me and stood up and held his arms out. I stayed where I was a second with my knee aching until I could breathe again and went to him, not knowing what to do with those arms—shake hands? Stand between them and get hugged? I couldn't remember us hugging before.

Sadie and Eddy were quiet a second, one of them poured another handful of the buttons back in the jar and they both said hi. Ray grinned from me to my dad. "She's big, eh! Skinny as a bloody Biafran, but she's gettin' big."

Dad was still grinning. "Com'ere and say hi to the old man," he said and put his palms on my ears. He didn't hug me exactly, he sort of patted my arms and shoulders like I just fetched a stick. He leaned down and we kissed each other's cheek. It was stiff kind of, and I was nervous about being there, telling lies and being a traitor, and worried the Shut Up Lady would start yapping at her dinner people again and I'd get all confused and he'd think I was stupid. So he said, "Hiya, how y'doin'? Sure *are* gettin' big. You're gonna be tall like your mother."

I smiled. Didn't know what to say. I wished he didn't bring her up. So Ray talked again. "She looks like you, though, eh Danny? Same kinda crazy eyes. Eilleen's always sayin' she looks like a wolf," and the two of them chuckled. Sadie and Eddy were back to arguing. Ray told them to simmer down and go play in the traffic.

"You like school?" my dad asked. "What're you in now, grade 3?"

"Four," I said, bugged that he didn't know. I stood a bit away from him now; I couldn't get comfortable being too near; I couldn't make him and "Daddy" go together. It would've been easier over the phone. Now it was all weird. He asked how my mum was. And then I got a big hunk of guilt where I used to have butterflies. She was fine, she had the flu today, I told him and felt like I said too much. He watched me and asked if I was ever going to come back to Toronto to visit him. I said maybe, then probably not, then that I probably wasn't allowed. The least I could do was show that she still said what went. Even if we were sneaking around behind her back right now, she was still Mum and he'd be stupid not to know it. I wanted to say how she was better than anybody he knew—smarter, funnier, prettier and taller, with redder hair and nicer nails and bigger boobs and higher heels, and she was crazy about me. And plus: if it wasn't for me she'd be dead because she told me so and that's more than I can say for you, buddy. "So I can't be here too long cuz I'm helping out around the house today." He smiled and nodded fast, then reached for his back pocket. I all the sudden noticed how perfect his slacks looked, how they fitted exactly to his waist, with no wrinkles except where his legs bent, and the shirt, how clean and orange it was. The collar was big and pointed and perfect. He took out his wallet and flipped it open.

It reminded me of this time in Toronto when I went with him

to the used-car place he worked at. Four or five guys were there in the office, sitting at a round table, smoking and telling stories, laughing crackly laughs and talking like the guys Mum pointed out in old movies. Guys she called heartthrobs, like Frank Sinatra and Tony Curtis. My dad's friends held their cigarettes and cigars the same kind of way, with their shoulders and heads tilted the same way, their eyes squinting, smoke curling up beside their noses. I wondered if they were like TV or TV was like them. Dad said, "Hi, what's doin'?" to the guys at the table and hung his coat on the rack. He told me to have a seat for a minute while he talked to Minky, in the back office.

I sat down beside Dad's friend Jacky. Jacky'd been at our house once. He took a drag off his cigarette and tilted his chin back to have a look at me. His eyes were sparkly blue and he had eyelashes like a pony. "How old are y' now, kid?"

"Seven."

"Huh. Got lots of boyfriends?" I shook my head and made a barf-face. They all chuckled and sipped their drinks, or flicked their smokes in the ashtray. Jacky reached in his pocket, took out a quarter and slid it to me with one finger. "That's for you." I grabbed it and said thankyou fast.

When Dad came out of the back room, I showed him and he made me give it back. I handed it to Jacky, grounding my teeth. From now on, I was keeping my mouth shut. Jacky picked some tobacco off his tongue, flicked it and winked at me. He glanced over his shoulder at my dad's back as he put his coat on. "Well, good to see you again, sweetheart," and he took my hand in between both of his, squishing the quarter against my palm. He winked one of his squinty eyes again. I winked back and dropped the money in my mitt before I put it on.

My dad's baby finger stuck out with a fat gold ring on it as he pulled a ten-dollar bill out. "Here. This is for you, yer birthday's comin' soon. Y'can get yerself a present." I took it and felt my chest falling into me. I wanted to get the money out of here before he changed his mind.

I said, "I think I'll put it in the bank."

His eyes sparkled up. "That's good. That's real good," as if I just did a perfect handstand or fetched a stick again.

I kept going. "Is my bank account that you opened for me in Toronto still open?" He said it was. "Cuz I was thinking maybe I should get that money and bring it to my bank account here. So I can really save it, you know? Could you maybe send it to me? Cuz there must be lots now, with the interest, huh?" I figured the five dollars he opened my account with would be around a hundred by now. After all, he told me he put a few more bucks in at my birthday last year and it'd been almost two years since we opened it. He chuckled and nodded.

Ray smiled hard and leaned against the counter, tapping a pen. "Chip off the old block, eh Dan—apple doesn't fall far from the tree." And they both laughed. I figured laughing was a good sign and I'd have my money in no time flat. As soon as he got back, he'd send it and Mum and I could use it to do whatever we wanted. I folded the ten and put it in my back pocket, then took it out again. "Maybe I should hold it so it doesn't fall out, huh?" My dad nodded and Ray laughed. "OK, um, well, I have to go, cuz I have to help out around the house." He patted my back and Ray told his kids to pipe down back there before he brained them.

Walking back home, I was all weird and quiet inside. I hugged my arms around my middle—sometimes that helped make the voices go away. They got tricked into thinking someone was with me, I guess. There were no voices then, but I just wanted to trick myself anyway. I wasn't with him hardly any time. And I didn't know if it should be a secret. Or nothing. Just a visit. Just another way to get ten bucks. And maybe she'd be proud of that. Or maybe she'd get mad and sicker.

Doreen was gone when I got back and Mum was curled on her side with a plate of chicken and rice beside her on the bed and a glass of wine on the nightstand. I stuffed the ten in my back pocket again. Mum said hi without moving. I asked where Doreen was. Mum said she took off without hardly saying goodbye but that I should have the chicken and rice she brought. I took the plate in the light to make sure it didn't have any spilled wine or hairs on it. Didn't look like Mum even touched it. I bit off some chicken and then spilled my guts—"Daddy's here. He was at Ray's store and I went down to see him."

She was quiet a second, then, "Son of a bitch," and quiet and then, "Why didn't you tell me you were going to see him? I probably would've said no."

I forked some rice in. "Well. Good that I didn't ask then." She glared at me and grumbled something in her pillow. "It was just for a minute and he gave me ten bucks." The chicken skin was the perfect crispiness and I folded it and stuffed it in my mouth.

She lifted her head. "Oh, he did, did he? Ten whole dollars. Stupid bastard." She reached for her wine, took a sip and set it back. "Ten bucks! Isn't that charming as hell. He doesn't pay a dime for child support but he can dole out a pittance and look like a big fucking shot. *This* ... shit hole—and he gives you ten bucks. La Dee Dah." That was twice she said la-dee-dah. It bugged me. Doreen said la-dee-dah. And usually Mum never said stuff like "shit hole" either.

I swallowed, "Yeah, but Mummy—"

"Mummy nothin'. Goddamn prick. Ten bucks. From now on you tell me if he calls here. I don't want you alone with him, and if he ever comes to your school, you don't go anywhere with him."

I kept stuffing my face. "Why not? He's my *father*," and she said nothing. "Mum!"

"Because. I said so."

"Why!"

"Because he might just grab you—that's why. Kidnap you and take you back to Toronto. You think you're so smart but that kind of stuff happens, you know, men stealing kids from their mother and nobody hears from them again." She reached for the wine and knocked a bottle of aspirin on the floor.

"He is not going to grab me. He didn't even hug me. He can't just grab me—I could escape! Nobody can just *grab*. You're being goofy." I scooped the rest of the rice up in my fingers, dropping some down my shirt and on the bed.

"I mean it, Grace, I mean it. I'm telling you, if I ever lost you, if you ever disappeared, if anything ever happened, I'd die. I. Would. Die," and her eyes welled up. "Just please do what I say and don't be a smartass ... please." She hugged the side of her pillow. I finished the rest of the plate.

The buzzer went. It was Doreen. Again. I didn't want her here. "Mum's just sleeping right now."

"Yeah, sweetheart———" (static scratched through half of what she said) "———OK, so I just gotta come up for a sec." I wiped my mouth and thought a second, then buzzed her in, listening by the door before I opened it. There were other feet; she wasn't alone. She was bringing people over? Fine, then—she was going to get the big kiss-off like the guys on the phone. I opened the door to her and two cops.

The cops smiled and scrunched their leather. Doreen's smile looked all like she felt sorry for me or something. "Let us in, sweetheart. You see this," she said to them and flapped her hand at me. She yanked one of the cops by his sleeve and I moved out of the way. She waved her arms and her silver coat around, yapping away in that voice of hers that sounded like a crow with a hangover. "She's got a little girl here and she's taking pills and booze—she's trying to kill herself. She's gonna end up dead and this little one here—just come on and take a look at this place, she's trying to kill herself." And they all clunked down the hall to the bedroom. My heart started going and I couldn't figure out how to stop them. Too many people. And there shouldn't be cops. And they shouldn't be looking at her when she's sick. I ran after them. Wishing Sadie and the Shut Up Lady would scream their guts out at them all.

One cop moved in to the head of Mum's bed, talking all slow and dumb, like she was about three. "Hi there, what's going on? You've got some people pretty concerned about you here. Have you been drinking?" And he picked the empty bottle that the yellow pills used to be in off her night table, while the second cop poked around and Doreen blabbed about dying and the child and pills and booze.

I yelled over her and the cop, cuz they were acting like I wasn't there—"She has the flu, she's just taking 222s. It's just, it's for a— she's trying to sleep and she had a headache." The second cop backed me out and took me down the hall while I tried to catch what else they said behind me.

He sat me down on the couch and I suddenly remembered Henry's litter box because of how had it smelled. Mum's voice was small and shaky from the bedroom. The first cop clomped back toward us and left Doreen in there. The two of them sat on either side of me on the couch with their belts and holsters squawking every two seconds. I got up and started back to the bedroom. "That's OK, maybe you oughta just stay here and have a chat with us." I didn't see who'd said that, but I stopped and sat on the arm of the chair. Henry jumped on the coffee table and tiptoed around it until they patted him.

"He's a pretty nice kitty. He's got nice stripes," the first cop said, and I wished he'd shut up so I could hear what Doreen was up to now. "Your name's Grace, is that right?"

"Yeah."

"I'm Officer James and this is Officer Duncan. Have you had anything to eat today? Did your mummy make you any dinner?"

"Um, yeah."

"What did you have?"

"Um, no, I mean, I'm not hungry. There's chocolate cake. Made from—would you like some Scratch Cake?"

"No thanks. Grace, your mummy's not doing too good. She might need to go to the hospital. Do you have any relatives you could stay with for a few days?"

"Um, no, I should stay here—she's just got the flu, y'know. Doreen doesn't know anything. She's not really that, um—there's just aspirin there and that's all she took. She's fine, though. We're fine. Everything's OK, y'know." They both nodded and smiled and patted my cat.

VANCOUVER

POLICE
DEPARTMENT

312 Main St., Vancouver, B.C., Canada V6A 2T2, Tel (665-3433) Telex 04/508501

R.J. Winterspoon
Chief Constable

November 1974

Vancouver Resource Board
Main Office
2075 W. 7th Ave.,
Vancouver, B.C.

Dear Sir:

The following report is forwarded to you
for your information.

Yours truly,

L.L. Dale
Staff Inspector i/c Information
& Communications Division.

V.P.D. 198-MLH-62

MISCELLANEOUS AND SUPPLEMENTARY REPORT

NATURE OF COMPLAINT Information re Neglected Child   CASE NO.

| COMPLAINANT | On View | PLACE OF OCCURRENCE | #7-4789 Main | PAT.AREA RPT.ZONE |

| ADDRESS | PHONE | DATE AND TIME REPORTED | October 28/74 | 18:30 |

A/m time and date u/s attended at #7, 4789 Main St.,
re a possible sick woman. Found Mrs. Eilleen Haufman, Nee
Ellison lying in bed in advanced state of intoxication.
The bed clothes were wet with urine and blood, as well as
spilled wine. The room was littered with empty beer and
wine bottles and the entire apartment filthy -- spilled
flour, pet excrement, dirty dishes, and clothing.

Eilleen

~~Grace~~ Haufman was so drunk she couldn't stand let alone
look after the child. There was no food fit for human
consumption in the apartment. It appears the child has
been surviving on a chocolate cake and little else and
that Mrs. Haufman has been drunk for several days.
Husband has left -- n/k whereabouts.

This situation needs attention form the Resources Board
Peolpe immediately if not sooner. The little girl cannot
be left alone and if there were an emergency the mother
is incapable of walking due to drink.

The daughter attends Wolfe School during the day.

TIME SPENT ON CALL _____ MINS.
HRS   TOTAL VALUE PROPERTY $_____

CASE DECLARED		BULLETIN
_____ UNFOUNDED	INVESTIGATED BY PC 370 Samuel CAR _____	
_____ INACTIVE - NOT CLEARED		FILE
_____ CLEARED BY ARREST	APPROVED BY _____ SQUAD _____	
OR SUMMONS	V. Resource Board Counsellors	COPY
_____ CLEARED OTHER MEANS	COPIES TO _____	
		APPROVED
BY _____	TYPED BY _____ TIME _____ INDEXED _____	RPT CPL
DET SERGEANT		

Hoffman, Anne Eilleen

28.10.74 (T. Baker) Police investigated Mrs.
Hoffman's apartment after complaint re neglect.
Mrs. H. in advanced state of intoxication, apartment
a shambles, unable to care for child. See police
report of this date.

29.10.74 (T. Baker) Visit in evening by social worker
and homemaker, Mrs. Anderson. Mrs. Anderson refused
to stay but later changed her mind and stayed for two
and a half hours, cleaning up the worst parts of the
mess. Mrs. Hoffman apparently incoherent for the du-
ration, and accused Mrs. Anderson of being a spy.
Social worker returned with police liason worker at
7pm but building was locked. Child involved is Grace
Hoffman, age 8, who attends Wolfe Elementary. She is
apparently very protective of her mother.

30.10.74 (T. Baker) Case assigned to me. Visit in
morning with Coordinator. Mrs. H. still drinking,
apartment a shambles. Mrs. H. at least ambulatory,
which was an improvement but she was not terribly
coherent. She agreed she needed help as she could
not manage things any more. Agreed to work with me
towards that end.

Back at the office in discussion with Coordinator, to
see hwat could be done to gx help Mrs. H. back on
her feet--perhaps homemaker could go in to clean up
mess, perhaps Mrs. H. could go into detoxification
center for a while. Decided to try this rather than
apprehend child immediately.

31.10.74 (T. Baker) Call to Homecare--they agreed
that they could go in to clean mess up, although only
once Mrs. H. was out of home. Mrs. Anderson refused
to go back with what I thought was good reason. I
went out and saw Mrs. Pong (Landlady) who told me that
she'd been receiving complaints for quite some time
regarding Mrs. H.'s drinking and carrying on. This
was confirmed by downstairs neighbor Sheryl Sugarman
and Mrs. Voigt, another neighbor. Apparently this
latest binge has lasted abut 3 weeks, xx and Mrs. H.
has been on previous binges in the last few months.
The neighbors regretted not having called us earlier.

Mrs. Pong had an eviction notice for Mrs. H. and asked me to go with her as she was afraid that Mrs. H. might get violent. Mrs. H. did become abusive and threatening (she is almost twice as big as Mrs. Pong) but I managed to calm the situation. Mrs. H. and I had a long talk. Her preoccupation is with herself, her problems etc. She agreed that she needs to go into a program-- she had been in AA and had managed well until this summer when she began popping pills again then drinking. Grace came home from school this afternoon and soon left to go to "Alice's"--a friend of her mother's at 4788 Quebec as tonight was Halloween and she was going out with Alice's children. Grace seemed very protective of her mother. After Grace left, Mrs. H. expressed various complaints about doctors and relatives and said she was afraid of the withdrawal associated with stopping her drinking. She continued to sip at it k her beer during the entire interview.
Sheryl Sugarman has agreed to look in on Grace over the weekend.

1.11.74 Spoke with L.B. Henighan, who has been Mrs. H's physician for some time. He does not really want to get involved, as he has worked quite hard with Mrs. H. but can see no motivation on her part to change her ways. He said she was hypoglycemic, which results from liver damage (alcoholism) and causes low blood sugar, anxiety/depression, tremors, etc. He has put Mrs. H. on medication to control this but she usually goes back to drinking. He suggested my getting her to VGH and getting in touch with a relative. (We have no addresses, however) Late afternoon -- Mrs. H. called to say she is willing to go into a program.

2.11.74 Called all detoxification centres on file including Dr. Amy Nielson of Metropolitan Health and Dr. Henighan again. All agencies simply referred me to other resources or each other. Mrs. H. cannot get into a treatment program until she is de-toxed and there is no centre for women alcoholics. Dr. Henighan still does not feel he should get involved.

Mrs. H. seen. After long talk, she agreed to sign non-ward consents, as Grace would need a place to stay if she were entering treatment program. Still drinking,

apartment still a mess but she was more lucid than on
Friday. Grace was there and understood situation.

After leaving Hoffmans, I interviewed Sheryl Sugarman
and son, Josh. They told me that about 2 weeks ago,
Mrs. H. came up to their apartment with a knife, quite
drunk and insisting that there was a man in her apartment who wanted to "get" her. She was satisfied only
after Mrs. S's brother, who was visiting at the time,
took her through the apartment. Mrs. H also bangs on
the Sugarmans` door at all hours and does the same to
other tenants. Was also seen by Mrs. Pong threatening
children out front of the building with broom handle.
She also prostitutes quite a bit --brings variety of
strange men home. Mrs. Sugarman said she brought in
four different men on Saturday night, said this was
common, this was how Mrs. H. got extra money. She expressed great concern for Grace in this respect as her
mother was constantly drunk and not very selective about
the type of men brought in. Also she said that Mrs. H's
sex was quite loud, and would be obvious to Grace in a
one-room apartment. She said there was at least one
occasion where Mrs. H. has come home at 4:00 am xdxxd
and that her coming home late was not unusual. (Mrs.
Sugarman must open the door for Mrs. H. who forgets her
keys). They said that Mrs. H. has collapsed in the
hallway as a result of drinking and pills.

Mrs. Sugarman mentioned that she had taken Grace in
quite often, stating that Mrs. H. had a very poor idea
of nutrition and that her housekeeping is very poor
even when she was sober. Mrs. Sugarman had had helped
Grace with her homework last school year, when Grace
received xx mostly A's (despite the fact that she was
in three different schools) but that Grace was (understandably) doing very poorly this year. It seems
Grace has trouble with the simplest math problems.
She also has noticed nervous reactions in Grace
(twitches, sudden uncoordinated movements) that had
not existed before. She believes that Grace may be
suffering from hypoglycemia as well as stress-related
reactions to poor nutrition and Mrs. H's lifestyle.
She described Grace as being "shell-shocked")

3.11.74 (T. Baker) Vancouver General is the only
resource for drying Mrs. H. out, but Dr. Henighan is

doubtful that she would be admitted. Foster home
arrangements being set up for Grace. VGH said they
would do nothing about getting Mrs. H. admitted but
referred me to Downtown Care Team who were sympathetic
but could do nothing until Mrs. H. was admitted to VGH.

Saw Mrs. H. again: she complained of internal pain,
sleepiness, dehydration, muscle stiffness. Agreed to
enter a ꞵꞮꞥꞡ program and agreed that Grace would have
to go into foster care. Agreed to sign into VGH.
Drinking somewhat less, mentioned that she felt
suicidal but that Grace kept her going.

Sheryl Sugarman seen: offered to take Grace in for a
few days but this is impossible with Mrs. H. still in
building. She said that Mrs. H. had come in after 4
am yesterday. Grace was apparently alone until then.

Mrs. H. is not making any effort to stop drinking.
Grace will have to get out of this environment soon.
NOte that Mrs. H. has told me that she will leave the
city with Grace if I try to apprehend.

CONSENT OF PARENT(S) TO CUSTODY
CHILD CARE AND MEDICAL ATTENTION

(Complete one for each child)

....

THIS AGREEMENT AND CONSENT made on the __3rd__ day of

___November___ 19 __74__ BETWEEN: The Superintendent

of Child Protection for the Province of British Columbia and

_____Eilleen Hoffman_____

Name(s) of Parent(s)

of___#7-4789 Main Street_____, ___Vancouver_____ in the

address   city

Province of British Columbia

STATES THAT

___Grace Hoffman_____, born ___November 24 1965___

(Name)

is in need of care for the reason that :

___Mother will be entering a treatment program for___

___alcoholism and will not be able to care for Grace___

___until after the program._____

_____

_____

Recognizing that the Parent(s) continue to be the legal guardians
of the said child, and the Superintendent Hereby Agree that the
Superintendent will provide care and supervision of the said child

for a period of ___three_____month(s)/~~week(s)~~ beginning the date of

___November 3_____ 19_74___ (initially not to exceed 3 months).

THE SUPERINTENDENT FURTHER AGREES:

1. To provide suitable food, shelter, clothing and health care for the child.

2. To provide the following specific services to the child: whatever services are needed in regard to continuing school attendance (General Wolfe Elementary)

3. To provide the following specific services to the parent(s): Arrangements for proper treatment program and ongoing service.

4. To consult with the parent(s) as soon as possible concerning any unplanned situation which the Superintendent considers to be of a serious nature.

THE PARENT(S) FURTHER AGREE:

1. TO CONSENT TO THE SUPERINTENDENT or his delegates authorizing and providing such medical or surgical treatment as necessary.

2. To keep the SUPERINTENDENT or his delegates informed of their place of residence at all times.

3. To maintain regular contact with the child as agreed.

4. To work actively with the SUPERINTENDENT or his delegates in resolving the difficulties causing the child's placement in care. These efforts will include: Agreeing to enter and complete a rehabilitation program for alcoholism.

5. To pay nil monthly towards the maintenance of the child or to authorize the SUPERINTENDENT to be payee, as trustee on behalf of the child for Family Allowance payments received during the period the child is in care.

The PARENT(S) and the SUPERINTENDENT FURTHER AGREE THAT THIS AGREEMENT AND CONSENT may be terminated upon one week's notice by either Party to the other, or upon an Absence Without Leave by a child of more than 10 days.

DATED THIS ___third___ day of ___November___ 19 74 ___.

Signed, Sealed and Delivered By The Parties in the presence of

_____   *Eillen Hoffman*
      Parent   Parent

_____   The Superintendent of Child
      Witness   Protection per

                      Todd Baker
                      His duly authorized agent

Inclusion of child—this Agreement has been shared with me and explained by the Social Worker

_____
      Child's Signature

Interpretation

1.   Time   (a)   The initial period of care under this AGREEMENT AND CONSENT cannot be longer than three months and may be renegotiated for no longer than 6 months. Any subsequent renewals cannot be for longer than 6 months.

           (b)   EACH renegotiation should involve a discussion among the social worker, the parent(s), and a third party mutually agreed upon and acting for the child's best interests. Where appropriate the child should be included.

2.   If parents do not keep the SUPERINTENDENT or his delegate informed of their whereabouts and contact with their child also lapses, and if efforts by the SUPERINTENDENT to locate the parent(s) fail, the child will have to be apprehended under the Protection of Children's legislation.

3.   Agreeing to TERMINATION ON ONE WEEK'S NOTICE BY EITHER PARTY recognizes the need to prepare the child for a move back to his own family, in terms of school, health reports, preparing clothing, etc.

4.   HEALTH CARE - includes medical, dental, optical, psychological and psychiatric services and prescribed medicines. While in the custody and care of the SUPERINTENDENT the child will be enrolled in the B.C. Medical Plan and be covered for all these services. However, when the AGREEMENT ends, so does this coverage.

Grace Nine

NOVEMBER 1974

M RS. GERBERT, the PE teacher, went off to the side of the gym when a man came through the doors and nod-ded at her. In a few seconds my name got called and I dropped my hula hoop, glad not to have to keep doing that thing with my hips. When I got close to Gerbert and the guy, I realized it was Todd Baker, the social worker who'd been over at our place lately. He was OK; I only talked to him enough to know he thought Mum should go in the hospital for a while to dry out and I should stay with some foster family even though Sheryl Sugarman, Josh's mum, said I could stay with them for a bit, but Todd wasn't that crazy about the idea so it made me not that crazy about him. Mum didn't like him period; she said he was a draft dodger. Cuz he was American and around his late twenties. *Draft dodger* started sound-ing like *weasel.*

He wanted to talk to me in the hall a minute and chewed on his thumb-skin when we were going out the door. "So listen, uh, I—there are some people I'd like you to meet this afternoon. The lady's name is Mrs. Hood and she has two girls around your age. I think you'll like them." He said it like they were pals of his and it took me a few seconds to figure out they were foster people.

"When? you mean, like, to go now?" I was nervous. About things like, *He could grab you; Never leave the school grounds with a stranger; Never get in a car; If your father comes around, don't go near him.*

"Yeah. Well, right, after you get changed. I spoke with your principal and it's fine for you to miss music class under these circumstances." He smiled. I didn't get how a person could smile like that after they said "under these circumstances."

On the ride over, Todd Baker made small talk, the usual: do you have any pets? how many sisters do you have? what is her name? So I started telling him about how Charlie had a baby and how she just moved down to Portland last week with her boyfriend to sell sportswear and that as soon as she had an address and got settled and stuff I'd be visiting her all the time. Then he asked how old she was. I told him eighteen. Then he goes, "Oh, so you were kind of an afterthought." As if I didn't count so much or something.

"No. If you mean like an accident, I wasn't. My mum wanted me, she wanted to have me. My sister has a different father and when my mum met my dad, they wanted a child together, that's all. She didn't have to have me if she didn't want to."

"So your sister is actually a half-sister, then."

"No. She's my sister, my real sister. She just has a different father than I do."

"Well, isn't that what a half-sister is?"

"No. She isn't. We both have the same mother, we both came out of her womb, so we're whole sisters. It's—that only counts if you have different mothers and you live with them and don't even see each other, and just have the same father but weren't all in the same womb. And we were. She's *not* a half-sister."

He said, "Oh," and dropped it, but it was bugging me the way he was trying to make me feel like we weren't really related, make us be less of a family so this wouldn't seem such a big deal. I was going to have to make sure he knew that I knew what was what.

It was a real house, not an apartment. And the street had tons of trees, orange and red leaves all over the place. It looked like a neighbourhood; no gas station on the corner and the houses were made of wood and brick, no stucco. A fat grey Persian lay in the window, still as a rock, and I half wondered if it was stuffed. Todd stuck his thumb in the buzzer and the door swung open hardly a second after.

She looked like a mum: her hair was blue-black, slicked back in a bun, and she had on an apron over her blouse and pants. Her nose had big sideways nostrils and she had fat lips that flattened wide when she smiled and helloed. She had little teeth, but there were a lot of them. We took off our shoes at the door and she patted her thighs before she led us in. Wendy and Lilly, her girls, would be home any time now, she said; the school was quite close.

Their kitchen was as big as our living room but bright with white see-through curtains. It reminded me of the kitchen at our house in Toronto, the one with my dad. Todd and I sat at the table and Mrs. Hood made us tea. I explained how my mum liked me to have it half milk. She smiled and said that was a good idea. Todd chuckled and chewed the inside of his cheek, then started asking Mrs. Hood about her girls and their hobbies and stuff; he told her about my baton lessons. And about Explorers. He kept nodding and grinning, making his eyes go wide, and I tried to act like it was interesting. A skinny cat with hardly any tail walked in the room and made it easier.

Mrs. Hood set the teapot on the table. "That's Spike," she said, "he's Lilly's cat—where's your ball, Spike?" Spike charged back to the living room right when the front door opened and slammed, shaking the windows. Mrs. Hood tilted her head toward the front of the house. "Hello-o?" and then a hello back from two girls. Then shoes clunking and sock-feet rubbing toward the kitchen.

The two of them came in and stood in the middle of the floor, all half-smiles and bored sort of hellos. Wendy and Lilly. Wendy was the bigger one, eleven. Lilly was eight. I'd be nine in two weeks, older than her. Todd said on the way over that Lilly was in grade 3. She looked it. I knew we wouldn't be friends. Lilly looked like what Mum called a sprite: a puny head, too-big black eyes, bee-size mouth and two black braids that hung long over skinny-boned shoulders. She looked tricky. She looked like she bit. Her sister was thicker: thicker lips, thicker hair, a thicker body. Her eyes were slower. Their mum introduced us and said, "Grace might be staying with us for a little while." Wendy nodded.

Lilly's eyes poked over me. "What school do you go to?" I told her. "Do you know a boy called Tom?" I didn't. Nobody said anything, so Wendy said she was going up to change and Lilly ran upstairs behind her—the steps to their bedrooms were in the kitchen like Sadie and Eddy's place. Todd gave me one of those fake kind of smiles like teachers use the first day of school and I copied it.

When we finished our tea, Todd told Mrs. Hood we had to get going. She stood and wiped her hands on her apron, said it was lovely to meet me and led us to the door, talking about umbrellas. Todd and I clomped down the wet steps; it'd started to rain. Neither of us said anything until we were back in the car.

He turned the ignition. "So? Did you like them?" And the wipers rubbed squeaks and grunts against the window.

"Yeah. They were pretty nice." If they were his friends I didn't want to talk bad about them. And they did seem pretty OK and

I'd probably like them better if I knew them. "Mrs. Hood was nice and I liked Spike." I waited. I wanted to meet whoever else he had in mind before I decided.

Todd watched me and rocked his head up and down. "Well, I mean, do you think you might like to stay here while your mom's in the hospital?" He said *Mum* like *Mawm*. It sounded fakey or prissy or something.

"Um, here? Well, I guess so. Yeah, sure. What about my cat, because I have to have Henry with me, so I don't know."

"Well, no, you couldn't bring Henry, someone else would have to look after him. It wouldn't be for long, I'm sure we could find someone." He looked so big on the whole thing that I didn't want to be a pain. Mum was always calling me a fuss-budget about stuff so I thought maybe I should just stick it out for a few days. Todd smiled and grabbed the pack of cigarettes from his pocket. "Good." He stuck one in his mouth. "OK, let's go back to your place and get your things together." He lit one and sucked it like there was milkshake on the other end. "The sooner you're taken care of, the sooner we can start taking care of your mom." The engine shook as he put it in gear and started down the street.

"Yeah but. Um. Well yeah, but does my mum know? I can't just go if my mum doesn't know," and I didn't think she did really. Of course she did, Todd told me, she signed the consent didn't she. Yeah, but. She changed her mind. She told me the night before that she didn't want me going anywhere, she couldn't bear it. Todd just talked about the hospital and her drinking and how much better things would be. I figured he was right; if I left, she wouldn't have any excuse, she'd have to go wherever it was she went when she quit drinking. And in a few days I could come home and the place would be clean and we could pack up and move. I could start a new school and maybe we could live on a street with trees.

When we got home, Henry slithered through my shins and made his chirpy meows at me. I kneeled and scratched his head, picked him up, and Todd asked if I had a suitcase. I stood still, breathing Henry's fur, and thinking how much worse everything looked when a stranger was in the house, how bad it smelled, how dirty it still was even since the Welfare sent someone over to clean it up. I was a traitor again and I kept my nose in Henry's shoulder. Todd looked fidgety. Neither of us was saying so, but half the game was getting out before she came home. If she caught us, if she caught me leaving with a bag of clothes, she'd go crazy. Henry wiggled away and jumped on the floor. There was probably a suitcase somewhere, but I didn't feel like stealing Mum's to run away from her.

Todd went to the kitchen and came back with a garbage bag. "OK, let's try to grab as much as we can so you can have a few things with you." We picked through my drawers and stuff lying around the bedroom. Todd winced when he picked my clothes off the floor. I didn't look at him again until he brought me back to the Hoods'. Then I didn't want him to leave.

He sat in the living room with Lilly and me while we watched Wendy show off Lilly's cat: she threw a red ball, the kind I used to play jacks, and Spike scrambled down the living room to get it. He pounced and bit and clawed it with his back legs before chomping it up and trotting back to Wendy's feet. He dropped it there and looked up at her. She threw it again and Spike fetched. I looked at Lilly; she sat straight like a spelling-bee kid, all proud of herself. The Persian never moved from the windowsill. She was Wendy's cat—her name was Marble and nobody said much else about her. Then Lilly squealed and said, "Show her hockey."

Wendy grabbed the ball and all of us followed her to the bathroom. Lilly was second through the door, said "Gimme," and took it out of Wendy's squishy thick hand. "Com'ere Spike, com'ere boy," and she threw the ball in the bathtub. Spike leaped in and fwapped the ball around the sides, then bounced back to guard the drain, batting it just in time to keep it out of the hole. Todd chuckled over my shoulder and I could hear teeth clicking from biting his nail. The ball boinged off the side of the tub and plopped in the drain. Spike pounced and growled, tore it out of the hole and ripped at it with his back claws, before he chucked it down the tub and went back to playing goalie. Todd nudged me. "Pretty good, eh?"

After he left, the house was strange and prickly. Nobody said much. We had hamburgers for dinner at the dinner table, not in front of the TV. And they didn't know how to play switcheroo, so we just watched *Happy Days* until it was bedtime for Lilly and me. It bugged me going to bed when she did. I was practically nine.

I took the bus to school the next day and daydreamed about Mum, what she did when she came home and found me gone. Todd said he was going over there when he left me. But he couldn't talk to her really, not like me. I wanted to be the one to talk to her, but he told me not to call. None of my friends even knew where I was. Nobody did. If I never went to school that day they would've thought I disappeared, which I kind of liked—the mystery of it—but then I still didn't have much friends at my new school, so they might not've even noticed. I wondered if Mum was in the hospital or in her bed right now. Probably crying. Maybe she had to cry, though, maybe she had to just cry out everything until she got better.

After school, Mrs. Hood picked me up and took me to get my hair cut. She scowled at me in the mirror while the hairdresser pumped my chair up. She didn't really look as mum-ish as I thought. She told the hairdresser to just try and make me look presentable, told me she was going to go have a coffee and left us staring at the mirror.

The hairdresser picked some hair from the side of my head, sighed, and let it drop before bringing me to a sink. I thought about the way Todd took my clothes up off the floor, like he was picking up snotty Kleenex. She tied a brown plastic bib on me, then wound a towel round my neck and lowered me back against the sink. My neck didn't go down the way she wanted, in the groove thing on the sink. She huffed and pulled me back up, pushed me back down, nudged the chair closer to the sink. She blew air out her nose, left and came back with three towels for me to sit on. When she finally had my head where she wanted, she soaped it up and then kinda stared around my ears and said, "When's the last time your hair was washed?" She sounded like her face when she first touched my head.

I didn't know. I said, "Probably day before yesterday." She hmmed and scrubbed harder. I shut my mouth and kept it shut till she finished the haircut. My eyes hurt from not crying and I imagined horrible things my mother would do to her for this.

Next morning was the doctor's appointment. We sat in the waiting room for around half an hour, Mrs. Hood flipping through magazines, her lips squishing up under her nose at stuff she was reading. I watched the glass door we came in through to see my reflection; see, if I looked quick and pretended not to know me, if my hair really looked like Keith Partridge. The receptionist called "Hoffman" and I went frozen. Mrs. Hood nudged me. I went to the counter; the receptionist smiled. "Hi there, how are you today? Here, maybe you can just go to the bathroom and bring me back a sample." I took the cup and the key and went down the hall. I figured she meant pee but I wasn't sure exactly, and if she meant pee, how much did she want? And how was I supposed to hide a cup of it coming back?

Then the key didn't fit the lock. I tried it upside down. Didn't fit. I went back to the receptionist, trying not to touch my hair again and draw attention. I asked her if it was the key to the girls' room.

"No sir!" She said it loud and smiled big like she was in a talent show or something. "That's for the boys'."

I put the key on the counter. "I'm not a boy."

Her face kept still a second till it went, "Ah—oh! I'm—" and she made tisky noises and shook her head and grabbed at my file. "Grr ... ace—of course you're not. Did I give you the boys' key? Here you go. Miss." Her smile was smaller.

I brought back the cup mostly full and a nurse took me in a room and asked me to take off everything except my underpants, said she'd be right back. She didn't leave me anything to put on. Mum's doctor always gave me a paper poncho. I took off my clothes and sat scrunched on the table with my hands between my knees, feeling the room breathe on me until she came back. She was pretty with a hoppy ponytail. She wrapped the black band thing around my arm, pumped it tight and asked about what I did that day, if I had a bowel movement. Figured it probably meant pee again, so I just said yes. She asked me what it was like, I told her regular. When the black band thing was loose again, she took it off my arm and asked about the colour; I said that was regular too. She asked me about sleeping, eating, aches and pains; anything I had to tell about, I called it regular. She seemed to think that was pretty funny and I liked her for it. I liked hearing someone laugh again and have it be cuz of me. When we finished she told me to sit tight, she'd be right back.

Kind of a while went by, and I was sitting there thinking how I was glad I ate lots of bacon and eggs and toast for breakfast and had good blood sugar cuz, God, it would've been crappy to hear the English Lady arguing or else whispers and stuff and be naked on top of it. I started thinking how Sheryl Sugarman was maybe right and smart and then I figured maybe I was supposed to get dressed and I was about to jump down, my chest all light again, when the nurse opened the door and came in with a little Chinese man. He was in a white coat and his face hardly moved. "Grace,

OK, this is Doctor Lee, he's going to examine you today," and she left.

I folded my arms. It was cold. He told me to lie on my back in not-that-great English and started looking over my whole skin and everything, pressing and knocking, asking if it hurt—breathe in, breathe out. Then he looked down my underpants. I was going to cry and I crunched my teeth together. He asked me to turn over on my stomach and asked where every one of the marks on my back came from. I fell and tripped so much, I couldn't remember how I got any, except for the big scar on my backbone that I had from sliding down the porch steps when Eddy chased me and Sadie. I said I fell, and Dr. Lee's face kept still and he sounded like he thought I was lying. He wanted me to explain better, but I didn't want to tell how Eddy was running after us with the *shitbag*, a paper bag of poo he said he found. I started making stuff up. Dr. Lee didn't look at my eyes; it was like I didn't have any.

I looked away and clenched some more and changed my mind: I wasn't going to cry, and I looked at the wall to think about something else. I saw his framed doctor certificate up there and two things cut out of the newspaper. I kept staring at the newspaper pictures until I figured out he was in both. One headline said "Child Abuse," and "Lee Heads C.P.A. Crackdown" was on the other; one picture showed just his face and one showed him at a table with some other people. He was some kind of famous doctor-guy. He wasn't just Dr. Lee, he was *the* Dr. Lee, Bad Mother Hunter. In my imagination I sat up and yelled, "She hits me." He wouldn't smile exactly, but he'd be glad or proud or something. I never said anything in real life though, so he pulled up the elastic on the back of my underpants and looked in at my bum. No one ever saw me without a paper poncho on and never without my mum in the room.

I closed my eyes. He was in on it too. They all wanted to trick me into saying something bad about her. She warned me. She said

it only took two doctors' signatures and they could put her away.
I kept my mouth as shut as I could; just yes and no. I wasn't going
to help him up on any more walls.

The next morning we sat over breakfast. I was taking more time
off school again because Mrs. Hood said I had to get new clothes
because Todd dropped off clothes vouchers and it would be best
if we got it over with today, especially if I was going to be switching schools. Lilly was crabbed. "How come I never get to take
school off to go shopping—you're the one who said I need new
shoes, but you take *her* instead."

Mrs. Hood brought a heavy black pan to the table, took her
flipper and slapped one pancake on each of our plates. I was only
half listening and couldn't figure out what she meant about switching schools. She told Lilly to stop being such a busybody. "You're
in nowhere near the situation that Grace is in." Lilly kept arguing
about the holes in her shoes and "you always do that" and "what
about me."

When it was quiet a second I said, "Well, I don't think it'll be
a big deal for me to miss a couple days of school and I'm fine taking the bus cuz it'll only be a few more days till my mum's better
anyhow and I can catch up on my normal school then. We're
probably moving anyway. We got evicted."

Lilly stopped chewing to stare at me. Wendy snorted and
started coughing on her pancake. Lilly giggled, drank some juice
and slapped her on the back. Wendy swallowed and said, "What's
it like to be evicted?" Mrs. Hood yelled Wendy's name at her and
Wendy kept going. "And who said anything about a few days, anyhow? You're here for way longer than that, kid, you're here till
February. Three months." She threw in that last part like it was
normal. Three months is three months.

"At least," Lilly said with chewed-up pancake practically falling out.

I tried to keep my voice normal. George told me one time about dogs and horses and how they could smell your fear. I could taste mine. I put my fork down. "No I won't. My mum'll be all right sooner than that. It's just for a bit." I picked my fork up again and everyone was staring at my hands and smelling their fear of forks, wondering what kind of idiot-kid has hands that can't use a fork properly. I didn't want pancakes anyway—Mum would've never let me eat white flour and syrup for breakfast. I'd get sick if I stayed here. I'd catch malnourishment. Adelle Davis's cookbook said children who aren't fed properly get misshaped bums and weird soft bones. My mum'd be mad if she saw me eating this way.

"No," Mrs. Hood said, "Wendy's right, you'll be here three months—until February."

I had a stomach ache. Todd Baker would have said something, he wouldn't have lied. I was getting dizzy cuz my bones were going soft probably and my blood was getting evaporated; there wasn't going to be enough left to hold me up that much longer. Mum always said I didn't have to do anything I didn't want. I wanted her so much. But she was probably in a hospital somewhere and I couldn't call her in front of them anyway. Wendy and Lilly glinted under the kitchen light, watching each other, cutting up their pancakes piece by piece. The air in my chest went thick.

"Will Grace be coming with us to Kingdom Hall?" Lilly asked.

Mrs. Hood put a bunch of pancakes on a plate and put them on the table. I whispered, "No thank you," and looked at Mrs. Hood to find out what Kingdom Hall was. It sounded fun, in a way, like there'd be a Ferris wheel and fairy princesses and stuff.

She said, "I don't know. We'll see if she'd like to. Have you been to a Kingdom Hall before, Grace?"

I shook my head.

"We're Jehovah's Witnesses," Lilly yapped. Loud, the same way she said "At least." I'd heard that name before and asked her what it meant. "It means we spread the message that Armageddon is coming soon and the lion will lie down with the lamb and birds will fly to your finger and me and Wendy are getting tigers after Armageddon!"

"No I'm not, 'member I told you I want to have a bear."

"Why do you wanna bear? They're all dumb and slow. What would you get, Grace? Except for you're not a Witness, so you won't be here when God puts Satan in chains. All the people who don't believe won't be, um, brought to life again after Judgment Day, like out of the ground, they just die and they don't get to be here when Jesus is building paradise and they just stay in death and get eaten by worms cuz, um ... but after the great battle, the ones of us that's—believe will be saved or they'll be, mm—resurrected if they already died, but the ones who don't will be killed when God gives Jesus the keys to rule the new earth. Only we get to live forever with Jehovah cuz we served him." She smiled like a pumpkin at me, threw a braid back over her shoulder and poured more syrup.

I looked at their mum. She was leaning back in her chair, sipping from her teacup. I looked back at Lilly, sick of her. "You can't have a tiger for a pet."

"Yes You Can!"

"Calm down, Lilly. If Grace wants to come to the next meeting, she can learn what it's all about then. You should go get ready for school anyway, and Grace and I have to get ready ourselves."

"Yeah Lilly," Wendy told her and whispered, "Little spaz," before she drank a whole bunch of orange juice to wash her pancake down.

"Shut up, Wendy, you're the spaz! I was just *telling* her! Cuz we're s'posed to! We're s'posed to *witness*, y'stupid!"

"OK, that's enough—get ready for school." Mrs. Hood stood and reached for Lilly's plate. "Grace, is that all you're eating?" I nodded.

Wendy let her eyelids droop at me as she came out from behind the table. "Won't get away with that for long," and she went upstairs; Lilly giggled and skipped behind.

Hoffman, Anne <u>Eilleen</u>

4.11.74 (T. Baker) Morning visit to Mr. Thompson,
principal at Wolfe Elementary. I had called previously
to briefly explain Gracee's home situation, her non-ward
status, and pending foster placement.

Two visits to Mrs. H. during the day -- not home.
Sheryl Sugarman did not know where she was.

Visit to Wolfe Elementary in afternoon. Grace seen
and new foster home placement explained to her.
This would be Mrs. J. Hood, 545 West 19th Avenue
(876-5374). Grace and I had quite a long talk then
went off to Mrs. Hood's. Mrs. Hood struck me as a
very warm, caring person, the house was very tidy, and
she and Grace got along very well. We returned to
Mrs. H's apartment and on the way, Grace was very
cheerful -- she liked Mrs. Hood very much, liked the
idea of having her own room. Mrs. H. not home when we
arrived -- we gathered up the basics that Grace needed
from among the clothing and junk strewn in tangles on
the floor. Many things were too filthy to take along,
or simply could not be found.

When we returned to Mrs. Hood's, Lilly (8 years, 3rd
Grade) and Wendy (11 years, 6th grade) were there,
Mrs. Hood's own children. I stayed for some time,
talked a great deal to both Grace and Mrs. Hood and
even played a game of "hockey" with the girls and one
of their cats. Grace got along well right away with
Lilly and Wendy, and seemed well settled by the time
I left.

I returned to Mrs. H's apartment and found her on the
floor at the bottom of the stairs leading to her
apartment. She was very drunk and had fallen down
the stairs. I had to help her up to the apartment as
she could not make it on her own. She explained that
she had spent the day in a hotel on Hastings Street.
Mrs. H. was wearing a very short-length, bright yellow,
sleeveless dress which mainly served to show off a
variety of bruises on her arms, shoulders, ad and
legs. Her face was also slightly bruised and she
could not remember how she got the bruises. I had
Wanted to take her to V.G.H. that afternoon but could

not see how that could be done without carrying her.
I explained that I had taken Grace to the foster home
and said I could not give her the address or phone
number now. I spoke with her for an hour,
without making any progress, then left asking her to
get some sleep.

5.11.74 (T.Baker) Sheryl Sugarman called to say that
Mrs. H. had called the police last night (after hours
of wandering the halls of the building calling
"Grace") to report her daughter missing. Luckily the
police saw Mrs. Sugarman first, who briefly explained
the situation. Call to Mrs. Hood -- everything all
right. Arrangements for initial clothing grant made.
Mrs. Hood was warned that Mrs. H. may cause trouble at
Wolfe, in which case Grace would have to switch
schools, to Edith Cavell.

Spoke to Mr. Pretty -- informed of situation, and that
Mr. Thompson, principal of Wolfe would call if there
is any trouble. Mr. Pretty made some calls and was
told that Mrs. H. has a record for soliciting, spent
some time in Kingston Penitentiary. He thinks this
problem could be solved if a complaint were made,
police could arrest her and then detox her. He
promised to call Downtown Care Team. I tried to call
our Health Care Team—no one available for a referral.

Later inday, received a call from the Downtown Care
Team, who said they wouldbe going out with their G.P.,
Dr. Klaus. Dr. Klaus later called saying x he and
Dr. Pantern (Now Mrs. H's psychiatrist) agreed to put
Mrs. H. in V.G.H. and to commit her if necessary.

At 5 p.m., I received a call from Alice Collingwood
(4788 Quebec) who had Mrs. H. with her and was about
to take her down to VGH immediately. I said I would
take her instead. Mrs. H. was very unsteady but we
made it to emergency but were refused admittance for
Mrs. H. Only after a two hour wait, when Dr. Klaus
showed up, was Mrs. H. admitted.

Eilleen Eight

NOVEMBER 1974

VANCOUVER GENERAL, in the basement. Seems like a
basement; green walls. Like snake innards. Walking down
tinny green-gone-wrong veins of a reptile. Baker's with you. He's
OK. Not so bad. You told him, call-me-Eilleen. Drove you down
here—he's helping you check in, trying to get you well.

It's echoey, wandering, nurses and patients all look out of
their minds. Weaving, everything's breathing and weaving until
you get to the counter. Baker talks to the nurse there; her smile
looks gluey. He's talking about admittance, this ward and Doctor
Graham, referrals, alcoholism, disorientation, blahahaha. Boring.
Let smarty-boots take care of all that crap. Your job is to dry out
like some boozy old grape. You'll get Grace back when you're a
raisin again. Kids love raisins.

Let's take a look round this rat trap; have a boo. Let them figure out the details. You poke your beak in a room. Jesus, nothing
in there but a mattress. And a basin, bleach-bone white. You
saunter in, see how the other half lives.

God almighty, what poor slobs end up in here? Hold tight to your purse, look up and down the box walls. White, everything white. Just a couple tiny smears, splotches, yellow-brown like baby shit. Dents here and there in the door frame; somebody took their boots to it. You get about the middle of the room—Christ knows how that mattress looks under the sheet—turn, swing your head in time to see the white door swing shut. And your heart hiccups, holds still. Oops.

Hey, you say, *heyy-ey. Yoo-hoo. Hey, open the door, you've*—and no knob on the door. There's no goddamn doorknob. Like the quiet room at the old Hollywood Hospital. You didn't *do* anything. You don't deserve the quiet room. *Hey!ey-ey-ey!* And you bang a palm twice. *You've locked the door here. Open the door.* Fist your palm. *Hey, open the door!* Baker. Baker did this. Fucking Baker—goddamn, let-me-help-you Baker. Yeah, he'll give you a ride. What a dear. Dear sweet Bastard Baker. *Open the f(ee-iz)ucking door before I bust it down. I mean it!* And you're kicking and punching and screaming and nobody's coming and nobody's talking, can't hear anything. Only takes two signatures. Two doctors could lock you away for good. Stand back, kick the door: nobody hears you, make more dents. FuckFuckFuck. Throw something, throw your purse. Slam it. Pick it up and slam it. Slam it again and say *Hear Me, you bastards.* Screaming, mascara and tears gluing your eyes, can taste blood in your mouth—kick the dents again. Kick them all. *You can't do this. You can't do this.* Nobody hears. They're going to get you this time. You signed your baby away. You didn't read the fine print. *Let me out, you pigs. You pricks. Can't do this.* What did you sign? You signed something for that nurse, didn't you? or was that just for Baker? Where did you sign? What did you say?

You drag your purse back off the floor, hurl it again and the door opens. Beefy boy in white: hospital bouncer—'member them? A nurse stands behind him, tight smile. *You'd best quiet down,*

Mrs. Hoffman, there are other patients on this ward, you know. And he moves in through the doorway, bends down.

Reason with him.

I'm not a patient here, I'm not—I didn't do anything. I'm not nuts. I'm hypoglycemic. And he stands up with your purse in one fisted mitt. You move towards him and stop. He looks like he could twist your arm, snap it off like Barbie's. You reach out your hand. He nods, passes your purse to the nurse, backs out. *That's— gimme my purse, you—Give Me My Purse!* Your voice rakes over the walls as you tackle the smooth door, banging, and trip. Your knees smash the floor. Two signatures, just takes two signatures. Get up, get up, don't stay down. Find something, a weapon. Baker must be there, he just can't hear you. You can't be in the psych ward, you're not a psych. Just a goddamn lush, that's all.

Nothing. No knobs. Think.

Thinking.

Fuck. Pace. Pace the room. The basin, grab the basin, make someone hear. Get them to the door. Someone will know when they see you, it's a mistake.

Throw it. Harder. Bash the door with the basin. White plastic bomb, banging and flinging itself back on the floor. Pick it up— see what happens, fuckers! I don't go quietly, rage rage rage against the white. Bash their knobless brains in, pick it up. Hollow plastic bangs and bangs and bangs until the door opens.

The bouncer's back, two this time, nurse behind them. He says, *You know what, lady, you're gonna hurt yourself is what, and annoy the hell out of me in the process,* and he yanks the plastic rim out of your clutch.

You wake up to the door opening. Don't know when it is, must have slept. You're on the mattress. Sit up. Look down at your prickly shins, salmon-coloured cotton from the knees up. Can't remember. When did they take your clothes? Did they put you out?

Or did you just pretend to be good? A nurse opens your door all the way. She's smiling that ugly basin smile. Bleach-bone teeth. She's a new one. *Would you like to come out now, Mrs. Hoffman?* Hard, fake cashier-smile.

Be good now. Be a good girl. Show them how docile you are, well-mannered, and bright, not crazy. Not one bit. You stand and hold your gown shut behind, hide your bum at least, dignified is halfway to sane.

In the hallway, a couple patients walking, heads down, hair stringing, old man's maggot-white legs wander bony down the hall, wrinkly squish hanging out the back of his gown, shaking his head back and forth. A young pretty thing sits in a metal-legged chair a few yards down, hands folded in her lap, eyes straight ahead. Looks like she's in primary school—straightest spine gets a gold star. The nurse goes into her station—wonder if she's the head nurse; must be, she looks stark raving. You sit in the chair outside *the quiet room* and look well rested and harmless.

What kind of get-up has she got on? She bustles behind the counter and in front: a brown cape, long brown skirt, starched white blouse, dark stockings, clunky sensible shoes. You want to tell her Florence Nightingale called— she wants her stuff back. Keep your yap shut. Just because *you* didn't know the nineteenth century had come back in such a big way … Don't forget where you are: the booby hatch. Takes one to know one is the rule of thumb, and you are no booby. Convince her lest she descend on you with leeches.

Butter the bitch up.

That's a lovely outfit, and you do something pleasant with your lips. She smiles back, not really at you, just stretching her lips to show the world a well-formed skull, and she says, *Thank you, I made it myself.* She did? And you think of that head nurse at Hollywood Hospital, years ago; saw her the first time you went in to dry out. Next time you ended up there, there she was again, except this time she was a patient. You look back at Turn-of-the-Century Theresa and her flowing brown skirt, cape flung back, gently kissing the ankles of her dark stockings. Jesus Christ.

Look away. Yes, start looking.

Look up, down the hall.

Look for neon red that smells *Exit*.

You stand up. The nurse glances, flesh pulls back to her ears again, just a little teeth this time. *Well*, you sigh passively, *think maybe I'll go take a walk*. She nods, makes a sunny *mm* sound.

Now walk. You reach behind again, trying to close the flap. Ridiculous—if they weren't so busy shooting your ass full of drugs, a person could have a gown that closed in front.

Find the exit, worry about clothes when you get home. Just nonchalantly, not-making-a-break-for-it. Hum. No, don't hum; too obvious. Be dazed, aimless.

EXIT.

Glance over your shoulder—no reason.

Quick. Throw your weight into the door.

It opens. You're out! It's a parking lot. Walk straight ahead. Act natural. Think. Now think. No purse. Well, hitchhike then. Surely to god someone will see you are in distress. Get through these cars, get to the road, just get the hell out of here.

Oh shit, you feel a pressure—patting. A heavy man-hand pats your shoulder. *OK, now*, and you stop.

Freeze.

Orderly. It's a goddamn orderly. The jig's up. *OK, now, let's just go back inside, you're not dressed for socializing. Gonna get yourself in trouble out here*, and he takes your arm in his huge meathook and you go limp like those wildebeests on *Wild Kingdom* when they realize they're dinner. He escorts you back inside.

She's waiting for you, brown drape cascading over her mean little breasts now, hiding her shoulders, just her forearms poking out, ring of keys in her hand. She shakes her head at you, makes a tut-

tut noise, you bad-bad girl. Turns on her heel, as only a nurse in a cape could do, and you feel like sticking a fork in that bun at the back of her head, letting the steam out. As you are being tossed back in the quiet room, you give her a snide glare. *You're a pretty tough broad, aren'tcha?*

And she slides you the closed-mouth grin of two-hundred-year-old paintings, the one reserved for heathens and heretics, and she says, *I'm a tough lady, yes.*

Hoffman, Anne Eilleen

6.11.74 (T. Baker) Call to Dr. Klaus in morning.
He said Mrs. H's Motivation was lousy, that she had
gotten violent in emergency after I had left last
night, throwing things around, etc., had left several
times, but had come back with him when he went out
after her (at one point, she was standing in the
middle of 12th Avenue, hitchhiking.) Dr. Klaus had her
agree to stay only after he threatened to commit her.
He said she was manipulative, looking for support,
sympathy, and continuing her dependency. He and Dr.
Pantern were going to try to get her into the psych.
ward, but did not know if anything could be done as
she was uncooperative. If a neighbor would press
charges against Mr. H. regarding the knife threatening
incident, then a court could order her into a program.
Otherwise not much can be done.

Clothing vouchers made out for Grace. A visit was
made to Mrs. Pong, the landlady, re Mrs. H. Mrs. Pang
does not want to get involved. I talked to Sheryl
Sugarman who seemed uncomfortable with the idea of
pressing charges against Mrs. H. and besides had never
seen anything that would warrant a charge, except
perhaps Mrs. H. ppummeling Mrs. Pong's door last
Friday night.

Visit to foster home; Grace was taken to see Dr. Lee.
Grace showed excess protein in her urine, otherwise
everything all right.

Received call that evening from Julie Smith of
Downtown Care Team at V.G.H. We talked a good deal
about resources for Mrs. H. but she was rather negative as Mrs. H. was uncooperative and manipulative.
Later I received a call from a nurse at VGH emergency
who wanted to inform me that Mrs. H. would probably be
out by tomorrow morning as she was insistent on signing herself out despite the wishes of her doctor.

Eilleen Nine

NOVEMBER 1974

YOU DON'T HAVE *to stay, Eilleen, I just really wish you would ... Of course you're not crazy—I've had a talk with them, things just got a little out of hand, on their parts, and maybe yours too or you wouldn't have ended up here. Calm down. I'm not trying to pull anything on you here, I just want to see you get on your feet so you can get your daughter back. I'll get you a room upstairs— it's not like this, I promise, it's nice.*

That was your shrink talking. Yours, not theirs. You finally got that Cuckoo's Nest bitch to call your psychiatrist—*Just call him, call him yourself and get him down here.* You requested your purse for the phone number; truth was, you'd only seen him a couple times, ages ago, and couldn't remember his name. Went to him at Dr. Graham's suggestion, when Graham got sick of your face, sick of handing out prescriptions. Pissed you off at the time, but now —thank God for boredom and loneliness, the need to talk. To a man who would say in a smooth gentle voice, *And how does that make you feel?*

So you gave in; this time too. Maybe he was right, maybe it was worth staying for a while and letting them look after you. And now you're upstairs, but only because Doctor—oh hell, why can't you remember his name: Pasteur, Pastern—anyway, your shrink told their shrinks that you don't belong downstairs, that you can be by an open window with little risk. Fact is, you just want to get the hell out of here. Want to find your baby. Want to know where they put her. And all you get is the runaround.

They've already sent one of their quacks in—Doctor Klaus—couple hours after you got up here. He sat down, asked a stream of questions and took notes and you tried to be good, be co-operative, but what's the goddamn point: you're a drunk, not a mental case. And it's been over a week; already been through the worst of it: the shakes and pain, the DTs, creeps and gremlins hiding in the corners. All gone. You're on an upturn now. So you look like shit. It's what's inside that counts.

And all during Klaus's inquisition, you tried to tell him you'd be better off outside, getting your affairs in order. You have to move and clean up the house and you have to find your little girl. His response? *Well, you're here now and here's where you're staying. If you were fit to look after a child, you'd be doing it.* And that bony German face registering nothing but the task at hand, the proper channels. So you tried *Yes, well you're right, I was having problems, drinking too much, and now I'm not, I'm sober, so I don't see the point in staying here. I don't need a shrink, just a kick in the pants and some AA* and you laughed, ha-ha, see how lighthearted I am, not crazy.

He didn't look up from his clipboard, stopped scribbling only to scratch his temple with the end of his pen, then, *When you feel depressed, do you experience insomnia or do you find yourself lethargic, sleeping a lot?*

When I'm depressed, I find myself depressed. Doctor Paster told me I could leave if I wanted and I've decided that I want to.

*If you're referring to Doctor Pantern, that's irrelevant. He's not
your attending physician, I am, I'm your doctor and only I can sign
you out, and frankly, I don't see fit to do that. If I were in your posi-
tion, Mrs. Hoffman, I'd be doing everything I could to make myself
a reliable healthy parent in order to regain custody of my child. At
the rate you're going, you'll never see her again.*

Is that a threat?

It's an evaluation.

And then he left. And you sat on your bed feeling like someone just clubbed your face in, thinking there's no fucking way he's
going to keep me here, no fucking way. But scared, heart flitting
around like maybe they could do anything they wanted. They
could take her permanently, find her father and give her to him.

You had your regular street clothes back on, so you went and
sat in the common room, ended up talking to some guy, kind of a
cute old thing, and chatted, and it turned out he'd spent time in
Hollywood Hospital too. Said he'd had electric shock treatment.
And he wanted it again because it was the only thing that could
get him off the booze for any length of time: the dizzy mind-blank
and the darkness afterward as if there were nothing but the very
moment he was experiencing; he kind of liked it. Said, *Christ,
maybe I just need it now and then—blots out everything the way
booze does me except it clears me out for a while and gets me off the
booze, 'cause I'm tellin' ya, the same as they told me—if I don't get off
for good, it's gonna be the—pardon my French—fuckin' death of me.*
He asked how you were making out, if you needed a Librium or
something for the shakes, *I got a whole barrel of 'em in my room.*
He told you his partner brought them by. He and his partner had
this scam going where they printed up their own prescriptions
with a fake doctor's name and the number of a phone booth in the
east end somewhere. One guy would bring it to a drugstore downtown while his friend waited at the phone in case the pharmacy

should call and double-check. It sounded so brilliant yet familiar
—Genius: it's always on the cusp of the obvious.

It's your fourth day in here, no, third, it was day before yesterday Baker brought you in and you're starting to lose your tem-
per. You don't try to escape for fear they'll sick the hospital thugs
on you, throw you back in the cubbyhole. The nurse said Klaus
would be back in to see you today at 3:00 p.m. That's your appointment. In five minutes. All day you've been putting in time,
figuring how the hell to get yourself out of this. Even called Baker;
tried yelling at him. Then you appealed to his Mighty Mouse sen-
sibilities, ones that might rescue. Told him that Klaus had threatened you with never seeing Grace again, threatened you with
being here indefinitely.

He had shit-all to reply, really. Baker—why bother. Said he
was sorry and that he was powerless at this juncture. Then you
started to cry and told him that there was no way that son of a
bitch was keeping you from your baby. He said a lot of nothing
and then he had to go. So you spent the next five hours puttering
and trying to think up a plan. A plan, a plan, my Librium for a
plan. That shock therapy guy gave you ten of them this morning,
brought them in on the q.t. and dropped them into your palm like
Smarties. Like Christmas. They don't do much, but they do soothe
the shakes and twitches, might help you feel more human in the
face of Herr Shrink—and speak of the devil—Germans, nothing
if not punctual.

He says, *Hello, Mrs. Hoffman, how are you today?*

Shit. no plan. So you say, *Fine. How 'bout yourself? ... Ah, I'd
like to talk with you about something, though. I've given a lot of
thought to it and I've decided that this isn't the kind of place con-
ducive to, uh, getting better, healing, for me and I'd like to discuss
being an outpatient.*

He jogs his head and rolls his eyes to the side before he looks
at you, and when he does, it's as if he's looking at someone so

nitwitted and swine-like, it's an annoyance to cast his pearls before you. *Look, Mrs. Hoffman, you better take a good hard look at yourself and what you've become. If you don't make some changes and pull up your socks, you will never see your daughter again. And that's not a threat, it's a fact.*

Your heart is crawling into your throat like something from a horror movie. If he'd just stop saying that, if everyone would just stop holding your child for ransom. Christ, now you're drizzling in front of him. He thinks he's trumped you now, that you're crying in remorse, that you're broke like a scrawny dusty old nag. He says, *Cry all you want, Mrs. Hoffman, if that helps. Realize, though, that you're not getting out of here and things aren't going to progress until you make some attempt to co-operate.*

You wipe your eyes. *Christ, you're a bastard. Well, how is it then that I'm supposed to get out of here?*

You get out when your physician signs you out. And I'm your physician and I won't be signing you out until I see enough change in you to warrant that.

He's your *physician.* Who died and made him your *physician?* How 'bout this: *Well, what if I were to tell you that I am releasing you as my physician?* His ice eyes go black. *How about if I were to tell you that I will no longer be needing your services and I'll be finding another doctor to care for me, how would that suit you?*

His chiselled face droops ever so flaccid, and you, my good woman, have become your own Mighty Mouse and, looking at this man, you wish he had a twisty dark moustache because it seems he is this far from clenching his fists and saying *Drat, foiled again.* But no, he has regained his composure and pushed the pen back in his breast pocket. *That is certainly your prerogative, Mrs. Hoffman,* he says, and walks out the door.

Hoffman, Anne <u>Eilleen</u>

7.11.74 (T. Baker) I received a call this morning
from a nurse in the psych ward at the VGH who said
that Mrs. H. had signed herself out of the hospital
against the wishes of her doctors and despite the fact
that firt first tests regarding her liver showed something was very wrong. I subsequently received a call
from Mrs. Sugarman who said Grace had come to visit
her and had just left when Mrs. H. came in. I called
Mrs. Hood who had not known that Grace was up to old
neighborhood and asked her to keep Grace within sight
for a while and asked her not to go up to her friend's
in her mother's building.

I called Sheryl Sugarman who said Mrs. H. had staggered
in, and that fMrs. Pong had fainted, then gone off to
see her doctor (apparently afraid of what might happen
with Mrs. H. back). Mrs. Png told Sheryl Sugarman not
to give the key (a spare) back to Mrs. H. but I
advised her that she had to as the apartment was still
Mrs. H's. I also asked her to send Grace back to the
foster home if she re-appeared and told her there was
probably little more I could do to help Mrs. H.

8.11.74. (T.Baker) I had a long talk with Grace,
both about her mother's medical condition and about
the necessity of her staying away from her old
neighborhood. I told her that her mother had signed
herself out of hospital despite blood sugar and liver
problems. I also asked her not to go up to visit
Sheryl Sugarman or Alice or any of her friends up
there until I have been able to get her mother into a
program. We discussed this for a while and she agreed
to stay in her new neighborhood. I also asked about
her her possibly attending a new school (Edith Cavell)
both because of possible interference by her mother
at Wolfe and because Edith Cavell is closer to the
Hoods'. Grace really liked this idea but largely
because she does not get along with her present
teacher who is apparently a strict disciplinarian and
has been very strict with Grace not realizing Grace's
home situation.

9.11.74. (T.Baker) Call to Mrs. Sugarman: Mrs. H. still drinking. Is cleaning her apt. some, feeling that this is all she needs to do in order to get Grace back.

Call to Dr. Klaus: Mrs. H. has liver impairment, will become jaundiced and may go into coma if she does not stop drinking. She had refused to accept Dr. Klaus as her doctor (she says he is "too strict") and once Dr. Pantern discharged her from Psych. Dept. as totally uncooperative, Mrs. H. simply signed herself out. Dr. Klaus stated strongly that Mrs. H. was incapable of caring for Grace. Said there was nothing more he could do.

Visit to Mrs. H. Still drinking. Refuses to see Dr. Klaus or Dr. Henighan, refused to enter any residential program. She had seen Dr. Person (unknown) and had gotten some pills (unclear what). She did not believe Dr. Klaus' test reust results and had gone to the lab at 750 West Broadway for other tests. She said she had no food -- I promised to return later with a voucher.

I next spoke with Mrs. Sugarman: She explained that Mrs. H had broken a window in her apamtment, had been banging on walls and doors in the building after midnight, etc. Apparently a bootlegger in the area supplies Mrs. H. Also Mrs. H. said, on Sunday night, she was going to get Grace and take off into the interior. I picked Grace up after school as I was afraid Mrs. H. would show up, took her to her foster home and there apprehended under section K. I also arranged to have Grace transferred to Edith Cavell effective Wednesday November 12.

I later visited Mrs. H. and explained that I had apprehended Grace, going through the reasons carefully. She was still in a stupor and became very maudlin, etc. I left a grocery voucher and the names of counsellors to call at some rehab centers.

12.11.74 (T. Baker) Grace taken to Edith Cavell in am. Grace was a bit nervous but overall happy with the change, as both Wendy and Lilly attend Edith Cavell. Grace told me of a dream she had, where a

"boyfriend" of her mother's chased her down a back
alley that was filled with beer bottles (like her
mother's apartment).

Arrangements made with Mrs. Hood (regarding Graces'
baton lessons, visits with friends, scout group,
ᴡ swimming lessons, etc.) to insure as far as possible
that Mrs. H. does not try to pick Grace up. Mrs. H.
has been informed that she cannot have contact with
Grace until she sobers up.

14.11.74 (T. Baker) Visit to Mrs. H.   She ws not at
home but her friend Doreen was there.   She told me
that Mrs. H. is in a deep depression over Grace.   She
feels it is her fault and has tried to help Mrs. H. by
cleaning the apartment.   Most things had been put away
and the floor had been washed.   She began to explain
that she had called the police that night NOT because
of Grace but because Mrs. H. had taken "about 15
different kinds of pills and was drinking like a fish."
She had been afraid that Mrs. H. would kill herself.
I explained what I had been trying to do -- especially
in getting Mrs. H. into a program for her alcoholism.
Also that our purpose was not to keep Grace forever
but only until Mrs. H. had shown that she was managing
and capable of caring for Grace.   I aso clearly
explained that Grace was now a child-before-the-court
under the guardianship of the Superintendant of Child
Protection.   I explained because Sheryl S. had called
this morning to say that Mrs. H. was trying to get
someone to drive her around to all the schools in the
area to try to get Grace at noon hour.

Called later to Edith Cavell -- the principal will
arrange things so that Grace will not be out at lunch
hour.

17.11.74 (T. Baker) Mrs. Pong called to complain
again about Mrs. H. who has been banging on doors
etc., keeping people awake. I referred her to the
Rentals man as there is really nothing more I can do.
Apparently Mrs. H. is still drinking.

Grace Ten

NOVEMBER 1974

ODD BAKER didn't have much to say about it all. He said he never told me "a few days," that *I* decided that. That he said a little while because "three months *is* a little while," and that I had a habit of interpreting things to suit my needs then acting surprised when stuff didn't get delivered as for my expectations, or something. He said my mum was going to need more than a few days to get on her feet and I had to be supportive by doing my best. That my mum had an unpredictable mind right now and if I wanted to really help I would switch schools, work hard and try to make things run smoothly instead of fight them every step of the way. I just said forget-it in my head and tried to think about how at least I wouldn't have to have Anus in my life now.

The worst part about the new school was having to walk there every morning with Wendy and Lilly. Mostly they talked about being a Witness. By around my first week, I knew Lilly was sick of me and couldn't wait till February. And then as soon as someone said anything about time and waiting for stuff, Wendy started

going on about Armageddon, and how you never know when
God's wrath is going to come, in three months or three minutes,
to kill the ones that are wrecking the earth. That was in Revelations; she was always saying everything about Revelations.

It was kind of weird about Wendy: it was like how you think
a bear is going to be slow and dumb, but really it's super-fast and
kills you—well, I thought Wendy being thick all over and moving slower meant she couldn't get me or something, and yappy
Lilly was the one to watch out for, but it wasn't Lilly who was giving me nightmares now.

Wendy told me on the way to school that there were signs
every day that Jesus was coming; that for now, Satan controlled
the earth but there would be a great war and the world would be
destroyed, not because of a flood, because God said he'd never do
it that way again, but probably nuclear war, she figured. "Because
it says, in the time of the end, the king of the South, that's the
Eagle, and that's for sure the States, will engage in a pushing with
the king of the North, the Bear, and that's Russia. That's how the
world'll end and you can tell now how they're going to have
World War Three. And plus all the famine and earthquakes and
false prophets—those are the signs, you know. Just turn on TV
and there's all these people pretending they're Christians but
they're not—Satan is their lord." I thought of Josh's living room
and the healings on TV. I could hear him giggling and giggling.
Wendy's voice came loud again. "Satan's like a prostitute, you
know, luring God's creatures to worldly religions like Catholics
and stuff so they think they'll be saved when Armageddon comes,
but really they'll be destroyed. God will once again rule the earth
and remember his servants and resurrect them." She took a
breath, did up her coat more and looked up at the rain dripping
off the trees.

Lilly rolled her eyes. "I don't think it'll be a bomb cuz that
would wreck the whole planet."

"So what, there'll be a new heaven on earth. God'll just fix it and the ones who were his servants will be resurrected." Wendy's lips pushed up under her nose the way her mum's did.

"So. I'm just saying. I think it'll be a different way. I think maybe it's gonna be The Killer Bees. It even said in the paper that Killer Bees are coming."

"Oh yeah, Lilly, like some bees are going to get all the wicked. Prime Minister Trudeau isn't gonna get it with a bee sting—duh!"

"Shut up. You don't know everything. It's not going to be a dumb war!"

"Do you listen? Ever? It says in black and white that there's going to be a war rulers and armies of every nation will be assembled in opposition to God. Must you contradict me at every turn?"

"You're not my mum, OK? Must you copy Mum at every turn?"

I cut in, "Well, where does it say you get to have animals?"

Lilly glared. Wendy drooped her eyelids at me again and said it slow as if I was retarded. "It says in Isaiah, it says how leopards and sheep will live together and lions will eat straw like cows, and babies can play with snakes and not be afraid. God said, that's who said."

Lilly joined in, her eyes all glinty and excited. "I can't wait! I hope it's tomorrow, it could be in five minutes, you know. Birds will come on my finger—I wanna owl or a hawk like the picture in homeroom at school. Heaven will have streets of gold and be way better than like it is here now. There'll be everything."

I didn't get what the big deal about gold streets was. "Will there be TV?"

Lilly frowned. "I don't know. Prob'ly. I'll ask my mum."

That night, the Hoods brought me to a Watchtower meeting in someone's apartment. There were nine or ten of us there and everybody was called "brother" or "sister" something. I wanted to

join in just so someone would call me Sister Grace, but kids got
their regular name. Everyone had a copy of this week's *Watchtower*,
a little pamphlet with a school kind of lesson and then at the bottom of each page there'd be questions. But it was super-easy, because the question had the same number beside it as the paragraph
with the answer in it. You didn't even have to figure out anything
or look for it; they told you. So anyhow, Wendy and Lilly had un-
derlined, in pencil crayon, the answers in their pamphlets, and
everyone else's was the same. After each right answer, the leader,
whose apartment we were in, would nod and say "yes, good" in a
low sort of brown-sugar-and-butter-sandwich kind of voice, as if
we were all little kids. He sounded nice, though, and I wanted
someone to say "yes, good" at me. The next question was whether
or not it's possible to be neutral about God and still be saved during Armageddon. I grabbed my *Watchtower* and looked fast for the
right paragraph, raising my hand at the same time. "Phyllis," the
leader said. I waited. He looked at me, then smiled gently. "Do
you have the answer, Phyllis?" Lilly bursted out laughing.

"My name is Grace." I felt stupid all the sudden for trying to
be one of them. Lilly mumbled something mean I couldn't hear.
The leader ducked his chin and apologized. "I don't know why I
thought your name was Phyllis. Grace is such a pretty name." Lilly
whispered, "Exactly," and started shaking from holding in her
laughs. The leader told me to go on in his yes-good voice. I read,
"Matt twelve-thirty—" and Lilly nearly blew up from giggling
inside. Mrs. Hood leaned into my ear. "Matthew, chapter twelve,
verse thirty." My neck burned, but I said what she said and read,
"He that is not on my side is against me and he that does not
gather with me scatters." I looked to the leader. He said, "That's
right. Number two: what will happen to young children at
Armageddon?"

I laid in bed that night, wondering how come no one ever
told me this before, that God was going to slaughter us all for our

sins. Us all who didn't believe this stuff, didn't serve Him, didn't go door to door and spread the word. And if it would hurt. And what will happen to young children at Armageddon? I wasn't sure if I still counted as a young child. What if Mum was left by mistake and God just slaughtered me? What then, what would she do, all alone? She'd cry by herself without me. I tried to think of a plan and prayed for God to kill us together so we wouldn't be scared or lonely.

Todd Baker took me to The White Spot for lunch and asked me who I'd like to spend my birthday evening with. My mum. He said that I knew that wasn't going to happen, that she wasn't well enough just yet, maybe in a couple weeks, after she moves, he could arrange us a belated birthday together. "Grace, it's not going to change anything if you sit there and glare at me—it's enough that you've insisted on being in your old neighbourhood this past while, knowing she's only a couple blocks away. Now, I know your baton lessons are important to you and your friends and swimming and all that stuff, so I work around it, but don't push. The fact of the matter is, you're not going to get everything you want every time you want it. Maybe you got away with that before, but not now."

I plinked my teaspoon against the saucer a couple times. Todd frowned and I dropped it in my teacup. "If you're trying to say I'm spoiled, I am not. I just wanna see my mum on my birthday. You didn't have to leave all your friends and your mother and your school and everything." I thumped my chin in my hands and my elbows on the table so he could see for himself I was upset. Except for one elbow caught the edge of the saucer and sent all my tea-stuff flying across the table.

"Grace!"

"It was an accident. I didn't do it on purpose." The waitress ran over with a cloth, saying things like "oopsy daisy" and "don't worry, happens to me all the time." Todd sighed hard and stared at me. I watched the waitress fling the cloth around the table. It always felt worse when someone felt sorry for you like how she was now. Like the way Anus acted when I cleared my junk out of homeroom my last day at my old school; she took me aside and said, "Grace, I'm so terribly sorry. Why didn't you tell me what was going on at home? why you had to leave early the other day?" and I shrugged at her. "Of course, it all makes sense now why you told the class on the first day that you'd gone to all those different schools."

When we left The White Spot, Todd asked me to come to Woodwards and point out what I liked in the toy department so he could get an idea of what to get me for my birthday. I wondered if that meant I'd have to get him something for his, whenever that was. Then I figured the Welfare was probably paying for it, so I tried to look happy and told him I'd like to have my birthday with Joshua and his mum. We were quiet through a couple red lights, so I changed the subject: "I had this dream last night that I was walking down the laneway to see Sadie and Eddy—you know, the ones whose father owns a furniture store?—and it was getting dark so I was kind of nervous, and when I looked behind me there was a guy, like a big drunk guy, and in the dream he was supposed to be my mum's boyfriend. Not in real life but in the dream I recognized him, and so anyway, he was right behind me and he tried to grab me, so I started running down the lane and I kept being scared that I'd trip on a—over a pothole thing. But I didn't. But every time I looked over my shoulder, he was getting closer and then the last time when I looked in front of me, in the middle of the lane, there was this humongous pile of empty beer bottles in cases, all piled on each other in practically a mountain. And there was a little green fishbowl full of kittens and they were all meowing and spilling over, you know, like their heads and paws hanging out over the sides. So I picked up the bowl and tried to climb over the beer bottles, but they'd keep rolling and falling and I kept sliding back down and the drunk guy was still coming. And the kittens kept meowing these little teeny me-ew me-ews, and I kept falling and I was so scared I was going to drop them. And then it ended. That always happens in my dreams, they just kind of end. Right at the important part."

Todd breathed out smoke and flicked his cigarette out the window. Then he started chewing on his thumb skin again. There was a big quiet, I guess cuz of how your dreams never sound as scary to the person you tell it to. I asked more about my birthday, what we'd probably do. He said he thought a movie would be good, that I could pick. I did my cheerful smile; I was getting a stomach ache again. "So. Um, where is my mum going to be, when is she moving?"

He took out another cigarette and lit it. "Uh, I'm not sure."

"How come you never told me she found a place, what's the phone number going to be?"

"Because she hasn't moved yet and things have been very tentative, very up in the air, and there is no point in giving you information before I have it all."

"Yeah, but how will I—Well, will you give me her phone number? or what?"

Todd shook his head and blew more smoke. "Your tone sometimes, Grace, I don't know. She hasn't moved in yet, OK."

"You don't have to yell at me. You said before that when she was better, when she got out of the hospital, and now you're just doing this—you're pretending like you never said anything. That's lying."

"I did not lie to you and I didn't yell. Just because you don't like what you hear, it doesn't mean you've been yelled at. And furthermore, just because your mother's getting another apartment doesn't mean she's fixed and everything's hunky-dory. I thought I made that all perfectly clear when I took you down to the courthouse and went before the judge for you. These things take time. Give her some space, let her get organized, let her find her bearings. She's got a lot on her plate and I don't think having you there or talking to you on the phone right now is such a good idea. Let the dust settle."

"I'm not dust."

"I—you know what I'm talking about, so there's no point in arguing. Or pouting. You'll see her. You'll see her when she's settled OK. And you'll see her Christmas vacation."

"So once a month till February?" He shook his head again and didn't answer. "What about Henry? My cat. Is my cat gonna be there?"

He changed driving hands and rubbed at his forehead with his wrist. "Yeah. Ah, here—" and he turned off Cordova Street into the Woodwards lot and we puttered around the echoey parking place, looking for a spot.

I folded my hands on my stomach and wished I could burp. "So can you give her my number then? She could call me when she gets a phone. Or she could use the neighbours' phone. She could call me on my birthday."

Todd pulled into a spot, wiggled the gearshift and turned off the engine. He held the steering wheel in both hands. "Sweetheart"—He never called me anything like that before. Usually he just said my name too much. He was about to pull an Anus. "She can't call you. She's not allowed to have your number. It's against the rules." I sat still, clenching and unclenching my teeth; my stomach hurt so bad I wanted to fold over. "I know it's your birthday, I know this is crummy and it's a drag, but there are rules and you have to be patient. I know you love your mom and I know she's nuts about you ..." He was quiet a second and breathed out his nose. "Look, just trust me on this, give it a few days, be patient. As soon as she moves, I'll have a phone number for you, OK? I'll get you her number. OK?"

"Yeah. 'K. As soon as she moves." I said it to the truck in the spot beside us. "Does Mrs. Hood have to be there when I talk?"

"I don't know. It's her house, Grace. It's up to her."

Todd picked me up around dinnertime on my birthday night. Me and my birthday, just more stuff for Wendy and Lilly to hate me for. They didn't have birthdays. At first I felt sorry for them, but then Wendy told me that celebrating birthdays was pagan, that lighting candles on the cake was what the Greeks and Romans did and it had to do with magic and was a ritual of the devil and that, on his birthday, King Herod ordered John the Baptist to get beheaded and that story was in the Bible for a reason. I looked at her head and wished for King Herod to come alive again.

We picked up Josh and Sheryl Sugarman and went to McDonald's for dinner. Josh was in a good mood cuz I let him pick the movie since I couldn't decide: *Young Frankenstein* by Mel Brooks. Having Josh with me felt like I got my clothes back on or my hair back on my head, but it was peeing rain again and cold and I missed my mum. I didn't hear much of what everyone was talking about at McDonald's and I wasn't paying very good attention to the movie. Afterwards, the four of us went to Todd's apartment. He had a place on Granville Street above a store.

His place was dark and skinny, like a chunk of hallway. Everything in the room touched the thing beside it. Squished against the short wall at one end was a single bed and beside it was a nightstand that touched an orange crate with some blue flowery cloth over top, a full ashtray and a tape player on top. The crate touched the back of a chair, which touched the leg of the table that touched the second chair that touched a miniature fridge with a lamp on top. His apartment was like, "There's a frog on the bump on the log in the hole in the bottom of the sea." The other short wall had cupboards and a counter with a puny sink and a hot plate beside it. Then on the other long wall there was

just the door to come in, a closet door and a bookshelf with tons
of books squished into it, and it was touching the foot of his bed.
I didn't know if I was going to be able to breathe so good with all
of us in there.

In the middle of the table, Todd had a little chocolate cake
with "Happy Birthday Grace" in blue swirly letters waiting for
me and ten candles—an extra one for good luck, he said. Sheryl
gave a "weee," then pulled a green box out from nowhere and put
it on the table. I never even noticed her carrying it. There was a
little chirpy noise behind us where Todd was scrounging in the
cupboards for matches. Then more chirpy noises and he twirled
around with a sheet-covered thing from under the sink. He said
"tah dah" almost like Mum would've, pulled off the sheet and held
up a silver cage with a blue budgie flapping its head off. "For you,
Mademoiselle," he said and put as much of it as he could on the
table beside the cake and Josh and Sheryl's present.

I didn't know what to say. "Really? Will Mrs. Hood let me
have him?" and I stroked the glimmery cage bars.

"Yes, ma'am, I've already spoken with her. Oh, here, and this
too." He handed me *The Handbook of Budgies and Budgerigars.*
"And I think I know someone who has a stand for the cage."

I couldn't hardly talk. I looked around the room; practically
half his apartment was taken up with his bed. On the nightstand
he had a double picture frame. One side showed a cracked black-
and-white picture of a lady and on the other side, a colour picture
of an old man. Then, lying on its own was a Polaroid of a pretty
girl with long honey-colour hair making kissy lips at the camera.

Sheryl nudged me with the present from her and Josh. "Here,
open ours, it's going to pale in comparison to a pet bird, but what
the heck." I smiled at her and said Sheryl Sugarman in my head,
just to hear the *shh*-sounds, tore off the paper and opened the box.
It was stuffed with shredded paper the same colour green as the
box. When I pulled it all out, there was a short fat cup-thing, green

with a spout and *For* in black writing across the side of it, a matching big bowl with a handle and spout that said *Tea* and another little one with *Two* on the side. Sheryl showed me how they stacked on each other. I stared at them. "See, *Tea For Two*," she said.

"And *Two For Tea*," Josh sang. She reached back in the box and grabbed a green lid. Josh looked at them and punched me in the arm. "Get it? Because you like tea so much."

Everything went numb. I wished I could understand what these little cuppy-bowl things had to do with tea. But I was super-thankful and I touched my fingers over the black letters. I kept trying to find words in my brain. "Thank you. It's—they're so nice. They're lovely."

Josh did a horse laugh. "Lovely! Hey Mother Hubbard, glad your present's so *lovely*."

Sheryl elbowed him. "Josh, don't be such a poop."

Hoffman, Anne <u>Eilleen</u>

23.11.74 (T. Baker) Mrs. Hoffman entered hospital
November 22nd after having been beaten around the
Little Mountain Project Area. She was apparently
drinking and had wandered out into the evening. She
was attacked by two men, and beaten especially bdaly
on the head, but was too drunk to remember clearly
what had happened. Dr. Klaus will be involved with
her now.

I have not told Grace what has happened -- Things are
going well for Grace in the foster home. Mrs. Hood
has had no problems.

7.12.74 (T. Baker) Great deal of contact with Dr.
Klaus, Mrs. Pong, Mrs. Hood and Mrs. HOffman in the
last two weeks.

I arranged with Mrs. Pong to pay Mrs. Hoffman's rent
for December, on the agreement that Mrs. Hoffman would
move by Dec. 31st. Mrs. Pong has been very cooperative. Dr. Klaus has been working hard with Mrs.
Hoffman but seems to be pushing her much too hard.
He has been telling her that she will never get her
child back, etc., unless she does what he says, and
Mrs. Hoffman is much too stubborn to respod to this
sort of approach. I have see Mrs. Hood several times,
arranging for Grace's activities (baton, swimming etc.)

Mrs. Hoffman herself was badly bruised in the face
by her beating but the experience paradoxically has
reulted resulted in her being completely dried out.
I saw her today (she was released from V.G.H. today)
and she is much better -- much more responsive,
intelligible and understanding of her experience.
She realized that the beating and the apprehension of
Grace were direct results of her alcoholism. Her
memory is still spotty -- many things she does not
recall and she believes that Grace was apprehended
because of her poor housekeeping. We had a long
discussion about her past, her relationships with her
first husband as well as Danny Hoffman, Grace's father,
and her problems with her other daughter. As far as
possible then, I focussed on the future, on her hopes

and plans and what we may be able to prebide provide.
She is still unstable in mnay respects, and physically
weak -- her hospital stay also provided her with the
first steady diet in six weeks or more as she had not
been eating.

Dr. Klaus has siad that Mrs. H's liver problem has
abated somewhat. He also said that she would become a
virtual vegetable in two years or so if she continued
drinking. Mrs. Hoffman does not want to see Dr. Klaus
again -- she is simply avoiding unpleasant facts as
usual.

9.12.74 (T. Baker) There is increasing pressure
from Mrs. Hoffman and from Grace for their seeing one
aether another. Mrs. Hoffman has started attending AA
again (some members visited her in the hospital)and I
have had some calls from AA members. I am trying to
hold off as long as possible on visiting, until Mrs.
Hoffman begins some definite program.

11.12.74 Mrs. Hoffman has found a new apartment at
2810 Carolina Street -- a basement suite with rent at
$200 per month. Arrangements for moving were made and
she is settling in. I expect that her separation from
her old neighborhood will do her a world of good.
The new apartment is brighter than her previous one.
Mrs. Hoffman has now talked to Grace by phone. I
expect increasing pressure for a visit.

I have had several very hard sessions with Mrs.
Hoffman and we have had our first substantial talk
about her problems --alcoholism and prostitution.
She has grown much more lucid, and the possibility of
Grace's coming home for Christmas has given her a goal
to work towards. She still denies that her problems
extend as far as they do (when I raised the question
of Kingston Penitentiary, she laughed and told me I'd
been misinformed. She said it was Jake Carrington,
her ex-husband who'd been imprisoned) She has been
responding, however, slowly, and has finally gone to
see Mary Allison at the Alcohol Foundation. She is
regularly attending AA as well. Her health is very
much improved; she doesnot have the "shakes," is not
as tired as she had been etc.

Mrs. Hoffman's central problem is in her role as
victim. From all she has told me, it seems she has
led a rather deprived life as an adult, chose partners
who closely mirrored the abusive and controlling nature
of her father. I don't have a lot of information
about her childhood but the abuse she suffered sounds
primarily psychological (Her interests all disparaged
or discouraged) Some physical abuse took place as
well, though, as her father was firm believer in
corporal punishment. She sees herself as a victim of
circumstance, misunderstood, lonely, etc. ~~Tei amntain~~
To maintain this image, she has repeatedly done things
to sabotage herself or chosen situations that would
guarantee failure -- and so reinforce her self-image.
She seeks dependency, and concomitantly, sympathy.
As far as possible, I have denied her these things,
and have directly or indirectly forced her to act on
her own. Her attitude from November (I can't do it
on my own) has changed appreciably She is getting a
great deal of ~~xuppnx~~ support and sympathy from AA but
she has also learned to accept herslef more and do
positive things that will enhance her life, rather
than destroy it. In this respect, I see her pill-
taking and drinking binge, which prompted her friend
to call the police, as actually a cry for help.

Grace Eleven

DECEMBER 1974

IT WAS AROUND two weeks after my birthday till Todd Baker called with Mum's number. He said other stuff, but the words were just like green shredded paper around the numbers for me. It was after dinner on Monday night and raining harder than ever. Mrs. Hood was ironing in the kitchen. Wendy sat at the kitchen table doing homework and Lilly was on the floor with Spike, chucking the ball across the kitchen.

"Lilly, stop throwing the ball so hard or go down to the basement," Mrs. Hood snapped all the sudden and sprayed the sheet on the ironing board with a bottle of water.

"Wha-a-t! I'm hardly throwing it! It just does it—it's rubber, you know."

Wendy looked up from her homework and stared at the back of her sister. Lilly's head whipped around. "You shut up!"

Wendy stared and didn't move her lips. Lilly pulled her whole self around and told her, "Quit it, Wendy, nobody asked you nothing! Mum, tell Wendy to quit it."

Mrs. Hood stood her iron up. "Why don't you both give me some peace and quiet. I don't want to hear any more—Wendy, stop doing whatever it is you're doing, and Lilly, go do your homework." Wendy gave a little smile and stared more at Lilly.

I hung up the phone, back on the wall. "Got my mum's number ..." I said it just to say it, even though they weren't going to care. Wendy pushed her lips up under her nose and went to her homework. I was saying it mostly to her and I didn't know why.

Maybe because one night a week, when Mrs. Hood was at the restaurant where she worked, Wendy was in charge of Lilly and me and I never knew what was going to happen. The week before, she took out a photo album and showed me pictures of herself from the summer. I told her she looked Indian, wondering what it would be like to have that dark skin and hair, like Sadie's. Wendy slammed the album shut and said, "I look Hawaiian—everybody says I look Hawaiian." Dinner was ready; Wendy made spaghetti and sauce from a recipe of her mum's and she put the album away and told Lilly to set the table. I had two things against me so far that night: first I told her she was putting too much salt in the sauce, and now the Indian thing. My stomach was twisting again. Wendy put the pot of sauce and spaghetti on the table and served us each before she bowed her head and said, "Dear Lord, we thank you for this food you have put before us, and we thank you for the rain today that makes the plants flourish and we ask that you give us patience in this trying period and patience that we may endure until the time of the end. Amen." Lilly *amen*-ed a little louder than she had to. Wendy looked at me. I whispered *amen* at my plate. We picked up our forks and twisted up some noodles. Lilly slurped hers in. "Lilly, don't be so loud," Wendy told her without looking.

"Yes'm." Lilly kept acting like one of the *Waltons* that night.

I picked up my fork and held it a second, wishing there was a way I could just eat with my hands. And wishing she hadn't gone and mixed it all in together; I'd've rather had just noodles with butter. It took me a while to get some in my mouth and it was salty all right. I looked at Lilly; she swallowed and gulped at her milk. Wendy watched me. I was going to gag. I held my breath for a second, took a drink of milk and washed it back. She said, "Well, how is it?" Lilly didn't say anything. Seemed like we were supposed to prove how good we were by not saying how sick it tasted. I moved around in my chair and there was a roll and ping in my stomach. Then a pop.

Lilly's head whipped up from her plate. "You farted!" and she was still using her *Waltons* voice, then she screamed it at Wendy, "She farted! Ew." My face got prickles. I dropped my fork and started to giggle. "Ew! She done it on purpose. That's disgustin'."

If it wasn't for the giggle, I would've been paralyzed stiff. Wendy pushed her lips under her nose, then put down her fork. I gritted my teeth and swallowed the giggle. "I'm sorry. It was an accident."

Lilly slouched in her chair. "You, miss, are the most disgustin' pig in the whole world. Ah cain't eat this now. Ah hate you. February is not never gonna come."

Wendy finally opened her mouth. "You're a heathen." Except she said it like Kingdom Hall, not like *Waltons*. But it made me do another quacky laugh—whenever Mum said "heathen," it was a joke. Wendy said, "I think it's your bedtime, Grace." I giggled a bit more, knowing it wasn't funny for sure now. "Grace. Go to bed. You don't eat what's put in front of you and then you do *that* right at the dinner table. Go. Now." I put down my fork, put my hand over my mouth and left. I laid in bed watching the clock, listening to Lilly stay up almost two hours past our bedtime.

"So. I'm going to phone her," I said. Wendy didn't even look at me and they all stayed doing what they were doing. I stood with my head against the phone, wishing I could rip it off the wall and drag it to a closet where the coats and clothes would keep my talking from going right into everyone's ears. I huddled around the phone and dialled, scared all the sudden that I wouldn't know what to say. The iron was spitting behind me and Spike slammed the ball into the cupboards.

When she answered, it was like I just fell into a giant tub of mum and her voice was gurgling around me. I could see her and smell her. I could feel her like breath on my face. Her voice smelled clean and like the olive oil she poured in her bathwater all the time. I could feel her patting the middle of my back, vibrating my ribs, and hear the amethyst rock clicking in her ring like crickets.

She sounded out of breath. There was a little shake in her voice when she asked how I was, how the family looking after me was and my new school, and if I missed her. I kept saying "fine" until it got to the missing-her part and my throat squeezed. I said, "Yeah," and I said it again because I couldn't speak hardly.

Her voice kept being all over me and she asked a zillion things about nothing and I wanted her to keep thinking up stuff to say, until she got to, "Well, let me get a pen, Lamby, OK, what's your number there and we'll phone each other ... oop, wait ... OK, what's her name, the woman looking after you?"

I tried to keep the butterflies down. Everything would be OK. Mum could call and maybe Mrs. Hood would like her and invite her here for tea sometimes and things would get better. I said, "Mrs. Hood," into the receiver and Mrs. Hood's head jumped up, her eyes all buggy. I thought maybe she burned herself, but I kept going. "It's 327—"

"No!" She stood her iron up, her lips stuck in an *o*.

"What?" I looked at her.

"What what?" my mother said. "What's the matter?"

Mrs. Hood shook her head and her lips pulled back like she

was going to get hit in the face with something. My brains went all quiet. I said, back in the phone, "Um, it's—"

Mrs. Hood hissed at me, "You cannot give out this number!" My throat squeezed again.

"Honey, what's the matter?" Her voice welled up in my eyes.

"Mm, I can't. I'm not allowed. Said I can't."

"What do you mean you're not allowed?" Her voice was snaking up.

"Mrs. Hood said I can't." Mrs. Hood hissed from me saying her name again. The line was quiet. "Mummy?"

"Well isn't that just lovely." Mum's words were like bites. "Baker says they're Jehovah's Witnesses—whatever happened to 'honour thy mother and father'—that *woman* forbids you to give your number to your own mother? What, pray tell, does she think I'm going to do for chrissake?"

"Don't know." I wanted to go stuff myself between my mattresses. "I'm sorry. I can keep calling you. I'm sorry."

"And stop saying you're sorry—Uh! I'm sorry, I didn't mean—I just mean it's not your fault. You can bet Baker's going to get an earful about this, goddamn little draft-dodging nothing. Bloody low-lifes trying to separate a child from her mother!" More quiet. "Are you still there?"

"Uh huh." My chest was going to fall out my back.

"Hmm, well, I guess you can't say much with them in the room."

"Uh huh."

She sighed. "OK, well, you've got my number now, right? So the next time you go over to see Sadie and Eddy, call me from there. You'll be over there, won't you?"

"Yup."

"I wish I could have been with you on your birthday, honey."

"Uh huh."

"Well, we'll have our own little celebration together, I have presents for you, you know. I don't know when he's bringing you, but soon, I think—don't be upset, angel, we'll get through this, we're tough, right?" and she sang a bit of "You and Me Against the World," by Helen Reddy.

"Uh hmm."

"Don't worry, OK? I love you—I love you to pieces." I said *me-too* and she said, "Just a few days till we see each other and then it'll be Christmas and we'll have all that lovely time together." I *uh-huh*-ed again and she let a big breath out with, "OK, lovey, I'll let you go. Call me, OK?—we'll do it on the sly, he-he."

Eilleen Ten

DECEMBER 1974

Y OU ARE IN your new apartment, trying to make it look cheerful, clean, at least, as you're waiting for the fruit of your womb. You've made a chocolate birthday cake; it's kind of low-slung in the middle, filled in with extra icing because Grace loves the icing more than the cake. Or is that you? Can't remember. Does she like pickles? and what kind of chip dip? and you've been saying things like, *it doesn't matter, just so long as we're together,* while wrapping her presents and wondering will she even like Silly Putty or is that too young?—but it's OK because you've compensated with a black-velvet-strapped Timex that looks grown-up as hell and shit, how does one wrap a watch box so it doesn't look as crappily slapped together as the rest of the loot? But she'll just tear it all off anyway; rip it like she's fighting her way out of a wet paper bag because that's half the fun. That much you remember.

She's due any minute and so you go back in the bathroom and check again. Do you look motherly? Is this what mothers look like? You blot off some lipstick. No, now you look sickly, you're not a woman who shines without lipstick. And you pace back in the kitchen, it's a huge kitchen, she'll like that. It's a basement, but at least it's in someone's house: safer, not so anonymous. Right now you're of a mind to have people know who you are, at least the you you are now. To hear *hello* followed by your name makes your backbone straighter, helps you feel here.

If you didn't have to sleep in that bedroom, it'd be better. The five days you've been here, you've waited till the very last second to get into bed because there's something about that bed in that room with nothing else but a dresser; it becomes apparent that your life is one empty Cracker Jack box and you really have nothing, not even a phone number to the only thing that you love. Fucking Baker, you let him have it for that, telling your flesh and blood that she may not give her whereabouts to her own mother. You'd hate him if there was enough there to hate, American weasel. Draft-dodging little turd. Wonder if he gets a nice gold star on his report card for this particular absconding. He barely addressed your demands, said he hardly thought it was an issue with which to concern yourself at this point in time and furthermore it was against the rules. The rules. What do the rules say about kidnapping? What do they say about dragging a kid out of her school, uprooting her, placing her with religious freaks?

There's a soft knock at the door. Then a snappier one and you breathe deep twice, too deep, and your first step's a dizzy one.

You open the door, fast and sweeping *à la* Harriet Nelson, and there she is. And him standing behind her. You say nothing to him and grab her, throw your arms in great octopus swings and suction her to your shoulder, lift her up just a little till your back shifts and maybe picking her up's not such a good idea. Baker says he'll be back at nine. That's three and a half hours. How to pack a birthday and four weeks and a million apologies and sobriety and a clean house and fresh breath and love and love and no crying and lightness and mirth into three and a half hours. You swallow and hold her at arm's length, even though it hurts to let her go that far, and think, *Let's join the circus, the Marines, let's run like hell and never come back again,* but instead you touch her new hair like a sheared lamb and say, *Whose idea was this?* Not hers, she says, they did it. Call them jerks and tell her she'll look good as new in a couple weeks. That's the good thing about mops, they grow back. You squeeze her again because she's rag-doll limp and you're trying to squeeze out her scares, squeeze back the miles and miles and years and years since you've hugged another living soul. Then, slide off her coat, some little burlap sack of a thing she says they bought her with Child Protection vouchers. *It's all right,* she says. *I'm not that crazy about it.*

You pat her shoulder and bring her into the living room, show her the pullout couch you got for twenty-five bucks and the TV—well, that was there before—but here, look at the bedroom; no, maybe not, it's kind of depressing. She stands stock-still in this bedroom, then walks to the bed, kneels on one pillow to look out the window into the laneway and says, *It's good how it's on the ground like this—you could escape, you could get out lots of ways—like if there was a fire or something.* Don't remember her being so concerned with fire safety.

You tell her that you thought you'd make pork chops for dinner and she could have raw carrots and radishes and a baked potato. *You like baked potato, right?* and you're embarrassed that you had to ask that. The brain cell with that information seems to be on the fritz just now and she says *Yes* politely, which somehow is more humiliating than regular Yeah-of-course-what-kinda-dope-are-you kid tone. *Or we could have snacky finger-food stuff like cheese and crackers and pickles and raw veggies with french onion chip dip and I got salt-and-vinegar chips too and peaner butter. For a nice peaner butter and jammitch sammitch?* She says it's o.k., porkchops are good. But she seems funny, her voice does, her soul is lagging behind. And you want to cry because you feel exactly the same way.

While frying and slicing, you ask if she's still taking baton lessons. She says it's over, with a sullen stare into the table. *We had this recital thing that parents and people came to where we got judged and marked and stuff. Sadie got first place,* she says. Sadie's beginning to piss you off too, but you brush it aside and say, *Well, how'd you do? was it fun?* and she says, *It was OK, I lost points because my mouth moved while I was counting and then I dropped my baton, except for it bounced on the tip and I caught it and the judges didn't see.* And she smirks, looks pleased with herself—putting one over on the judges: a proud family history. She got Honourable Mention in the end and you expound on how fabulous that is. She's not offering a whole lot of information, so you ask about Explorers and she says that they had a party at Halloween, *and we were all supposed to bring a dessert thing and I brought digestive cookies because I, well, first I went to the bakery and it was kind of expensive for just twelve cookies except if you buy twelve you get thirteen and it's called a baker's dozen, so I bought that so I could get the extra one and then I kind of ate some of them and then there weren't enough, so I bought digestive ones because I like them, but then at the party the other girls' mothers all baked stuff for them and two of the girls looked at me and said, "Nice baby cookies—Smooth move Ex-Lax." And they all started laughing at me, about bringing stuff out of a package and ... I don't know, I went a couple more times and then I quit.* Alas more evidence of your not-up-to-snuff mothering, but who do those brats think they are anyway, so you say *Well, who needs a bunch of crummy little creeps like that around? I don't blame you, I'd've quit too.*

When the pork chops are ready and the potatoes are soft and the margarine's on a dish beside a bowl of raw vegetables and cheese is cut up waiting to sit down on a comfy cracker, you say,

*So would you like to eat at the table or in the living room and watch
TV?* and she says maybe we should eat at the table as if that might
be the wisest because what if the dinner cops pull up, we'll be
screwed.

It's quarter to eight before she seems remotely like herself. It happens in mid-bite of chocolate cake and comes out in the shape of
a squiggly giggle and before you can stop yourself it's out your
mouth: *Did you tell Todd Baker about a dream you had with a man
chasing you down an alley?*

Chocolate gooed *yeah.*

Oh, Grace, why?

What d'you mean? Why not?

*Bec—Sweety! Don't you get what—don't you see how he took
that? He reported it, you know, he said, "I'm sorry, Eilleen, but I don't
feel that I had a choice." And he was insinuating that you could've
been molested by "one of my men," as he put it—not to mention the
fact that he thinks that my drinking may have caused you irreparable
damage. I don't know—maybe he was right. But honey, things are
different now—I'm better and I'm scared that if we're not careful, they
won't give you back to me. Please be careful, if they—just—I couldn't
stand to lose you for any longer.*

She looks pissed off, stares at her icing, scrapes off a forkful
and sloughs it on the side of her plate before taking another bite
of cake. *But I dreamed it! And it was kind of a weird dream and it
was like a story and I felt like telling it and I never—and anyway,
you weren't even in it. I didn't say anything about you!*

Why have you done this; she's nine years old; how the hell is
she supposed to know? *I know, Angel. I'm sorry. I'm sorry things have
been so bad that you would have nightmares like that, but I'll make
it up to you. I feel like he tricked us into this whole thing, anyway.
Neither of us thought you'd be away this long and look what they did,
that … snotrag's got you there for three months—and* suddenly she

chokes on her cake, laughing and coughing and laughing and laughing. *What's so funny?*

Snotrag! You said snotrag, and she coughs and says, *I think I got chocolate cake up my nose.*

By quarter to nine, she's sitting in a pile of ripped-up wrapping paper and a pencil crayon set and felt pens that smell like fruit and a novel called *The Lion, the Witch and the Wardrobe* and The Game of Life while the face of a Timex glints off her wrist. And as if on cue, as if suddenly someone had yanked blinders off this part of her brain, her head jolts up and her mouth says, *Henry! Where's Henry?* She looks embarrassed and ashamed like a bad mother and you know the feeling because that name has just made you feel like the worst one on the planet. She stands up, then sits back down. *Where's Henry, why didn't he come? Is somebody else looking after him?*

Yeah, that's it, someone who had to move to Texas and needed a cat. Think. Shit, it's almost ten to. Baker'll be here. Not now. *I don't know. He's a cat. He's around.* And you suddenly wish your child had narcolepsy, just for now. But there's nothing to do but stutter and ask her if she'd like a cup of tea with you and she says, *Mum!* and you crack, turn off the faucet and say, *Damn. Oh angel, I'm sorry, I lied. I just—Henry fell. At least we think that's what happened. After you went to stay with the Hoods—and that's a fitting name for them if I haven't said so already—h-huh, ah, well, I went into the hospital and George was in town, so I got hold of him and asked him if he'd go over and feed the cat. And, uh, you know how Henry used to get outside from the window by climbing the stucco up and down the building? Anyway, George said he found the cat lying out on the grass below the living-room window and his back was broken. And George didn't want me to see him, he thought I should let him handle it and he thought it'd be better if we didn't tell you, or I thought, if we just made something up for a while. Until things settled down. He was dying, sweety—so George took him and had him put to sleep. I'm sorry.* Oh god—you're a liar and an asshole: your children get broken and your children's children. Even if you'd sent him to the SPCA he might've had a better chance. And your voice cracks when you say, *I didn't know what to do, I didn't want to tell you. If I could go back and change things I would. I promise. I'm sorry.*

Her face is dewy, a river is flowing underneath. It's five to nine. Shit-shit-shit. There's no time to be who you were trying to prove you were. She nods and folds her arms and nods until her whole body is nodding and she looks like someone in a nuthouse. *Please, baby, honey, it'll be all right—Henry knew you loved him and it was—we'll get a new cat, we'll get a kitten together.* You've got her on your lap now, rocking her yourself; if she's going to rock like this, you want to at least pretend it's you who's rocking her. Then she starts to shake and sob and the tears come in a torrent. They pop from every pore on her face, her arms limp so you have to pick them up and tie them around your neck. *Oh, honey. Shhhh, it's OK, I promise everything'll be OK. I promise-promise-promise. Please, Lamby, Todd Baker'll be here any minute, and if he sees you so upset, he might not bring you back, he might think seeing me is too upsetting for you. Please don't cry, please. Shhh, it's OK. There, honey, there, it's OK,* but this is four weeks' worth, or four months or years, or it's all the tears of all the stolen babies in the world. And there's a rap on the door. On time, of course—why the hell do these fuckers always have to be on time? Doesn't anybody dawdle any more? *Listen, lovey, we'll get a little fluffy kitten and we'll—and in a couple weeks it'll be Christmas—*and you toss *Just a minute* over your shoulder—*and we'll have lots of time, just the two of us. We can do anything we want, please, angel, please don't do this. I know you're sad—me too, but they might not bring you back.* And the knocking starts up again, so you ease out from under her, sit her back in the chair before you go to the door.

Todd Baker's standing there, uncomfortable and sheepish, smile plastered on. He looks down as if he's about to kick at the dirt with his toe, then ambles into the kitchen. You titter and tap fingers on your breast plate, say, *Grace is a little upset, I just told her about Henry, her cat, and*—you shrug at the room to say the rest is obvious. Grab a Kleenex off the table and kneel in front of her to dab, run your fingers back through her hair, and her arms come forward and she flops face first into your neck. And you say, *Oof, sweety*, and hug her and thump your palm slow against the rhythm of her panting tears. *Sorry, we just need a second*, you say to him, carefully reading the I-Feel-Like-A-Dolt printed in block letters across his forehead.

He rubs the corduroy patches on the elbows of his blazer, jams hands in his pockets and pulls them back out. *Yeah, oh course, take all the time you need. Grace, did you tell your mom about the bird you got for your birthday?* She snorts and chokes a yes. *Oh*, he says, pulls the left hand out of his pocket and stuffs it back in again.

Hoffman, Anne <u>Eilleen</u>

13.12.74 (T.Baker) Grace went to visit her mother
today and stayed for the evening. Things went fairly
well. I have spoken at length to Mrs. Hoffman, asking
for her help in insuring that Grace does not run
from Mrs. Hood's and she has been cooperative in this
matter.

Grace Twelve

DECEMBER 1974

I COULDN'T STOP FEELING like I was going to cry after being at Mum's. Seemed like I should've been able to stay; she was sober now and she had a new place and she was going to AA again. I thought that was supposed to be the reason I had to go to the Hoods' in the first place. And you could tell she was better cuz of how much she got done by herself, got everything moved, got the phone hooked up, got us a pullout couch, and got me birthday presents on top of it. She was still kind of shaky, but she was her again. And still I wasn't allowed to stay. At night, I lied awake and made up dreams about racing down the street with nothing but a bag of clothes and Lyle. That's what I called Todd Baker's budgie, Lyle. He lived beside my bed in his cage hanging from the stand Todd brought me.

The night after, I decided I had to work harder at training Lyle. I was doing it by sticking my hand in his cage every once in a while like *The Handbook of Budgies and Budgerigars* said to do to get him sitting on my finger like the bird in the picture. I wasn't doing it that good, though—I was supposed to use a pencil or a stick to bring him along slowly, but I wanted him to like me now. I wanted him to sit on my shoulder and go with me everywhere. Anyway, I kept sticking my hand in and Lyle kept screeching and flapping until I gave up and read some of *The Lion, the Witch and the Wardrobe*. But I went back to the cage because I figured if I did it super slow, if I moved really slowly to the cage, put my hand in, really slowly—then Mrs. Hood yelled up the stairs for lights out and I yanked my hand and sent Lyle squawking his head off.

I flicked the light out and went to look out my window. Maybe Mum was doing the same in her room, kneeling on her bed, staring out at the laneway. She wasn't anything like Mrs. Hood, the way she told me about God. Mum's God was nice and gave presents and stuff—"Every unselfish good deed you do will be rewarded threefold." She never said anything about the end of the world or lions and lambs. I stood there and tried to yell a prayer in my head and get God to give me a sign, like whisper in my ear or make Lyle talk. But Wendy made it sound as if God didn't even like me. He was getting rid of me and all the stuff I wanted: there was going to be a new heaven and a new earth because this earth would pass away and there would be no sea. Didn't even make sense; didn't He like the beach? And fish and seagulls—why didn't He like seagulls? And if there was no more death, where would He put everybody? They were always talking on TV about the population explosion and how there was too many of us already. Except for, first, He was going to kill everybody, though, so maybe that's just what He does, lets it get really crowded and then kills everybody.

I let go of the windowsill and backed up to do this thing that I did every night where I ran and jumped on my bed with the lights out so that it was like being blind and flying through the dark until my bed caught me. Except tonight I leaped wrong and went crashing down on the floor. My shins hurt so bad I could feel it in my ears and Mrs. Hood hollered up the stairs. I curled up and held myself, saying "Nothing" as loud as I could, but I could hardly make my lungs move. Then I pulled myself onto my bed and laid there trying to breathe pain-butterflies out of my chest. God seemed creepy all the sudden. Snickery. Like a drooly lizard-thing sitting on me, waiting.

The next morning Mrs. Hood said that if I was going to be crashing around upstairs all hours of the night, then maybe I'd like to go to bed a couple hours early and get it out of my system. I tried to explain but I couldn't get my words right lately, and she cut me off. "That's fine, Grace. From now on, bedtime's at seven." Lilly smiled with her lips sucked in and Wendy looked like I got what I deserved. Eight days left till Christmas vacation, till going to Mum's.

The next Sunday, when there were five left, I sat on my bed and copied cartoons out of the newspaper onto Silly Putty. I had sheets and blankets over my window and mirror, and Lyle was flying free. I hoped he was going to love me more every time I gave him freedom, and eventually he'd fly on my finger the way Wendy said was going to only happen after Armageddon. We just came back from Kingdom Hall a couple hours before and Mrs. Hood was in the kitchen baking; the smell of banana bread fumed under my door and Lyle walked across my dresser, pecking pencils and one of my socks.

Then the doorbell bonged because Wendy and Lilly's sister, Julia, was coming today. I met her once before. She was around the same age as Charlie and she wasn't a Jehovah Witness. In a way I kind of wanted to see her again because she was more like normal, but I didn't want to come out of my room. Todd Baker's voice was in my head, saying, "I'm sure it's your imagination, Grace, of course the Hoods like you. You're just feeling insecure because you're a little homesick."

I listened to them kissing and *hello*-ing and I imagined the hugs. It was making me be homesick for Charlie. I couldn't even write her a letter if I wanted to cuz we didn't have her address. And now she wouldn't have ours either, so I started thinking about all the ways she could find me again—she could call directory assistance and find Mum's new phone number or she could write a letter to Welfare and ask them to give it to me or she could hire a private detective who would go from school to school asking if Grace Hoffman was there. I left my Silly Putty, opened *The Lion, the Witch and the Wardrobe* and reread the same sentence over and over until I gave up. Plates clacked downstairs, then a kettle whistle and laughs here and there, mumbling and Lilly's voice going loud and high and Julia's over top. More mumbles, some clear words. Julia sounded mad all the sudden. "Oh Christ! For God's sake—every goddamn time I call or come into this house, all I hear is *Grace this* and *Grace that*! You torture the hell outta that kid!" and Lilly's voice, "No way! It's her. She's the one who starts it. And plus—she farted! Right at the dinner! And one time in Kingdom Hall!"

My face went prickly and I held my stomach. Then Julia said, "Well, big friggin' deal. I'd like to go fart in Kingdom Hall myself. That poor little bugger, God knows what living in this house does to her digestion. Try leaving her alone, for God's sake! And if she's so bad, she's got an ass, smack it and be done with it!"

Then Mrs. Hood went, "I don't believe in hitting children."

"No? but you believe in torturing them. I don't know how the kid survives—it's a psychological hellhole ... what!? Well, so what, she's not a Witness, so where do you get off trying to—" and her voice quieted off.

Then more mumbling and Lilly squealing, "Huh! Alls I know is I'll be glad when it's February," and Wendy saying something about testing patience until Julia hollered over top, "Listen to them! Obnoxious little brats—the Grim Reaper and her little dog too—and You! *You're* the foster mother! So *foster!*" and Mrs. Hood made hissing noises and the *shush* voice, and mumbles again and more of Julia's sighs and snorts.

I was on my hands and knees listening at my door by then, wishing it wasn't squeaky so I could open it. Then suddenly there was running thumps on the stairs and I ran back on my bed till the feet passed and Lilly's door slammed. I opened my book and stared at a page, all weird cuz of feeling like, Huh-I-was-right and then Oh-no-I-was-right. It was still only December fifteen.

I wanted to hear my mum's voice so bad, but the only time I could talk to her was over at Sadie and Eddy's. Even Josh's place didn't feel safe any more, Sheryl Sugarman looked funny or sounded funny at me about my mum now. Sadie and Eddy's mother, Alice, liked Mum, though, and always had messages to tell me when I came over. It was getting to be the only place I didn't feel scared, but it took two buses to get there and Mrs. Hood wouldn't always let me. She said it was too much to ask of their mother, for me to be there all the time; it was hard enough dealing with two kids never mind a third.

The day after Julia was at the house, I called my mum after school from a phone booth and listened to her voice and the television in the background. I kept a finger in my other ear so traffic wouldn't drown her out. I started asking her about Charlie and if she wrote us a letter yet. Mum said no but not to worry, that it'd only been a month and she was probably really busy getting settled and taking care of the baby. Then she started talking about Christmas and how she already had two Christmas presents for me. I told her about Lilly being mad because a kid in her class gave her a Christmas card. Mum said that was ridiculous, that my Great Aunt Judith was a Jehovah's Witness and she *sent* cards to family at Christmas. Then she asked how it was going over there anyway. I told her, fine. I didn't want to upset her and part of me was worried maybe Mum was *unpredictable*, maybe it'd make her explode so big, Armageddon'd be nothing compared. Plus she had all this getting-better stuff to do; the whole point was not to have to worry about me while she was getting better. She said, "You sound a little blue, angel. Sure everything's all right?"

"Yup. I'm just counting days till I get off school. This school where I'm at now's boring. And I miss you and I want time to hurry up so we can have Christmas time together. Did you get a tree yet?"

"Well, actually, I was wondering what you'd think about an artificial tree this year? Alice was saying that Ray could get us a pretty nice cheap one."

I got all scrunchy inside again. "No. We have to get a real one. Cuz it smells good and it'll feel like a fakey Christmas if the tree's all fakey."

"Okey-dokey, far be it from me to have a fakey Christmas." Then she said that she loved me to pieces and was marking off the days too. She asked what else I wanted for Christmas.

I called her the next day and the next day that week and she still never got a tree. The thing was, what if when it came down to it she didn't get one, or what if she got us one of those skinny-boned old Charlie Brown trees? And maybe she'd hurt her back if she had to carry it all by herself.

Two days before school got out I took the bus up Main Street, got my thirteen bucks out of my bank account and went to a Christmas-tree place. It was like a secret mission, creeping between Christmas trees, scared Mrs. Hood would drive by or Wendy would see what I was doing and tell her mother or tell me I was pagan and that Armageddon was coming before Christmas anyway. I wrapped my scarf higher, for a mask, and looked over the trees until this skinny guy with sunglasses and a leather jacket came out of the trailer, folding his arms from the cold. He walked over with a goony kind of grin and went, "What can I do you for?" I told him I needed a tree, that I was getting it for my mum cuz of her being sick. He nodded and lowered his sunglasses to look at me. His eyes were red and like he just got woken up, and he said, "Huh. So you're the family tree-shopper, huh?—what were you lookin' to spend?"

"Um, around five dollars." He nodded and showed me the five-dollar trees.

I looked at him and at them. "They're kind of ugly, these ones."

He chuckled and looked down, kicking the dirt. "Yeah, they ain't so hot."

"I'll just have a look around, if you don't mind," I told him and he snorted and nodded, rubbing his arms and said, "Hey, be my guest."

It took some looking until I found one that wasn't that huge or too beautiful, and I reached in and tried to pull it up. The stick-guy came over and stuffed his hand in to the middle of the tree, lifted it up and stamped it down a couple feet back. He brushed its branches and gave it another stamp. "Yeah, this old girl's not bad. Nice shape to her."

"How tall is it?"

"Huh, well, around six foot. You picked a good-lookin' tree. Not too glamorous, just good-lookin'."

"Well, is it way more money than the other ones from over there?"

"Well, yeah, it's—well I'll tell ya, you're kind of a funny kid, how 'bout I mark her down on special since your mum's sick and all that. Today only, five bucks."

"Oh."

We stared at each other a second. "Well? what d'ya say, kid?"

"OK. Thank you," and I gave him the two twos and a one out of my coat pocket. I had the rest hid in my boot so he wouldn't think I was rich or anything.

He scrunched the bills up and stuffed them in the hip pocket of his jeans, then said, "So what's the deal here, you carryin'?"

"Um, can I use your phone? And if I arrange for a guy to come get it, would you hold it for me till he comes?"

"Sure thing. Y'gotta like a kid with connections."

I called Sadie and Eddy's dad, and told him I just got a good deal on a tree and could one of his furniture guys come get it and bring it over to Mum's. Ray laughed in my ear and I thought I heard him slap the table. "You're Danny's kid all right. Okey-dokey, just gimme the address or the intersection or whatever the heck you got goin' there."

The next day I came home after school, planning to make a list of all the stuff I wanted to bring to my mum's. I'd called her from school and she made a big deal over me for getting the tree and I was super-excited about Christmas. One more sleep left. I wasn't going to be able to take Lyle, but I didn't know if I could trust them to feed him while I was gone, to change his water. I ran upstairs, thinking about how Lyle probably got more freedom than any other bird he knew. I opened the door and closed it behind me so he wouldn't get out and get us both yelled at. I called his name. Then looked in my closet. Then went over to see under my bed, when some blue caught my eye and Lyle was lying under my window. My unsheeted window. My unsheeted mirror. I kneeled and picked him up; he was still limp and soft. Tears started coming in my nose and I told him how sorry I was for letting him fly against glass he couldn't see, and stroked his wobbly neck.

My face was burning wet when I came down to show Mrs. Hoffman. "And it's my fault cuz I didn't cover stuff up," I told her.

She was sitting at the kitchen table drinking tea. "Aww. I'm sorry, Grace, that's too bad. You should get rid of him, though; there's all kinds of mites and parasites on birds, so you better throw him out." I looked at her then him and kissed his head before I put on my coat and went out back to bury him. Then I stayed in my room until the next morning.

In the morning, they sat across from me over breakfast. Lilly had baggy red eyes, and she stabbed her pancakes then slammed them on her plate and Wendy took deep breaths and chewed slow. I was tired too, from crying most of the night, and I stared into space.

"Shake your head, your eyes are stuck!" Lilly spat at me, pancake flying out her mouth. My brain snapped back to the room and I looked down on my plate. "A-duhh!" she said and clanged her fork down.

"I'm—I wasn't looking at you, didn't see you, I mean."

Lilly rolled her eyes. "Well, maybe if you weren't *bawling* all night over a dumb bird—stupid gomer, you didn't even have it long enough to cry—and did you have to cry so friggin' loud?"

"Lilly!" Mrs. Hoffman gave the warning voice. "I don't want to hear that kind of talk."

"What! I said *friggin'*!"

"We all heard what you said."

Lilly looked at me and did yowly imitations.

Wendy breathed out hard. "Lilly, shut up, I had to listen to the real thing all night," and reached across her for the butter.

Lilly smacked her arm. "Wouldja don't, that's rude!"

Wendy stared at her arm and then at Lilly, put the butter down and, really calm, said, "Don't ever do that again, Lilly." Lilly got one of those stunned shudders in her face and neck that only Wendy could make her have and told Wendy to get lost. Wendy cleared her throat. "You know, Grace, you're not supposed to advertise your grief. Jesus said you're not supposed to show it because if you make a sad face, you're just like the hypocrites and your face gets ugly and then everybody knows. You should act natural when you're sad, so only God knows, and then you'll get rewarded."

Lilly chewed and looked at me. "She's got the same ugly face all the time, how're you s'posed to tell the difference."

"Lilly!" Mrs. Hood turned off the stove and brought the last of the pancakes to the table. "I told you I don't want to hear that kind of talk. At the rate you're going, Judgment Day will be a pretty scary one for you, won't it? Grace's pet died. How would either of you feel if one of the cats died?" and she stomped back to the stove and plopped the pan down.

"Uh! You always take her side." Lilly slammed herself back in her chair.

Wendy joined in. "Yeah, you kinda do. Grace is just trying to get attention. She only had the thing a couple weeks and it always sounded like she was torturing it. And anyway, she killed it herself letting it fly around her room like that."

A wiggle went up my throat in my mouth. "Can I go get ready for school—I don't want to eat—this—I'm, um—" and I crunched my jaws together.

Mrs. Hood was sitting back at the table now with tea. Her voice was calm. "Oh, no? Well, you're going to. I don't get up at seven a.m. for you to turn your nose up at the breakfast I make. I'm sure you're having a hard time right now, but honestly, this is ongoing and it's getting ridiculous. I don't know how your poor mother ever tolerated your pickiness."

Wendy looked up at the ceiling, chewing. I said, "It's not cuz it's bad. I'm just—" and clenched my teeth again.

Mrs. Hood stared at me, waiting. Then she said, "It's my responsibility as your guardian to make sure you're fed, and you're skinnier every time I look at you. And I don't want to hear about what your mother fed you and how you're not allowed to eat white bread or Kraft Dinner—I'd like to know just how a woman on Welfare managed to feed you steak every day and whole milk and fresh juice and fresh vegetables. And she should be ashamed of herself for not forcing you to eat like a normal person—dumping vitamins down your throat. Not to mention your table manners. Half the time you're eating with your hands, and when you do use utensils, it's like you never held one before in your life." Lilly sucked in her lips and got dimples in her cheeks.

Christmas vacation started and Todd Baker drove me to my mum's. He was trying to make peppy happy conversation on the way and I wasn't in the mood. It seemed like he thought it was some big present, bringing me to my mum's place, like I should be grateful or something. But it was mine and I deserved it and I didn't want him thinking he was supposed to get thanked.

He was talking about Christmas in Oregon, his mother and his cousins and their dogs and cats dressed in Santa hats for Christmas pictures. He wished he remembered to bring the one his uncle sent. And then Christmas in New York: the lights and music everywhere; his brother and the wife and how they were Jewish there and they had Hanukkah; did I know what Hanukkah was? Josh never said anything about it. I stared out the window and said, "Uh huh."

He was quiet a second, then, "I haven't been home in more than four years." I wondered if he meant I should feel lucky again. Then he said, "Next year for sure—I think, anyway—I'll be able to make it down; last year my mother came up here."

"What's a draft dodger?" I asked and didn't look at him.

Quiet again. "Where did you hear that?"

"Mm, I don't know. I heard someone say it. Just wondered."

He patted pockets until he found cigarettes, flipped the lid with one hand, looked, then chucked the empty package on the floor. He shifted gears hard and switched lanes. "It's someone who believes so much in the strength of their convictions that they leave their homeland in order to avoid compromising them."

I looked at the Player's Light pack beside his feet and said,

"Hm. I see …" He looked over and chewed inside his lip. I figured I must've nailed him a good one and it was like eating chocolate cake made from scratch.

We came to a red light and both of us stared at it. He lowered his chin and straightened up when the light turned green. "So. How's Lyle? That's such a great name, what made you think of it?"

The Hoods must've said something to him. He was getting me back. I did my no-big-deal voice. "Dead."

Todd watched over the steering wheel till it sunk in. "Pardon?"

"Dead."

I watched him without turning my head. He squinted like something really hurt. "Dead? He died?" He didn't know.

"Quite." I was doing my best Mum imitation. "Last night, as it were." I was sophisticated like crazy.

"Well, why didn't you tell me earlier? Did the cats get him?"

"Nope. Musta got a bad bird. Probably had a short." I got him with a Mum-and-me joke on top of it. I was stomping him.

"What? What is that supposed to mean? What's with you, Grace? Something on your mind? Because I'm sensing a little hostility here. You know, because if you've got something to share or get off your chest, then you needn't be sarcastic with me." I looked out my window. He kept going. "I feel as though you're acting out at me sometimes, Grace, and I don't feel I deserve it. I know it's a drag what's happened to you; I know you've had it rough, but at the same time—you're so damn used to getting your own way, you just make it harder on yourself. Maybe you're used to adults thinking it's cute, your precocious snide little remarks, but I'll tell you right now, it's not going to get you very far. My politics, my job, my life are none of your business."

I couldn't think all the sudden, so I said, "Me too," and my stomach hurt like maybe I would fart and then Todd Baker would win because I'd be ugly and disgusting and riff-raff.

"What?"

"Nothing." Tears ached under my eyeskin.

Todd Baker turned to me as we pulled up in front of the house my mother's place was in. "Grace ... what is with you? You are so—moody. Sometimes you're such a great kid, you're bright and funny, and other times you're nothing but aggressive and manipulative. Don't start crying, it's—forget it, it's no big deal. You're here. Maybe you just need a little time out. You won't have to see the Hoods or me again for another four days." I sat straight, gulping myself back. Todd watched me and wobbled his gearshift back and forth.

I shoved open the door and climbed out, grabbing in the back seat for the suitcase Mrs. Hood loaned me. It caught on something and I banged it back and forth to get it free. Todd told me to hang tough and he'd be right there while he ran around to my side, hanging on to the car so he wouldn't fall on the ice. But it was too late, the slush slid out under my feet; everything flipped up and sideways and slammed me down on my bum.

Todd got there just as I landed. "Aw Grace, com'ere, let me help you. If you could ever be patient." He smiled and tried to catch hold of my arms.

"Lemme—just leave me alone, I can do it myself." I slid around in the dirty slush and grass until I got standing enough to hold on to the car roof, then backed up to the sidewalk.

Todd picked the suitcase out of the slush and tiptoed through it. "Here, Grace, let me help you in—I'll carry it."

"No. I'm fine—just—I don't need help." I grabbed the suitcase, doing my best not to touch him. "God. I'm going to see my mum, OK? so I'm fine—just—Thank you," and dragged it up the walkway. Todd stood there and I didn't look back until I heard both car doors slam and the engine go burping down the street.

Eilleen Eleven

G ET READY. Peering out your window, moments ago, there appeared to be a war on your sidewalk. You open the door and glee *Lamby-Pie* at the soggy lump on your doorstep.

Your child is grey-slushed from ground to elbows, her eyebrows arm wrestling above her nose; there is a glob of mud sticking hair to her jaw. *Don't you look lovely,* you say and pull her in by the coat collar, await the tirade, the stomping ...

Nothin': she just stares at her boots, tight-mouthed. You undo buttons, thinking, *Christ, those foster people have cruddy taste in clothes*, then slide the dismal brown coat down off her and say, *Wanna step out of these?* Her eyes are welling as you pull off black gumboots, stand them on the doormat and heap that coat over top. *What's wrong?* and you take her jaw in your hands and kiss her smack on the mouth. *What's wiff oo? poor antface* and tears fling themselves out of her ducts and you're half-surprised she hasn't taught them to shriek as they go. You wish for her sake she could say, *You should see the other guy*, but you saw him yourself and he was dry-dry, just a bit of social-worker dismay stuck in his teeth. You put your arms around her bony body—it's bonier than usual —and hug, kiss three times: temple, cheek, neck, and say *What's the matter? Say something. What were you and Baker fighting about?*

I don't know, she says and squashes herself against you, stuffs her face in your neck.

Uh oh. What did you say? and she yowls and pulls off; you've stepped on her tail. Well shit, it's not really an accusation, it's just—*Well, don't get your shirt in a knot, come back here. I just wondered, just seems like he's too nerdy to actually* start *a fight with a beast like you.*

She likes being called a beast and this has a calming effect. She takes a breath, then, *I asked him what a draft dodger was.*

Gasp here. You and your big mouth. *Oh, Grace! Gees.* That's all you can think of before a laugh squirts out of you. *What a bugger you are!*

Oh well, a girl's got to survive and you hold her to your chest and pat between her shoulder blades, the loose amethyst in your ring giggling against her back. She gurgles and slurps tears over your shoulder and you pull back to look at her, kiss her cheek as you pass it, say *Ew, are you getting me all snotty?*

And her gurgles round into giggles and she shudder-breathes and says, *And he asked why Lyle died and I said that he must've got me a bad bird and maybe there was a short in it.*

Ack! That's all you have to say to that. And all the giggles— yours, hers, your ring's—turn to cackles because nothing is more hilarious than flipping a family joke about men on a man like Baker, since Baker's just the kind of man who started that joke: the kind of man who picks up any broken household appliance, cocks his head and then, like a belch after beer, must follow with, *Ah huh, well, must be a short in it.*

Well! you say, *enough about him, let's talk about us ... Looky-looky*—and you reach into your blouse and whip an envelope out of your bra. And her eyes splash at the frivolous oh-so-naughty gesture. She squeaks *Charlie?* before you can open your mouth again.

She snatches it out of your hand, tries to rifle it open, drops it and looks about to cry again. She *sorry*s, picks it up and pulls out the pages, scans Charlie's looping squirrel script and asks you to read it to her:

Dear Mum,

I hope you get this. The last one I sent came back. I'm going to try mailing it to Lilly Darling at Welfare. She'll probably know where you are. I hope you guys are doing OK. God I miss you. I feel like I'm going to die of homesickness. But guess what, I'm coming home soon. I wanted to call you so bad and tell you but Ian won't let me have a phone. He says I'll just run up long-distance bills. Everything's kind of weird right now. I'll tell you when I get back. Oh god, I can't wait. Every day takes a week but at least I know I get to see you guys soon and Sam'll get to see his Nana and his Aunty Grace. Probably after Christmas, around the beginning of January. Tell Graceface I love her like crazy and I can't wait to hug her again. I love you.

Love Charlie
xoxoxoxoxox

P.S. Do you think you could call Lilly Darling when you get this and ask her if I can get Welfare again when I come back?
P.P.S. And also tell Grace that I'm sorry I won't have money for Christmas presents this year. I wish I had bags of money to buy her everything in the world. xoxox

Grace looks like she's about to hyperventilate. *Did it come in the mail?* she says, *Who's Lilly Darling?*

Lilly Darling is Charlie's old social worker. Remember, she was over last year when we first moved to Vancouver. Maybe you were out. Anyway, I guess she dropped it off because it was under the door this morning.

Well, are you gonna call her, Lilly Darling, are you gonna call and tell her Charlie needs a welfare cheque at beginning of January?

Yes. Yes I am, in fact I already did. So they know she's coming. They'll do up an emergency assistance cheque when she goes into the office.

Her face looks stunned, stuck in limbo, as if she's too scared to get excited. So you grab her and start to waltz round the kitchen— *Charlie's coming soon, chachacha, her boyfriend's a baboon, chachacha, we're gonna sing a tune, chachacha, 'cause we're crazy like loons, chachacha.* And she giggle-shrieks at the ceiling as you dip her.

You realize the first night how uncomfortable she is discussing the Hoods, and you're not sure who she's scared of: you or them. Or Baker. But she won't come out with much in the way of details. You must infer things, deduce from the way her body buoys up when you suggest making popcorn in the middle of the afternoon, to watch *The Newlywed Game* and *Match Game* back to back, that this isn't the way things go in her current abode. Must assume that Steve Lawrence and Eydie Gorme's announcement on *Tattletales* that they would probably live together first if they met today would not be tolerated in the Hood house by the way Grace glances from the screen to you and back. By the way she suddenly plunks a television trivia question on the table: *Rhoda slept over at Joe's sometimes before they were married, right?* And you say, *Sure.*

She looks vindicated—*Just cuz Wendy and Lilly said no way that Rhoda never did that before she was married or they wouldn't watch the show.*

Well, the yoke's on them. Is there a lot you're not allowed to watch over there?

She shrugs, mumbles and clams up.

And so that's how it goes, she drops crumbs and you try to make stuffing. It's good, though. Mostly. You gave her the bed and you've been sleeping on the pullout couch—figured it would benefit both of you, since you can't sleep and end up pacing around the house at all hours and you don't want to bomb yourself with the pills it would take to put you out because—well, just because.

Because it feels good to be awake sometimes and hear her squeak and the blankets ruffle, to be able to go in there and say *there there*, ask what she dreamed. The second night with you, she woke up and sat staring out the window. When you came to her, she said, *I feel like I'm forgetting something, like I'm supposed to be somewhere. I feel like someone's coming.*

Just Charlie, you said and kissed her.

Nights you can't sleep and nights you can, you dream schemes of driving away, and it's so real the steering wheel just floats under your hands and the top is down and Grace is bouncing on her side of a white leather bench seat, playing with the radio dials. You're somewhere on the Prairies and there's a breeze and the two of you are getting pink in the sun and she's singing that song, that one she used to sing about a brand new pair of roller skates. "I ride my bike, I roller skate, don't drive no car, don't go too fast but I go pretty far. For somebody who don't drive I bin all around the world; some people say I done all right for a girl."

"Christmas wouldn't be Christmas without presents." That was the first line of your favourite book when you were Grace's age. *Little Women.* Maybe you were older. But you bought it for her anyway. And you bought her one of those little Kodak cameras and two games: Payday and checkers. And goofy things like a straw that coils around in circles before it gets to your mouth, and you were going to get her a Pet Rock but the really goofy thing was the price. And she got you these enormous fluffy purple slippers that you'll never wear because they make you look like Carol Burnett. There's one last one to open; it's for you from her. *Wait,* Grace grabs the camera while you examine your present, wondering what in god's name she's picked out: shiny and flat and could only be a record. You shake it anyway, gaze up at the lights on the tree. She says it's a new basketball and laughs uproariously, looks through the camera and tells you to be Christmassy. *Flash!* she yaps. You bring the present down on your lap and start lifting the edges of taped paper. *Faster!* she orders and reaches over as if she's going to help.

Get lost, goofball! you say. She rolls her eyes and leans back to flash another Kodak moment. *Quit it, you, I was busy savouring and now I'm going to look like an old hag in that picture.*

And it's—who? You smile at the Cellophane-covered jacket, say, *How do you know who the Ray Charles Singers are?*

I don't. You said it once and I wrote it down.

It's one in the morning, Christmas Eve, and you've never been so grateful for another human being in your life.

Hoffman, Anne Eilleen

22.12.74 (T. Baker) As by agreement, Grace taken to
her mother's for the holidays. She will be staying
until December 26th. I have already made arrangement
to go to court on January 6th to request an early
return of Grace to her mother, as Mrs. Hoffman is
managing very well now. We had talked of a V.I.P.
placement earlier in the month, and now that she is
physically stronger, she has taken to the idea of a
job quite well. She is still attending AA.

Except for pressure to visit her mother, Grace has not
had any requests and has been doing very well, except
for minor conflicts with Mrs. Hedd's Hood's little
girls.

26.12.74 (T. Baker) Grace taken back to Mrs. Hood's.

27.12.74 (T. Baker) Grace had tantrum over her
allowance, slamming doors, etc.

Grace Thirteen

DECEMBER 1974

W E ALL COUNTED the days until February third, when I'd be gone for good. Mrs. Hood still tried to make me feel included, though: she told me one morning, while Lilly and Wendy were arguing about Jews and whether they'd survive through Armageddon, that their family vacation was coming up. Lilly'd been explaining to me, "We don't get blood transfusions cuz it's wrong. Or any bloods at all, even. Like in the war, Hitler tried to make us eat blood sausage but we wouldn't but the Jews ate them, plus they fought amongst themselves. See, they're not at peace with each other and they prob'ly won't survive Judgment Day." I was wondering if I should tell Josh that or if he rathered not know. I couldn't stand it if God hurt Josh. Then Wendy yelled at Lilly that she shouldn't talk about the Jews because they were God's chosen people. And Lilly yelled back that she never said anything bad about them and "I can say Jew any time I want— Jew-Jew-Jew!" Mrs. Hood told everyone to simmer down and changed the subject with this thing about a trip to Harrison Hot Springs. She said they had friends there with a place and there would be room if I wanted to join them. Lilly rolled her eyes and I suddenly got a jumping under my jaw, like a big hopping nerve, while I tried to think of an excuse not to go. "I don't have any money, though; I don't think I can do trips."

"Child Protection makes allowances for things like that. I've already asked Todd about it. So you give it some thought. We can probably make arrangements for you to stay somewhere if you don't want to go. By the way, I'm working tonight, I switched evenings with another lady at work, so you kids'll have to get your own dinner this evening." She poured herself some more tea.

Lilly groaned. "I hate when we have to make ourself dinner— stupid Grace won't eat anything."

They kept on about McDonald's and I tried to picture Mrs. Hood working at the White Spot, waiting on tables, smiling the way she did the first day I met her. "If you only work one night a week," I asked her, "how do you pay for stuff? Do you get other money? Like, for me?"

"You're rather inquisitive this morning, aren't you?" Mrs. Hood looked at me like I was a cockroach on the counter.

"What's that?"

"It Means You're Nosey." It would've been funny if Mum said it. My mind went out of the room and into a story about a dead cat a boy in school told me about. He said his brother went to the SPCA, got a cat they put to sleep, boiled its skin off and put back together the bones. I wondered where it was, all skinless, put back together wrong, teetering till someone figured out all you had to do was flick it right and it'd clatter all over the floor.

Stuff seemed better if I wasn't around the house. I spent as much time as I could at Sadie and Eddy's or over with Josh and his mum, but then Mrs. Hood got it in her head that I was spending too much time at their places. So she decided she needed to give my friends' mums something to show her thankfulness.

I watched her lining up batches of perogies on cookie sheets and tried to ask why without being inquisitive. I told her she didn't have to: "Sadie and Josh's mums invite me."

"That's fine, but it's important to show gratitude."

I stared at the white blobs. She was going to give Sheryl Sugarman and Alice a prize for being able to stand me. I went up to my room and waited until she called me down and loaded Wendy, Lilly, me and two trays of Saran-Wrapped perogies in the car and drove away.

We weren't on the road that long before I forgot where we were going. Couldn't remember if it was bowling or skating; one time we talked about bowling.

Or a meeting in someone's house. Phyllis—my name's not Phyllis, kept going through my mind, loud then soft, hard then slow. Who was that—where were we when I was Phyllis? Then nothing. It was like one of those blank-space-in-my-brain things. But giant.

We pulled up in front of a house and Mrs. Hood told me to go on. I looked out the window and reached for the door handle, except there was food on my lap, a thing of perogies.

Space.

Something about perogies.

Maybe if I felt around, asked questions like normal—"With these?" I pointed my nose at my lap.

"Yes! Go on, we haven't got all night. I want to get home by a decent hour. And for goodness' sake, don't drop them."

I walked up the path like a tightrope. I knew the house, I knew where I was; it was in there somewhere. On the tip of my brain. I went up the steps with the tray, wondering if I'd fall. With the perogies in one arm, I got the screen door open, but the tray started to go and *Phyllis!* I yelled that in my brain so God would hear, caught the tray against the door and knocked. Feet banged towards me, inside, and the door swung away and I grabbed hold of the tray with both hands.

Then Eddy, standing there. Eddy. This was Sadie and Eddy's house. Sadie came up behind and they smiled and said Hey! and What're you doing here? things like that. I smiled back. I was mostly glad someone I knew opened the door. Sadie and Eddy and me looked at each other and I looked back at the car, opening my mouth in case the reason might come out. Mrs. Hood's shadow was hunched, her head ducked a bit so she could see me. Because I was supposed to do—something …

Alice came up behind Sadie and Eddy, wiping her hands on a dishtowel, saying, "Hey, what the hell're you kids doin', tryin' to warm up the neighbourhood? Close the bloody door." I smiled at her the way she was doing and Sadie and Eddy were doing until I figured out I must've made a mistake. Alice bounced her eyebrows at my tray and said, "Hey, are those for me?" and I looked at them.

"I think I'm in the wrong place, I can't—just a sec," and I ran back down the stairs to the car.

Mrs. Hood rolled down her window. "What are you doing?"

Just. Nothing. Space. And a tray. "Am I supposed to give these to them?"

Wendy watched straight ahead at the headlights on the road. Her mum leaned across and snapped, "Yes! Of course. Go! What are you doing?"

I turned slowly. Really slowly. Like a hand going in a birdcage, walking, and walking faster because maybe it was that I was in trouble. I came to the door where the three of them were whispering at each other. The screen door opened again and I tried to make my tray into words. "Yeah. These. These're made—she made them for you." Sadie and Eddy looked at each other and *duh*ed me at the same time. I nodded and laughed because that's what you do when you're dozed-out and someone says, "Duh."

Alice took the perogies. "Wow, that's terrific! Well, thank, uh, what's her face for me, that's very nice of her—you comin' in or what? It's colder than a witch's tit."

In. "I don't know." And I looked back at the car and saw Mrs. Hood's arm waving or pulling something towards her. Me, maybe. I looked back at Alice. "Um. No." Eddy laughed. Sadie smacked him and he called her a lez. "'K. Um. Bye," and I walked away.

Next was Josh's place. I did it fast and quick and didn't talk that much to them.

The day after the perogie night, I called Todd Baker about Harrison Hot Springs and told him how I'd rather do something else with my vacation money. After that, I kept going over it in my head, what I was going to tell Mrs. Hood and how she wasn't going to get mad. The next day in the afternoon, after Kingdom Hall, I figured it was a good time. She was baking.

Just act natural, I figured.

And I went into the kitchen where she was putting spoonfuls of dough on a cookie sheet. "Um. I was talking to Todd and—I said—well, he said that if I wanted to go do a different kind of thing, I could. And it didn't have to be Harrison Hot Springs."

"Uh huh." She either wasn't listening or it was going good.

"Like fo—the money they give for me doesn't have to be for Harrison. I asked him and he said that if I didn't want to go, that you'd be getting money and that I could get it from you."

The air went different. She turned and stared. I went over, in my head, what I just said. Her eyes squinted and her teeth opened. "I do not believe what I just heard. Can you have the money? Is that what you just said to me? You want the money? You ... have got to be the nosiest, most money-grubbing, intolerable child I ever—Your poor mother. How she ever managed to put up with you. Where you get the nerve is beyond my comprehension—that you dare!" She turned and yanked open the stove door, then went back for her cookie sheet, slammed it inside and banged the door shut. "That's it. I've had enough. I'm through dealing with you and I'm calling Todd this afternoon. Maybe your mother could do it for nine years, but I can't. I can't stomach this another day," and she left the kitchen.

Space.

Eilleen Twelve

IT'S SATURDAY AFTERNOON and you're doing your roots, naked from the waist up, stained towel round your neck, plastic gloves on, covered in nut red goop, consistency of egg white, toothbrush in hand, bristles slimed and ready for the next parting of the hoary sea. You've just started working your way towards the back—hate the back, can't see a bloody thing—when the phone rings. Shit. There's crap on your ears and on your neck. And it's ringing again. Shit. Drop your toothbrush in the goop cup. Oh, forget it, just let it ring. Nobody important ever calls you anyway. And you pick up the brush again, but the phone keeps ringing. Thing's already rung half a dozen times; if you grab it now, they'll hang up for sure.

Well, crap, hang up!

So you start pulling at the tips of the gloves—and then rinse them off instead. Swish them around and listen to the phone scream fire. Scream *fire*; does that mean someone's being raped?—

what is that thing again, if you're on fire (dry your hands on your neck towel)—if you're being towelled, scream rape. If your towel's screaming—*Hello!?*

Mummy?

Oh! Grace! For goodness' sake, didn't even occur to me it might be you. Hello, angel, where are you?

Sadie and Eddy's.

Oh, because I'm just doing my roots. Can I call you back? And there's a pause while your child hums like she hasn't heard a word. *Sweety, what's going on? anything wrong?* And she pauses from the not-tuneful melody and says Huh?

I said, what's wrong, you sound funny.

Yeah. Mm.

Grace?

And she's humming again.

Grace, what the heck's going on? Alice said you were over there the other night and you didn't know whether you were coming or going, you could hardly put a sentence together. What's wrong?

Pause. *Yeah. um. I think I have to go?*

What?

I think Mrs. Hood is going to tell Todd I have to go cus, um, she doesn't want me there any more. And then she starts something close to singing, can't figure out what. Sounds like the radio is on in the background.

What do you mean, she doesn't want you there? What's going on, what did she say?

She said, um, I asked if I didn't go with them to Harrison, could I have the money that the Welfare was giving for it, and she said that I was nosy and money-grubbing and how could you have ever put up with me for nine years. And more singing—sounded like she said "They're searching for us everywhere, but we will never be found, na-na-na ..."

Grace! Stop it—what are you singing?

Just this song—and she said she couldn't stomach me any more. And then your child sings, "Band on the run, na-na-na, band on the run ..."

Grace! Listen to me, stop singing! Stop it.

And it's quiet, just music in the background and one of Alice's brats screaming its smelly head off in the distance. Then small and gravelly, *I'm scared to go home.*

Miss Clairol *Flame* is dripping down your neck, which has heated up to your ears.

Bullshit! Your kid is your kid, and that's the bottom line— goddamn bitch. Swallow hard and say up-your-ass to the system: *So don't go.*

What? The voice is bug-sized with tiny paper wings.

Don't go. Come home. To me.

Grace Fourteen

THE CLOSEST BUS STOP was three blocks away, on Main Street. I sat on the bench breathing into my mittens, watching all the cars for Mrs. Hood or Todd Baker. They knew for sure I wasn't just late. I stomped my feet on the ice and pulled my scarf higher up my face and walked back and forth in front of the bench.

Every time I pushed my mitt down to check my watch, my stomach crittered up my ribs. It was after four o'clock and getting darker. Someone pulled on my coat and whispered "Grace"—I spun around, and smashed down on the ice. No one was there, just one of those big rusty bench screws caught on the hem of my coat. I looked around again to make double sure they weren't there and, before I could get up, the bus splashed up to the curb and slushed me all over. The doors opened and the driver chuckled, watching me stomp up the steps. "Sorry, kid—what the heck were you doing on the ground?" and his neck jiggled like his belly. I was crabbed and thought of mean fat stuff, but I was too scared to look at him in case he recognized me. Maybe the police were looking for me. I dumped my money in the box, then went and found a window seat so I could see them before they saw me.

When Mum opened the door, we stood there a second with our eyes sticking on each other. She grabbed me and pulled me to her stomach. "Quick, get inside," and she slammed the door closed behind me, "it's cold." She straightened up and put her hands on my shoulders, then put one hand on her hip and the other one on her forehead, then dropped both by her sides. She pulled my toque off and patted my head cuz of it being sweaty. "Well, actually, no. Here," and she pushed the toque back on, looked over her shoulder to the living room. "I'm packing the couple things you left here and I called Stewart. Remember Stewart? I thought maybe we better get out of here, and stay the night there. I don't think it's a good idea if we're here tonight—OK? Are you OK, sweety, you look a little peaked?"

I nodded. "Did they call here? They're probably gonna come. Should I phone and make something up or something? Or—did Todd Baker call?"

"No, but I'm sure we'll hear from him. I should threaten to turn the bugger in if he doesn't mind his own goddamn business. I s'pose he's got some kind of asylum here, though. Come on, come in the bedroom while I get our things together—oh shit, I suppose I should call a cab."

I followed along behind her. "Did you say he's in an asylum?"

Mum giggled a scared laugh. "You're a dandy, MaryAnne. It—I'll tell you later. Now ... there's a bag on the bed with underpants and pyjamas and a pair of slacks, and that crummy yellow dress that Mrs. Hood got you—don't worry, I'll call her myself later and let her know where you are, and I'll call Baker too—don't worry, angel," she did her accent like Carol Burnett being The Queen. "Darling, don't let's get in a tizzy, it'll all come out in the wash."

"I'm just scared they'll come."

"No one's coming—they'll just think you're late. You're a kid, kids do that. OK, OK, hmm, OK, I think that's it, go call six-six-nine, seven-triple-seven and ask for a taxi. You know the address?"

We took the elevator up to floor seventeen in Stewart's building. When the door opened, he had a drink in his free hand. "Wellll! ..." His voice was so low and big, it rumbled. "Look at you! look at you, Gracey! Jesus Christ, you're big. Last time I saw you, you were like this—" he brought his hand way down as if the last time he saw me I was as big as a cat, "and now look atcha! Growin' like a weed!" He chuckled and nodded, and he was really bald. I noticed cuz he took his hand off the door to scratch some hair still at the back.

Mum and I stood in the hall; I looked at Stewart's belly and she patted it, then pulled me past him inside. "Oh, Stewart, you silly old thing. Have you got anything in the fridge, I'd like to make Grace something for dinner. We've been rushing around so much, we haven't really had time to eat."

Stewart hung on to the door, smiling still, after Mum dropped our tote bag on the floor and started looking through the cupboards in his kitchen. "Oh," he swung it closed, "uh, hmm uh yeah, well something, yeah, there must be something. Maybe Kraft Dinner or something."

Mum stared into a cupboard. "Hey kiddo, you want some Kraft Dinner for a treat, or what? Or-r-r, here, hey, here's some corned beef—I could make you a corned beef sandwich. Stewart? Bread? Have you got any bread? and mustard?"

Stewart closed the door and went and leaned on the counter-top that was between the puny kitchen and the living room. He squished his fingertips in his forehead and looked at Mum's bum.

She turned around. "Stew? You OK? You look like you've been into the hootch pretty good tonight."

He burped like he meant to and smacked his hand over his mouth when he looked at me. "Excuse me, Miss," and smiled. "Yeah, I got bread. I think I got rye! Make her a corned beef on rye—hey, that's a damn good idea," and he slapped his burp hand onto the counter. "Yeah, make me one too. A corned beef … on rye. I'd like that." He looked at me again and clapped his hands together. "Yessirreee!"

Mum winked at me. "OK, you two kids go sit in the living room and I'll make sandwiches. Stewart, leave your drink here and I'll freshen it."

Stewart and I sat on the couch in front of a hockey game. He looked from me to the TV. "Y' like hockey?—naw, you don't like hockey; this is no fun for you, geez. Let's take a look-see in the old boob-tube guide here, and see. See, see, see … hmm … hey, there's a *Get Smart* rerun on. D'ya like that? I like that guy." He held his thumb and finger close and said, "*Missed it by* that *much.*"

I laughed even though it wasn't that good an imitation and looked at the TV. Mum brought in sandwiches and tea a few minutes later. Stewart looked in the teacup she gave him and said, "Tea? Tea. Where's my—" and he looked over at me.

Mum said to him, like he was my little sister or something, "Oh, sorry, honey, did I forget milk and sugar?"

Stewart looked all pouty in his cup and then tried to act natural just like as if another kid punched him and he didn't want to go crying in front of everybody. He was super-like-that—like a big dumb kid, especially with his slow goofy voice—he said, "Huh, ohh, no, I'm—I like it black. Yeah, this is nice." As if.

Then we started eating our sandwiches. They were pretty good for scrounging-in-the-cupboard sandwiches—corned beef tastes way better than it sounds. It sounds like it'd have sloppy corn all over it and taste sick. Sometimes the worst thing about stuff is its name. I started thinking that about Stewart while I was eating—*stew* and then *wart*. Then I felt sorry for him, sort of, even though I still didn't want to hang around with him or anything; he kept sighing between bites of sandwich and wiping mustard off his mouth with the back of his hand. Then he noticed the big smeary glob of mustard on him and starting looking around the room like he got punched again. Mum grabbed a paper towel and put spit on it and wiped his hand. He smiled with his stuffed mouth closed, and sighed through his nose. You'd think it was the hardest thing he ever had to do, eat a corned beef sandwich. He took a sip of his tea and winced-up his face like he was sucking lemon. Then he said, "This is good, Eilleen, I think, though—I'm, uh—I'm just going to have a nap. And have this rest later. Okey-doke?"

I must have had ESP for a second cuz I was right then thinking he needed a nap time. He got up and bumped into the wall on his way to the bedroom. It wasn't even that funny, really. It was how Mum was a lot of times when she used to come home from being out with him. And then I felt sick cuz of suddenly remembering Mrs. Hood hating my guts and probably sending the police out looking for me. And Todd Baker would hate me too, and they'd be looking for me in police cars and stuff and we couldn't go to any of our normal places or they'd find us. Stewart's was our only secret place.

I think Mum got ESP then too—she picked up the phone and put it in her lap. Mrs. Hood—she was reading my mind and she wanted to call Mrs. Hood and I'd have to tell her the number or she'd hate my guts too. I looked at my last hunk of sandwich and ate it. Chew each bite twenty times—I kept thinking that in my head, over and over—chew each bite twenty times, twenty times, twenty times. Mrs. Hood told me that once after I got another stomach ache.

Mum reached over and flipped my hair behind my ear. Her hands smelled all clean and like bread. "I think I better call and let Mrs. Hood know you're all right."

Fifteen chews, sixteen, seventeen—my mouthful was like goo, so I just swallowed before twenty. Except my teeth kept clacking together looking for stuff and biting inside on my cheeks. What if Mum went like a tornado and yelled and screamed at Mrs. Hood, and screamed and yelled and swore, and then they traced the call? And stupid Wendy would say I told you so—and the lion will lay down with the lamb. You can't have a tiger for a pet.

I squeezed everything tight, my toes and teeth and armpits and bum, until it hurt as much as possible, and then I let go. Mum said, "Would you feel better if I let you dial?" No. Nope. And the lion will lie down with the lamb. "OK, how about if you tell me the number, and I'll dial." No. No way. You can't have a tiger for a pet. Mum touched my cheek again and I jumped. Her hand jumped back a little and she came in close and put her arm around me. "It's OK, honey, I just want to let her know you're OK, that's all. She's probably worried."

"No, she won't care. Let's just go."

"Go where? Sweety, listen, we have to call and come clean so they don't think you've been kidnapped or something."

"Yeah. Yah. 'K."

"Do you know the number?" She was talking to me like I was even younger than Stewart.

"Yeah." Just say it, and the lion will lay down with the lamb. And Jesus will take back the keys to the world. "OK. It's eight-seven-six." Their numbers—*You cannot give out this number!* Numbers, Deuteronomy and Matthew and Joshua. I missed Josh. Why couldn't we've just stayed with Josh? "I can't re—I'm not allowed," and my plate has to go in the sink. I got up and went in the kitchen and sat on the floor behind the counter. I forgot my plate. Just rest for a while. Like nap time when you're little. What will happen to little children at Armageddon?

Mum came in the kitchen with the phone and a long snake-cord dragging behind. She sat down on the floor beside me, then she put the phone beside her and held my hand and kissed it. She said, "I just don't want her to worry."

"I'm not allowed."

"I know. But you're with me now, you're safe."

"Yeah. Don't tell, 'K? OK. Eight-seven-six. Um—" Mum looked at me like I was the best thing in the whole world. "Eight-seven-six, five-three-seven-four."

She started dialling. I watched the circle of the dial float back around after each number. Then, "Hello!" Loud, too loud. "Is that Mrs. Hood? ... Hi, this is Eileen Hoffman." And quiet. Then, "Oh yes. I, well, Grace dialled the number so I could let you know that she's here with me and you wouldn't worry." My chest went tight when she said my name. I turned my back away and put my forehead on my knees, squished my eyeballs hard. Then Mum said, "Pardon? No, I'm not—she's fine, she was just a little home-sick and wanted to stay with her mum for a while and I wanted you to know." Then there was a big pause and Mum took a breath like she got punched too, and she stuttered all flabbergasted and went, "Wha—just a second here, a child like what?—Grace is not a child like anything—she's terrific, she's here because I want her here, because I love her, and as a matter of fact, *I* told her to come home ... No, listen, I don't appreciate your tone or what you're saying or, furthermore, what you've put my child through. Grace is what keeps me alive. You may believe in death, but I happen to believe in life!" And then she said "Merry Christmas" and slammed the phone down. Quiet.

My chest hurt, so I breathed and Mum said, "Gee, hon, she's lovely. Why have you been keeping her from me?" She was trying to be funny, so I smiled a bit and asked what Mrs. Hood said. Mrs. Hood told Mum she shouldn't have to deal with a child like me in her condition. That's why Mum got so mad. Then Mum said to me, "Well, may's well keep going while we're on a roll," and started dialling Todd Baker. It was kind of the same, except she didn't get as mad when she got to the mad part. She just said, "Look, she was afraid to go home. What did you expect me to do, send her away?" And then she told him to never-mind and hung up on him too.

I felt sort of smiley butterflies a bit after she hung up on Todd Baker. Now he could just see how it feels, getting told off when you're upset. Plus, he shouldn't even have got upset; she was *my* mum. Then I asked her what he said. And she said he told her she was going to get charged with kidnapping and to send me right back where I came from.

Mum swooped over and went "Nap!" when she hugged me. We got snorty giggles and I grabbed her back. "Nap!" We kept napping each other on the kitchen floor. Then she pulled me onto her lap and said, "Kidnapping my own kid—huh! Draft-dodging little turd." And I started laughing like crazy. Mum always had good words like *turd* to call people—and she said it some more, only like The Queen—"Yes, a turd, I say, a turd without a country! Poor goof, probably scared they'll ship him back to Ohio or wherever the hell he's from." I told her he was from Oregon. And Mum went, "Ew—an Oregonian turd. They're the worst!" Mum's hilarious when she's being funny. "Well, screw 'em all; it's just you and me, kid. Come sit and watch TV with your old Tigress ma," and she growled and we went and laid down on the couch together.

Grace Fifteen

M UM WANTED US to keep moving. Like Butch Cassidy and the Sundance Kid. She didn't say that and I never saw the movie, but I heard that's what they did. And plus, I really wanted to be called The Sundance Kid.

Stewart's head hurt and he was sad that we were leaving. He seemed kind of bugged that Mum wouldn't say where we were going. I figured she couldn't tell him cuz then he'd know too much, until we were sitting, all set to go, in the back of the taxi— turned out she didn't even know. All she could think of for telling the driver was *downtown*.

We were in the taxi for around ten minutes' worth of driving when he finally said into the rear-view mirror again, "So, where d'you wanna go? Do you *know* where you wanna go?"

Mum kept looking out the window. There was rain again and it made everything blue—the trees and people and streets. "No, just go downtown ... somewhere cheap."

"OK, you mean a hotel or something; now we're gettin' some-where. Whereabouts? Like *downtown* downtown? or Broadway and Main? or—I mean, we'll be downtown in another seven, eight minutes, eh … so, uh—" He wiped the back of his hand across his nose and sniffled. I looked at his black hair curling down on his shoulders, then in the rear-view mirror at his eyes, blue and shiny and right in this little clean space between the curls on his forehead and the beard creeping up his face. He opened his mouth and closed it again, then went, "A cheap hotel."

"Yeah, nothing fancy, just a cheap clean place to stay the night."

He was quiet a second. "Well, hey, y'know, the Child Protec-tion's got a place where y—"

"No!" bursted out of Mum and me at the same time. We gig-gled at each other and fidgeted.

The driver-guy watched us in the mirror. "Hey, no problem, whatever you like," and waved his hand at the idea as if it was a bug on the steering wheel. "We'll just keep drivin', that's no prob-lem … So how cheap?"

"Cheap!" We said it together again like we were the chicken sisters.

"Right." He nodded, "Cheap." Well, we'll be coming up on the Ivanho Hotel on Main. Shitty area, but it's somethin' around ten, twelve bucks a night."

"Sold!" She held my hand and said, "Just think, you can look back at this someday when you have kids and tell them we ran away and stayed at the Ivan-ho-ho-ho Hotel."

I looked up at the place as we stopped. Mum leaned over the seat and paid the driver with some of the money Stewart gave her, saying, "Umm, just the bills, please—I'm sorry, that's not much of a tip, we're in sort of a tight spot right now."

"Hey, I understand, completely, eh—I know the scene. You guys take care," and he patted the back of the seat.

We got out and Mum took me by the hand under humongous neon letters that ran up and down over the doors. "IVAN O," it said, with the burned-out "H."

The lobby smelled like cigarettes and beer. We could hear yelling and glass clinking in the bar behind us through the swinging doors, like the kind of doors in a western movie except for made of metal. The carpet was black with giant red flowers, and had a dirty crusty part right outside the bar doors and a worn-out-carpet path going from the outside door to the front desk.

I looked around while Mum did the talking at the front desk. The bar doors smashed open and a skinny guy, kind of like the guy who sold me the Christmas tree, tripped out and sloshed his beer, yelling over his shoulder at the bar, "Oh yeah, eh, well fuck you too, buddy, and your fuckin' cat, y'fuckin' ..." He laughed himself into a cough and said, "Shit, I got beer up my nose," and swung his head around, whacking it into the door. "Ah shit, man, my fuckin' head!" He looked at me. "Good thing I'm pissed or it'd hurt like hell," and he cough-laughed again, and rubbed his cheek and looked around the lobby. "This isn't the fuckin' can—hey man, where's the can?"

The desk-guy looked up from where Mum was filling out a card. "Look. Don't come out here with your beer, it's illegal. Go back in the bar," and he took the card and handed Mum the room key. He changed his voice to nicer when he said, "It's number two-twenty-three and the doors lock automatically. You can take those stairs up."

The drunk guy was still standing in the door with his hand inside his rumply shirt. "Hey Asshole, I didn't come out here t' drink, for fucksake—I wanna take a piss and you're talkin' about drinkin'! Well, s'cuse me in front of the kid, but fuck you," and he giggled and shook his head and took an imaginary hat off at Mum and me and backed into the bar.

We went up the stairs, down the hall. The wallpaper was glued tight on the walls, no coming-loose parts, just yellow and brown splotches. The carpet was green; there was a dresser and a bed covered with a gold bedspread that looked like it used to be some drapes.

Mum threw her purse and our tote bag on the floor and looked around. I went to the blinds and banged and clanged them to the side so I could look down at the street.

"Grace, get out of there! Don't stand in the window like that, OK."

I banged back out. "Why?"

"Just—It's better not to." She was standing by the door, trying to wiggle the back of a chair under the doorknob. It was too short. Her eyes went around until they stopped on something bigger. "Here, come help me with the dresser." She pushed our stuff on the floor and started nudging the dresser out from the wall.

"Why? What are we doing?"

"Putting it in front of the door—give me a hand."

"Why?"

"Because. *Because-because-because, because of the wonderful things he does.*"

"What?" I figured so Child Protection couldn't break in, so I pushed the dresser hard as I could.

"Because this is what you do in an eleven-dollar-a-night hotel."

I remembered about the drunk guy downstairs and looked for more furniture.

When all the chairs and end tables and stuff were piled on, I asked if we were going to move the bed.

"Uh, no. I think that's enough."

"'K. Now what? There's no TV."

"I don't know. Let's get ready for bed and play Twenty Questions or I Spy or something."

Eilleen Thirteen

ALMOST SEVEN A.M., according to your watch. Still dark out. Grace is sleeping. You're not. Not that you did at any point, just lay on your back listening for footsteps of cops, social workers or rapists, because that's what you do when you and your baby are holed up in an eleven-dollar fleabag.

All night you've been running scenarios. You've pondered the interior, running to Kamloops or Penticton. But what's the coast for, if not stowing away on ships, floating to Hawaiian islands, floating … Tried to fall asleep floating on breath last night. No dice. Imagined them banging on the door of your apartment. *Mrs. Hoffman, we know you're in there.* Same words, different faces.

Is this rock bottom? The one they yammer on about, the one you hit and float from, ears popping, lungs exploding, busting a new glassy surface, a new woman crashing out of the water towards the light, the sun that finally came up?

Must be. Must be, because it makes no sense to keep running. Makes no goddamn sense unless you plan to go through this again,

run again to hear about yet another door they've banged their
heads against looking for you and your kid. Keep running and
they'll grab her in mid-stride when you're least expecting.

You've broken the surface, now get back to shore. Go and get
your feet planted; you need roots; you need roots so deep, they
can yank till their teeth ache.

Your daughter's kid-plump mouth takes air in and out. Her
baby skin looks like a word could pierce it. If you don't give her
this, if you don't give you this, what good's it all, anyway?

Sit up. Breathe. Breathe deep and feel your lungs explode, feel
the sun make your cheeks rise like dough. Swim for it.

You get dressed and Grace lifts her head, mumbling at you.
Go back to sleep, angel, I'm just going to the store to get us some juice.

She looks to the furniture piled against the door and at the
ceiling, asks the time, rolls over, rolls back, asks, *Can I 'ave orange
juice? and, um ...* But she can't think through the haze.

I'll get us something. I'll be right back, and you start taking
down the barricade.

The next thing you know, you are in front of a pay phone, the
dime has dropped and someone groggy picks up on the second
ring.

*Hi. It's Eilleen Hoffman. OK. I've given this some thought and
we're going home. Grace stays with me, that's the deal. You're not taking her back there. You can send social workers every day if you want,
to monitor the situation, I don't care, but she stays with me. If anything happens, if you try to take her, we'll just run and you'll never
hear from us again. So. There. That's my offer.*

There's a sleep breath on the other end. A tongue cluck. Todd
Baker says, *OK, Eilleen.*

ACKNOWLEDGEMENTS

I would like to express my eternal gratitude to the wonderful women who, as both friends and editors, believed in me from the start, encouraged me, pushed me along, and without whom I would have been lost. In order of their appearance: Susan Musgrave (for your philanthropy and jolt of courage), Rhea Tregebov (for your endless generosity and continued status as Deadeye Tregebov), Maya Mavjee (for helping me cut to the chase), Sarah Davies (for your provocation and nurturing hand) and Anne Collins (for taking a chance).

To Irene Livingston and Lenore Wildeman for your inspiration, love and experience, I thank you. To Ken Kirzinger for your all-encompassing love and your generous heart.

Thanks also to Melinda Menkley at the Ministry of Social Services, the staff at the Addiction Research Foundation in Toronto, the staff at the Metropolitan Toronto Reference Library and the Vancouver Public Library, David Franco for touring me through Vancouver General Hospital, the congregation at the Tsawwassen Kingdom Hall of Jehovah's Witnesses, and the members of various Alcoholics Anonymous centres who graciously shared their knowledge, literature and memories with me.

For their support, I am grateful and indebted to the Banff Centre for the Arts, the UCROSS Foundation, the Money for Women/Barbara Deming Memorial Fund, and the Canada Council for the Arts for both the now-defunct Explorations Program and the Grants to Professional Writers Program. And, finally, thanks to the Writers Union of Canada for its Mentorship Program and commitment to fostering novice writers. Were it not for the Union I would not have had the privilege of working with my mentor, Sandra Birdsell, who not only gave me encouraging critique, but took the time to teach me about the business of being a writer.